A Matter

of

Identity

I0563171

Susan Tuttle

Published by: WriterWithin Publications

Copyright © 2015 Susan Tuttle

A WriterWithin Publication

All rights reserved.

ISBN: 1941465129
ISBN-13: 978-1-941465-12-7

DEDICATION

For my parents' dear friend, Jean Roberts, whose enthusiasm for this story kept me going until it was finished, and pushed me to get it into print. I miss you. Won't be long now, we'll have a reunion. Keep the bar open for me.

CONTENTS

ACKNOWLEDGMENTS

Without the help of a good writer's group, no novel worth its salt would see the light of day. To this end, a huge thanks goes out to SLO NightWriters, and my critique buddies: Ginger Lasher, Dennis Eamon Young, Claire Gordon, David Georgi, Evelyn Cole, Richard Sudden, Judythe Guarnera, Diane Smith.

And especially to Sandy White, who always has time to listen to my chicken scratching, and who's always there whenever I need her, encouraging me. Thanks for being my friend and neighbor. You're the best.

A Matter

of

Identity

SUSAN TUTTLE

Chapter One

I sat erect, motionless on the hard horsehair settee, facing Mr. Marlowe, a solicitor, I believe he is called. It was he who had just pronounced my doom, spelling out the 'myriad' options open to a penniless female left orphaned in the heart of London. In other words, I could hire out for service, go on the streets, or starve.

The room that had so intimidated me at first faded away. I was no longer aware of the aged oak paneling on the walls and ceiling that lent a musty air to the surroundings, the candled sconces burning without giving off much light. I barely saw the massive oak desk piled high with legal papers from among which he had taken what was left of my life, nor the leather-bound volumes which lined the walls. Despite the hushed atmosphere I felt like screaming, though I knew I was not capable of making a sound.

I stared at him in silence as his words sank in, hating him not only for what he had said, and would still say, but also for the supercilious air with which he said it. He reminded me of a ferret; thin to the point of emaciation and not over-tall, his dark hair slicked back like a shining cap. He wore a pearl gray sack coat of the latest, almost-lapelless style over an elaborate brocade waistcoat. The striped bow tie clasped round his neck looked as sharp and narrow as his face. His pointed nose seemed to sniff tragedy wherever he looked. Brown eyes bulged in their sockets, prying into my private feelings, and his pursed lips and nervous fingers gave the impression that he enjoyed destroying helpless females. Little did I know how right I was in that estimation.

"I don't understand," I said. "There is nothing at all? Surely, there must be—"

"I assure you, Miss Weston," he interrupted, his lips downturned at the fact that I dared question his pronouncement, "there is nothing at all. Upon your Father's demise, no more than 30 pounds were discovered on his person. After careful investigation, not one further asset has been uncovered."

He sat back in the embroidered armchair with a self-satisfied smirk. I looked down at the papers on the table between us, then back up at him.

"But," I began, but Mr. Marlowe would allow me no further opportunity for question or doubt. It was, after all, unseemly of a woman not to unconditionally accept a man's word.

"My dear young lady." His drawling tone rang with exasperated impatience. "I am well aware of the home you claim to own in Boston, Massachusetts."

Claim? My eyes widened at the implied insult to

my honor.

"And," he continued, clearing his throat and adjusting his pince-nez with a delicate gesture, "I am also aware of the business interests into which your Father told you he had invested."

He paused and his look of melancholy pity froze the breath of protest in my throat. I knew then, with absolute certainty, that what I had most dreaded since my Father's suicide really was true. There was nothing left, neither here nor at home. Father's tales of partners in England, the need for a quick trip overseas to finalize important investments, the promise of shopping expeditions to replace clothing and items there hadn't been time to pack—all were lies. Lies! Disaster had finally overtaken him, and in true coward's style he had fled with me to England and then killed himself, leaving me penniless and alone with no way to return to America, and nothing there for me even if I could. Oh, Father!

I sat staring at Mr. Marlowe as I tried to force myself to breathe, to get my heart beating, my mind working. Only dimly did I hear his contempt-tinged words.

"I received Tuesday week a letter from a Mr. Alcott, in response to our enquiries. I believe he is your family solicitor—ahhh," he corrected himself, "attorney?"

He glanced at me for confirmation but I could only lift my shoulders in ignorance. I knew nothing of any details of Father's finances.

"He has informed our office," here he removed a page from among the many on the table between us, "that all personal family holdings and possessions have been liquidated in order to pay debts incurred by one George Arnold Weston, Esquire."

At the mention of Father's name in connection with such scandal, shame washed over me and tears filled my eyes. I bowed my head, not wanting Mr. Marlowe's ferret-eyes to watch while I strove to bring my vision into focus. As I struggled, I listened to his dry, detached voice drone on.

"The monies realized from said liquidation have discharged all but a sum of just over eight thousand dollars." He shifted in his seat and made an odd sound low in his throat. "That is eight thousand *dollars*, Miss Weston, not pounds. I am afraid that, as your Father's only child and heir, his debts have now become yours. However, the international aspects of this case may somewhat alter the legal ramifications. Mr. Alcott and I are enquiring on your behalf."

The words expressed some hope, but his tone clearly indicated that, no matter what, I would, of course, bear complete responsibility for the repayment of the entire massive sum. How ironic, I thought, pressing a handkerchief to my misty eyes, that a woman could not have property or money of her own —indeed, she was owned herself by either father, brother or husband—yet she was responsible to repay the debts any of them incurred. But since gainful employment was beyond possibility for most women, just how was that repayment to be accomplished?

He had ceased speaking; the silence deafened me. I raised my head but I could not meet his eyes. Would I ever, I wondered, be able to meet anyone's eyes again? I felt trapped. My breath shortened and my head lightened as I turned my gaze to the window and the sky-blue promise of freedom glimpsed through it, a promise as false as all of Father's. What would become of me? How could I ever pay back such a vast sum of money? How would I even live from day to day?

Mr. Marlowe must have been touched by something in my plight, for he leaned forward and covered my tight-clasped hands with one of his own. Like his voice, his hand was soft but authoritative.

"I understand how difficult this must be for you, Miss Weston. Such a shock, coming on top of your Father's sudden.... ah.... demise. And for a gently bred lady, the situation in which you find yourself is quite difficult. There are so few options available."

He rose and paced about the room, crossing to his desk, to the window and back again to the chair placed opposite me in an endless round. I could do naught but follow him with my gaze, my mind in turmoil. What more would this day bring?

"Let me see, now," he said, "do you sew? Cook? Are you fluent in any foreign languages? Are you well-traveled? Do you paint? Sing? Can you play the piano? Do you play any instrument? What is your knowledge of geography?"

The questions flew at me, on and on, forever, it

seemed to me, while I could only shake my head in negation or whisper, "Some... a little... barely..." in answer. At last he stopped faced me and exploded in frustration.

"My word, Miss Weston, what *do* they teach young ladies in America?"

I could only stare at him, blinking back tears. How could I explain that Father did not approve of girls (me) learning or knowing anything other than basic reading and writing, and how to cater to a man's (his) whims? I most certainly could not tell Mr. Marlowe in which directions my skills lay, such as they were, for, excluding marriage, they equipped me only for the more disreputable of occupations. Another wonderful legacy from George Arnold Weston, Esq.

"I–I do have some knowledge of mathematics, Mr. Marlowe," I said at last. He merely stared at me, his opinion clear in his face. Knowledge of mathematics, indeed! Mathematics was a man's subject; no woman could possibly understand such things.

"Well," he sighed after a moment of silence, "we can *try* for governess, although I hold but little hope for success." He seated himself in the chair opposite me, once again taking charge of my life. "Aside from your obvious lack of accomplishments, you have no references and no one to speak for your character, which is more than imperative given the manner of your Father's death. Also, the fact that you are an American is certain to cause difficulties in all but the least-desirable posts. And," he added with a very definite note of disapproval in his tone, "you are much too lovely to be allowed near most wives' husbands."

The silence lengthened as we pondered his words. I felt hysteria begin to rise. Being pretty was what every girl hoped and prayed for. Father had often told me I 'would do', as did my own mirror, although I had not truly trusted my own judgment nor that of Father or his business associates. Now it seemed to me astoundingly comical that I should have clear, objective confirmation of beauty from one such as Mr. Marlowe, while being told that self-same beauty made me ineligible for gainful employment. Perhaps I was more suited for the streets; the idea of genteel starvation held no appeal for me at all.

He must have seen how close I was to the breaking point, for he rose, took my hands and helped me to my feet.

"Yes, yes," he said almost to himself, "most assuredly a companion post will do, if we could only find one. Indeed, yes. They are quite difficult to come by, you understand; most widows and elderly spinsters have a flock of poor relatives from which to choose. But surely there must be one or two who would consider taking you on. At reduced compensation, of course. After all, given your history," he shuddered a bit at his veiled reference to Father's suicide, "you could not expect the same wages as one with an impeccable background. A good selling point; yes, indeed, a very good selling point."

He steered me toward the door, patting my hands with what, I'm sure, he thought was a soothing gesture.

"Well, now, after my fees are paid, there should be enough for you to live on for perhaps three more weeks at the hotel, if you are quite frugal. Perhaps if we found you a small room, somewhere, we should not be so hard-pressed. Yes, yes... We shall see what can be done there, also."

Still speaking, he opened the door and handed me out before I could frame a reply, a comment, or a question, not that I was capable of speech at the moment.

"Just leave everything to me, Miss Weston. Something is sure to turn up, eventually." He turned to his clerk. "Please see that Miss Weston is returned safely to her hotel, Pickering. Good day, Miss Weston."

He gave me a slight bow and shut the office door in my face.

Chapter Two

In numbed silence I sat in the cab the mute Pickering procured, seeing none of the passing London streets. I could feel myself slowly dying at the thought of being a hired companion to some crotchety, wealthy old widow or spinster, resented for my youth and good looks, despised for my penurious state, and tolerated only in so far as I jumped at every beck and call, no matter how unreasonable or humiliating. Always seeing life as an onlooker, never allowed to participate. And, most important to me, kept bound because of my 'unsavory' history, paid less than the post was worth so that I could never save anything, never repay that debt, never be anything more than an old maid's nursemaid. I wasn't sure my spirit could long survive such degradation.

When we reached the hotel I begged Pickering to return immediately to his place of employment, as I was quite recovered and well able to find my room by myself. He agreed with alacrity; shepherding frail young ladies to hotel rooms appeared to frighten him no end. As his cab pulled away I realized I could not stand the thought of sitting in my lonely room, placidly awaiting my fate to befall me. These could possibly be the last moments of freedom I'd ever have.

And so I turned my back on the bustling hotel lobby and began to walk, drinking in the commotion and the crowds, letting the purposefulness and direction all about me drain away my fears and confusion. How I loved the sights and sounds of those busy streets! I couldn't give up all this to molder away trailing after a self-centered, domineering old harridan. There must be another way for me to earn enough to put a roof over my head, clothes on my back, and food on my table. Another respectable way, that is. And repay Father's debt? I drooped at the unwelcome thought. It seemed hopeless.

At last I stopped outside a small bakery-tea shop, whose delicious aromas tugged at my empty stomach. I knew that it was not seemly for single young ladies to venture into any public establishment unchaperoned, but what was a very alone stranger like me to do? Accost a likely-looking lady on the street and beg that she take tea with me? Or live like an outcast in my room until a 'respectable' position snatched away my freedom to ever enter such a place again?

Taking a deep breath to stiffen my resolve, I opened the door and entered. I stood at the threshold a moment, knowing I at least looked presentable in my rose-and-green striped chambray dress with its pagoda sleeves and lace collar. I looked around to locate an empty table, aware of the curious stares and surreptitious comments my solo entry had evoked.

Well, let them talk. It was certainly no choice of mine that left me stranded alone in London, and as it seemed that would be my state for quite some time to come, I had better begin to get used to people's stares and comments. Lifting my chin higher, I threaded my way to a small table in the corner of the window, sitting down amidst a babble of low voices. I stared unseeing at the menu for some moments before I became aware that the proprietress was standing at my elbow.

"Oh. Good afternoon." I gave her a tentative smile that was not returned. I wasn't quite sure how to go about ordering, as I had rarely entered such establishments even in Father's company. And I certainly had never come in alone before.

"Would it be possible to obtain a pot of tea and a small plate of those lovely looking cakes in the window?" I asked. "They are so tempting I simply cannot resist them."

She merely stood there staring at me, sizing me up with her eyes, her hands buried in the pockets of her big white apron. She was a tall woman of middle age, big and soft, with gray-sprinkled red hair, green eyes, and a pale complexion reddened from the heat of the ovens. I felt her face was warm and kindly for all that she sent a stern glare at the vacant chair opposite me.

"No," I said in answer to her unspoken question, "I am not waiting for anyone. I am quite alone, a stranger here in London—in England, actually, although I am sure you could tell so from my speech."

I gave her another tentative smile, but found no answering softening in her face. My shoulders, and my spirit, drooped.

"If you want, I shall not stay. I just needed a quiet place in which to think, and I could not bear the isolation of my hotel room. You see," my smile was rather wry this time, "I have been left quite alone and friendless by my Father's sudden death, and nearly penniless, and I must discover what I am to do to live. I truly wish I had a friend to sit with. I could use one."

To my mortification, I could feel my throat tighten up again before I finished speaking, saying much more than I had intended. I looked away as tears pricked the backs of my eyes. I could not—I *would* not—allow myself to cry in public. I could not bear the humiliation. I felt her stir at my side and had gathered myself to rise and leave when she laid a soft hand on my arm.

"I am Mrs. Mollie O'Leary," she said, a sweet Celtic cadence to her voice, "and this is my shop, mine and Mr. O'Leary's. Stay as long as you'll be wanting."

She hurried away to bring my order.

The cakes were as delicious as their looks had promised—*at least something keeps its promises*, I thought —fresh, sweet and delicate. The tea was hot, brewed strong as only the English know how. It warmed my body and calmed my spirit. I sipped slowly at cup after cup and nibbled on those lovely cakes as I watched the world pass by outside the window, a world I seemed now forbidden to join. Forbidden because Father's death left me penniless. Forbidden because being a woman left me no freedom. It was all so unfair.

Unnoticed by me, the shop emptied of its customers and still I sat on, trying to bring my mind to focus on my main problem. Employment. It grew dark outside but my eyes, wrapped in an inner darkness of their own, did not see. Try as I might I could not make myself even begin to ponder a solution. All I could see were long years of hopelessness stretching ahead.

And then Mrs. O'Leary dropped into the chair next to me.

"You surely do look like you're needin' a friend to talk to, sweeting," she said in her lilting Irish accent, her voice gentle and musical. She gave me a warm, shy smile. "Why not try tellin' old Aunt Mollie about your troubles? Perhaps together we can think what you should be doin'."

And so I found myself talking to Mollie O'Leary and her husband, Eamon, a small washed-out man with soft skin, gray hair and sky-blue eyes, who turned the sign on the door and came to join us at the window table. Watching London hurry by outside in the darkness, I told them of my life in America with my Father, George Arnold Weston, Esq.

Chapter Three

Mother died just before I turned five and I have few clear memories of her. I remember mostly laughter and gentleness, the scent of lavender and glossy dark curls. I did not know why she died. Father rarely spoke of her again, would answer no questions, kept no mementos. It was almost as if she had never existed. But she had, for I was here and I looked just like her. "The exquisite Diedre," Uncle Joseph called her.

He lived with us for a time after Mother died, Father's half-brother Joseph, in our big old gloomy house in Boston. Father was almost never home, always out on some business or other. He never said what it was, and I learned not to ask. When he was aroused, his hand could be very heavy, indeed. I was allowed scant freedom, and no friends. What little schooling I had during those years, Father allowed me on the rare evenings he stayed home. Had it not been for Uncle Joseph, I would have been quite an ignorant girl.

He conspired to teach me things behind Father's back: reading, penmanship, and 'unwomanly' subjects such as mathematics. His health was delicate and so he kept an office at home, working on ledgers for various small business establishments. By the time I turned eleven, I was able to help him with the entries as his strength failed more and more.

He taught me songs, and how to dance after a fashion. We read poetry to each other and shared what the pieces meant to each of us. He taught me to watch, to listen, and most of all to think. He would brush my hair, fuss over my clothes, and stand up to Father for me. He was family and friend, Uncle, Father, Mother, brother, cousin, all rolled into one. I loved him so deeply it hurt, and I wished with all my heart that he had been my Father. I still struggle with the painful guilt of not loving the one I had.

It was not entirely all my fault, however, that I could not give George Arnold Weston, Esq., the love a daughter owes her Father, for he was not a very lovable man. Indeed, he became less so as each year passed, seeming to take pleasure in being as perverse as possible. When I was small, as long as I kept quiet he barely noticed me, though when I provoked his displeasure I would be banished for days at a time to my small attic room. But one does not remain small and unworthy of notice forever.

On my twelfth birthday Father sent for me, an almost-unheard-of occurrence. He had been away for just under a week, having returned very late the night before, after I was sound asleep. I could think of nothing I had done while he was away that could have roused his wrath, and certainly there had not been time in the half hour since I rose that morning. I shivered with dread as I stood outside his study door, nerving myself to knock.

I was bade enter immediately he heard the sound, and my courage almost failed me when the door swung open. He was seated in the big embroidered chair before the fire, long legs stretched out to the warmth. He motioned me in without turning his head to look at me.

"Close the door, Daughter, and stand before me."

He pointed to where he wanted me and I moved quickly to obey.

"Well, girl," he drawled, and lifted his gaze from the fire to mine. It had long been his habit to stare directly into my eyes. His were so dark a brown as to appear a fathomless black, and I always felt as though I were an insect impaled upon a board, soul laid bare. From experience, I knew the harsh penalty for looking away first, so I merely stood as still as possible on the outside while I squirmed with fear on the inside. I had never been able to outstare him. It always ended painfully for me.

But this time he broke contact first, letting his gaze roam over my body as he analyzed the changes and growth so apparent beneath the too-small gown I wore. Startled by the unexpected intimacy of this scrutiny, I stepped back. In a flash his slender, strong hand shot out and grasped my wrist.

"Hold!" His fingers tightened cruelly as the echo of his growl faded.

"Yes, sir," I whispered, dropping my gaze to the floor at my feet and keeping it there. I think I was more frightened then than I had ever been in my life.

Father rose and began pacing the book-lined mahogany room, passing the floor-to-ceiling mullioned windows and returning to stand beside me or behind me, continuing his piercing inspection. Finally, he gave a non-committal grunt and strode behind his desk. Sitting, he pointed to the hard wooden chair on my side and barked orders at me.

"Come here!"

I came.

"Sit!"

I sat.

The silence lengthened. At long last I raised timid eyes to see him lounging back in his high leather chair, sunk in reverie, half-closed eyes seeing something a long way or time from where we now sat. A gentle half-smile played about his sharp lips, his habitual ill-tempered scowl replaced by a look of quiet joy. Years had seemed to drop away from him. He looked young and gay and handsome with his lean, lanky body, impeccable dress and patrician features. My eyes widened in astonishment.

But I must have made some small noise or movement that recalled him to the present, for he blinked and I watched the peaceful quiet flee, to be replaced by the frowning dissatisfaction with which he faced every day.

"Your Uncle Joseph has reminded me that today is your birthday, Daughter." His voice was odd, almost a gentle caress. Only later did I realize that the underlying tone was one of quiet malice. "He has remonstrated with me concerning my lack of caring and interest in you, my own dear Daughter."

He paused and pursed his lips as again he caught and held my gray eyes with his bottomless black ones in his deadly game of nerves. My heart quailed when his eyes narrowed on mine. Questions came then, fast and furious, stepping on my frightened answers.

"Do you lack care?"

"No, sir." I tried to answer firmly, but the shaky whisper betrayed my fear.

"Are you neglected?"

"No, sir."

"Are you starved?"

"No, sir."

"Do you lack clothing?"

"N-no, s-sir." I began to stutter as the inquisition's tempo increased.

"Are you unhappy? Is your room not adequate? Do you complain about me? About how I treat you? About what I don't give you? Complain to your precious Uncle Joseph? Do you talk about me, you two, behind my back?"

He gave me no chance to answer now. The fury of the questions pressed me back in my chair. I could only shake my head while my eyes remained locked on his. As he spoke, he rose, leaned across the desk and shouted at me.

"Do you want more, you ungrateful little wretch? More than all I've given you? More than this house? More sustenance? More clothing? A bigger room? Do you want to leave here? Do you? Are you sick of me? Are you? Then go live on the streets, both of you! You and your precious Uncle Joseph!"

On and on he ranted at me, shouting words I could not even understand, until I sat sobbing in the chair, head buried in my hands. I don't know how long I cried, but suddenly I became aware that there was silence around me and I fought to control the hysteria, to still my sobs and bring my breathing under control. I dared not look up until my emotion was completely spent, for I knew Father would break me for it. When I felt calm enough at last, I lifted my ravaged face to find Father sitting serenely behind the desk, waiting with deceptive patience for my attention as though nothing untoward had happened. So great was my fear that he was about to put me out, alone, on the streets that I had to blink back betraying tears. I had no idea what to say. What could I have done to deserve this?

"I believe that now the time has come," he said, almost to himself, frowning at me in a thoughtful way as though he decided his course of action as he spoke, "the time has come for your free ride to end. Now you must begin to pay for all the benefits you have derived from my generosity." He leaned forward, resting his arms on the desk, and sneered at me. "As my dear brother has so correctly pointed out to me, you are growing up, Daughter. Becoming a woman."

He sighed and shook his head, again letting his dark stare rove over my body. I wanted to cringe away, cover myself with my arms, but I dared not move. I barely breathed.

"It is time to begin teaching you just what a woman is," he stated.

I swallowed in fear as he stood and came around the desk to stand in front of the chair in which I cowered. I didn't understand then what he meant, though I soon did, for I was educated in subjects few ladies are even aware exist. He perched on the desk in front of me and I sat listening to him speak, listening to the shape of the years to come, listening to my world fracture into tiny pieces that could never be put back into a whole.

The house would be divided in half, Father and I to live in one side, Uncle Joseph in the other, alone. I would no longer be allowed to spend my days with Uncle Joseph. Instead I would now take tea with him only twice a week during two-hour visits—in the company of Father. Father would now choose my clothes, decide my hairstyle, approve my reading matter, set the hours of my rising and retiring. I would learn to be content to be a woman whose place is in bondage to a man. The longer he spoke, the more I wished I were dead.

Finally, he stopped speaking and stared me.

Reaching out a hand, he stroked my hair, my cheek, with gentle fingers, saying nothing when I flinched at his touch though three days later I was punished severely for that disrespect. Then he smiled at me.

"It is true," he murmured, "you do look like her. More and more each year. That is what makes it so very hard. Pray God you have not inherited her nature. Then I should truly have to crush you." He leaned forward and kissed me on the top of my head. "I do love you, Marina," he said, using my name for the first time in many months. Usually he avoided it as much as possible. For years I had been merely 'Daughter' to him. "Love does not stop when the object of it becomes unworthy. You would do well to remember that, Daughter."

Thus having spoken, his last words again in his usual steely tone, he bowed to me and strode from the room.

Chapter Four

I have no idea how long I sat on, in numb shock and disbelief, futilely wondering what had brought all this on, wishing I could reverse time and grow small again. Most of my childhood died that day I turned twelve. The rest died six months later with Uncle Joseph, who never recovered from his brother's wrath nor the loss of our togetherness. I have never understood Father's reasons for what he did, and I have never forgiven him.

It was easiest to simply acquiesce, to learn bewildering lessons that came clearer as time passed and my maturity grew. I did resist at first, and often felt Father's heavy hand in the six months before Uncle Joseph's death snapped my will. My resistance was more unconscious than overt, consisting mainly of inattention, a moping attitude and slow obedience to Father's orders. But he recognized it immediately and dealt with it as severely as he dealt with everything concerning me from that time on. I spent most of my days in my tiny room beneath the eaves, nursing the massive bruises his fists raised on my body. He had no compunction at all about beating me, and we both knew that it was merely a matter of time before I would give in completely. The day Uncle Joseph died, I capitulated.

From that moment on, I learned. I learned how to pamper a man, how to dress and undress him, to light his cigar, pour his wine, massage his back, serve his meals. I learned to fetch and carry, anticipate his needs, and listen to him sympathetically without ever giving voice to any of my own thoughts, ideas, suggestions or plans. I learned how to care for him in illness, how to handle overindulgences, and how to be his scapegoat, abused and beaten in silence. I learned quickly and I learned well, for it was by far the least painful route to take. I learned to disappear into the woodwork, to see but not be seen, to be a woman according to my Father's definition: a person who exists only as long as the man who owns her allows her to.

By the time I was sixteen, I began traveling with Father on his 'business' trips, the purpose of which I never knew. I only asked once. The beating I received for my 'audacity' left my shoulder dislocated. I learned to flatter his business acquaintances, to act as his quiet, gentle hostess, to put prospective 'customers' at their ease. I also learned how to while away the great lengths of time I spent locked into hotel rooms, sometimes for whole days without food. I learned to always pack a book or two with which to occupy my mind, although many of those of which Father approved were deadly dull to me.

I lived with the secret hope that someday I would marry someone like Uncle Joseph and again become a person in my own right. I held desperately to the memory of that gentle man and what he had taught me about myself, that I had a good mind, a sharp wit and a sensitive soul. When Father found and burned the journal in which I kept my private thoughts and dreams—I spent a full month locked in my room and from then on was allowed pen and paper only in his presence—out of defiance I began writing in an imaginary book in my mind. My body might be owned by my Father, and my outward actions controlled by him, but my spirit belonged only to me. Father had, of course, read my journal before destroying it, and he often used the information it contained to mock and humiliate me in front of his acquaintances. But I bore it in stoic silence, knowing how much worse it would be if he thought I still harbored such thoughts. From all outward appearances, it seemed I had been thoroughly cowed by his male power, and as the years passed I did lose sight of much of myself. But I was never completely broken to his will. If he could somehow have fully broken my spirit, I would not have survived. Knowing that gave me the strength to hang on through the darkness.

It was not all tears and unpleasantness, though, for Father also began taking me to social affairs. It was a necessary part of my 'education', true, or I would not have gone, but it was also time spent with him, moments of laughter, of sharing each other's company, when I could pretend he was the Father I needed him to be. I also began to see in him a haunted child, one he tried hard to hide, and I think that, in spite of himself, he began to see me as an individual person and not only the 'slave' he wanted me to be. I found it quite ironic that our country was fast approaching a war to end Negro slavery in the South while, because I was merely a woman, Father continued enslaving me unimpeded and unnoticed by everyone but me.

However, I would never dare express such a thought. I was forbidden even to listen to the men when they spoke of such things as war and slavery in front of me. Still, we went to the opera and the theater, to art museums and for walks on the common simply to enjoy the fresh air and sunshine. We did not go often, but it was always pleasurable when we did, the only truly pleasurable time we spent together. Of course, no other man was ever allowed to approach me.

He also taught me to play chess and, although I always took pains to pretend my successful moves were simply luck, as I had been hard-taught to do—and I never, ever allowed myself to win—I believe he not only knew my skill but also was proud of it. We began, at the rare times when alone and he not 'teaching' me something, to enjoy each other's company after a fashion. But I never did come to love him. And then things started to go wrong.

For almost two years before he announced our hasty trip to England, his temper became more and more unpredictable. He left me home alone oftener, and more often he returned drunk and abusive, both verbally and physically. The quality of his 'associates' deteriorated, became rougher, cruder. He grew increasingly concerned with money, refusing me even the most necessary of expenses. But what frightened me most was when he started asking what I was prepared to suffer 'for love of my Father,' and bringing up what he called the most important part of my education, the physical nature of a man's relationship with a woman.

I had, of course, no practical experience of such a relationship, for Father guarded my virtue zealously, not allowing any but a selected few within a block of me, and even then he never left me alone with any of them. But he had made sure I had a thorough academic knowledge of the subject, and I knew things that no decent woman knew existed before her wedding night, and more besides, things Father said would be indispensable in successfully pleasing my future lord and master. I had suffered in silence through his many lectures. The pictures he showed me had left me feeling sick.

Now I began to be frightened that perhaps he would marry me off for money, marry me not to whomever would be kind to me and love me, but to the one who bid the most. I grew even more frightened when I thought that perhaps he would not hold out for marriage, only money. I refused to allow myself to think any further. He was, after all, my Father. But then he began bringing men home with him, an unheard-of occurrence, for he never conducted business at home or in my presence.

It was clear from the start that it was me he was showing off. These were wealthy men in the extreme, most of them old though one was middle-aged, all of them crude, disgusting libertines and rakes unworthy of being called gentlemen. He paraded me before them and watched them undress me with their eyes. Most were hard-put to control their hands. As much as I dreaded Father being away, I now dreaded his return even more. It was always a relief when he arrived alone.

He was drinking so much so often, and was so rarely sober, that I had no opportunity to cajole what little information out of him I had learned to do through the years. His wildly swinging moods undermined my sense of safety and sanity. I knew we could not go on this way much longer.

And then he disappeared for three weeks. I had no word from him, no idea where he was, no inkling of how to reach him. He arrived home suddenly, laughing, excited, talking of partners and investments and Europe. Two days later, just after my twentieth birthday, we left for London, leaving behind all but two small trunks, one for him and one for me. Three days after we arrived here, he hung himself in his hotel room. He left thirty pounds in his pockets, an eight thousand dollar debt in America, and a note addressed to me that read, 'Has love stopped? I have become unworthy. Father.'

* * *

Silence descended upon the three of us as I finished speaking. I knew not what Mollie and Eamon O'Leary were thinking, but I sat amazed at my own lack of feeling. He had been dead less than three weeks, and I had felt as though I were speaking of a stranger, not my own Father. I realized at last how very much a stranger he had been. I had never really known him at all, not his reasons, his thoughts, his feelings—if he had any—nor the devils that drove him. Now I never would, and it surprised me how little I cared.

Deep beneath the anxiety about my future I could feel a sense of freedom, freedom from the bondage in which he had held me and to which he would have committed me in the marriage partner he chose. I had no doubt that he would have found a man who thought exactly as he did. But I knew this sense of freedom was false, a lie, just as everything else in my life had proved to be. It would have no chance to grow, but would be crushed from the start by the bondage of the paid companion position my gender and poverty— and that enormous debt—would force upon me.

My sigh broke the silence.

"So you see my dilemma," I said, looking from Mollie to Eamon. "I have no money and an enormous debt to pay off. I have no skills with which to secure a respectable position, and am too well-bred for any un-respectable one. I cannot sew, or weave, nor even cook well enough to fool anyone for long. And I cannot go home. I've no money for passage, no home left in Boston, and no relations to take me in. And I'm not sure that they wouldn't throw me in jail because I cannot pay back all that money." I gave a half-hearted laugh that ended in choked tears. "If only I could sell all these silly tears, my troubles would be over," I said in a wry attempt at humor. "I seem to have an endless supply of them."

Mollie held me close as I brought myself under control, then I wiped my eyes and rose to leave, my heart still beating quickly from the feel of Mollie's arms around me. Not since my fateful twelfth birthday had anyone held me in their arms. I'd forgotten how wonderful it felt.

Mollie would not hear of my paying for the tea and cakes, and Eamon insisted on escorting me to my hotel through the dark and dangerous nighttime streets. We walked side by side in silence until we stood before the ornate front doors. I thanked him for his time, his generosity, his sympathy.

"I have been so alone for most of my life," I told him. "This is the first time since Uncle Joseph died that I have told anyone what is in my heart. God bless you, Eamon O'Leary, and Mollie, too. I am proud to know people like you. Whatever happens to me, I shall never forget either of you."

I bent forward and kissed his cheek, then turned and hurried into the hotel and up to my room, leaving him astounded and tongue-tied on the walk. I seemed bent on doing non-respectable things lately: Entering tea shops un-chaperoned; telling my life story to perfect strangers; kissing men on a public street. *Well,* I reflected as I readied myself for bed, *if I have to spend the rest of my life slaving away to repay Father's debt, having no life of my own, I might as well have something to look back upon.* I wondered just how exciting I could make the time that was left to me.

Giggling at my reckless mood, I climbed under the comforters and slept deeply and dreamlessly all night, very much to my own amazement.

Chapter Five

I awoke early a week later, as I did every morning, and dressed quickly although I had nowhere to go. Accordingly, my costume was more modest than what I had worn to Mr. Marlowe's office, a pique affair in pearl gray that had a high lace neck and full pagoda sleeves. The skirt swayed gracefully with my every movement even though, being one of my older dresses, the hoop beneath was not as wide nor as elaborate as those currently in vogue. Father had detested female fashions, and had never gone to many lengths to dress me more than adequately. Indeed, most of what I had brought to London seemed more serviceable for the position to which I would soon be relegated than that of a lady. But my lack of style really did not bother me. Perhaps I had inherited some of Father's disdain for the artificial enclosures into which women were forced to hide their bodies. In any case, I certainly found my abbreviated hoops and less-full skirts much easier to move around in.

But I had nowhere to move. I sat at the window of my hotel room, watching London awaken. Men streamed from coaches into buildings and from buildings into coaches. Street vendors melodically hawked their wares up and down the avenues. Charwomen, maids, cooks and shopkeepers bustled about, bent on the morning's errands. Street urchins ran everywhere, beneath everyone's feet. Later, as the sun rose high to burn off the damp night air, elegant ladies in elaborate dimity and chintz sailed forth to partake of early luncheons or patronize the very best of London dress, millinery and jewelry establishments.

My reckless mood of a week ago had vanished with the fog. How I longed to be a part of all that vitality below me. If Father were still alive, if his business interests had only been real, then someone else would be watching *me* alight from an elegant carriage. *I* would be the one to lunch with Lords and Dukes and Earls; *I* would be the one to create a sensation in all the very best shops.

I looked around my room and my fantasy collapsed about me like a house of cards. I knew that even if Father were alive and his business real, there would be no hope for my dreams. I would still be here, at the window of this hotel room, watching life pass by in the streets below just as I always had at home. The only difference between then and now that I could see was that Father was no longer here to lock the door. If I wanted to, I could go out and stand among all those people on the street. It would not matter. Life would still pass me by.

As if to underline this thought, a large carriage stopped just opposite my window, quite distinctive in its shiny black lacquer with bright red and gold trim. The coachman and footmen were liveried in like colors, looking grand enough to my eyes to be gentry themselves. My eyesight was not keen enough to make out distinctly the crest on the door, but even though I would not recognize the family I knew enough to realize that a very aristocratic personage, indeed, occupied the interior of that vehicle. As I watched, an elderly dowager emerged amid great flutter and attention from her servants.

She wore the very latest fashion of the day, a striped blue lawn gown whose wide skirts took up most of the sidewalk. It dripped with lace and ribbons, the skirt looped up to reveal a flower-patterned petticoat beneath. When she tilted her head imperiously to demand something of the coachman, I could see, beneath the ribbon and flower-bedecked spoon bonnet, that I had been mistaken in my first estimate. She was not elderly but late middle-aged, and perhaps had been somewhat pretty once. But her long narrow face had soured from an ill-temper that even I, so far away, could see. Her strident, superior, haranguing tone beat at my ears as she turned again to the carriage door, gesturing with impatience to whoever still sat within.

Due to my position, I could not see clearly who she upbraided so strenuously until that person had fully alighted from the carriage and stepped aside. I started forward with a gasp, for it could have been myself at whom I stared. Young, meek, obviously downtrodden; hair pulled back tight into an unbecoming bun in a transparent attempt to downplay inborn loveliness; a drab brown dress a bare step above a scullery maid's costume; shoulders and head bowed beneath the onslaught of words whose derisive tone carried all the way to my half-opened window.

The paid companion.

Beggared, destitute, desperate and hopeless.

As her 'benefactor' sailed on into London's most exclusive jewelry shop without a backward glance, the poor young woman sighed deeply, then straightened her shoulders and steeled herself to follow. Two fiery red spots burned high on her unusually pale, gaunt cheeks.

And that was to be *my* fate? Oh, heaven forbid!

I put my hands over my face and pressed hard, hoping to find by sheer force some other solution to my problem hiding in my brain. I knew that not all such positions were quite so demeaning, but at the very best they were not calculated to leave one any pride, freedom or independent choice. And my position would be even worse, having to save every scrap of money I could to repay that debt. I rose to pace the room, whether hoping to overtake a solution or outrun the problem I did not know, but the very act of movement gave me a feeling of accomplishment, a sense of control, false though it was. Somehow, I knew

I would have to talk myself into accepting my lot before Mr. Marlowe deposited me, defiant and resentful, before my new 'employer.' Such an attitude would only make a bad situation worse.

A knock on the door interrupted this gloomy cycle of thought. I opened to a maid who told me a visitor awaited me downstairs in the dayroom. My heart sank. So soon? How could Mr. Marlowe have found a jailor for me so quickly? Was I not to have even a tiny amount of freedom to savor through the long, lonely years ahead?

"Yes, I-I'll be right down," I managed to stammer, and shut the door again to still my heart and steady my nerves for the confrontation. As I checked my hair in the mirror and straightened the gown covering my slender, five-foot-three-inch height, I gazed at my reflection, seeing large, dark gray eyes staring back from a pale oval face framed with the glossy black curls I'd inherited from Mother. There, too, were her thin arching brows, high cheekbones, delicate straight nose and rosy lips saucily turned up at the ends; altogether an effect which Father once, in a rare mood, had called enchanting—as did the admiring glances of his men friends. Definitely distinctive among the many fair-haired, peaches-and-cream complexioned beauties I'd seen here in London. More than a slight disadvantage to gainful employment. And much more than a small goad to an aging, bitter, lonely and perhaps homely woman forced to pay for companionship. This beauty that should have been my joy would most likely make me more than miserable.

I stood before my door, willing my hands to open it. The sooner it was over, the better. And at least, no matter where I ended up, I would always be able to open my door. There would be no more locks. Taking a deep breath, holding that thought for starch and hesitating only slightly as I approached the dayroom, I strode out to meet my future.

Chapter Six

It was not, however, Mr. Marlowe who awaited me, but Mollie O'Leary, perched like a nervous bird on the edge of a brocaded sofa. She had stuffed her pudgy body into an old-fashioned pelisse of green and black Irish poplin. The wide white collar emphasized the rosiness of her skin. An ancient matching bonnet trimmed with wilting ribbons hugged her head. It framed, indeed almost hid, her face from view. It was obvious she had donned her best attire for this foray into 'society,' and I wondered if, perhaps, this was one of the dresses which she brought with her from Ireland, thirty-some years ago. She jumped up with alacrity when I entered. I blinked back my surprise at seeing her and missed her first words.

"W-what?" I stammered. "I-I'm sorry, Mollie. I didn't hear you." I sank down gratefully on the sofa she had just quitted, for the shock of reprieve had sapped my strength. "What are you doing here? Is your shop not already open at this hour?" Although I saw both Eamon and Mollie at the shop each afternoon for tea, I had never expected to see her in my hotel.

"Himself has sent me to fetch you. He has decided what it is you are to be doing with yourself." Mollie smiled and on impulse embraced me. "It is not very much, mind you, and it won't be making you rich, but who knows what does? Himself is convinced it is just what you need, and I'll be losing my wits if I don't agree with him! Now, you just come along. And don't be sitting there with your mouth hanging open, 'tisn't becoming a lady."

She rose and pulled me to my feet, and I tried my best to close my mouth. Thousands of questions crowded into my head, but my lips were not capable of forming any of them.

"Let us go and fetch your wrap. Himself is waiting most impatiently." She gave me an amused wink. "And I have not seen Mr. O'Leary so excited in many a year!"

We went to my room where I quickly donned a muslin burnoose. Mollie refused to tell me anything more, even when my tongue finally loosened and I deluged her with questions. She left me in suspense as she chatted about the shops we passed, how she and Eamon had met, and about her latest grandchild. She was so warm and expansive that I felt my anxieties slip away. I began to hope that wherever I ended up, I would somehow be able to stay in touch with these dear people. When we entered the shop and Eamon's beaming face greeted us, I realized with something of a shock, pleasurable in the extreme, that in this past week Eamon and Mollie O'Leary had become my friends, the only besides Uncle Joseph I had ever had. The warmth of that thought was, I'm sure, reflected in my answering smile.

"Here, haven't I saved your table for you." Eamon escorted me to the same window seat I occupied each afternoon, and Mollie disappeared into the back of the shop to don her working clothes. "Now, sit quiet and eat something, while I'm bringing what I have to show you."

He bustled away and returned with hot tea and fresh-baked cakes, lingering close until Mollie finally returned in a green work dress covered with a large, snowy-white apron. Exhorting her to watch over me as though he expected I would run away the moment his back was turned, he then disappeared himself into the inner recesses of the shop.

It was not very busy at this hour, though in a short while the tables would all be filled with laughing, chatting customers. The one young girl who waited on the tables and served behind the counter had no trouble tending to the place by herself. I sat looking at Mollie, astounded that the gentle, quiet man of the past week was now beaming and bubbling and bustling all over the place. Mollie winked at me as she kept a surreptitious eye cocked at the young table-maid.

"I was after telling you he is excited," she said, laughing at both my expression and Eamon's behavior. And soon he was back, carrying a small sign which he placed in front of me with a flourish.

"Well?" he asked. "Well? And so, what is it you're thinking? Will it work? Can you do it? Ach," he answered himself, "such foolishness I'm talking. Of course you can do it."

He sat down and stared expectantly at me. Mollie stared back and forth between the two of us. And I sat staring at the sign in complete bewilderment. No one said a word.

'Help wanted,' the sign read. 'Clerk, able to read and write well. Mathematic ability necessary. Book knowledge helpful. Room and wage. Enquire within.'

I became aware of the silence surrounding our table, an island of calm amidst the chatter in the shop, and I lifted my head to find both my new friends watching me closely. I sat on in silence, trying to understand what was desired of me, what this sign meant, what I was supposed to say. Finally, I simply raised my hands and shook my head.

"I don't understand," I confessed.

"Oh, yes, it is perfect for you!" Eamon's enthusiasm fairly bubbled over. "A small bookseller, new and used volumes in the one shop. He has just lost his assistant, emigrated to America, as so many do now. You told us only last week, Mollie and meself, how you would help your Uncle Joseph, God rest his soul, with his ledgers and so forth. Mathematics!" He tapped the sign for emphasis. "And you love to read. You told us so, you did!"

He nodded his head vigorously in self-satisfaction. The glitter in his eyes dared me try to protest, and the words stuck fast in my throat.

"Now," he said with a disarming smile, "I know old Jacob Chadwicke, he's a bit old-fashioned, and of course he is looking for a young man. But I know you could do the work, and t'would be good for the old coot to have a woman around him, civilize him, it would, and he'd grow to love you just as we do, and it will solve all your problems, it pays two-and-six the week, enough to live on and still pay some back on the debt, slowly mind you, but—"

Eamon broke off as much for breath as for the fact that Mollie was half-fainting with laughter while I sat with hands pressed to my cheeks, letting the tidal wave of words wash over me and sweep harmlessly away. Mollie slowly wheezed to a stop.

"Oh, Mr. O'Leary," she gasped, still short of breath, her face bright red, "I haven't ever heard you say so many words in all the thirty years we've been married! Truly, you've been saving them all up, you have!"

Eamon glared at her as she began to laugh again, this time much more quietly, shaking her head over this never-before-seen facet of her husband's personality. He turned a mock frown on me.

"Well?" he demanded, trying his best to be gruff. "Have you nothing at all to say for yourself, lass? What d'you think of it?"

Yes, what *did* I think of the idea? I stared down again at the sign, pondering Eamon's rush of words.

He was right. If the position entailed listing, cataloging and selling books, and making simple entries in the shop's ledgers, of course I could do it. But a shop assistant? Me? I looked up at my two friends, hope kindling in my breast. Why *not* me? I would be free and independent, making my own way in the world. Eamon had even said there would be a small amount left to begin paying back the debt I was legally—and, I felt, morally—responsible for. I supposed it would take most of my life, but at least it would be a free life and not one dependent upon another's whim for day-to-day existence. My future would be entirely in my own hands.

The idea was exciting—and overwhelming. Could I *really* do it? After all, it had been long, long years since I had done any work on ledgers, or with mathematics. Deep inside I heard Father's voice begin its familiar litany, and doubts began to flood in: *Like all women, Marina, you are worthless unless a man guides you... You make a shambles of everything you touch... Look at yourself! You cannot even dress properly without my help... See how ignorant you are... You will never count for anything, Daughter, never.... never...*

Father's voice rang in my ears as I glanced at Eamon, fastening on what he had said of this Mr. Chadwicke.

"But you said he wants a young man. Not a woman, a *man*. Even though we are all sure I can do this work, he will not take me on. I'm not what he wants. I'm—I'm just a woman," I ended in apology, looking down so he could not see the fear and doubt standing stark in my eyes. "It wouldn't work," I whispered, echoing the voice in my head. "I'm no good. I couldn't do it, I couldn't. I can't!"

Eamon gripped my arm, forcing me to look at him.

"Yes, you *can*," he said. "I *know* you can. Have faith, little one. Believe in yourself. We do."

So saying, he rose and went back to the business of his bakery. I watched him march away, back stiff, obviously upset and disappointed by my reaction, my fear. I thought about what he had said. Believe in myself...

I looked at Mollie who still sat staring at me, and gave her an enquiring look as if to say, dare I? Dare I believe as Eamon would have me do, against everything taught me by my Father? Could I truly do this thing, in spite of what he'd always said about my incompetence?

As if I had spoken aloud, she rose and kissed my cheek, murmuring, "Of course you can do it. 'Tis perfect and you know it."

She hurried away to help Eamon, for the shop had begun to bustle. The tables were now full and a line had formed at the counter. I watched her work for a few moments, then turned my gaze back to the sign Eamon had left on the table in front of me. I read the words over and over until when I lifted my eyes to the window there they were, burned into the glass for me to read yet again.

Some time later Mollie brought me a fresh pot of tea, and I sat sipping the scalding liquid and arguing with myself, my drive for independence and my timidity each trying to best the other. I thought about which would be worse: allowing myself to be chained into a lifetime of grudging servitude without ever having tested myself to see what I was capable of; or reaching for the stars, taking this position only to fail miserably and then be forced to become a paid companion, or worse. I couldn't decide. Both frightened me utterly.

Memories paraded before me: locked doors, cruel beatings, Father's vicious sarcasm; Uncle Joseph's encouragement, the neatly kept ledgers, his pride in my intelligence and the joy of sharing ideas, of singing and dancing; the years of bleakness following Uncle Joseph's death, Father's tyranny and brutality, his denial of my individuality, my worth as a person, a human being. I discovered in those memories that what had sustained me after Uncle Joseph's death were the memories of what we had accomplished together, the contributions I had made to his life and business. I had believed in myself then, had known that I had value in this world. I had lost sight of that value; it had almost drowned in the ocean of Father's crushing savagery. I very nearly had become the slave he had wanted me to be.

Slowly, a calm certainty grew within me. I knew what I had to do. Now that I had an opportunity to be my own person, if it were taken away before I could at least try, it would kill my spirit. Trying and failing would be infinitely better than never trying at all. Whatever the consequences, they would be preferable to moldering away in a non-existence of despair and regret. And maybe, just maybe, I would not fail.

I signaled to Eamon who, with Mollie, had been anxiously watching me all this time, and when he stood solemn and expectant at my elbow, I smiled up at him. I laid my hand on the sign still on the table in front of me and spoke with a firm, confident voice.

"When can I meet with Mr. Chadwicke?"

Chapter Seven

Mr. Chadwicke was definitely old-fashioned; rotund, short, with myopic blue eyes peering through small round spectacles, watch chain dangling from waistcoat pocket, white hair fringing a bald pate. He was gruff and grumpy of manner, with an off-putting way of merely staring at one in silence, as though incredulously inspecting a strange insect that had suddenly begun speaking in a foreign tongue. It was, as I discovered, his defense for a warm and sensitive heart. Also, women intimidated him to the soles of his feet.

Eamon and Mollie O'Leary escorted me to his shop after theirs had closed for the night. It was difficult to wait, for not only did I continue to struggle with Father-inspired doubts, but also I found that having made my decision, I was anxious lest someone else filled the position before I arrived. Eamon tried his best to set my mind at ease. The clever Irishman had told Mr. Chadwicke last night he would bring me round this evening—he had been so sure of me—while neglecting to mention that I was female and, as added insurance, he had taken away Mr. Chadwicke's advertising sign when he'd left. He felt justified in this for it could only enhance my petition. With no one else even applying, old Mr. Chadwicke might be more willing to consider hiring me.

I agonized over what to wear to that interview, not that I had much from which to choose. We had left in such haste that the bulk of my wardrobe remained behind in Boston. What had been left was most likely sold by now. Luckily, what I had brought tended to be more serviceable than frivolous, and at length I chose a plain deep blue day dress with simple lace collar and cuffs. A starched crinoline instead of a hoop added some volume to the skirt, and I appeared quite businesslike when I looked into the mirror. The blue added a spark of color to my gray eyes, and with excitement tinging my cheeks pink I knew I looked attractive enough. I hoped I also would look competent enough to Mr. Chadwicke.

We did not speak as we left the tea shop and walked the few blocks to the book store. I felt alternately flushed with confidence and chilled with dread, my poor stomach in knots I feared would take years to untie. So much rested on the success of this venture. Such positions were close to impossible for a referenceless young man to obtain, and a lady's place was strictly in the home or, in dire need, as teacher, governess or companion. Anything less made one less than a lady. But so, to my mind, did abject servitude, which was what awaited me through Mr. Marlowe. At least this way I would be able to make my own decisions. Besides, my upbringing did not exactly inculcate pride in social standing.

The shop seemed very small and dark on first impression, but as my eyes grew accustomed to the semi-gloom of the interior I realized it was much larger than it had first appeared. We entered into a long, narrow room lined floor-to-ceiling with bookshelves jammed with volumes of all types and sizes. In the back wall I saw a curtained doorway, and on the left opened an archway leading to another room. From the little I could see—the dim lighting did not penetrate very far into the darkness—this room, too, was filled with books.

The atmosphere surrounding us was solemn and church-like and, even with my nerves jumping like horny toads, I wished I could bury myself here forever, devouring the contents of the shelves for sustenance. Within moments of entering, I knew it was even more imperative that I obtain this post, for this wonderful, cave-like asylum felt like home. I had never expected that feeling to be mine again.

In a few moments the curtain masking the back room twitched aside to reveal one of the shortest, roundest persons I had ever seen. At first glance he seemed an elderly elf, an impression quickly dispelled by his gruff manner and unusually deep voice. He strode toward us, smiling a delighted welcome to the

O'Learys, first embracing Eamon and then bowing like a courtier over Mollie's hand. His smile broadened as she flustered in embarrassment. He glanced timorously at me from time to time, and acknowledged my introduction with a curt bow, but otherwise made no further reference to my presence.

He ushered us into his private rooms behind the curtain, chatting of mutual acquaintances the while, and seated us on the sofa before a table set with tea. It was a large room, though the clutter made it seem small and cramped. Bookcases lined the walls, filled to overflowing with old, time-worn volumes. Heavy draperies masked tiny windows, giving them the impression of more size. A wood stove in the right front corner gave off stifling heat, baking to a crisp the rug-covered rocking chair that sat before it.

A large old mahogany dining table with six chairs took up the right rear corner, in front of a huge kitchen dresser on which sat plates and utensils of all types. Chairs, tables and reading lamps stood in the other back corner, an array of pipes ranged neatly in a rack beside a small pile of books. In the front corner to the left of the curtained entry was the sofa on which we perched, faced by two stiff armchairs separated from us by the low tea table.

Two doors broke the line of the wall to our left, and another stood heavily barred in the rear wall. The space left clear in the center of the room looked like a narrow aisle threading through the furnishings. The lighting was dim, the colors somber, the murky atmosphere added to by the dark burgundy carpet underfoot. Everything in this room was well-worn and obviously well-loved for all that it was old, shabby and mismatched.

Mr. Chadwicke entreated Mollie to pour for us, and handed round cakes and breads bought from Eamon's shop. Then he sat back, rubbing his palms together in anticipation, and fixed the Irish baker with bright, twinkling eyes.

"Well, Eamon O'Leary, I am in a state of complete suspense," he said. "I have never known you to fail at anything you have said you will do, but I must confess I am baffled this time."

He paused and turned his blue eyes on each of us in turn. The twinkle began to fade when his eyes met mine and I smiled faintly. He looked at the curtained doorway that led out to the closed shop, quickly shifting his gaze back to Eamon though it snagged again momentarily on my face.

"You told me distinctly that you would bring 'the perfect employee' with you tonight, but I see no one here. We must keep our ears open for the sound of a knock. No doubt he will be along at any moment. Though this tardiness does not endear him to me. No, no, not at all."

As he spoke, Mr. Chadwicke's countenance gradually darkened with suspicion, his tone growing sharper as his fears deepened. His eyes shifted once more to me and away again; his last sentence sounded more like a question than a statement.

Silence reigned for some minutes while Mr. Chadwicke slumped in his chair, glowering at Eamon who merely waited, calmly eying his friend back. And then Mr. Chadwicke's head snapped around to where I sat at the end of the sofa. Blue eyes glared into mine, and I took a deep breath in an attempt to steady nerves which tried to disintegrate as the staring-contest lengthened.

My heart pounded. I remained still, enduring the bad-tempered glare and grimaces my hopeful employer shot my way, until at last I looked down at my hands folded in my lap. Why did Eamon not say something? He could at least explain why he brought me here.

My resolve began to falter under this elf-like man's animosity when suddenly I remembered that scene this morning on the street below my window. If I did not secure this position, I would be faced with one such as that. Mr. Chadwicke might be as bad-tempered as they come, but at least when the shop was closed I would have the freedom to do as I wished. My room, my food, my clothing, my *life* would be all mine, and not hired out on sufferance. I had to win this opening. I had to!

I sat up straighter, put on the 'I won't tolerate any nonsense' expression I had seen so often on Father's face, and raised my eyes. If it worked so well for Father, I thought, then perhaps it will work for me. But I was unprepared for the shock I received as, armed to fight tooth-and-nail—metaphorically speaking—my eyes made contact with Mr. Chadwicke's. Centered in his brooding, stormy face, almost hidden beneath lowering, bushy brows, rimmed with ill-tempered wrinkles and ridges, his eyes were not glaring. They were not fuming. They were not even angry. They were frightened. They held the look of a man who had finally been presented with the fate he had dreaded and eluded for years. All the gruff, ill-tempered sharpness was a cover-up, a bluff. He was intimidated. By *me*!

My mind raced. This was the opening, the clue, the edge I needed to gain the employment Mr. Chadwicke offered, albeit not to me. How to use this to best advantage? I could sense Mollie's look shift to me as excitement burned two spots of red into her cheeks. She put her hand on Eamon's arm, and in answer he covered it with his own hand as though to tell her to keep silent. He never shifted his gaze from Mr. Chadwicke, who now appeared totally unconscious of their presence. His entire attention was riveted on me, concentrated on driving me out by the force of his displeasure without a word being spoken.

As quickly as possible I assessed the situation and my options, for I knew I must make the first move, and make it soon. I could use my new-found knowledge of Mr. Chadwicke's weakness and simply bully him into giving me the job. But that would surely make him resentful and bad-tempered in truth, and the work, therefore, no pleasure when it should have been. If I became the totally helpless female in dire need of a gallant male rescuer, it could unman him so completely he would become a bumbling incompetent around me, and that bode ill for the business and my future alike. But if I could strike the right balance of competence and deference, appeal to his business sense while bolstering his male ego... For the first time I began to feel the least bit grateful for Father's training. I was sure I could handle this sweet old fake glowering in the chair before me.

I leaned forward to set my teacup down, breaking eye contact and demurely lowering my gaze to the floor, at a spot a few inches in front of Mr. Chadwicke's feet. He shifted them hastily. I counted to five, slowly, then raised a hesitant glance to his face and gave him a shy smile.

"I must confess, Mr. Chadwicke, you have guessed correctly. It was, indeed, not a young man that Mr. O'Leary intended to bring with him this night. It was me."

I paused here and cast a grateful look at a quietly amused Eamon, catching sight of an astonished Mollie beside him. When I turned my attention back to Mr. Chadwicke, I found his face had hardened, his inner defenses strengthened. And so I laced the truth with humility and a touch of Eamon O'Leary's famous Irish Blarney.

"I was quite fearful to come, Mr. Chadwicke. I am a woman in quite difficult straits and am well aware of the near-impossibility of anyone meeting my needs. But Mr. O'Leary convinced me that, being the kind and compassionate man that you are, you would have no objection to at least listening to my story, to our proposal. If it does not satisfy, perhaps you could even discover another solution to my dilemma."

I sat back then, gaze fastened on my clasped hands, hoping I had not overdone it. The silence stretched. Finally, Mr. Chadwicke rubbed his face with his hands and heaved a deep sigh. He turned his eyes on his friend again, a gleam of amusement sparking in the bright blue.

"I see," he murmured, his voice so low I had to strain to catch his words, "kind and compassionate, am I?" Eamon shrugged, his brows raised. Mr. Chadwicke turned back to me, his voice now at full volume. "All right, young lady. I'm waiting."

He settled himself into his chair as mentally I crossed my fingers and began to speak, telling him essentially what I had told the O'Leary's. I dwelt more heavily, however, on Uncle Joseph, reliving many of our special times, relating much of the advice I could remember him giving me, sharing what he had taught me of record keeping and the love of books. Mr. Chadwicke listened with an attentive air, grunting and nodding in places, shooting a cryptic look at Eamon when I spoke of my work with Uncle Joseph's ledgers, shaking his head in sorrow as I told him how Uncle Joseph and I had been separated and the emptiness his death had left in my life. Somewhere I became lost in my tale, forgetting to mold my words to suit my purpose, speaking instead from my heart, from the pain and joy buried deep inside me.

I skimmed my years with Father, omitting details but letting Mr. Chadwicke understand clearly that this father-daughter relationship left very much to be desired. My voice trembled with the strain of keeping in those things I no longer wished to speak of, much less remember. When I related the tale of Father's disintegration these last two years, Mr. Chadwicke grew very still, watching me in silence, his expression enigmatic. At last I came to the events of the past four weeks that had brought me here to him. Mr. Chadwicke leaned forward toward me. He seemed to be holding his breath. Finally, I stopped, not knowing what else to say, no longer sure why I felt it important to manipulate this wonderful old man who listened so patiently to a stranger who meant nothing to him.

We sat in silence for a time. I listened to the companionable voice of the Grandfather clock ticking in the reading corner, my gaze again on my clasped hands. When the clock began to chime the hour I looked up at it, startled, for I had been lost in my memories, unaware of the silence that surrounded us. I took a deep breath and let it out slowly, facing Mr. Chadwicke with my back straight and my gaze steady on his face.

"I believe Mr. O'Leary has great hopes that you will ask me to work for you, Mr. Chadwicke. I believe that is what was behind his deviousness in bringing me here only partly announced and completely undescribed." I smiled at him and, although he did not smile back, he did nod his agreement. "I cannot but hope the same, for it would solve a great many of my problems, as well as give me the chance to live for myself. And you *would* get a competent employee."

I looked again at Eamon, sitting beside me with a smug look on his face. I smiled at him, too, before turning back to the bookseller.

"Mr. O'Leary assures me that on the salary you propose to pay I would be able to make a start," I spread my hands in acknowledgment, "a tiny one, admittedly, but a start nevertheless, on Father's debt, which I am convinced is mine morally as well as legally."

I sighed as the enormity of the debt hit me again, and paused to search Mr. Chadwicke's face, looking for something to tell me whether or not I should go on. He merely sat watching me as well, searching my face for I knew not what. *Well*, I thought, *in for a penny...* and continued.

"I will be very honest with you, Mr. Chadwicke." I hoped my calm, low voice did not betray the high-strung state of my nerves. "I would truly love to work here with you for many reasons, not the least of which is hopefully an opportunity to read these books. It has been so long since I have been able to read anything worthwhile; Father did not believe in substance, or intelligence, not for women. This is a wonderful place, warm and homey and comfortable."

My gaze traced around the book-lined shelves which filled every space even here in Mr. Chadwicke's private sitting room, then again I looked him in the eye and gave him a shy smile. "I could stay here forever. And I know I could do very well at whatever you need done, although I would need a little time to become used to your monetary system. To become used to so much."

My throat dried up, stopping the flow of my words. Suddenly nervous, I licked my lips and bit at my lower lip. All the while, our eyes remained locked. Mr. Chadwicke sat with an air of expectancy, as though urging me to bare my soul. I started to tremble. Now I was the one frightened, intimidated. Tears misted my eyes and again my lips parted.

"I guess what I want to say is that what I need most of all is an Uncle Joseph," I said, startling us all with my words.

Someone gasped, Mollie or Eamon—or perhaps me—I do not know, but now that I had begun to speak my heart I could not have stopped had I wanted to.

"I know that I can do the work, I have no doubt at all even though I keep hearing Father's voice telling me I am no good at anything. But I do not know if I can live on my own—being alone—making decisions that I-I don't know even exist." I began to stumble over my words in my need to be understood. "Father t-taught me only to do for him, n-never for myself. Without advice, without friendship, I don't know if I could survive on my own. I-I don't know the first thing I would need to do, much less the second or third. But I do know that if I do not try, if I am again caught in bondage before I have a chance to find the me that Father tried to throw away, then there will not be a me left. I would simply... cease to exist."

I bowed my head not to hide tears for there were none, but because I could not bear him to see any longer the pain and desperation I knew stood clear on my face. Once again the silence lengthened, became more and more uncomfortable. I was terrified to lift my head, terrified to hear what he would say. Just as I could bear it no longer and was on the point of rising to flee, I heard Mr. Chadwicke thrust himself to his feet and begin muttering and complaining under his breath. I sneaked a peek at him and saw him puttering around back and forth from desk to table to bookcase to drawer, searching for something. Eamon, Mollie and I sat watching him, our mouths open in surprise. The whole while he continued to shake his head, grunt, utter such unintelligible sounds as, "Ha!" and "Ho!" and "Hoo!" and mutter incomprehensible phrases and complaints under this breath. I watched him in complete astonishment, wondering if perhaps he was mad. I was unaware that anxiety and bewilderment had caused me to hold my breath as I watched and wondered.

Suddenly, he turned and headed for one of the small doors near the reading corner, the one closest to the front of the room. Just as suddenly he stopped and pivoted about to face us. He stared at us in silence. We stared back.

"Ha!" he exclaimed, making us all jump. My

breathing started again on a gasp. "Well, what are you sitting there for? Do you want to see your room, or not?"

With those words, he spun about, opened the door and vanished through it. We hastily rose, smiling and shaking our heads at each other in bemusement, and hurried after him into a narrow hallway that ended in a staircase. Eamon beamed at me in self-satisfied elation, and Mollie squeezed my arm for congratulations and encouragement. But there was time for nothing else. As we reached the bottom of the stair and looked up, we found Mr. Chadwicke, surprisingly light and quick on his feet, already halfway up, key poised to unlock the door at the top. His words floated down around our disbelieving ears as we climbed after him.

"Compassionate and kind, ha? ... Help and advice ... Hoo, ha!... Uncle Joseph? Uncle? Ha!"

Chapter Eight

For three wonderful years I worked with Mr. Chadwicke—Uncle Jacob as I came to call him. He offered me warmth, solace, advice and friendship. They were the best years of my life.

The room into which he showed us that first eventful evening was large and spacious, running across the front of the building above the book rooms beneath. Tall windows that lined the street wall afforded an enchanting view of the lamp-lit London street below, and would flood the room with light by day. It was well-furnished with old but quality pieces, containing not only a large four-poster bed, wardrobe and writing desk, but also, situated before the fireplace, a charming seating group of settee, table and two mismatched chairs with footstools.

I stopped at the threshold, staring at the room in wonder. Even bare of ornament, with threadbare draperies masking the windows and no carpet to cover the worn oak floor, it looked luxurious to me. This would be mine, to live in? I could not believe it.

Silent, in awe, I moved around the room, absorbing its soul though the tips of my fingers, beginning with the fine old oaken wardrobe and the warm cherry of the wainscot, rubbed satin-smooth by years of polishing. I stroked the glossy depths of the mahogany four-poster bed and swept my hand over the nubby whiteness of its counterpane. I skimmed my hands along the bookshelves and the silken softness of the leather bindings contained therein. As I passed by, I ran the heavy soft shimmer of deep blue velvet bed hangings and window drapes through my fingers, and laid both palms against the cool luster of the fireplace marble. Feeling giddy with disbelief, I sank down on the settee and felt beneath my hands the varied textures of the embroidered covering. I could smell a comforting mix of wood polish, dust, old ashes and aged vellum.

I sat silent, overwhelmed by the beauty of the room, the like of which I had never before occupied. Father's room had been filled with beautiful wood and silks and satins, as were many of the other unoccupied rooms on his floor, but I was rarely allowed to even enter any of them. My small attic room began life as a servant's room, stifling in summer, freezing in winter, and bare of any necessity except bed and bureau; no curtains, no carpet, no chair. Even when we traveled, Father had always requested a tiny, top-floor room for me, one that contained the barest necessities and nothing else. That was what I had expected now.

I looked around the room again. True, it was not elegantly appointed as were those in the homes of the wealthy, probably not even designed originally as bedchamber, and the disparity among the age and condition of the furnishings spoke of a great many inhabitants over the years. But there was a feeling here of happiness, of contentment and peace. Each addition had been made with love, to give quiet pleasure to whomever would next reside within these walls. And now it was mine.

At last I looked at Mr. Chadwicke, who stood at a window looking down into the shadowed London street. Faint sounds of carriages, horses' hooves, laughter and coachmen's calls floated up to us. He must have sensed my eyes on him, for he turned a quizzical look upon me. I could not trust myself to speak, and so I merely smiled my gratitude to him, my eyes aswim with tears.

"Well, now," he said, rubbing his hands together. I was soon to discover it was a habitual gesture with him, one done when he felt gratitude or full of amused satisfaction. "It is not much, I know, and what is here is quite old and worn, but it has done very well for my former employees and I daresay it will also do so for you."

He strode to the cold fireplace before which I sat and indicated the swinging rods and iron pots.

"You can cook here in the fireplace if you wish, although it will take some getting used to if all you have worked with is a range cooker."

He went on bustling about the room, opening wardrobe doors and drawers, pointing out what he felt I should know, as though I were wavering in my decision to accept this miraculous offer. *Or, perhaps, to give me time to recover from the rapidity of it all*, I thought. Finally, he stood before me, feet planted wide and fists bunched on hips. He tried his best to glare at me.

"You have not said a word, Miss, not one word. I am offering you the vacant position in my humble establishment," he bowed as gracefully as he could without removing his hands from his hips, "much against my better judgment, I will add. Which offer includes this room to live in for as long as you may be in my employ. The very least you could do in return is to tell me when you would condescend to start."

He tried his utmost to act affronted, but the dimples in his cheeks and the sparkles in his eyes utterly betrayed him. I smiled to smother the happy laughter bubbling up inside me, rose to my feet and curtseyed to him.

"Mr. Chadwicke, I do most humbly and gratefully accept your offer of employment. I love this room. I cannot wait to move in, and as I have very little to bring with me, may I do so tomorrow? You are so very kind. This is all so wonderful, I can scarcely believe it!"

On impulse, I stepped forward and embraced him. Realizing the audacity of what I had done, I stepped back almost immediately, my face, I am sure, flaming red. I murmured an apology, to which Mr. Chadwicke responded with a quite gruff, "Humpf!"

and a very convincing affronted demeanor. He led the way back downstairs and we followed slowly, I terrified that now he would withdraw his offer.

I kept my head bent and my trembling hands clasped tight as we took our leave, and walked between Eamon and Mollie unmindful of their chatter, fighting tears the whole way. It was not until Eamon had escorted me to the hotel, having left Mollie off at their rooms behind the pastry shop, that I began to suspect that Mr. Chadwicke had given me a tiny hug in return. The more I thought of it, the more sure I became. His arms actually *had* come up and quickly but gently pressed upon my back. I knew for certain then that he would play the biggest part in making this new place a home for me.

Eamon arranged for two men to move my trunk and bags from the hotel the next morning, and I wrote a note to Mr. Marlowe asking that he settle the bill for me, as he still had possession of the bulk of the money found with Father. I also indicated my new address, and requested that he send any remaining monies to me there. I asked to be advised to whom I was to begin forwarding payments on Father's debt, and thanked him for his efforts on my behalf. I assured him that my future was now in capable hands—my own—well aware of the shock those words would produce. Were I not so anxious to settle in my new home, I would have greatly enjoyed conveying these sentiments in person. I dispatched the letter and set off for the bookshop, dismissing the solicitor from my mind. Aside from receiving from him, most likely by messenger, the money and information I had requested, I did not expect to see or hear from Mr. Marlowe again.

I settled into my new room, a process which took barely over an hour though I lingered for two, rearranging my meager belongings in joyful freedom—Father had even dictated the arrangement of my possessions—then went down to the bookshop below. Mr. Chadwicke was busy with a customer over some rare old editions, but he excused himself when I appeared in the curtained doorway to come over to me. He again expressed his pleasure in having me there, although I could see lingering reservations in his eyes. He bade me look around and familiarize myself with the contents of the two rooms while he concluded his business.

I could not have asked for a better suggestion. The thought of all those books at my disposal had kept me awake with excitement and anticipation most of the previous night. I stood quietly for a few moments, looking around and simply absorbing the atmosphere. Finally, not wishing to disturb Mr. Chadwicke and the well-dressed gentleman with him, who sent curious glances my way, I decided to begin my explorations in the other room. As quietly and unobtrusively as possible, I left the main chamber.

Again, just a few steps inside the archway, I stopped to absorb the atmosphere. This room was more square than the main room, paneled in dark wood, with heavy beams traversing the ceiling. Rich dark carpeting, old and worn in spots, covered the floor. The feeling here was very different from that in the larger room, less church-like and awe-filled, radiating instead more a sense of adventure and impatience. *Hurry, open us, read!* these books seemed to be saying, and as I stepped closer to the shelves I discovered why.

Each volume I saw was of fairly recent publication, and most were unread; many, I was to discover, with pages still uncut. There was much to uncover here, knowledge of subject matter, of each author's thought processes and beliefs, as well as his writing style. But the most important thing waiting to be discovered was knowledge of one's own self, learned through one's reaction to and use of what one has read. It is this self-knowledge that books themselves absorb. A part of each person who reads them remains behind in the pages, and they become more and more imbued with the spirit of the people they are written to serve, educate, entertain or instruct. That is why the large room, containing only old editions, radiated a solemnity and reverence lacking in this room. The old books chamber not only represented humanity, it contained humanity.

As I circulated the new book room, scanning the shelves, I realized that there was no order here. Everything seemed to have been dropped willy-nilly into the nearest available space with no regard for content or author. More than once I saw copies of the same volume occupying quite disparate places on the shelves. Some books lay flat upon the boards, placed one atop the other. Untidy stacks littered the floor. The first of my duties, obviously, would be to try to make some sense out of this room.

I learned some important things about Mr. Chadwicke as I explored that room and handled volumes still smelling of printer's ink. Those volumes were there simply as a convenience for his customers. It was obvious he had no real interest in them himself, and it appeared that his former employee had not, either. I had not had time to thoroughly investigate the room in which we had sat last night, but all the volumes I had seen had seemed quite old; precious books smelling of time and life, and not of printer's ink. I was willing to bet there were no new books in Mr. Chadwicke's personal rooms for, as much as he tried to hide it behind ill-tempered gruffness, he was most definitely a people person, a man whose life was shaped and defined by those who passed through his doors. I was sure I would come to love him as much as I already loved this sanctuary.

For that is how I thought of this shop, even on that first day, as a sanctuary, a haven from the cruel dictates of social custom that places a woman, however capable or intelligent, in the category of chattel, at the mercy of those in power: men, who cosset and treat women as pets created for their amusement; and wealthy women, who take out their frustration at their social captivity on those less monetarily fortunate than they. My growing up years with Father might have been hard and cruel, but at least he had not imbued me with a sense of social status which would have made it impossible for me to even consider a position such as this. He had imparted no sense of standing at all, merely made me feel invisible and worthless. Indeed, Uncle Joseph's loving support and encouragement of my sense of independence, lying fallow all these years, equipped me better than most to recognize and quickly grasp what was surely the only other acceptable way out besides marriage. And marriage, as defined by most men, was not acceptable to me. It was not a way out, merely a continuation of enslavement.

My education at Father's hands had taught me how hard it was to be a woman and maintain any sense of self, or fulfill any needs save those of others. Unable to own property, have business interests separate from a husband's, father's or brother's, or to control money; educated and equipped for nothing other than marriage, household management and child-bearing; kept literally and legally under father's, brother's or husband's thumb, women were trained to become—and believe themselves to be—non-entities. Very, very few escaped. Even those whose favors men paid for, on whatever social level, were controlled by their men and dependent upon their keepers' whims. I thanked God every night for the great blessing He had given me in the person of Mr. Chadwicke, and I prayed it would continue forever. It never occurred to me that my own blindness would be my downfall.

We worked well together, Mr. Chadwicke and I,

sharing quiet times and laughter, uncertainties and accomplishments. It did not take me long to understand the British monetary system of pounds sterling, and soon I was able to take over most of the shop entries, a burden Mr. Chadwicke found trying at best. He left me to my own devices concerning the new-book room, but told me in no uncertain terms that the rest of the place belonged to him. He would tolerate no outward interference from me.

"Miss Weston," he said one day when I had been there about two weeks, "we need to sit down together. There are a few points which must be made clear if we are to continue our, ah, association."

Again there was no mistaking the twinkle in his eye which belied his gruff manner, but I did miss it, for I still had not become fully used to his way. I was sitting surrounded by volumes from the new-book-room shelves, attempting to bring a semblance of order to chaos. I was covered with dust from head to foot, my hair escaping in wisps from the kerchief in which I had bound it. My heart sank as I gazed up at him from my place on the floor. Was he about to let me go? I knew I had not been there long enough to prove myself, but neither did I think I had been there long enough to prove a disaster, either.

But I had learned from Father never to trust my own judgment and, since two weeks was not long enough to undo that damage, it was with a sinking heart that I rose and set aside the books on which I worked. I dusted myself off as best I could and followed him into his private sitting room behind the curtain. I was becoming quite acquainted with it, for not only did we often take our noon meal there together, but I also, at Mr. Chadwicke's insistence, used it as a pass-through from my room above the shop. There was a separate outside entrance at the building's rear, but to use it meant incurring the inconvenience of a long walk down the mews and around the building at all hours and in all weather. And I had been right that first day. There were no new books at all in this room.

I sat at my accustomed place at the table as Mr. Chadwicke indicated I should. That he chose to stand I interpreted with foreboding. I folded my hands on the table, mainly to stop their shaking, and waited for him to dismiss me.

"Now, Miss Weston," he began in a hard, sharp voice, pacing to and fro before me, "I am well content to allow you free reign in that side room of mine." He waved an indifferent hand in the general direction of the room in which I had been working. *"But,"* he emphasized, turning to pierce me with his best mock-glare, "I will *not* tolerate *any* interference with my old books! Not any!"

He broke off and strode to the curtained doorway, standing there to gaze with love at all the room contained. I sat aghast at the table. What had brought this on? I would never dare to presume on any of his business. I never had. I had simply asked if he would mind if I re-shelved the new books into an order that would be easier to work with, and get them up off the floor. That the old volumes were in as chaotic a state I was certain, and doubtless they could also benefit from a systematic structure. But Mr. Chadwicke seemed to have no trouble finding what he needed, and so I had not mentioned my thoughts to him. And as I was forbidden to clerk in the old-book room, my employer having stated emphatically only a week before that the accounts and the new books were more than enough for me to handle, I could not understand why he remonstrated so with me. But he spoke on, adamantly refusing help I had not offered, and slowly I began to wonder if Mr. Chadwicke's bombast was merely a cover-up for his inability to ask for the help he might need. And want.

"*If* I should feel," his hard, gruff voice lashed at me, "and I said *if*, you will please note, *if* I should feel the need for a classification of any sort—which does not mean I do, mind you—then *I* shall decide and take charge of it. I shall decide how it is to be done, if it is to be done at all, which I can assure it will not need to be. But *should* it ever come to that, it is possible I *might* allow you to assist me, though I doubt it will come to that, I most sincerely do. These volumes are very important to me, Miss Weston." His voice began to soften and his eyes glazed with sentiment. "They are like my children. I cannot have just anybody fussing about with them, moving them here and there. It is very difficult for me..."

He stopped abruptly, cleared his throat and

tugged on his lapels. He stiffened up and glared at me once more. This time, however, I did catch the gleam in his eye, a very definite twinkle, and the dimples that flashed off and on in his cheeks. I heard the softness in his voice clearly under the gruff overlayment. I began to relax, and smiled to myself as he continued.

"Ah, hrumph! I mean, I will not have any *young woman* coming in here trying to tell me how to run my business. How can I run a business if you are forever moving my things about? Even if a new arrangement would make things easier." He paced back and forth in mock agitation, waving his hands about. "What kind of dealer would my customers think me if I had to keep asking some young slip of a thing where my own stock is? It would never do! I simply could not have that!" He looked at me and asked, seeming completely unaware of the plaintive, pleading note in his voice, "You do see, do you not? This is my shop. I simply cannot have that!"

I smiled at him and rose, pushing back my straggling hair. I saw perfectly, and I knew now where my duty lay toward this sweet, gentle soul with the so-rough exterior.

"Of course, Mr. Chadwicke. I am here to learn from you. I know so little of the world, or of life. I cannot tell you how grateful I am that I have you to guide me—in all things."

I paused and smoothed my skirt with my hands, trying to find the right words. When I looked up, I looked straight into his warm, sparkling blue eyes,

eyes that had failed so miserably at glaring.

"I am sure to make mistakes, and I will be so grateful for any correction you give me. I want only to help you in any little way you decide I may. But I do know that taking this position with you is the best thing I have done, or am ever likely to do. Whatever you may need of me, I am yours to command."

I curtsied, smiling at him with great affection, and he actually began to dither, the old fake!

"Oh!" He turned red and waved his arms around. "What are you standing about for? Have you not much work to do? Well, go on! Go on! To work with you, to work!"

He actually shooed me off with flapping hands as though I were a chicken.

"Yes, sir," I managed to say through the laughter I tried very hard to choke down. "Right away, sir."

I went back to my gargantuan task with a light heart and a gay spirit. What a deer, sweet old man. Unless I was quite mistaken, and I would be very surprised if I were for Father had taught me well how to understand a man's mind, my employer had just let me know how desperately he needed order brought to his complete inventory, including his precious antique books. But he also just as desperately needed to retain his hold on authority, the necessary male domination of all the decision-making processes of his business. In other words, he needed to save face.

Well, I considered, replacing Mr. Dickens' latest works on the shelf, it should not be too difficult to suggest ways to improve things while allowing him to believe the ideas were his own. It was simply a variation on how I learned to cajole information out of Father. True, it did not work very well with Father, but a tiny piece won from him equaled smashing success with anyone else. I had no doubt about my ability to give Mr. Chadwicke the help he needed in the way he needed it given.

Two months later I passed through the sitting room on my way out to the new-book room, where I continued slowly but surely making progress on the classification project. I stopped behind Mr. Chadwicke, who sat reading in his favorite chair before the fire. I leaned over to see what it was he read, resting my hands lightly on his shoulders as I did so. He held one of Marcus Aurelius' volumes—in Latin. He neither stiffened nor pulled away from my touch, but I felt him grow very still beneath my palms. I spoke, a quiet breath beside his ear.

"Mr. Chadwicke, I do not believe I can go on having you call me 'Miss Weston' every time you speak to me. If our, ah, association is to continue, I must ask that you call me by my given name. It is Marina. Marina Elizabeth." I smiled behind his head. "But just 'Marina' will do."

I bent down and gave him a gentle kiss on the top of his bald pate, then sped away before he could recover his wits. He avoided me for most of that day, turning red and speechless when, as always, we shared our noon meal. I ignored his red-faced, helpless silence and chattered on about the wonderful things I was discovering hidden away on the dusty new-book-room shelves. We had every volume as yet published by that marvelous Mr. Dickens, the latest, *The Cricket On The Hearth*, having only just arrived. Now that Mr. Chadwicke had suggested, with a little subtle nudging on my part, that we put a sign or two in the window, we were doing a brisk business in Mr. Dickens' works. His popularity seemed to be growing every week, surprising Mr. Chadwicke who, though he still had no use for the new books contained in that room, at least now acknowledged their existence.

As we closed up for the night, we spoke of the work ahead of us on the morrow, as we were wont to do. I turned out the wall sconce in the new book room and walked out to where my employer was lowering the lamp on his desk.

"I am almost finished with my work of classification on the new books, Mr. Chadwicke," I said, but he interrupted me abruptly, an occurrence I was fast becoming used to.

"Oh, no, no, no, no, no." He shook his head as though annoyed; I knew by now, however, that he rarely was. "This will never do. Never, never, never. It is entirely impossible for you to call me Mr. Chadwicke if our, ah, association is to continue."

He shot me a look of pure, twinkling enjoyment. I smiled back at him, knowing full well what was to come and enjoying it as much as he.

"It is entirely too long a name, the bane of my life.

Think of all the time you will waste saying it, day-in and day-out. No. No, it will not do, not at all!"

He stood looking at me expectantly and it was all I could do not to throw my arms about him in a huge hug.

"Well," I said, trying to look thoughtful, "what do your friends call you?"

"My friends?" He tried, and failed, to look both flustered and affronted. "My friends call me 'old man' or 'old Jacob,' most of them."

I stared at him in disbelief.

"Well, I most certainly refuse to call you 'old' anything!"

He merely harrumphed. I paused and watched him for a moment, knowing I loved him more with each day that passed.

"I shall call you Uncle," I declared, smiling at him. "Uncle Jacob." Dropping him a small curtsey, I turned and danced through the shop up to my room, leaving him red-faced and pleased as punch at himself that his little subterfuge had worked—as had mine.

And thus we continued, growing closer with each day for three wonderful years. Uncle Jacob was there through all my joys and sorrows, difficulties and accomplishments, sharing in them and giving me guidance and advice. He taught me how to manage my salary, how to budget what little I had left after sending my monthly payment to Mr. Alcott in Boston, a task not easy for the only money I had ever handled were mere figures written in ledgers and spent by someone else. I learned how to judge the value of the goods I desired against those I needed, a lesson hard in the learning, especially at the beginning. A weekly salary, paid monthly, seemed like a fortune to me, and it took many hungry nights when I had nothing left with which to buy food, and many cold ones when I went without firewood, before I learned just how quickly a fortune of any size can disappear.

But with Uncle Jacob's understanding and help, and his forbearance in advancing me money or offering unwarranted feeding, I did learn, becoming indeed a good manager. And we grew ever closer, feeling more and more like a real Uncle and Niece. Though we strictly observed propriety during shop hours, addressing each other as 'Miss Weston' and 'Mr. Chadwicke' in public, when alone together we remained on a first-name basis. Uncle Jacob often joked with me about my name, calling me 'Just Marina' as he claimed I had requested. I loved my life. I never wanted it to end.

Chapter Nine

Six months had passed since I began my work for Uncle Jacob, and I found it difficult to remember any other way of life. I had just begun to start—at his suggestion, of course—systematizing the used and antique volumes, when I received a visitor. I had become accustomed to the fact that customers, the women as well as the men, would ignore me even if I stood square in their way. Not one had ever condescended to allow me to wait upon them; what could I, a mere *woman*, possibly know about *bookselling*? A few would politely acknowledge my presence with a nod, and one or two would occasionally ask me a simple question, such as, "Will Mr. Chadwicke be very long, do you think?" It had yet to occur to any of them that I might have some knowledge of the work upon which I was engaged.

Therefore, when the heavy front door opened and closed to admit yet another expensively dressed gentleman sporting cape and cane, I did not so much as glance up from my place in a dim corner of the room. I heard Uncle Jacob hurry forward to greet his customer, and so I dismissed this latest intrusion and immersed myself back into the problem at hand, the classification of a work by Ovid.

I looked up, startled, when a shadow obscured the light. Uncle Jacob stood over me, an expression of concern on his face.

"Marina, my dear," he said in a low voice, extending a hand to help me rise, "there is a gentleman here to see you." He cast a quick glance over his shoulder toward the man standing with his back to us, seemingly scanning a bookshelf. "A Mr. Marlowe, he said. I believe it is something to do with your Father."

I understood his worried look. I had told him portions of my life with my Father, more so than I had told the O'Leary's, and all about the enormous debt which I must shoulder. I brushed the dust from my skirt and smoothed my hair. I tried to reassure Uncle Jacob—and myself—as I did so.

"I am sure he is here only to deliver whatever money is left from what was found after Father died," I said, "though it has been so long I did not think anything *was* left. Do not worry, Uncle Jacob. I am paying on what I owe, and as long as I continue to do so, I do not believe they can drag me off to jail. May we use the sitting room?"

I had no intention of discussing my personal matters in the shop, and I was certainly not about to take this cold, arrogant man up to my room. His very presence would destroy the calm, serene atmosphere I so treasured.

"Of course, of course," Uncle Jacob murmured, giving me a comforting pat on the shoulder. I smiled my gratitude at him and took a deep breath, then moved slowly toward this last link with a past I wished very much to forget.

"Mr. Marlowe," I said, touching him gently on the arm, "this is quite a surprise after all this time. What has brought you here, to Chadwicke's Books?"

He turned his head and looked me over in silence, noting with unconcealed displeasure that I did not seem distraught at my circumstances, but rather content, and not the least grateful for his appearance. With studied movements he turned his body to face me and took my hand in greeting, bowing over it while taking in with a distressed expression the plainness of my simple green wool dress, the disheveled appearance of my hair, the dusty state of my work- and ink-stained hands.

"My dear Miss Weston," he said, seeming quite disconcerted with what he saw, "I am obviously come only just in time." He looked around the dim, time-worn room with distaste. "Is there somewhere we may speak privately?"

I bowed my head in acquiescence and led the way into Uncle's sitting room, motioning Mr. Marlowe to a seat on the settee. It was somewhat perverse of me, I must admit, for I had noticed that most men seemed to be quite uncomfortable perching alone on a hard seat. For some reason, most likely his superior male attitude, I had taken a dislike to Mr. Marlowe upon our first meeting, and nothing had yet happened to change my mind. Something told me I would enjoy watching his discomfiture.

I busied myself preparing tea and he chatted amiably about various subjects which it seemed he considered suitable for delicate female ears, the cold, pre-Christmas weather being foremost. Smiling with feigned innocence as I poured tea and handed him his cup, I enquired, "Have you read Mr. Dickens' holiday works? I have just finished *The Cricket On The Hearth*. I have found the title to be quite symbolic, although the story does not intrigue as much as does that of *A Christmas Carol*. Any Christmas story is wonderful, I suppose, but I would like to see that such conditions as exist in *Oliver Twist* be abolished completely. That would make a true gift for Christmas, don't you agree?"

I gave him a sweet smile as I awaited his reply, all the while knowing it would be quite unlikely that Mr. Marlowe would have read any of Mr. Dickens' works, especially *The Cricket On The Hearth*, for the bound volumes of the original serials that had appeared in periodicals twenty years before, had been out for less than a week. He merely sat aghast that I would have read such a scandalous work as *Oliver Twist*, that I would be aware of the conditions to which I referred. One does not mention such things in polite society.

"But of course," I continued after an awkward moment, "you did not come here to discuss literary accomplishments or social change. Tell me, pray, what is it that has brought you here?"

I sat sipping my tea, outwardly calm, waiting for him to find voice, all the while wondering what did bring him here in person, especially after all this time. Surely, had he simply a few remaining pounds to convey, it could have most easily been done by messenger. Mr. Marlowe did not seem to me the altruistic type, concerning himself unduly with the fate of destitute young women. And I could not believe he had come merely to enquire after my health and happiness. My curiosity mounted as he let the silence lengthen.

At last he cleared his throat and spoke, his tone one of supercilious disapproval.

"I must confess, Miss Weston, that I was completely nonplused upon receipt of your communiqué six months past. Needless to say, I have been quite concerned as to the state of your welfare. I can see now that I was quite right to be concerned."

He paused to sip some tea and I watched him through eyes grown wary with disbelief. *If he has been so concerned*, I asked myself, *where has he been for the past six months? And what brings him here now?*

"To begin with," he said, setting his cup on the table, "I have here the concluding settlement of your Father's, ah, estate. It is nothing for you to bother your head about, I am sure you will not even clearly remember this confusing business about money and such things. But you will, of course, appreciate that many fees and bills have had to be paid from the meager monies recovered at your Father's death. So many, so many; doctors, funeral expenses, taxes, and of course my rather modest fee—"

"I remember perfectly the state of the financial matters concerning my Father, Mr. Marlowe," I interrupted, my tone rather cold, for I did not appreciate being treated like a dim-witted child. I had told him of my employment in the letter I had sent him. What did he think being an account clerk meant? "It was made crystal clear to me by yourself a mere six months ago, and I have never had trouble with my memory. I consented to allow you to handle this for me because I had been assured of your diligence and honesty by the managers at the hotel."

I paused, sipping tea with a demure air while my insides quaked at my audacity in thus addressing a personage such as Mr. Marlowe. He sat staring speechless at me. Had I suddenly turned into a viper, I'm sure he would not have been more surprised. I held the cup with both hands so that my shaking would not be noticeable and spoke on, determined to finish what I had begun.

"You have no need, I trust, to explain your actions or the disbursements to me at this time, Mr. Marlowe. If you will simply leave an itemized account with whatever monies are left, I will study it later. If I have any questions, I will notify you."

We sat staring at each other, each unable to believe I had said what I just had, and for much the same reason. I have no idea what had prompted me to behave in such an unladylike manner, but perhaps it was because for the past six months the life I had led had freed me from the restrictions society placed upon women. Uncle Jacob treated me with the charming deference due my femininity, but he also scrupulously respected the intelligence that was beginning to flourish under his care. For the entire time I had been here, he had not once turned aside a thought, idea, suggestion or feeling of mine simply because I was a woman. I was living on my own, making an invaluable contribution to Uncle Jacob's business, and earning enough money to buy clothing and food and pay back, albeit slowly, that enormous debt Father had left me with. It did not seem to me that I needed a man to guide my life and make my decisions any longer, and that gave me an incredible feeling of self-confidence and self-worth. I was certainly not going to allow the likes of Mr. Marlowe to take that away from me.

Mr. Marlowe, looking quite uncomfortable, shifted on his seat, crossed his legs and coughed. Finally, he placed a small purse and an envelope on the table between us.

"Yes, well, ah," he stammered, trying to find his way back into control again, "as you wish, Miss Weston. As you wish. It is all there."

He gestured at the purse and envelope, his face showing his firm conviction that I would not understand a word written on that paper. I merely nodded my thanks.

"Now, Miss Weston," he continued, his voice strengthening, gaining firm ground once again. Uncrossing his legs he leaned forward on the settee, putting on an incongruous avuncular expression. "What I am really here for is to discover how I can help you to... how shall I put it?" He gazed about the cluttered, shabby room with great distaste. "I have come, and only just in time, I can see, to rescue you from the unfortunate circumstances in which you find yourself trapped. Forced to labor like a common drudge! To dress—" He lifted his hands in a helpless gesture, as if unable to find words strong enough to convey the disreputable state of my completely unstylish work dress. "Oh, the indignities to which you have been subjected. The, ah, accommodations you have been compelled to endure." His eyes lifted to the ceiling as though he could see through the wood and plaster to my room above. He shuddered. "I weep inside when I think of it. Why haven't I come for you sooner? I shall never forgive myself, my dear Miss Weston. The change not only in your appearance but also in your... personality is simply appalling."

He shook his head in sorrow, holding his hand up for silence as I began to speak. Though I was outraged at what he had thus far said, I sat back to listen. I was curious, in spite of my emotion, to hear what further nonsense he had to impart.

"You will, I am sure," he gave me a self-satisfied

smile, "be overjoyed to hear that I have continued my enquiries on your behalf for a situation more suitable than that under which you are suffering at present. I know you sent to request that I abandon the search," he added quickly, for I had started to interrupt again, "but I knew you were not in your right mind at that time, your Father's death being such a shock. I knew that, given time, you would come to your senses. Gently-bred ladies, especially young ones such as yourself, cannot possibly have full awareness of the world in which we live, much less take care of themselves adequately. They are bound to fall prey to those who will take advantage of their tender, trusting natures, and sink into a deplorable state, in need of rescue. As indeed you already have.

"Now. I have found you a position which will be of mutual benefit to both yourself and your employer. It has been a very long search, and I most deeply regret the delay which has forced you into such dire necessity. A shop assistant."

He gave another condescending shudder and cast his gaze again around the room, as though afraid he would take a mortal illness merely from proximity. It was transparently obvious that the cluttered, aged condition of the room quite offended his sensibilities. He leaned back against the hard settee cushions and permitted himself a small wintry smile.

"At long last," he stated, his tone a smug purr, "my efforts on your behalf have paid off. Your sufferings here are at an end. I have secured for you a position of which most young ladies in your circumstances would find themselves quite envious. You will travel extensively, and your opportunities to be on a nodding acquaintance with our most elite personages will be almost boundless. There may even be occasions when you may partake in very minor social affairs, teas and such."

He paused to shoot his cuffs in a self-congratulatory way, giving me ample time to fully appreciate what he perceived to be my good fortune. Truly, I was struck speechless—not from awe as he thought but from wonder that I had so narrowly escaped this fate. Seeming to assure himself with a glance of my complete, wide-eyed attention, Mr. Marlowe continued to apprize me, in an oily, self-preening voice, of the details of my impending bondage.

"As well as living in a most elegant mansion here in London, and a marvelous country estate of vast proportion,"—his eyes twinkled; evidently these were wonders not to be missed for a poor unfortunate such as I—"there is also, I believe, a country estate in the south of France and an Italian villa to which you will often travel."

Yes, I thought as he spoke further on the unbelievable places and experiences soon to be mine, *and I will sleep in a tiny, airless servant's room under the attic eaves as I used to*. Resented, of course, by the servants for usurping their already too-inadequate space. I would be higher than a servant in social standing, and lower than everyone else, fitting in nowhere, too respectable to be considered a servant, and not respectable enough for anything else. Owned and controlled by a wealthy 'benefactor,' I would become a non-entity's non-entity.

"Your duties will be extremely light, I have been assured," he told me. "Some correspondence, aiding with entertainment, making travel arrangements, assisting on shopping expeditions. And I have been promised you will have much free time, at least one full day a month." *To do what?* I wondered. "As to salary, et. al., there is an allowance of two gowns per annum, chosen by your benefactress, which is extremely generous, I do assure you, and a most adequate annual salary of twenty pounds, for personal expenses. I do realize that there will be very little left of that to send to the Boston solicitor, but there will be small Christmas bonuses and such, perhaps as much as half a pound, which you can then send on to America."

He sat back, well-pleased with his recitation, watching me digest in silence this overwhelming offer of salvation. I could imagine just how flattering and appropriate those gowns would be, and I was sure they would be ill-fitting as well. And how long would it take me to pay off an eight-thousand dollar debt on a Christmas bonus of half a pound or less? I would be enslaved for the rest of my life.

He sat there, waiting for me to exclaim or faint with gratitude, becoming more and more annoyed when I merely sat staring back at him. I felt no gratitude. I no longer even felt outraged, for his words had smothered me completely. I felt nothing, actually, so I merely sat waiting for him to leave. Finally, he spoke in a tone sharp with exasperation.

"You have not even asked for whom you are now employed, Miss Weston. Are you not the least bit curious?"

Now that he mentioned it, I did begin to feel the stirrings of curiosity. I did want to know who this paragon of generosity might be. My erstwhile savior.

"Oh, yes, Mr. Marlowe," I said in a voice dangerously soft. "Pray tell me, please, to whom I owe so very much for the offer of a—companion post, I take it to be?"

He nodded his confirmation not only of my words, but also of his patent belief that I was in a state of euphoric shock over this. He was right; I was shocked, but not in the way he believed.

"I know this will seem incredible to you, but I do assure you it is true, every word," he said, building unnecessary suspense. I was not *that* curious. "Your new benefactress—she prefers to be thought of thus, for 'employer' is so vulgar a term, don't you agree?—is Lady Braithwaite, Countess of Morewood. I could hardly believe my—ah, *your* good fortune when she contacted me about locating, for a substantial fee, of course, a new protégé for her. That she would consent to take you, a foreigner, without references, without family, without skills—and knowing of your Father's unsavory death about which, of course, I had to enlighten her. As you can imagine, I was simply overwhelmed. I have rushed to you directly after confirming with Lady Braithwaite that you will begin immediately, this evening if possible, for she is in dire need." He looked around the room again and shuddered. "I am sure you will consent to gather your scant belongings and come away with me now, and leave this, this—nightmare behind you."

I let the silence grow as I savored the moment. Lady Braithwaite; she of the black, red and gold carriage I had seen below my hotel window six months before. She had passed by our shop in her carriage only three weeks ago, running down a child and berating the coachman for stopping to give aid. It was then I discovered the name of the great, obnoxious noblewoman who had sailed forth beneath my window, shadowed by my 'twin.' I wondered what had become of that poor young thing. Then, remembering the great lady's acid tongue and vile temperament in the street outside the bookshop, I discovered I truly did not want to know. I smiled in gentle triumph at Mr. Marlowe, a feeling that had more than a trace of malicious enjoyment in it.

"First, Mr. Marlowe," I said, struggling to keep a sweet tone, "I beg you to let me tell you that I do appreciate your continued efforts on my behalf. However, they have been futile. Had I known you were continuing your search, I would have repeated again that you call it off. I always say what I mean the first time."

Mr. Marlowe had begun to preen himself at my words, but as they continued he grew very still, sitting in astounded silence. He obviously could not believe his ears. I was not swooning with gratitude. I was, instead, cool and indifferent. Were he not the gentleman he was, his jaw would have dropped open.

"I must sincerely and most firmly turn down this offer of employment from the Countess, for employment it is, whatever she chooses to call it. I have seen how she treats those who surround her, and I would have to be desperate, indeed, to ever allow myself to fall into her hands." I paused a moment to consider, then added, "And I find it impossible to believe I could ever be quite desperate enough. The streets, Mr. Marlowe, offer more desirable opportunity than does the Countess."

I poured more tea for myself, although by now it was lukewarm. I did not offer Mr. Marlowe any.

"Contrary to your belief," I continued in a firm voice, "I am quite content here with Mr. Chadwicke. I have a lovely, large room in which I can be at peace, work that is stimulating and challenging, and a salary much larger than that the Countess condescends to pay. In short, I have my freedom. But freedom is not what the Countess offers, is it? Here at Chadwicke's I can choose my own clothing, cook my own meals, and spend each evening as I desire, as well as all day Sunday, *every* Sunday. *And* a half-day on Wednesday. I am also paid enough to make steady monthly payments on Father's debt. I have found good friends, and a mentor who is fast becoming family to me, and I am free, Mr. Marlowe. My life is my own, and I am finding that for the first time in many, many years I am happy." I paused to contemplate the stunned expression on the solicitor's face and again smiled. "I do apologize, sir. I know you have no way to comprehend all this, and so I will simply tell you that I am most gratefully staying here."

I rose, which forced him to do likewise, and began to move toward the curtained doorway. He strode quickly to my side, so obviously unnerved by my words that he actually forgot himself and grasped my arm, holding me in place.

"But my dear Miss Weston, you surely have taken leave of your senses. What have they been doing to you in this place? How can you possibly turn down what has just been offered? I do not believe you fully know what you are saying. Do you truly realize what the Countess can do for you? The opportunity, the travel, the people you would meet—the money!"

Ah, I thought. *He can see his fee slipping away.*

"Mr. Marlowe," I replied, easing my arm from his strong fingers, "I do assure you that I have all that and more right here. I can travel to any land I desire whenever I want through these books, and even travel back in time. Can the Countess do that for me? A great many wonderful people come through our door, and I can meet countless others in these self-same books, people such as Alexander, Cato, Dante. Can the Countess introduce me to such as these? Here I have the opportunity to expand my mind, sharpen my mathematics skills, and learn about myself as well as others. From the Countess I would learn nothing except how to cater to her selfish whims. And as for money..." I lifted my hands in mock apology, "here, I earn almost four times her pittance. I do not see that what she has to offer is all that desirable."

He took a step back as though I had just sprouted two heads, and then drew himself up in a posture of wounded dignity.

"But-but I have already accepted this position for you. I have given my word. My word as a gentleman. You cannot do this to me."

"But I am doing it, Mr. Marlowe. And I would strongly suggest that in the future you confer with your client first, even is it is a woman, to prevent your so embarrassing yourself again. It is not always prudent to make another's decisions for them, and I, for one, have no intention of ever leaving Mr. Chadwicke's employ." I dropped a shallow curtsey and held the curtain aside. "Thank you for coming, Mr. Marlowe. Please convey my sincere regrets to the Countess."

The look he sent me was one of pure loathing as he clapped his hat on his head.

"You will regret this, Miss," he whispered with venomous fury, "I promise you will regret it!"

He spun on his heel and stalked out of the shop in as foul a temper as I had ever seen Father in. The great manipulator had finally lost a battle—and to a woman.

I wondered if he would ever fully recover.

I followed him out, reaction making me shake like a leaf, and walked up to Uncle Jacob who stood looking after Mr. Marlowe in vast amusement. It was obvious that he had eavesdropped at the curtain, silently cheering me on. He opened his arms wide and I walked into them, for comfort, for solace, for safety, for love. He embraced me for a few moments, then held me out at arm's length and looked me over carefully. Shaking his head he began to chuckle, then laugh out loud in genuine merriment. I could feel it begin to bubble up in me, also, and soon I was laughing with him.

Finally, we gulped to a halt. Uncle Jacob wiped tears from his eyes.

"Oh, Just Marina, that was indeed a memorable performance. The poor gentleman never had a chance. I think I have adopted a tigress, not a niece."

He hugged me again, then sent me back to work. Periodically throughout the day I would hear a quiet chuckle from him, which I just as quietly echoed. We neither of us had any notion of the vindictiveness of Mr. Marlowe's nature. Had we known, we would have found nothing at all to laugh about.

Chapter Ten

Mollie, Eamon and I kept in close touch, for beside these two and Uncle Jacob I knew no one else in London. Mollie would fret because I knew no people my own age, but I did not feel the lack for I had never known any. On Sunday afternoons in the warm summer months, when the two shops were closed, we four would walk in the park and watch the Ton in their carriages and riding their horses. I spent many a rainy and winter Sunday teaching Mollie to read. Eamon refused on the grounds of age, which immediately brought vigorous protest from the rest of us. He remained adamant, however, enjoying instead the cajoling and argument. Mollie and I engaged in stimulating exchanges of thoughts and ideas such as Uncle Joseph and I used to do, leaving Uncle Jacob and Eamon to their chessboard. Most Sunday evenings, Mollie and I would converse with the sounds of chessmen clicking in the background.

Uncle Jacob and I grew so close that it was hard to

remember that we were only adopted relatives, not born kin, and I think we both began to wonder if love and caring were not more binding than blood ties. With Mollie and Eamon we formed a family of sorts, celebrating Christmas, Easter and birthdays with great joy in each other. Mollie taught me to sew and embroider, which I found very soothing and enjoyable. It gave me great pleasure to be able to make gifts for the people dearest to my heart, and the first Christmas I went cold for three days because I overspent on each of them and could not afford firewood. But it was worth it, I found. Most anything done for love is.

I took great interest in the London streets around me, abounding with wonderful architecture and charm beneath the dirt and tatters. On Wednesdays, our half-days when the shop closed at 1:00 pm, if the weather was clement I often walked to St. Paul's Cathedral to study both the inside and outside of Christopher Wren's magnificent edifice. It was hard to imagine how anyone could even envision such beauty, much less be able to construct it. To me, it looked like a hymn carved from stone. And the people who came there fascinated me almost as much as the building itself; flower sellers, penitents, thieves and ragamuffins. I would sit for hours watching them and comparing them to the characters in the many books I read. I discovered that Mr. Dickens came closest in realistic portrayal.

One day about six months after I began working in the main room, when the classification was finished to Uncle Jacob's satisfaction, two ladies entered the shop when Uncle was busy with a very important male customer. I knew that he would not hurry for, his association with me notwithstanding, Uncle Jacob still considered women as bubble-headed and satisfied with whatever came to hand, probably because most of those who frequented our shop were interested in the newer releases. It never occurred to him that a woman could be as much a connoisseur of literature as a man. I often wondered what he did think of me in that respect, for I read everything I could get my hands on, new or old. I think, perhaps, he considered me an aberration.

Rising from my place behind the desk where I was engaged upon the week's entries, I approached the women. Even in the dim light I could see how well-dressed they were; obviously ladies of some standing. The older of the two, a woman I guessed to be about thirty, wore a beautiful challis gown in the newest Polonaise style. Her deep fuchsia skirt had three tiers of ruffles at the hem. Borders and ribbons that matched the skirt trimmed the pale fuchsia overdress. Three large, lovely bows gathered the overdress skirt into graceful scallops in the front. Her long sleeves were slit to the elbow and inset with ribbons and lace, as was the collar of the bodice. Her small, plumed hat nestled amid luxurious auburn curls that reflected the color of her costume and added a touch of rose to her pale complexion. Sparkling, intelligent green eyes looked out from a round face, in which her delicate nose and tiny mouth looked a trifle small and somewhat lost.

Beside her the other woman, younger I thought by perhaps six or seven years, seemed pale and washed out. Her blond hair was light enough to appear almost white and her blue eyes reminded me of the sky just after sunrise, misty and delicate. She, too, had dressed to best enhance her looks, in a silvery blue that set her eyes aglow. In a style similar to the older woman's, her dress was less frilly, less ruffled, but no less elegant for all that. There was something about the way the fabric fell from her shoulders, free to the looped-up hem without a seam at the waist, that gave her the look of royalty. Hers was a classic face, chiseled in pale marble, every feature in perfect balance with the others. I felt too highly colored beside her, and dowdy in my dark green wool dress with its plain long sleeves, diminutive lace collar, and single narrow-hooped petticoat beneath. Practical for a shop assistant it might be, and even luxurious for my financial state—it was the very first dress I had ever bought and I was thrilled with it—but there were times like now when I did long fleetingly for the costumes left behind in Boston. Though I had never owned anything on so exquisite a scale as the dresses now before me, I did miss the softness of quality fabrics and the gentle beauty of ribbons and lace.

I stopped before the two women, smiling, though I expected the usual rebuff or condescension. In the nine months I had been here, only half a dozen times had anyone let me find a book for them, and only after Mr. Chadwicke had told me which one to choose.

"Good day," I said. "Welcome to our shop. Mr. Chadwicke is occupied at present. Perhaps I could show you around, or even help you to find whatever it is you seek."

I waited patiently while they inspected me, trying not to stare at their lovely gowns, and was startled when they replied not only in a civil tone, but also as though I were worthy of their time.

"Thank you," the auburn-haired beauty said, her voice soft and sweet. "We have been attempting to find a rather obscure play by William Shakespeare for my husband's birthday. He collects Mr. Shakespeare's works, and does own a copy of this play, but I am hoping to find a very old edition, for he also collects antique books. It has been rather a long search, and it is disappointing to find that Mr. Chadwicke is busy right now, for I need it in somewhat of a hurry. You see," she ended with an apologetic smile, "it is his birthday today, so I am quite desperate."

I smiled back at her, for her smile was very infectious.

"I think, perhaps, there will be no problem, for we have an extensive collection of Mr. Shakespeare's works, both plays and sonnets. Which were you interested in finding?"

I ushered them down the length of the room to where the plays were shelved—they actually followed me!—and found three copies of the play in question, one of which was handsomely bound in red leather in a volume with two other plays. The second and third copies were in folio, but the older of the two was suspect; there were many alterations and juxtapositions of text in it, and a few places that did not seem to read in the flowing style of William Shakespeare. As I explained all this they stared at me, amazed.

"Elizabeth," the pale blond woman exclaimed, "do you believe that this young woman has such knowledge? Why, I wonder, was it stressed that we deal with Mr. Chadwicke only? Honestly! Men can be so tiresome at times."

"Jane." Her companion laid a restraining hand upon her arm and turned to me. "I am Lady Elizabeth Teasdale, and this is my irrepressible sister, Lady Jane Creswell. And what she is so indelicately attempting to say is that it is most unusual to discover a woman in such a position, and in possession of such knowledge, as are you. It certainly is refreshing."

I laughed, seeing her discomfiture at what she assumed to be an awkward situation.

"I am well aware of the unusualness of my employment, my lady," I told her, then leaned forward and lowered my voice. "Do you realize," I added with laughter in my tone, "that this is the first time in almost nine months that a customer has allowed me to wait upon her? It does say a lot for Mr. Chadwicke's reputation that everyone wants his personal service, but, alas, it is not much help for mine."

We smiled together, and Lady Jane requested that I show them around the shop. I pointed out the various departments into which we had specialized our stock, explained our reference system, and came at last to my own special love, the room full of new books. As we scanned the shelves and I compared the various points of merit of the sundry authors, Lady Jane clapped her hands and exclaimed in delight.

"Elizabeth, I do believe we have discovered the perfect bookseller! I, for one, will make this a regular stop, and I intend to keep this delicious creature all to myself. I shall pick her brains, and become the toast of the intellectual elite!"

"As shall I," echoed her sister.

True to her word, Lady Jane did return every two to three weeks, and we would spend a happy hour sorting through the new arrivals, for her first love, like mine, was contemporary literature. We became as friendly as possible considering our social differences and her upbringing. I was, after all, only a shop assistant. Her sister, Lady Elizabeth, would occasionally come with her, but neither Lady Jane nor Lady Elizabeth kept their word to keep me a secret. Gradually, their friends began to come in, both men and women, and either I or Uncle Jacob would assist them, though there were a few who still would deal only with him. Our business picked up considerably, and I was very gratified to be treated as an intelligent, competent human being instead of an empty-headed, frivolous woman. My life was immensely full and happy, despite occasional yearnings for the fine clothes I saw all around me. Then I met Andrew, and things began to change.

I had been with Uncle Jacob for almost a year and a half, and had made it my habit to stop for tea at Mollie and Eamon's shop on my Wednesday afternoons off. I had noticed the young man a few times, staring at me from across the room, but as he was not always there when I was, and made no move to speak to me nor even to sit at a table near mine, I thought nothing of it. I was becoming used ignoring the stares of the male population, and in any case I always sat in the window and he always took the back corner table.

He must have worked on Mollie's desire for me to know people my own age, though, for one day they appeared at my table only moments after I had seated myself. She stood red-faced and uncomfortable, and introduced him in halting, short sentences, saying he was the son of an old friend in her native County Kerry. He was only recently arrived in London to apprentice at an apothecary shop, and he was quite alone and lonely.

He was very tall, this Andrew Sykes, his extreme thinness evoking, I am sure, Mollie's motherly instinct to fatten up the poor lad. Indeed, she always gave him twice what he ordered and insisted he clean his plate before he could leave. In looks he could be taken for Irish, with red that glinted saucily in the sandy-brown hair that waved about his ears and blushed across a complexion kept pale from long hours shut in a chemist's back room. With sparkling hazel eyes, quick, grinning lips and a pert, turned-up nose, he looked like an overgrown street urchin. Indeed, beholding the childlike delight that bubbled from inside him, one almost expected to see Mr. Sykes in short pants rather than the coarse, ill-fitting checked suit he wore, the best he could afford on his meager salary.

He executed a sweeping bow, presented me with a small spray of violets and requested permission to sit with me in the most flagrantly false Irish brogue I had ever heard. I shot Mollie an amused look as I granted permission for him to sit, laughing silently at such an obvious ruse. Mollie bustled away, unable to look me in the eye. She was a terrible liar. How she expected to get away with such a ridiculous story was beyond me. Mr. Andrew Sykes, who I was sure had never seen the countryside outside London's environs much less Ireland's County Kerry, was certainly no country bumpkin recently transplanted all agog to the big city. His very air of assurance and the clothes he wore gave him away instantly. I may not have had much life experience nor met very many men, but I was well aware of the difference between city-born sophistication and country-bred naiveté.

We sat quietly together for five minutes or more, sipping hot tea and nibbling on Eamon's special cakes, which Mollie brought us still warm from the oven. Mr. Sykes, having successfully gained the introduction he craved, seemed, in spite of his city sophistication, unsure of how to proceed further. I merely sat avoiding eye contact, amused by his discomfiture and determined not to offer him an easy way out. He had gotten himself into this situation, and I was quite curious to see how he would get himself out.

Finally, he looked up at me and gave me an unabashed grin.

"I suppose I might as well come right out and confess," he said in his native, lower-class London accent, "that I am not from County Kerry, nor even from Ireland. I met Mrs. O'Leary a mere six months ago when I saw you sitting here in this window and began coming in just hoping to meet you. It is true, though, that I am an apothecary apprentice in the Staley Road, but I was born and bred in London. In fact, I have never been out of the city."

He grinned at me again, supremely confident that his open frankness would win me over completely, as indeed it nearly did. But who was supposed to be the country bumpkin here, him or me? For all his engaging charm and good looks, I did not appreciate being played for a fool. Frankness up front, not when caught out, counted most with me.

I fixed him with an icy stare I had to struggle to maintain and sat back in my chair.

"Just as I'd thought," I said in an indifferent voice.

His grin froze in place. He seemed momentarily taken aback by the coolness of his reception and the obvious failure of his ploy. I watched with amusement tempered more and more with liking as he quickly recovered his wits, not losing one iota of his high spirits.

"Ah, then," he confided, leaning across the table toward me, "you must be aware that my sole objective in this elaborate charade was to meet such a vision of loveliness as yourself, the epitome of my dreams, the queen of my heart. In truth, from the very first instant I laid eyes upon you, eyes dazzled by your beauty as though by the sun, I— "

He broke off abruptly, looking startled by the expression in my quite undazzled eyes. He certainly would not last long if he intended to treat me like an empty-headed country girl! Although I loved to hear compliments as much as any woman, I would much rather they not be rehearsed before a mirror as these most certainly had been. I was also sober and objective enough to realize that my effect on men was not quite as earth-shattering as Mr. Sykes would make it out to be, and intelligent enough to appreciate a more level-headed approach based on friendship and not effulgence. Besides, Father's training had accustomed me to a more subtle, sophisticated approach; I could recognize sheer nonsense when it was served up on a platter, even if Mr. Sykes had spent six months trying to gain an introduction.

He had the grace to look sheepish.

"All right, no more malarkey, Miss Weston. But I really was struck at my first glance, and that is not malarkey. Each time I have come for tea I have prayed that you would also be here, although sometimes you were not. I have been dying of curiosity. Who are you, what is your given name, where do you come from, where do you live, are you married, will you marry me?"

Now it was my turn to stare at him, completely taken aback, unable to believe I had heard what he had just said. Mr. Sykes himself appeared to be in a state of shock, as though he had had no control over what had come from his mouth. I began to laugh, unable to dampen the hilarity bubbling up inside me. What an interesting way to meet someone! Mr. Sykes dissolved into laughter also, and we sat laughing all the harder for trying to stop. Each time we began to breathe normally, a mere glance would set us off again, amid affronted stares, amused smiles and much whispering from the other patrons. At last we wheezed to a halt, sides stitched and faces aching from the uncontrolled merriment.

I took a deep breath and sighed aloud.

"Well," I said, still somewhat breathless, "this has most assuredly been the most unique and enjoyable introduction it has ever been my fortune to be presented with. And in spite of your rather unorthodox method of securing acquaintance, I fail to see how two people who have shared such amusement can simply part, never to meet again."

He did not trust himself to words, for grins were still tugging at the corners of his lips. He gave me a look of such pure, overacted ecstasy that I almost went off again myself into gales of laughter. I raised my hand to him in a 'Stop!' gesture.

"No, Mr. Sykes," I said, trying to speak clearly

through the giggles that kept breaking my voice, "I will not marry you. But I will meet you for tea again, if you would like."

And that was the beginning of a wonderful friendship, for I found Andrew—we were soon on a first-name basis, neither of us desiring to be hampered by staid social convention—a very sympathetic listener. He always seemed to understand when I would describe my feelings about whatever subject we discussed, even if his own were completely different. And they often were when we spoke of the place of women in life, for Andrew was very much a male product of his environment. I found it amazing that he could sympathize with me without agreeing even a little. He loved to hear me talk of Uncle Joseph and life in America, although I told him more of life in general than the specifics of my own upbringing. He merely knew that Father and I had not gotten along, and that George Arnold Weston, Esq., was not very successful as a father.

Most wonderful of all, Andrew Sykes was a fascinating storyteller. He could take the most commonplace occurrence and raise it to great heights, enthralling his listeners for hours. We often found ourselves surrounded by an audience when at the bakery; indeed, many began coming in just in hopes of hearing another of Andrew's yarns. Thinking of the wonderful tales told by Mr. Dickens, I kept encouraging Andrew to try his hand at writing his stories down. He slowly began to do so, but for a long time he would not show me anything he had written. He said he felt too shy and embarrassed, and was not yet satisfied with his work.

When I finally cajoled him into showing me a finished piece, I was astounded by the lyrical quality and the pixie-ish sense of humor his words portrayed. I was sure he could get his work published, that people would clamor to read his stories as quickly as he could write them down. It was then, as I urged him to send the story to a publisher, that he confessed it was his lack of penmanship, and not dissatisfaction with his work, that stopped him from trying. It had taken him three months to get those words onto the paper. I immediately offered to help him learn to write properly, and to copy down his stories for him until he was better able to do so himself, and thus stopped his excuses.

But he could not put much time into writing, for his apprenticeship kept him occupied twelve hours a day and six on Sundays, with a half-day every other Wednesday. Any time he had left over Andrew wanted to spend with me, not cooped up in Uncle Jacob's back room, writing. He took me to Covent Gardens and the Crystal Palace, to plays and concerts. We walked in Hyde Park on sunny winter Sunday afternoons, and picnicked once on the bank of the Thames on cold chicken, Eamon's biscuits, and a wine which cost Andrew most of a week's salary.

He told me of growing up in London, helping at his father's small drapery shop when he was very young. By the time he was twelve, it had become clear that the shop would not support his father's family—there were six girls—his two older brothers, now both married, and himself. And so he began looking around for what else he could do, finding very little available for a young lad with little education and training only in fabric measuring and cutting. Realizing that luck aided by a quick mind would be his only way out of grinding poverty, Andrew concentrated on learning all that he could, both from books and from everyday experiences. He prowled the streets, poking his nose into everything, testing different occupations to see what suited him. He discovered an affinity for the chemist's shop, a fascination with compounds, herbs and medicines, and began haunting those establishments in hopes of finding permanent employment in one of them.

For four years he ran errands and delivered medicines for five different shops, earning a mere pittance, barely surviving even though he still lived at home, for he had to provide his own food and clothing. Somehow, he found time both to improve his reading skills and to study the chemist's art. He learned about the healing and soothing properties of the numerous herbs and substances available, and how to dry, mix and infuse them.

One day, while waiting for the chemist in the workroom to finish mixing a cough remedy and package it for delivery, Andrew sold two preparations for sprains and cuts to a very distraught nobleman, explaining the proper use each one. He also sold the gentleman a special calming tea to aid both his loved one and himself to relax and sleep well, for sleep is the most effective cure for almost everything. A week later, this gentleman was back at Abernathy's Apothecary Shoppe, complimenting Mr. Abernathy on his polite, sympathetic and extremely intelligent assistant. Lord Merrick was well-known to be harsh and critical; rarely did a compliment or kind word pass his lips. But Andrew he praised highly, not only for his knowledgeable handling of his apothecary needs, but also for his kind sympathy in a time of distress. Mr. Abernathy was properly shocked, for he had no apprentice. Who could this possibly be who had so admirably waited on the great Lord Merrick? Casting his mind back, he recalled Andrew, the runner, who had been waiting to make a delivery, and sent for him. He hired Andrew immediately.

Mr. Abernathy, however, proved a harsh taskmaster, for he did not actually desire an apprentice; he hired Andrew only to keep Lord Merrick's custom, and that of the friends the great man would send to him. He gave Andrew very little time for himself, and very little money for the work he did. But Andrew did not mind. He truly loved the work, and he knew that eventually the shop would belong to him, as Edgar Abernathy had no heirs. And so he slaved in Mr. Abernathy's back room, squandered his pitiful salary on me, and spun stories full of pathos and laughter for me to write down, all the while loving his life with a wild enthusiasm that made it seem he remained untouched by the poverty and squalid conditions in which he moved daily. I often wonder even now what would have happened to him, to us, had I not written down his stories; had I not wanted more for him than he himself had wanted; had I not had Father's enormous debt dictating so much of my life; had I been able to love him as he loved me. My dear, dear friend, Andrew Sykes.

Chapter Eleven

It was my fault, I fear. I began the entire chain of events with a simple, innocent remark, though I often wonder if perhaps it would all have happened anyway. Most probably not in the same order, the links of the chain rearranged into an alternate and varied pattern, but leading still to the same ending. How different life would be could we only see the ripples our words will cause before we speak them. And yet, in the dead of night when darkness closes 'round me like a smothering velvet glove, and my heart aches for the empty places inside me that can never be refilled, I question whether anything we do can affect what surely will be. There are times, even now, when Father is very, very near.

It began in January after my second wonderful Christmas in my adopted home, surrounded by my new 'family': Uncle Jacob; Mollie and Eamon O'Leary; and dear Andrew who was fast becoming the brother I had never had. I had done much better this year with my expenses, and managed not to spend all my wood money on gifts, difficult though that was. Father had never celebrated any holiday or anniversary; he did not believe in giving pleasure to anyone, least of all to me. At Christmas and on my birthday, Uncle Joseph would gift me in secret with a hair ribbon or a diary or a slim book of verse, which of course I had to leave in his apartments lest Father discover it. But I had never once, until my first Christmas with Uncle Jacob, been able to offer anyone a token of my own love and esteem in return. The joy of giving is still so wondrous for me that even now I must take care lest I bankrupt my purse completely.

That January of 1868 was unusually cold, and I wished I had not sent my Christmas bonus to Mr. Alcott in Boston. Though in the end I had sent it all to be put against the debt, I had debated keeping some of it for a warm flannel dress, for I had only two dresses that were winter-weight: the plain green wool I had purchased the year before; and a deep gray foulard with blue velvet trim on the pagoda sleeves and at the hem. When I had seen a picture of it at the dressmaker's, I simply could not resist it, even though it was a trifle elegant for the shop. I had had it made only last October, having saved scrupulously all summer, for since Father and I had traveled to England in late April, I had packed only spring and summer clothing. I did not truly need new things for those seasons, even though most of my American dresses were not appropriate for the shop. I had minimized that problem by setting aside my hoops and wearing only two starched petticoats, my new-found prowess with a needle enabling me to turn up the now-too-long hems on the skirts. But there was nothing to be done about pale colors that soiled so easily, and pretty lace trims that caught on book corners and tore and had to be removed. Nor was there anything to do about money sent away; it could not be called back and turned into wood for my fireplace. This winter, not even good management could save me from the piercing cold.

Lady Jane Creswell arrived one morning mid-way through January to inspect what merchandise had arrived since Christmas. She stood just inside the door for a moment, brushing snow from her fur-trimmed burnoose with delicately gloved fingers. Her striking, pale blue eyes inspected me with a curious air, and I wondered what she was thinking as I walked toward her, a welcoming smile on my face. I again had on my green wool dress, which she had seen on me the last six times she had come. I am sure she believed it the only one I owned but it was merely coincidence, and nothing more, that had me in that unbecoming costume each time she arrived. That, and the fact that I saved the gray dress for 'good,' wearing it seldom in the shop, keeping it for Sundays and my half-Wednesdays off. The green wool had become almost a uniform, as it was too cold to don my one dark summer gown as I had during last year's milder winter, a deep blue dimity with long sleeves and a high neckline that didn't look completely out of place in the winter months.

Today Lady Jane, too, was wearing green, but her warm, luxurious cashmere skirts looped and swirled in the latest fashion atop wide hoops, the color as soft and gentle as her complexion. As usual, there was a dearth of frills and fuss; Lady Jane Creswell needed no lace or ribbons to enhance the perfection of her beauty. I felt plain and dowdy beside her, very much the penurious shop assistant. Being constantly cold did not help. I almost wished she would stop coming in.

"I cannot stay long today, Marina," she said in her high, breathless voice. "Lord Creswell needs me at home, some tiresome reception he insists on giving. He is helpless without me."

She smiled, shaking her head as if to say, 'Men!' and moved purposefully into the side room. We chatted a while about the newest arrivals, and she set three aside to take with her. One was *A Tale Of Two Cities* by Mr. Dickens, which had just arrived bound into a single volume. Lady Creswell had read it in installments when it first appeared nine years before, and she felt it was one of his better works. She did not care much for Mr. Dickens' writings, especially his newer pieces which dealt with the abuse and suffering of the poor of London and poked fun at the moneyed aristocracy, but she wished to have a copy of this tale for her own. She also chose *Vilette,* by Charlotte Bronte, and a slim volume of verse by Morgan Carruthers, who was all the rage at that time although I did not care for his style. His work seemed falsely gay to me, artificial emotion aping true feeling.

When I wrote out the bill and wrapped the books for her to take, Lady Creswell again studied me with that curious air, one slim finger tapping her full lips. I kept my head lowered, my hands busy with their work, but still I saw her glance quickly around the shop to see if we were observed. We were quite alone, Mr. Chadwicke being occupied beyond the curtain. There were no other customers.

"Marina, my dear," she said, "is that your only dress?"

I could feel my face redden. I looked down and with trembling hands smoothed the coarse, dark green fabric that covered me.

"No, my lady. Of course not. I do have a gray foulard also, though it does not seem so, does it?" I smiled bravely into her lovely, frowning face. "It is much nicer than this dress; there is even velvet trim on the sleeves and at the hem. It is my favorite of the two."

I gave her a small shrug, praying that the tears which pricked at the back of my eyes were not visible from where she stood. It appeared they weren't; she shook her head, oblivious to the painful emotion she had evoked in me.

"Then why haven't I seen you in it, Marina? It is hard to believe you favor the foulard over this, if you never wear it."

"I do wear it, my lady," I assured her, forcing the

words past the lump in my throat. I looked down and retied the string on her package, thus hiding the tears I had to blink away. "It is just that, having only the two dresses, I try to keep one for occasions other than work."

"Only two? I don't understand, Marina." She frowned, a pretty moue of confusion that creased her pale brow. "You have so many pretty, if outdated, things for summer. How can you have only two winter dresses? Surely the winters are also cold in America."

"That is easy to explain, my lady." I hoped she didn't realize how forced my smile was. "When Father and I left for England, it was late spring. I only brought summer clothing with me, for I expected to return by August. All my winter things were left behind in Boston. And now," I added, forestalling her next question; why did she not simply leave! "I haven't enough money to send for them. It is quite expensive."

Though I had told her that my Father's sudden death had stranded me in London—but not, obviously, the manner of his demise—I was not about to detail my full shame and reveal how my wardrobe had been sold at auction.

"Then why don't you simply replace what you left behind? If you like, I shall introduce you to my dressmaker; obviously, you need better guidance as to fabric and style. And I do wish you would wear the foulard the next time I come. I am so tired of seeing you in this green thing!"

"That is very kind of you, my lady," I replied,

suppressing a wince at the way my voice shook. "Perhaps I should send you a message the next time I wear the foulard. Or you could come to O'Leary's Bake Shop on a Wednesday. I usually wear that dress when I go there for tea on my free afternoon." I forced a half-hearted laugh. "I daresay Mrs. O'Leary thinks I have only the *gray* dress to my name."

I held out the package of books, a false, bright smile on my face, knowing tears would fall at any moment. The clock in the corner softly chimed the hour and Lady Creswell started, glanced at the hands pointing to 1:00 pm, and uttered her high, breathless, careless laugh.

"Oh, dear, I have overspent my time here, as I usually do. Lord Creswell will be roaring like a bull. Thank you, Marina dear, for all your help. I will see you again, soon."

She took the package and with a sweep of her full, elegant skirts glided from the shop without a backward glance. I stood staring after her, shaking like a leaf in a winter gale, hearing Lady Creswell's words blend into Father's disparaging voice: *You need better guidance as to fabric and style... You cannot even dress yourself properly, Marina... Why don't you simply replace the dresses... You are so useless, you never do anything right!*

I stood unaware of Uncle Jacob, who emerged from the back room to lock the door and turn the closed sign around as he did for half an hour each day while we lunched together. My hands clenched at the rough material of my skirt. I had been so proud of my dresses, both of them, of the money I'd painstakingly saved to purchase them, the choice of color, fabric and style. I thought I had done so well, I who had never seen the inside of a dressmaker's shop. And I *had* chosen well, my head knew that, for I had acquired clothing admirably suited for my work and still stayed within my budget. Frills and lace and voluminous skirts would only hamper me.

I was not a social butterfly; even could I afford it, I could not use clothing such as Lady Creswell's, appropriate only for gracing an idle drawing room. And yet I ached inside, my heart weeping as it yearned for something I did not really want. I would never trade my free, happy life, poor and unglamorous as it was, for one of social bondage, of idle uselessness, wrapped in elegance and glitter though it might be. Of the two of us, I knew that I was the lucky one, for all that Lady Jane Creswell sat cradled in wealth. But there were times, like now, when my heart rejected the truth and longed for the false comfort of soft feminine fabrics, large elegant mansions, sumptuous meals, gay parties, and the flattering attention of a handsome, sophisticated man. There were times when being alone felt merely cold and lonely.

Uncle Jacob returned to me and laid warm hands on my shoulders.

"Clothes do not a gentleman make, Marina," he told me in a soft voice. "Nor even a lady."

"I know, Uncle Jacob. I know. It's just that sometimes..."

I lifted my eyes to him, eyes swimming with tears that splashed down my cheeks to darken the bodice of my dress. Uncle Jacob gave me a sad smile.

"Ah, sometimes," he murmured, pulling me into his arms. "We all suffer from 'sometimes,' my little Marina. It is a disease that never goes away, no matter how wealthy, or how old, we grow."

I had forgotten Lady Creswell's visit by the time I met Andrew at the bakery shop that next Wednesday afternoon, for almost a week had passed. We had barely ten minutes alone together before two young gentlemen, who often came in to hear Andrew's yarns, prevailed upon him to spin yet another tale, a summons Andrew never could resist. He was halfway through a rollicking adventure story about a thief and a draper's daughter when the shop door opened, letting in a gust of cold air. Shivering, I looked up from my place at the edge of the crowd gathered around Andrew to see Jane Creswell and her sister, Elizabeth Teasdale, standing just inside the door.

Lady Creswell's pale eyes fastened with bright alertness on Andrew, inspecting him with a curious, almost covetous air. But Andrew, so deep in his tale he did not even look up, seemed unaware of the scrutiny. Lady Teasdale searched the gathered crowd until her gaze met mine. She touched her sister's arm and spoke into her ear. I rose to greet them even before Lady Creswell took her gaze from Andrew and turned my way.

"You see, Marina, I did come to inspect your

dress," the exquisite blond woman exclaimed, acknowledging my tiny curtsey with a regal nod. "But I expected tea and cakes, not a literary entertainment!"

"That is the most wonderful part of O'Leary's on a Wednesday, my lady," I replied, "for then you are offered both. Please, sit here with me, and when Andrew has finished I will introduce him. I am trying to convince him to send his stories for publication. I am sure he would soon be as famous as Mr. Dickens, for he tells absolutely wonderful tales. And you must have some of these delightful cakes, they are the very best in all of London."

I knew I was babbling, but could not help myself, I was so astounded to see them here in Mollie and Eamon's humble shop. As wonderful as their baking was, and their shop well-patronized by the rising merchant middle class, still it was not in the best part of town, the part frequented by the social elite. It had never occurred to me when I had spoken of my Wednesday outings that the grand Lady Creswell would actually condescend to sit in person amidst her social inferiors. How often now I wish I had not said those words. And yet I believe that had I not spoken, somehow it would have made no real difference. What was to be would not be avoided by mere silence.

"You are right to favor the gray over the green, Marina dear," Jane said now, her dark-haired sister smiling sweetly at me as she took the cup of tea I'd poured for her. "Though the style is a bit old-fashioned, don't you think? And the skirt not full enough; whatever were you thinking, to order it that way? Or were you, perhaps, cheated?"

"Jane," Lady Teasdale said in gentle reproof, laying a hand on her sister's arm, "I do not believe Miss Weston's taste in clothing is quite our business."

"Oh, nonsense! Just because she is a lady fallen on difficult times does not mean she must abandon all propriety. I do applaud her courage in obtaining the position she has—-it is truly refreshing to see a woman's intelligence finally recognized—-but if she sinks completely into the mire of the lower classes, how will she ever get out? She could be caught in that dingy old bookshop all her life!"

They spoke as though I was not sitting there with them, the way they would were I one of their servants. Humiliated, I looked down into my tea, biting back the temptation to be as rude to Lady Jane as I had been to Mr. Marlowe. I would love nothing more than to be caught, as it were, in that dingy old bookshop for all my life. But I believed she spoke more from ignorance coupled with true liking for me, and not from malice or self-gain as had Mr. Marlowe, and so I curbed my tongue though my face, I was sure, flamed red under her disparaging tone.

"Still, Jane," Elizabeth patted her sister's hand, "it is her life. She may not welcome your interference."

"Don't be ridiculous, Elizabeth. Look at her! It is obvious she is no good on her own, so I shall simply guide her until I find the right man to take over. Starting with an acceptable wardrobe!"

I looked up, then, a protest on my lips, and suddenly Andrew materialized at my elbow, looking awkward and gangly with his grinning face and great, reed-thin height. He clapped a hand over his heart, lifted his eyes to the heavens and sighed.

"If I died tonight it would not matter," he intoned solemnly, "for I have seen perfection. Indeed, double perfection. I am content."

The two noble ladies exchanged an amused glance; I gave Andrew's shin a surreptitious kick.

"Please, my ladies," I said, looking first at Jane Creswell, then at Elizabeth Teasdale, "may I present Mr. Andrew Sykes, master apothecary apprentice and story-teller extraordinaire. Andrew, this is Lady Jane Creswell, and her sister, Lady Elizabeth Teasdale."

To his credit, Andrew bowed with courtly grace, greeting each woman with the deference due her rank. Lady Creswell granted him permission to sit, and Mollie bustled over with great importance to set fresh, hot cakes before us, and another pot of tea. We passed a pleasant half-hour in idle chatter, or I should say Andrew and the two ladies did, for I suddenly felt shy, not quite knowing how to conduct myself in such a social situation. I had never been allowed to speak to anyone when I was out with Father, and he kept me far away from any social affairs that would requite polite conversation. So I merely listened and smiled as the three bantered words about so quickly I had trouble following them. Andrew flattered, flirted and beguiled the two women, without seeming to fawn or grovel before them. Then Lady Creswell asked for a story, her request seconded gently by her sister, and Andrew soon had us laughing in delight over an extempore tale of two noble ladies caught in a magical tea shop. They were rescued, at last, by a hero who looked suspiciously like the author himself.

We sat chuckling while the gathered audience broke up, returning to their tables. Elizabeth Teasdale rose and drifted to the counter to settle the bill and choose some luscious pastries to take home with her, leaving the three of us alone. Andrew laid his hand on mine where it rested between us on the table, his fingers warm and possessive. I smiled at him, my face heating, and turned my gaze to the window where I caught sight of Jane Creswell's face in the glass. She stared at our hands, her body very still, her face closed, speculative, almost angry-looking. She sent an enigmatic look my way, then shifted her gaze to Andrew and gave him an angelic smile.

"Mr. Sykes," she said, her voice a seductive purr, "I am having a literary soiree on Saturday week, at eight in the evening. It will be small and intimate, only a few close friends. Lord Creswell will not even be there. He has decided to go to the country, for he finds these affairs quite tiresome. I expect it will be quite amusing, and very Bohemian. I have persuaded Mr. Morgan Carruthers to attend, and Mr. Huntly-Grey, with whom I am sure you are familiar. Mrs. Deborah Satchel will also attend, as well as three or four of the more prominent serial publishers. I would so love to have you come and entertain us. I daresay they have never heard anything quite like you."

My mouth had dropped open in very un-ladylike fashion as Lady Creswell casually dropped the names of the most popular authors and poets currently in vogue. I knew that she read them, but I had no idea she actually knew them, had connections in the literary world. I looked at Andrew, who sat looking as stunned as I felt, a wondering smile of awe growing on my face. He would be in the same room with, even be able to speak to, Morgan Carruthers, Huntley-Grey, Deborah Satchel! They would hear Andrew's stories. Perhaps one of them would even take him under his wing, as protégé. Our dream of being published might soon come true.

"Oh, Andrew!" I whispered.

He looked at me, then smiled at Lady Creswell.

"Thank you, my Lady. We will be happy to attend," he said.

Jane Creswell's smile froze, slowly fading as her eyes shifted to me. I turned to smile at her, knowing my excitement shone on my face, but the cold, calculating look in her eyes caught me up short. I knew, clearly, that I was not wanted. Then her eyes dropped and she rose gracefully, Andrew rising also to bow in farewell. Lady Teasdale stood near the door, waiting for her sister.

"By all means, Mr. Sykes, bring Marina with you." Jane's high, breathless voice belied the look she had given me. "I am sure she will find it enjoyable also.

And, Marina, my dear," she said to me, oh, so sweetly, "do remember to wear the foulard you have on and not that green thing. Please."

She dimpled at Andrew once more, then swept from the shop, leaving me sitting in numbed disbelief, wondering just what I had done to deserve her honey-coated venom.

Chapter Twelve

It was a dreadful evening, though Andrew did enjoy it.

I had not wanted to go, but Andrew begged, finally declaring that he would not himself attend unless I accompanied him. I agonized over what to wear, knowing full well I had no choice but the gray foulard, which was totally inadequate, leaving Andrew to cool his over-anxious heels in Uncle Jacob's sitting room until I descended at fifteen minutes past eight. I had tried my best with the little I had to work with, parting my thick black hair in the center and sweeping it into long curls at each side. I had bound the hair at my nape into a mesh snood, and added the gray ribbon I had purchased two days before and could not really afford. I wore no jewelry, for I had none; Father had not allowed me any such decoration, nor did my meager salary. After one final glance at myself in the mirror, I threw my second-hand brown wool burnoose about my shoulders and went down to Andrew, knowing I looked exactly like what I was: a lowly shop assistant, a mere step above a servant. And though I knew it was nothing to be ashamed of—indeed, I was truly proud of my accomplishment in the business world—I also knew I could not long hold out against the pitying, condescending looks that were sure to be directed at me this night. And in that, I was right.

Lord Creswell's mansion in Mayfair was the largest, most elegant building there, pale, gleaming stone that seemed to go on forever. Huge windows ablaze with light glittered like gigantic diamonds, shedding sparkles on the polished carriages ranged in front, awaiting their titled owners. Wide marble steps swept up to a massive carved entry door, and as I alighted from the cab that Andrew had hired, spending an entire week's salary, I dreaded ascending to where the uniformed doorman waited, fearing we should be sent down again and around to the servant's entry. But Andrew appeared to have no such reservations. He grasped my arm, smiled his excitement at me, and paced solemnly up those wide stone steps as though it were not the very first time he had ever done so in all his life. At the top, I discovered my fears were groundless. Andrew gave his name, the doorman bowed, and the ornate portal swung open to admit us into an incredible fantasyland.

I had no idea such places truly existed outside the pages of books. Everything was marble, carved stone or soft dark wood that gleamed like satin. Rich embroideries covered chairs and settees ranged along the walls in the reception hall; heavy thick velvet draperies looped gracefully back from shining, multi-paned windows. A staircase as broad as that outside rose into the air, then divided, curving both left and right to the balustraded balcony that rimmed the immense hall. An exquisite crystal chandelier depended from the central dome overhead, ablaze with what seemed a hundred candles.

One could have put my room above the shop into the alcove beneath that staircase, Uncle Jacob's whole building inside just this one hall; this hall, a mere tiny portion of that immense structure. I thought my heart would stop when I pictured myself, in my shop assistant's gray foulard and hand-me-down, fraying brown wrap, standing here amidst all this elegance. Then a maid curtseyed, eased the burnoose from my shoulders with reluctant hands and an incredulous look, and a butler in livery more splendid than even the very best of my summer gowns stepped forward.

"Mr. Sykes? Lady Creswell awaits you in the private salon. Please, follow me, sir."

He bowed and turned and, with measured steps, traversed the echoing marble hall to a door in the rear of the right-hand wall. Andrew winked at me, his grin so wide I thought his face would split in two.

"Did you hear, Marina? He called me sir!"

I smiled in response to his delighted whisper, unable to find voice in my trepidation but glad that he, at least, seemed to feel nothing but excitement. The disparity between his coarse, cheap clothing—the same brown checked suit he wore every time we met—and these grand, almost royal surroundings did not seem apparent to him. I wished I could feel as confident and at ease as did he.

The butler enquired as to my name when at last we stopped outside a set of double carved mahogany doors, which he then threw open with a flourish. We stood on the threshold, raised up three steps from the floor of the room, the center of all eyes while our names were announced in solemn, ringing tones.

Had Andrew not been holding me tight, I would have turned and fled. The room, large, square and paneled in rich, carved wood, with thick Persian carpeting on the marble floor and luxurious red velvet drapes masking deep window seats lining the outside wall, was filled with elegantly dressed titled nobility. The gowns on display made what Lady Creswell wore to the shop seem like rags; silk, satin, brocade, velvet and moiré abounded. Precious gems glittered in hair, on fingers and wrists and on bosoms, catching the light of the myriad candles burning in elaborate sconces and crystal chandeliers. My gasp of disbelief echoed loud in the sudden silence. This was not at all the small, intimate gathering of a few friends of which Lady Creswell had spoken. Then she was gliding gracefully toward us, her smile for Andrew as intimately welcoming as the gathering was not, and voices rose around us as ladies leaned their heads together behind concealing fans, their laughing eyes still upon me in my shopkeeper's dress.

Lady Jane greeted us both with equal warmth, nothing in her manner betraying any awareness of the impact her change in plans had upon our sensibilities. Nor, indeed, did Andrew seem aware of it either, caught as he was in the dazzling glitter of the moneyed assemblage before him. She swept us into the room and introduced us to everyone there: Viscounts and Earls, Dukes and Duchesses, Lords and Ladies; the peers of the realm. *The only one missing is the Crown Prince!* I thought in a panic, curtseying as gracefully as I could on shaking legs, and enduring curious, disbelieving stares and soft laughter that tapped at my back.

They were hard put to place me into a category, these noble women, for I was neither servant nor lady but fell somewhere in between, into a mysterious netherworld that before now had not existed. Lady Creswell assured each of them that, lady though I once had been, I did indeed work with mathematics—imagine that!—that I lived quite alone, by myself, with no one to care for me; and that I made all my own decisions without benefit of male guidance, including the purchase of my clothing. She told everyone about my astonishing knowledge of books, her words gracious and her lovely face smiling with pride as though I were her protégé. And yet, a subtle undertone made it clear that no true lady would have stooped to the disgrace that I had most willingly sought. Lighthearted wit in the drawing room was quite one thing; astonishing male acquaintances with one's feminine intelligence merely an amusing game to play. But for these women it would be better, indeed, to starve in truth, than to actually forfeit social standing for freedom and independence as had I. Once again Father's voice arose to echo in the pitying stares and head-shakes that followed my progress around that elegant room.

I had no man to identify and define me, to give me worth. In their eyes, I was worse off than even a servant, who at least caught the reflected glory of the house she served. But I served no one, be it father, brother, husband, lover or master. In turning from acceptable behavior by seeking a man's independence and freedom, I had slipped between the cracks of life. I belonged nowhere, and I ceased to have any social value except as a curiosity. My identity had long ago faded away; certainly it was not for me to define. In society's eyes, I truly no longer existed. I was not a lady, not a woman, not even a person. I was nothing. And I was told so with every arrogant look, covert stare and derisive snicker as I progressed around that salon.

Somehow I got through that first hour of introductions, smiling sweetly while I fought despairing tears, listening to Father's tone echo beneath Lady Creswell's laughing, breathless voice. Her husband, Lord Edwin Creswell, Count of Buckfell, had not gone into the country as she had stated. He bowed over my work-roughened hand, a portly, graying man of sixty whose indifferent brown eyes looked through a very invisible me while acknowledging an introduction I knew he would forget within moments of our moving on. I glanced at his wife, flirting rather openly with a bemused Andrew as we toured the room, and wondered what it was like being married to such an old man. Though I knew, now, that my original estimation of her age had been wrong—she was the elder of the sisters, being twenty-nine to Lady Elizabeth's twenty-seven—still there were more than thirty years between she and her husband. Thirty years! It would seem like being married to one's father. I shuddered at the thought, knowing that had he lived, my own father would have consigned me to a like fate. To my mind, not existing truly had its small advantages, however painful it did sometimes feel.

I lost Andrew to the men once the introductions had been completed. Lady Creswell pressed a glass of champagne upon me, and I sat sipping the bubbly, slightly bitter liquid while I listened to the ladies talk of things unknown and incomprehensible to me. Distracted by the laughter ringing from where the men clustered around Andrew, I kept glancing their way, sure he must be off on another tale and wishing I were with them. Each time I turned my head, Lady Creswell would prevail upon me to enlighten the women gathered on some obscure point of comparison between two authors of whom most had never heard. They listened with bored, polite condescension, turning again to fashion, travel and servant problems immediately I had finished. Then, after pressing a second glass of the potent wine on me, Lady Creswell jumped up, clapped her hands, and organized the evening's entertainment.

The promised authors were there, though due to their popularity and mounting wealth one could not readily distinguish them amidst the company by their dress. Servants pushed settees and chairs into a rough semi-circle before the massive marble fireplace, leaving bare an area fifteen feet square in which the performers would stand. Clutching my half-empty glass, I looked around for Andrew, but could not find him in the press of gentry searching for seats. Quietly, I moved away to the side wall and seated myself on a deep window seat between the panels of a pair of half-opened velvet drapes. Cold radiated from the panes close to my back, chilling me to the bone, a chill unalleviated by the fire roaring on the other side of the wide room. And yet, cold as it was, it still felt warmer to me than the embrace of those elegantly clad and dazzlingly bejeweled ladies.

Morgan Carruthers began the entertainment, standing stiffly poised before the assemblage, thick-jowelled head thrown back so that his beady hazel eyes stared unblinking at the heavy ceiling beams. Firelight glinted on his carefully coiffed light brown hair, and the way the shadows fell on his long face, emphasizing his broad brow and hooked nose and plunging his eyes and receding chin into darkness, he reminded me of an owl. His voice, when he declaimed, sounded incongruously high and tinny. It grated on my nerves.

He recited from memory a long narrative poem which he said he'd finished just that day, the meaning of which I could not discover though I listened carefully. Whether it was due to his annoying, whiney voice or the fact that it was sheer gibberish and nothing more I could not tell for sure, though I leaned quite heavily toward the latter. He spoke on for almost half an hour, his tone stilted, his gestures awkward, his pauses incomprehensible. I sat shivering, trying to make sense of his words and slowly finishing the wine. I was glad to have it, for though it made my head swim it did minimize the feel of the icy window at my back.

Next came Mrs. Satchel, wearing elaborate blue moiré with feathers in her dark brown hair. She read an essay on Mr. Disraeli's rather unpopular Reform Bill, which just last year granted the right of vote to small farmers and city workers, men who did not own property. She wrote well, with a biting wit, and the audience chuckled in appreciation at the chaos she predicted would come from such foolishness as giving the ignorant masses a hand in government. I twirled my empty glass in icy fingers and wondered what might happen should women be allowed an opinion at the polls. It was hard to believe they could mess up things any worse than men already had. I sighed and set the glass on the window seat beside me, not listening as Mrs. Satchel concluded with three short, amusing and rather risqué ditties about secret assignations gone wrong. As long as women were owned by men, I decided, there could be no possibility that anything they said, did or thought would be taken seriously.

Mr. Huntley-Grey, resplendent in a black tail coat, rose-and-white waistcoat with a raised matelasse design, and green and black striped trousers, then told a tale of terror on the high moors, reading in a nasal monotone from the text of his latest book. He looked like a character from the story, his tall body solidly muscled beneath the fancy dress, his long, square face more reminiscent of a highwayman than a writer. But a writer he certainly was, for despite his droning voice he told quite a good tale, chilling in the extreme. Twice I found myself peering over my shoulder at the darkness behind me.

When he had finished, leaving the company shivering despite the warmth of the room, Lady Creswell called a break, ordering champagne sent around while restless guests stretched cramped muscles. I took advantage of the confusion to seek out Andrew, finding him in close conversation with Mr. Huntley-Grey. Not wishing to disturb him, I turned away and found myself face-to-face with Sir Henry D'arcy, Lady Jane's handsome country cousin who was staying with the Count and his wife for the winter season. Indeed, I found myself more than face-to-face, for the sudden warmth of the nearby fire had combined with the wine in my head to tilt the room about me alarmingly. I staggered as I turned and knocked against the glass he held, spilling champagne down the front of his elaborate brocaded waistcoat.

"Oh, Lord D'arcy, please forgive me!" I cried, a wave of heat washing over me. How I wished I could vanish through the floor. "I am so sorry—"

'No, no, Miss... Weston, isn't it?" he interrupted, smiling at me as he dabbed a linen handkerchief on the stain. I nodded, my eyes aswim with tears. "There is never any reason for a beautiful woman to apologize. I assure you, I enjoyed this encounter immensely, damp though it was."

"You are too kind, my lord," I murmured, my face lowered. He reached out and placed a knuckle beneath my chin, tipped my face up until I looked into his deep blue eyes. Blond hair waved across his forehead, long sideburns adding width to his already round face. His lips were thin, and a trifle cruel looking, his nose straight and narrow, his chin cleft with a deep dimple.

"Sir Henry, please," he whispered, his gaze caressing my face, lingering on my lips. "And you can be sure I will frequent Chadwicke's Books from now on, now that I know its attractions are so... delectable."

He turned away and grasped two full glasses of wine from a passing tray. Handing me one, he raised his in a toast.

"To literature, Miss Weston. And the surprises it holds."

I nodded and sipped from my glass, wondering how to extricate myself from this predicament. At that moment, Lady Creswell clapped her hands and called everyone to gather around, for her newest find and the star of the evening was ready to regale them with marvelous tales of romance and adventure. I had turned, startled at the abrupt sound of the clap, and when I looked around again at Lord D'arcy, I found myself quite alone among the moving guests who were already re-seating themselves. He was nowhere in sight.

Sighing with relief, I took a last sip of the bubbly wine and slowly made my way toward the door. I stood there a few minutes, listening to Andrew spin an enthralling yarn about a little flower seller, then turned and left the room. I was sure no one would miss me, for Andrew was caught deep in the spinning of his tale, his audience enraptured by his every word and movement. He stood in that elegant, luxurious room, before that wealthy, intimidating crowd, as completely natural and at ease as though he sat in O'Leary's Bake Shop, or on the steps of the Thames, weaving his story for this assemblage of titled nobility with the same enthusiasm with which he approached all of life.

Smiling happily, for I knew this night would be a turning point for Andrew, I stopped a passing maid and asked where I could refresh myself. She led me to an upper room where the ladies' wraps had been set and left me to my own devices. I sat long before the mirror, trying to ignore the magnificent room, thinking about the exchange with Lord D'arcy. I knew what his eyes had been saying, what he would want from me should he visit the bookshop. I did not feel flattered, I felt angry; angry that he would assume I would rush to drop my life, my identity, at the merest suggestion from him. And yet deep inside I could feel an ache, a formless yearning that left me confused and wondering. *What is wrong with me?* I asked my mirror image. *Other women seem to be content to be a man's toy, a mere mindless plaything. Why can't you? Is a life of want and poverty, of never having anything more than bare necessities, really worth giving up what he offers?*

I looked around at the rich furnishings, the powders and perfumes on the dressing table, the elegant wraps waiting to cover the scintillating, shallow women below—and thought of Uncle Joseph. And the neat, efficient ledgers in Uncle Jacob's shop. And the debt that a man had incurred, but that a woman was paying off. And I saw just how empty all this wealth and social standing truly was.

Yes, I decided, rising to return to Andrew, it was worth it. I might be invisible, but I most certainly was not empty. Or shallow. Or without value, however much other people shut their eyes to it. The ache, I finally realized, was for an impossible dream, an echo of the 'sometimes' sickness Uncle Jacob said plagues us all. It was time to go home, to reality.

I made my way to the top of the grand staircase and paused, smiling at the laughter emanating from the salon. Trailing my left hand on the smooth marble railing, I slowly descended, my head turned to the left as I gazed at the slightly open salon doors and listened to Andrew's expressive voice. Looking forward again as I gained the floor, I found Lord D'arcy standing to my right, watching me with intent eyes. He leaned against a narrow doorframe, arms crossed, a slight smile curving his thin lips. I returned his smile and bowed my head in greeting but I did not stop. I turned away to my left to approach the salon. Before I could take more than a step he had crossed the twenty feet between us and laid a firm hand upon my arm.

"Miss Weston, there is something I must show you. Please."

Though he gestured a polite invitation to the room he had just quitted, his strong fingers held me tight, permitting me no escape. I was forced to accompany him.

"I thought of this when dear cousin Jane mentioned your knowledge of antique books," he added. "I am sure you will find it quite intriguing."

"I really haven't much knowledge of antique volumes, Lord D'arcy," I protested as he guided me across the hall to what I discovered was a library. "Mr. Chadwicke would be of more help in that respect than I."

"It is there, on the desk," he said, ignoring my objection. "Please, step in further, take a closer look."

He let go of my arm and I stood a moment looking around the large, book-lined room, a room very similar to the one in our Boston home. Though the ceiling here was higher, the room twice the size and the appointments richer by far, still the atmosphere recalled sharply my twelfth birthday. I turned and, as bidden, walked closer to the massive desk, half-expecting to see my Father sitting there.

"And I am not Lord D'arcy, Marina. Not for you. For you, I am Sir Henry."

I spun at the insinuating words, the intimate tone. He turned the key in the lock and moved toward me, his eyes burning on mine. I stood frozen, my heart pounding in fear, until he was within arm's length of me.

"No!" I cried, dodging to the side, but he caught me and spun me into his arms.

"Yes, Marina. I want you. I have since Cousin Jane first spoke of you."

His lips crushed down on mine, his arms pinning me tight against him. I struggled and squirmed, unable to lift my arms to strike at him. He moved me back until I pressed against the desk. His lips still on mine, he bent me back onto the gleaming oak surface.

He broke the kiss. I gasped, breathless with fear.

"Please, let me go!" I begged.

"No, Marina. I will take good care of you, my little bird, you know that, don't you?" He twined his fingers in my hair, pulling at my curls. His gaze caressed my face. I pushed at his shoulders with fisted hands, to no avail.

"I will take you away from that dreary shop and find you an elegant house. I will buy you clothes, jewels, give you money. You'd like that, wouldn't you, Marina? Beautiful clothes and money?"

He kissed me again, oblivious to my pounding

fists. Keeping me pinned in place with his body, he slid his hands to the neck of my dress and began pulling at the buttons.

"No, please, stop! Don't, please! Let me go!" I cried, renewing my struggle for freedom.

He bent his head, his lips caressing my neck, the swell of my breast above my camisole, and I froze, terrified. He must have taken my stillness as acquiescence, for he lifted his head and smiled at me, then opened more buttons until my bodice gaped to the waist. Gently, he caressed my breasts with his hands, his fingers impatient to remove the thin camisole covering them.

"So beautiful, Marina," he murmured, his eyes aglow. "You should be surrounded by beauty, not drudgery. And you shall be. You will be my love, my beautiful toy. You will give me pleasure, and I shall buy you whatever you desire."

He stood and pulled me into his arms, his hands sliding in my hair, holding my face to his, his fingers pulling my long locks free of snood and ribbon. I could feel tears leak from beneath my closed lids and desperately I pushed at him, twisting in his iron grasp. At last he lifted his head and laughed.

"What a mistress you will be! What fire runs in your veins! We will have many wonderful years together, sweet Marina. Starting tonight."

"No!" I shouted, pushing him with all my strength. He stumbled back a pace, taken unawares, then reached for me again with a low growl.

"You think you have a choice in this? I'll break you if you refuse me, Marina," he threatened. "Do you hear? I'll break you!"

He grabbed my left wrist. Instinctively, my free hand closed around a crystal paperweight sitting on the edge of the desk. My arm swung, and the heavy glass cracked against the side if his head. He staggered back a few steps, dazed, though his fingers did not loosen on my wrist.

"Let me go!" I demanded. "Don't touch me!"

He stared a moment, shocked, then his hand rose and pressed on the left side of his head. It came away spotted with blood. His face twisted and he yanked me close, laying the back of his hand across my face with stunning force. My knees buckled. He pulled me up by my wrist and hit me again, this time allowing me to drop onto the floor. He stood staring down at me, curled sobbing on the thick carpet, blood from my split lip staining my fingers. Then he spun and stalked to the door, wiping the blood from his temple with his handkerchief, neatening his cuffs and smoothing his hair before he unlocked it and left, without looking again at me. He shut the door firmly behind him. Not five minutes had elapsed since we first entered the room.

How long I lay there I don't know, but I do not think many minutes passed before I forced my sobs to still and sat up. With shaking fingers I re-buttoned my dress, noting with despair that fully half the buttons were gone, yanked off by Lord D'arcy's anxious fingers. I ran my hands through my straggling hair, trying to smooth it back into order, and pressed my handkerchief to my lips to stem the bleeding. After a moment, I rose on weak, trembling legs and made my way to the door. I was so terrified I could barely breathe. What if he waited out there in the hall? What if I left the flimsy safety of this room, only to have him grab me again? I looked at the key and knew I could turn it in the lock and remain where I was until Lord Creswell came, and I was sorely tempted to do so even if I waited all night. It would serve that arrogant bastard right for the Count to discover just what sort of man he was.

My hand was actually on the key when I realized the futility of the action. I was merely a shop assistant; what made me think the Count would believe a word I said? That I had been beaten was obvious, for I could feel my cheek and lips swelling from Lord D'arcy's heavy hand. But who would believe that he had done it, and done it because I had refused to let him rape me? He could easily claim I had trysted with a servant who had been rough with me, and that I hoped, by blaming Sir Henry, to wheedle money out of the Count. Or perhaps he would say he had caught me stealing something upstairs, and had struck me in self-defense when I attacked him, after which I fled in here to hopefully escape capture. His words came back to me with sudden clarity; *I'll break you if you refuse me, Marina.*

My heart pounded with fear. I had to get away

from this place. I couldn't let anyone see me, not like this. I daren't even go upstairs for my wrap, lest I meet one of the ladies or a servant on the way. What I would do, where I would go, I knew not, but I had to leave this house.

I held my breath, eased open the door and listened. In the hushed stillness I could hear Andrew's voice; from the tone, it seemed he now spun a tale of tragedy and woe, his audience enraptured and silent. Carefully I peered out, my gaze searching the hall. It was deserted. The front door stood to my right, thirty feet away. Taking a deep breath, trusting that Andrew would hold them all spell-bound a few minutes longer, I slipped out of the library and walked quickly to the beautiful entry door.

No one saw me, save the chilled, bored doorman half asleep in the dark night outside the entranceway. I kept my battered face turned from him and hurried down the broad steps into the gently falling snow, putting the bright lights and false security of the lovely house behind me. Crossing the wide drive that curved around the front of the mansion, I passed between two elegant carriages waiting to convey their owners home, before the cold penetrated my desperation and shock. I stood in the deep shadows near the carriages, unable to control my shivering, staring up and down the avenue. Which way should I go? Where was Uncle Jacob's shop? How would I ever get home?

"Oooh, you look so cold! Come 'ere, little darlin'. I'll warm ye good!"

I whirled to see a footman, his rough, ugly face leering at me. I shook my head and backed away, his coarse voice and suggestive laughter following me in the dark. Shaking with cold, I stumbled past the long line of vehicles, accosted by a few of the bored, waiting men, tears of panic freezing on my cheeks. Not until I had left the coaches behind and stood on the dark street, with the rising wind whipping snow in my face and swirling my hair about my head, did I realize I would never make it alone. I had no idea which way to go or how far it was, but remembering the lengthy cab ride earlier, I realized that even if I did know I could not walk that far all alone in the cold darkness without even my worn wrap to cover me. My fingers and toes were already numb, the snow almost ankle-deep; even with the burnoose I would freeze to death long before I drew near the shop.

A hand touched my shoulder and I jumped, biting back a scream. An elderly coachman, bundled in an amazing array of clothing, gave me a gap-toothed smile and put a comforting arm around my shoulders.

"Come out of the wind, Miss, that's right, behind the carriages here," he crooned, leading me into the lee of the second-to-last coach. "Me name's Willie. I drive this carriage 'ere, 'ave done so for thirty-some years, and that's a fact. Now, din' I see you go in the big 'ouse earlier wearing a cloak? Not a night for going without it, no it i'n't. Let me send someone over there to fetch it for ye. What's it look like?"

Willie coaxed the story of my abrupt departure

from me, his solemn eyes dark as the words tumbled from my lips amidst great tearing sobs. I felt so grateful to him, for he believed me. He sent a young footman to the servant's entry to wheedle my cloak from the parlor maid, and while we waited Willie fed me sips of the harsh, cheap liquor he kept in a flask in his tattered greatcoat pocket. For emergencies, he said. Though it tasted terrible and made me gag, it did spread a burning warmth throughout my body that helped combat the shudders that kept rippling through me.

In less than half an hour, the footman, Robbie, returned with my wrap, having left a message with the maid to tell Andrew where I was. But I was so thoroughly cold by then, despite the liquor, that I was not even aware when Willie draped the warm woolen fabric around me. It was more than an hour before the grand lords and ladies emerged from the warm depths of the mansion to be taken home, and Andrew stalked to where I stood waiting, numb in body and mind. His eyes glittered with anger in the lights from the great house. He barely spoke to me all the way home in the cab he procured, clearly not seeing in the deep shadows beneath my hood the darkening bruises on my swollen face. Despite being out of the wind, I could not stop shaking.

"You embarrassed me terribly, running off like that, Marina," he said when the cab at long last pulled up in front of the shop. "I needed you with me, yet you left the moment I began to speak. Why? Are you jealous of the attention I received, is that it? I know you did not want to be there, but did you have to go and spoil the evening for me? Did you?"

I opened the cab door and forced my aching body out, unable to find words to explain. I looked at his pained, angry face, my heart breaking.

"I am sorry, Andrew. Truly I am," I whispered, then turned and walked on unsteady legs around the shop to the back entrance. Andrew did not come after me; the moment I disappeared from his sight I heard the the cab drove off, and I feared it would be a long while before his emotion cooled. I was shaking so hard I could barely fit the key into the lock. But I persevered, and somehow managed to drag myself up to my cold, shabby, lonely room.

Chapter Thirteen

I grew very ill from my long sojourn in the cold, snowy night. Uncle Jacob found me Sunday morning on the hard bare floor of my room, the street and room doors both open wide to the frosty air. I still wore the threadbare burnoose atop my gray dress, both clammy with damp and cold. But my body burned red, hot to the touch, and I knew nothing and no one but fever-induced phantoms for long days. Uncle Jacob told me later, when I was almost fully recovered, that many times he had been sure that I would die.

But I didn't. I lay fighting the nightmare demons that assailed me. For five days, Lord D'arcy blended into my Father's brutal form, their fists pounding at me. Lady Creswell together with Andrew pursued me, their words slashing at me, trying to erase me, to destroy my life. Uncle Jacob and Mollie O'Leary took turns nursing me, laying cool cloths on my burning head and dosing me with preparations a frantic Andrew sent round almost hourly. From what I said in the delirium, both Mollie and Uncle Jacob were able to piece together the story of the bruises on my face and arms, as well as a good part of my life in America I had not spoken of before. They said nothing to me of what they had learned for three weeks, not until the letter arrived from Lord D'arcy.

When the raging fever finally broke and I was coherent once again, I pretended surprise at the livid, swollen bruises and declared I must have hit my face when I had fallen unconscious on the floor. Mollie and Uncle Jacob humored me, not wanting to upset me in my weakened state, and I congratulated myself on successfully fooling them and thus avoiding a painful explanation. It was over, anyway. What was the point of speaking of it? Nothing had actually happened, no permanent damage was done, and surely I would never see Lord D'arcy again. My abrupt, rude departure from the Creswell mansion ensured I would never again be invited, not that I would accept if I were. The whole episode was best forgotten.

It startled me then, when two days after the fever broke, as I lay trying to breathe past the obstruction in my chest, my body racked by a deep cough, Uncle Jacob reported that Lady Creswell had come by the shop to inspect the new arrivals. She seemed genuinely upset at the news of my grave illness, and appeared unaware of my precipitous flight from her home. The next day, a large load of firewood arrived for me, and three warm wool blankets for my bed. Uncle Jacob refused to let me return them, and though I was angry at first in the end I was grateful to him, for without the extra warmth I may not have survived. It was, he told me weeks later, the very least that woman owed to me.

Three weeks after I woke I was breathing much easier, though the cough still plagued me if I moved around too much. I insisted on coming down to work for the mornings when my meager energy was at its peak, agreeing with Uncle Jacob that I would sleep each afternoon. I tired very easily and found that if I did not ascend to my room immediately after lunch, I did not have the strength to mount the stairs later in the day. Thus, I was behind the big antique desk in the old-editions room, a thick blanket tucked tight around me, working on the neglected ledgers when the messenger arrived.

"You Miss Weston?"

I looked up at the young lad and smiled, for he reminded me of how Andrew must have looked at twelve or thirteen; tall, gangly, with sandy hair sprouting in every direction and a voice unreliable in pitch. I acknowledged his question with a slight nod. Uncle Jacob was busy with a customer.

"I have a letter for you," he told me in a tone full of self-importance. "I am instructed to put it directly into your hand, and no one else's."

He pulled an envelope from a pouch at his waist, thick creamy white vellum, the flap held closed by an ornate wax seal. There was nothing written on the outside, not my name, nor an address, nothing. I held it in my still-shaky hands a moment, studying the seal, but being unfamiliar with British crests I learned nothing other than that it was very expensive paper, indeed. I had moved to break the seal when I realized the boy still stood before me.

"Do you need something?" I asked, wondering why he had not left. Perhaps I was supposed to pay him for the delivery.

"I am to wait for a reply, Miss," he said, his voice now fallen two octaves and sounding rather official. "He said there would be a reply."

I looked back down at the letter in my hand. A reply? What could anyone want with me that would require a reply? Mr. Marlowe? Something to do with Father, with the money I owed? It was the only thing I could think of, and it set my heart fluttering. What if they demanded an increase in the payment, what would I do? I was already sending almost more than I could afford each month. My hands shaking now from more than weakness, I broke the seal on the envelope.

It was not from Mr. Marlowe.

My darling Marina. The copperplate hand looked lazy and elegant. *You left behind your hair ribbon; a pledge, my dear? I have engaged the rooms of which I spoke.* Here followed an address in a semi-fashionable part of town. *I shall be waiting tomorrow night, to return the ornament in person. And add many more to it. Don't dare fail me, Marina, my love. Come to me. D'arcy.*

I stared at the graceful, spidery lettering, waves of hot and cold flushing over me. My hair ribbon! I had not given it a thought, had forgotten in my fear and panic that he had pulled it from my head. It must have remained behind on the desk in Sir Edwin's library when I fled. Lord D'arcy must be mad—or incredibly arrogant—to believe I had left it as a sign of willingness. How could he think, after what he had done to me, that I would fly to his embrace? Don't dare fail me, he had written. Was this, then, just the beginning? Would he hound me until I could stand no more, until I at last gave in? Once again I heard his angry, threatening voice: *I will break you if you refuse me, Marina.* He had beaten me to the ground the last time. What would he do to me now?

"Well? Where is the answer? He said there would be one," the boy's impatient voice demanded, his tone again soft and high like a girl's. Startled, for I had forgotten he stood there waiting, I looked up at him and frowned, blinking in confusion.

"No," I said, my voice almost a whisper. "No, there is no answer. No answer at all."

The boy sighed with the great exasperation of youth faced by incomprehensible adult behavior. Then he shrugged with total unconcern and left the shop. I stared down at the haughty, self-assured words looping across the luxurious paper. Tears misted my eyes. I was so tired it was hard to think how to fight this. I knew the easiest route to take was simply to give in; Lord D'arcy had the time, wealth, social impunity and commanding arrogance needed to make my life miserable for weeks, months, years even, until he forced me to his will. He might even take out his ill-temper on Uncle Jacob in some way.

I re-folded the thick white sheet and laid it aside, sending my gaze around the dim, warm, book-lined walls, letting the peace and tranquility that radiated out in soothing waves embrace me. I was, in a way, saying good-bye. Desperately weak as I was, I knew I could not long fight Father's ghost within and Lord D'arcy's importunities without. Drowning in darkness, I was unable to see any solution other than compliance. That my weakness, a heavy racking cough, and the painful constriction in my chest combined to drain my concentration so that I committed mistake after mistake on the ledgers only added to my hopeless feeling, confirming as it did the incompetence of which Father had so often accused me. It was true; I was no good, useless, a failure, of value only as a plaything for a rich, self-centered man. Father had been right. My bid for freedom was over.

"Come, Just Marina," Uncle Jacob called from behind the curtain. "Our meal is ready."

The gentle voice abruptly pulled me back to the shop. I must have sat long sunk in despairing reverie, for I had not seen Uncle Jacob's customer leave, nor Uncle Jacob himself lock the door and turn the sign in the window. With a deep sigh I pushed myself to my feet. My gaze fell on the open ledger book; great blotches marred the pages where my tears had fallen, destroying two days' worth of work—one more confirmation I did not need. Feeling empty inside, I folded the blanket onto the chair and moved slowly, like a very old woman, to where Uncle Jacob would be waiting at the dining table in the back sitting room.

He was not at the table. He stood in the center of the room, staring solemn-eyed at me, the letter from Lord D'arcy clutched in one pudgy hand. How very far away I had been, indeed, that I had not seen him take it from beside me on the desk. And now he knew, or thought he knew, what had happened that Saturday night—why I had left Andrew, who I had met, what I had done, the 'reward' I was to reap for the compromise of my virtue. It was there in Lord D'arcy's own hand. It never occurred to me that the torn state of my dress, my straggling, disheveled hair, the ugly swollen bruise on my cheek, and the strong blond man I'd fought against over and over in my delirium, all told a tale more eloquent—and truthful—than all of Lord D'arcy's imperious words.

Uncle Jacob said nothing, merely enfolded me in a warm, comforting embrace. I cried a long time, my head resting on his shoulder, letting out through those silent tears the pain and fear and confusion I had wrestled with these last three weeks. Finally, he dried my eyes, fed me warm soup and bread, and helped me up to my bed. With a tender smile he snugged the blankets around me, then chuckled as he turned Lord D'arcy's letter over in his hands.

"It is his supreme confidence that amazes me so, Marina. You would think he would recognize a 'no' when it clocked him on the head, would you not? How he could beat you for refusing and then expect you to run to him is beyond me."

"You've known what happened, Uncle Jacob? How?"

"I did not know who had done it, my dear, but it was obvious what had happened from the moment I found you with your face all swollen and your dress half-undone. It was obvious you were not a willing participant. Despite your Father's heavy-handed attempts to crush you, your moral fiber has survived strong and intact."

"My Father? Uncle Jacob—"

He laid a finger on my lips, stopping my words.

"You spoke of many things in the fever, Marina. Things best forgotten. We'll not waste precious time rehashing them, for there are too many good things of which to speak. Now. Shall we give this the treatment it deserves?"

He held up Lord D'arcy's letter, a wry expression of distaste on his face. I frowned at him and he winked, held a finger to his lips, then tiptoed to the fireplace and, with a flourish, dropped the exquisite paper into the hungry flames roaring on my hearth. We smiled at one another with conspiratorial delight, and I fell asleep with a heart light and hopeful. Though self-doubt and despair still lurked at the edges of my mind, I was no longer alone in fighting them. Until my body fully recovered and my strength returned in force, I would have Uncle Jacob for support, his fortitude to keep me safe and strong.

Two weeks later, Uncle Jacob closed the shop as

usual at one p.m. on Wednesday, tucked me securely into the rocker before the stove in his sitting room, a stack of books and a pot of tea beside me, and donned his heavy overcoat. He kissed me good-bye but did not tell me where he was going. He returned three hours later with cakes and bread from Eamon's bakery and the gray hair ribbon and mesh snood that had been lost in Lord Creswell's library. I never asked how he had gotten them, and he did not volunteer the information. I did not hear from D'arcy again, not for two long years, but his lordship did not forget the grave insult I had paid him.

It was spring before I fully recovered, the late April sun warm on my face when at last I felt strong enough to walk in the park with Andrew. The cough and weakness had lingered through the winter, affording me the perfect excuse to refuse the three invitations to literary soirees that had arrived from Lady Creswell. I could not believe she would expect me to overlook her cousin's behavior and put myself into a position where it could happen again. But Andrew, who knew nothing of Lord D'arcy's attack that night and who regaled me with details of these as-promised small, intimate and truly literary evenings, convinced me that Lady Creswell did regret my enforced absences and looked forward to my presence when I fully recovered.

I decided finally that she must not know the truth of what had happened in her house that night, and yet I could not decide what she did think of me. I had written to apologize for my hasty departure, blaming the sudden onset of my severe illness, and thanked her for the kind gifts of firewood and blankets. The reply I received seemed indifferent, even cold, but when she visited the shop for new books, as she continued to do, she was her usual, breathless, careless self, running on happily about Andrew's growing popularity and truly pleased that he kept me abreast of the myriad excitements in his life.

Still, in late March, after hearing from Andrew of the time he spent at my side on his days off, she began holding her gatherings on Sundays, or on Wednesday afternoons, the only time Andrew and I had together. I missed him desperately, the few moments we did have leaving me yearning for more. But he was happy, enjoying the adulation and in constant demand; my new-found brother was growing up, away from hearth and home. I was pleased for him though my heart ached inside. I was not yet ready to let go, since I had only 'found' him such a short time before. But it seemed I would have no choice in the matter, for if I protested I knew Lady Jane Creswell's jealousy would only pull him further and further away. I contented myself with the few stolen moments we had together.

We strolled in the park one April Sunday afternoon, savoring the rarity of togetherness. Four of Andrew's tales had already been published, and two more were ready to be sent. I had, as my strength gradually returned, continued copying down his stories—which he then gave to Lady Creswell—and encouraged him to practice his own hand, which he did but reluctantly. Andrew did not care that his tales appeared in print, other than that it earned him money. He relished more the gatherings where he told his stories in person, where he was surrounded and adulated by his audience. Now I walked arm-in-arm with him, listening to him relate how Lady Jane Creswell had stolen another piece of him away.

"When at last I confessed to her, Marina, that I could not write, not well enough to get my stories down on paper, that it was you who wrote them down for me, she laughed, absolutely delighted. 'A writer who cannot write!' she exclaimed. 'How delicious!' I couldn't believe it."

He threw himself onto the grass, pulling me down with him. He held my hands in his, his eyes shining with excitement.

"Do you know what she did? She hired a secretary. For me!"

"A secretary? Oh, Andrew, you wouldn't need a secretary if you would learn to write properly yourself."

"Ah, but Jane says that is part of my charm," he replied, his brows lifting into a comical angle. "'The illiterate literate,' she calls me. Learning to write would spoil my 'atmosphere of spontaneity,' Jane says."

"*Jane?*" A frisson of fear shivered through me. American though I was, even I knew the dangers of flaunting propriety. "Andrew, you cannot call her Jane. She is *Lady* Jane, a Countess."

Andrew gave me a smug, somewhat supercilious smile. I stared at him, my heart sinking.

"Andrew, you are not getting involved with her, are you? Do not forget she is the wife of Sir Edwin, the Count of Buckfell. He is powerful, a Peer of the Realm. He will crush you if overstep the bounds."

Echoes of Lord D'arcy's nasty threat sounded in my head; again I felt his heavy hand upon my face.

"What bounds, Marina? Jane says there *are* none, not for us creative types! Besides, he's just an old man, what would he care?"

"Oh, Andrew!" For all his experience of life, despite being born into deprivation, poverty and want —or perhaps because of it—Andrew Sykes was blindly naive, oblivious to the dangers beneath the glittering wealth he sought. "There are *always* bounds. It would not do for you to forget your place, no matter how much money you earn. We are not real people, we of the lower classes, not to those born into wealth and social standing. We are toys, mere playthings, curiosities that exist for their amusement. And they grow bored very easily, Andrew; bored and angry. Poor and humble as we are, we have no way to fight them. Don't let your success and the excitement blind you, Andrew, please."

"My eyes have never been open wider, Marina." He threw his head back and laughed. "I have Jane eating from my hand. I'm her golden boy, I can do no wrong. And soon, soon all of London will be mine."

He went on, weaving an amusing but touching

tale of a waif-like orphan who becomes the toast of London, which attracted a small crowd around us, as Andrew's tales always did. I sat beside him, watching his shining face, listening to his enthralling words, seeing how he blossomed beneath the adulation of the crowd, and all the while my heart beat with fear. Andrew was on a collision course with a fate he thought he could control. There was a fanatical look in his eyes when he spoke of the way the moneyed aristocracy sat before him, spellbound by the force of his words and ideas. He could not see it for the chimera it was, would not hear me tell him over and over how quickly the fame and adoration could die. He saw only his success, and Lady Jane Creswell, who for a lark helped him spend the money he began to earn, guided him in his choice of clothing and jewelry, and introduced him to the finer things of life: gourmet foods, expensive wines, sporting games and gentlewomen's boudoirs.

Still, Andrew somehow found time for me. As the weather grew ever warmer and my strength at last returned in full, he again took me to plays and concerts, though now the seats were grander, more expensive, and Andrew recognized wherever we went. He gave me ribbons and lace, flowers every week, and a beautiful cameo to wear around my neck. But it was not until the beginning of that July, in 1868, that I discovered he had left Abernathy's a month before. We were again in the park and I stopped beneath the trees, astounded at the news.

"Andrew, what are you thinking? How could you leave your work, throw away all your hopes, your dreams? That shop is your future! You can't—"

"No, Marina, you're wrong." He grasped my shoulders, turned me around and pointed. Across the rolling lawns, London's buildings glimmered in the late-afternoon sun. "*There* is my future, out there, where life really happens. What kind of life is it, slaving away twelve hours a day for barely enough money to keep body and soul together?"

"But someday, Andrew, the shop will be yours. And it will be there long after the stories have faded and the nobility have forgotten your name."

"Damn the shop! What good is it? What will it give me, Marina? Nothing really worth having. Six tiny, dingy rooms above the rank smell of medicines and herbs, in a shabby part of town where the sun almost never shines and no one worth knowing ever goes. And twelve-hour days that will rob my youth, sap my strength and leave me old before my time. And for what? Barely enough customers to make ends meet, many of whom can't afford to pay the whole bill, and are too ignorant to use the preparations properly, anyway. It would be hell, and you know it. Never anything more than mere existence, Marina. Is that what you want me to be, a simple, poor shopkeeper a bare step above destitution, not worthy of anyone's notice, fawning for scraps that fall from other people's tables? A nobody?"

"An honest man who works hard is never a

nobody, you know that. And the things that really count in life are not bought with money. You thought the shop enough once, Andrew. More than enough," I reminded him.

"That was before I knew what life could be, Marina, before I tasted what is out there. Before great ladies curtsied to me, and gentlemen shook my hand. Before servants started calling me sir, Marina. Me! Sir! I want it all, to walk with lords and dukes and earls, to sit at their tables and drink their brandy; to laugh with them, play with them, be equal to them. I want a fine house and fine clothes, and finer friends. And I want ribbons and lace, Marina, silks and satins, and glittering jewels for your hair."

He pulled me close and kissed my lips with wild, feverish passion. I stared into his glowing eyes while his hands caressed my face and he stared at a vision of the future created by his own desperate yearning, a future not based on reality.

"I am as good as they are, Marina, despite my low birth," he said, "and soon I'll have money enough to prove it. I'll have a big mansion, an elegant carriage, and the most stylish, expensive clothing. And the most beautiful wife, dressed as she should be, sharing it all with me, right by my side. I love you, Marina. I always have, right from the first moment I saw you. Please marry me, Marina. Marry me."

I stared at him, stunned, for, our first meeting notwithstanding, he had given me no cause to think he felt this way about me. We were friends, family, confidants, but certainly not lovers. Confused and dismayed, I turned away and shook my head. I didn't want to hurt him, but I couldn't marry him.

"I–I don't know what to say, Andrew," I finally managed to choke out.

"Say yes, Marina. You do love me, don't you? Don't you?"

"Of course I love you, Andrew." I turned and looked at him, at his bewildered eyes. "I love you like a brother, you know that. You're the family I never had, you and Uncle Jacob, and Eamon and Mollie. I never expected you would feel this way. I don't know what to say to you. I can't marry you, Andrew, I don't love you like that. You're my brother. That's how I love you."

"Your... brother? That's all I am to you, a brother? When I love you so desperately?"

His voice sounded so tiny, so forlorn, inestimably hurt. Tears misted my eyes at the look on his face, the pain I could see stab his heart.

"I'm sorry, Andrew," I whispered. "I didn't know."

"Didn't know? *Didn't know?* After all this time? How could you *not* know?"

His hands curled into fists; I couldn't speak, I could only shake my head and cry.

"You've just been using me all this time, haven't you?" he said, his bitter tone a knife in my heart. "Using the way I feel about you, keeping me dangling while you looked around for better. Jane warned me about you."

I gasped. "What?"

"Oh, yes, she warned me. She told me what you did that night at her house, where you went, who you met, but I didn't believe her. I didn't want to. Because I trusted you, Marina. I loved you."

"No, Andrew," I whispered. "It's not true. No."

I backed away a few steps and Andrew followed, snarling now, too angry to heed my words, his face twisted.

"I'm not good enough for you, am I? Jane was right, wasn't she? You went after D'arcy and threw yourself at him, didn't you? What happened, Marina? Didn't he want you? Weren't you good enough for him? Didn't he think you were worth even cheap trinkets like this?"

He reached out and snatched the cameo from my neck, breaking the chain with a quick snap. He stared at the delicate filigree with an anguished expression.

"I would have given you the world, Marina. The world. Damn you. Couldn't you have pretended, like you would have for him? For a real lord? Couldn't you have pretended?"

He opened his fingers. The locket slid from his hand to the ground, glittering in the grass in the slanting rays of the sun. I bowed my head, burying my face in my hands, my shoulders shaking with sobs. Andrew stared at me a moment in silence, then shook his head.

"You deserve to stay where you are, Marina, in

the gutter. It's where you truly belong. A shop assistant, with the soul of a whore."

I moaned, sinking to my knees on the hard ground. But Andrew did not hear. He had already turned away to stalk across the grass in blind anger. I forced my tears to stop, aware of the public scene I created, the attention I drew from passers-by. Picking up the locket, I rose and walked among the trees until I had myself completely under control once more, then I walked home alone, clutching the broken cameo. Not even Uncle Jacob could ease the ache in my heart.

We did not see or hear from Andrew for more than three weeks, though in that time two more of his stories appeared in London's most popular publications. My smile eventually returned though the sadness deep in my heart never fully abated. The locket, broken chain gleaming in the candlelight, lay on my desk, untouched. I hadn't the money to have it mended, nor would I have worn it if I had. Every time I looked at it I saw Andrew's twisted, betrayed, hurting face. *He was right*, I thought. Though he had neither said nor done anything to let his inner feelings show, I should have known. Somehow, I should have known.

When at last he came it was with lavish gifts, off-handed apologies, and amusing tales of his latest adventures among the Ton. His clothes were more elegant now, his jewelry richer, his eyes shining with feverish excitement. But there was a desperation in him, too, a nervous, almost fearful agitation as he raced after a dream that constantly eluded him. I tried again to talk sense into him, as did Uncle Jacob, but Andrew was flying too high and fast to hear the words of those who truly loved him. Our love was tied to the poverty which he felt tainted him, and it no longer was enough for him. Maybe it never had been.

As though he held a tiger by the tail and could not let go, Andrew plunged into society with wild enthusiasm, trading on his wit and his talent with words to gain him what he sought most, the unqualified love and acceptance of the aristocracy. His visits grew farther and farther apart until at last, by January of 1869, he ceased coming altogether. Nor did he answer the messages we sent. He was in constant demand, the pet of the nobility, and lived as though he were one of them, his life an endless round of parties, entertainments, sojourns at country estates, and travel in the company of dukes and earls and their ladies. Always, there were the ladies.

But it could not last, and finally the life overwhelmed him, as I had feared it would. Scandal was whispered about, his name linked first with this lady, and then with that. He grew reckless; he accepted every challenge, faced every dare, no matter how dangerous. He drank to excess and gambled insatiably. The rakes and roués, the wastrels, black sheep and troublemakers of the greatest houses became his constant companions. He stopped writing.

The dream he so cherished, and grasped at with both hands, proved a nightmare in the end. It turned on him and swallowed him whole, crushed his childlike, trusting spirit beneath its relentless, merciless heel. The gambling ate up what money he had made, and ruined him completely. Not one of his noble companions stood by him, or helped him. Constant drinking destroyed his health; the fall to the depths was as rapid as the rise to the top had been. All he had wanted was love and respect; he found only heartlessness and betrayal.

Three years after he proposed to me in the park, Andrew Sykes, broken in body and mind and spirit, died in the squalid London slum where he had been born, alone, forsaken, destitute and friendless. He was twenty-seven years old.

Chapter Fourteen

Lady Jane Creswell stopped coming to our shop once she had Andrew completely in her power, and gradually our business fell off as the friends she'd brought with her followed her lead and also stayed away. With the exception of a few serious collectors who continued buying from us—Lady Elizabeth Teasdale among them—we were soon back to our regular clientele, the growing merchant middle class who still found quality and service of more importance than a bookseller's name or address.

I breathed a sigh of relief, for unlike Andrew I had never had any illusions of friendship with the titled women who used to come in, however friendly they seemed. I was content to have my life return to the dull safety of work, quiet evenings reading by the fire with Uncle Jacob, and tea on Wednesdays at Mollie and Eamon's bakery. I remained aloof from everyone and everything but these, for I was determined to never let anything threaten my security again. I was free,

SUSAN TUTTLE

independent and in control, and so would I remain. I would not be like Andrew, and overstep the bounds.

But we all suffer from our own brand of arrogance and blindness, and life has a way of pulling us rudely from the pedestals we erect for ourselves. It waits in silence until we are confident and secure, sure of what we want and our ability to hold onto it, for it is then that we are the most vulnerable.

It was Mr. Marlowe who set it in motion, though I did not discover that fact until it was all but over. When apprized of the dilemma his client was in, what he needed to extricate himself without the loss of his freedom—indeed, the solution would enhance it, for it would remove all responsibility from him—the solicitor immediately thought of me. It is easy even now for me to imagine how his lips curled with enjoyment and his eyes lit with malicious satisfaction as the long-awaited chance fell into his hands. Revenge. I would like to think he would have refused had he known the full fate to which he consigned me, but I know that is not true. He surely had to have known enough to guess at whatever details were not spoken of, but still he sent him to me, aided willingly in my destruction. And, no doubt, congratulated himself on a job well done.

I have wondered these last years if it would have made a difference had I known Mr. Marlowe was involved, if it would perhaps have rung a warning bell somewhere inside me. I do not think so. It would not have mattered to me at all, for I loved him. From the very first moment I saw him, standing inside the shop door waiting for his eyes to adjust to the dimness, I loved him with every fiber of my being.

He was tall and lean, with broad shoulders straining at the stylish dark gray cutaway he wore, the sweep of the fabric emphasizing his narrow waist and hips. Long legs stood encased in trousers striped in pale gray-blue and charcoal, making him seem even taller. From where I sat I could see only his profile, but that was enough.

My heart ceased beating as my gaze traced the line of his wide, clear brow, along the proud arch of his nose, across lips that curved sensually beneath the half-concealing mustache, down around a chin strong with confidence and determination. He had removed his black top hat upon entering, and stood holding it in slim-fingered hands that looked both gentle and forceful at the same time. Dark brown hair curled about his ears and waved onto his collar, gleaming softly in the light from the wall sconce near his shoulder.

I could not tear my gaze away from him, nor move, nor speak, nor even breathe. How long we remained thus, frozen in time, I do not know; but I felt eternities had passed before Uncle Jacob bustled forward and Matthew Palmerston—that was how he introduced himself, as Matthew Palmerston—bowed, smiled and followed Uncle Jacob out of my sight, his movement breaking the spell that held me motionless.

I blinked, gasping, and looked down in confusion

at the book I held. What had happened to me? Who was that man? I felt as though I had died, only to be instantly reborn into a world where colors were brighter, sound more melodic, the air sweeter than ever I had known it to be. Trembling, I forced myself to finish cleaning the shelves, setting the books back in place while his deep, vibrant voice rolled like muted thunder from the rear of the shop where he conversed with Uncle Jacob. I kept my head bent when he left carrying a small bundle of books, acutely aware of the cat-like grace with which he moved, the potent virility he exuded. For days, thoughts of him filled my every waking hour, and I accomplished little of what Uncle Jacob set for me to do. Matthew Palmerston haunted my dreams at night, and I began to wonder if I were not, perhaps, a trifle mad.

I also wondered if I would ever see him again, if he would come again to the shop. He did, but not until his third visit did I meet him, and speak with him. The second time he came, four days later, I was busy with a customer of my own in the new book room, and though I felt his gaze upon me, when I looked he was absorbed in whatever Uncle Jacob had shown to him, oblivious to me.

You fool, I chided myself, watching my customer leave. *He does not even know that you exist.* I seated myself behind the desk and opened the ledger, hoping to make some sense of the marks therein. I was shamefully behind in the accounts, unable to see anything but Matthew Palmerston's gleaming dark brown hair, the curve of his square jaw, the slant of wide bones above smooth, hollow cheeks. Sighing, I shook my head, pulled the bills closer, and dipped my pen into the inkwell.

I had made three entries before I again felt his gaze upon me. I looked up and our eyes locked. A tingling shock ran through me at the contact. Then he smiled and bowed his head in a remote, indifferent greeting. Blinking, I nodded back and bent again to the ledger book. Despair filled my soul. I had been right, he had not noticed me, not at all. I was nothing to him.

In this, I soon discovered, I was quite wrong.

Three weeks passed before he came again, and I had begun to fear he never would. Then suddenly there he was, shrugging the warm June rain from his broad shoulders and wiping his face with a snowy linen handkerchief. His wet hair glittered like diamonds in the lamplight.

I was again behind the desk working on the accounts, Uncle Jacob having retired behind the curtain to ready our midday meal. Despite my protests to the contrary, he still refused to allow me to cook for us. He had been doing for himself for almost forty years, he declared, and saw no reason to change his ways now. I knew he would not come out to wait on whomever had entered; he would expect me to handle it myself. Carefully, my heart thudding in my chest, I set aside my pen and rose to meet the man whose face I could not forget.

"Good afternoon, Mr. Palmerston. May I help you

find something?" He smiled at my trembling, breathless voice, and my heart stood still. "Uncle—uh, Mr. Chadwicke told me you are interested most... in Jacobean... drama..."

My words trailed off as again his eyes met mine and my thoughts flew from my head. I stood staring into the golden-brown depths oblivious to everything around me, wishing only that he would kiss me. Of course, he did not.

"Yes, indeed, you are amazing, just as Mr. Chadwicke said." I heard his voice as from a great distance; the words held no meaning for me. "How, pray tell, do you remember the preferences of customers whom you have never served? Have you a secret formula hidden away in your account ledgers, Miss—?"

I did not answer, nor enlighten him as to my name. I merely stared on at him, unaware even of his question. Gently, he touched my arm.

"I am after Ben Johnson, today, Miss—?"

"What?" At his touch I gasped, blinked and the shop and my work again flooded into my consciousness. "Oh, yes. Johnson. Yes, of course. Please, follow me."

I led him to the place where the plays were shelved, and we spent a pleasant half-hour sorting through the leather-bound volumes. He had extensive knowledge of the plays we searched out and I felt a bit out of my depth, for I had not yet read any of them myself. There was very little I could say to advise him about one particular volume over another except, perhaps, the quality of the paper or the method of the binding. He chose four books, two handsomely bound in tooled leather, the others plainer, older, and showing more wear. I wrapped them with care and wrote out the bill with shaking hands, acutely aware of his intent scrutiny as I did so. The clock chimed quarter past one when at last he turned to leave, and I accompanied him to the door to turn the key in the lock for the time Uncle Jacob and I would lunch. Matthew Palmerston paused with his hand on the knob and raised arched brows at me.

"I cannot leave without knowing," he said, "though I attempted by subterfuge to discover it, so as not to be found lacking in memory. That, alas, shall now be my fate, it seems."

"Discover what, Mr. Palmerston?" His words mystified me.

"Mr. Chadwicke told me once, I am sure he did, when I expressed my pleased surprise at your presence here. If all employers were as enlightened and courageous as he, the business world could only benefit from feminine wit, intelligence and charm."

I could feel my face heat, I fear, from the gentle compliment. I shook my head, still bewildered.

"I still do not understand," I confessed. "Told you what?"

"What you seem determined to keep a deep, dark secret. Your name."

"It is no secret, Mr. Palmerston," I said with a

laugh. "It is Marina. Marina Weston."

"A beautiful name, Marina." He nodded, his eyes solemn above lips that smiled. "And quite fitting."

He took my hand in his, his fingers warm and strong on my palm, and raised it to his lips. When he kissed my fingers, his eyes never left mine. Then he was gone, leaving me alone in the empty shop, unable to breathe or move until Uncle Jacob called me for lunch. I reached out, locked the door, turned the sign and floated back to where Uncle Jacob held the curtain for me, an amused chuckle rumbling in his chest.

That was the beginning, and even had someone told me the course upon which I was set, I would have listened to them no more than Andrew had to me. Matthew acted his part perfectly, left no clues over which I might stumble. Even Uncle Jacob and Mollie believed him, were almost as taken with him as was I. Eamon sounded the only warning bell, for he took an instant dislike to Matthew Palmerston. Mollie laughed at him and declared Eamon would not like anyone who interested me, for in Mr. O'Leary's eyes no man on the face of this earth would ever be good enough for Marina Weston, the daughter he'd always wished to have.

And so I dismissed Eamon's misgivings without even listening to them, because I wanted to see only what I wanted to see. I had learned my lesson well and was convinced I would never again fall into the traps life sets along our way. I believed I had paid my dues already, suffered through the years of Father's cruelty, my abandonment and the loss of Andrew, and thus had earned my reward: love, and the cessation of struggle and want. I had forgotten, or perhaps did not yet know, that some dues are never fully paid. Without struggle and want there can be no change; and without change, there can be no life.

The next week, Matthew Palmerston met me as I left the closed shop on Wednesday afternoon, bound for O'Leary's Bake Shop and St. Paul's Cathedral. It was a warm, sunny summer day, and I wore a light muslin shawl over a sky-blue gown. Though it was several years out-of-date, having been made three years before we left America, and I had only starched petticoats to give volume to the skirt, I had sewed dark blue ribbons and white lace at the hem, the neckline, and on the wide sleeves to add a touch of elegance to an otherwise plain dress. I felt both pretty and competent when I snapped the key in the front door lock, knowing the color of the gown enhanced my pale complexion and added interest to my plain gray eyes. Mr. Palmerston's compliment—wit, intelligence and charm—still echoed softly in my ears.

I clutched my book tight and smiled with happiness, looking forward to seeing Mollie and Eamon and to spending a peaceful hour in the sun on the steps of the church. I turned and promptly bumped into Matthew Palmerston. The hat flew from his head; the book fell from my hand.

"Oh! I am so sorry!" I exclaimed.

He bent and picked up the book, handing it to me

with a small flourish.

"No, it was my fault entirely," he said. "I was not looking at where I was going, my head in a cloud, as usual."

He retrieved his hat and I watched the bright sun pick golden highlights from his softly waving hair. I could see now that it was a lighter color than I had thought it to be in the dim interior of the shop, and I felt a pang when he set the stylish bowler back on his head, covering the shining brown waves. He smiled at me and I watched his eyes, fascinated by the tiny flecks of green in the rich, golden-brown irises.

"You are doing it again, Miss Weston. Not listening to me."

"I'm not?" Once again, I could barely breathe.

"Indeed, you are not. You are simply staring at me, while I am attempting to make polite conversation. What have you to say for yourself?"

"What?" I blinked, his voice finally penetrating my benumbed state. I felt my face flush as I realized my rudeness. "Oh, I am sorry, Mr. Palmerston. Please, forgive me."

"I most certainly will not, Miss Marina Weston. That is, not unless you agree to take tea with me. It is the very least you can do," he added upon seeing me shake my head, "given the grave nature of the insult."

With an engaging smile, he held out his arm. Laughing, I agreed, tucked my hand into the crook of his elbow and allowed him to lead me down the street. As we strolled, he chatted about the wonders of

London. He had a farm in the northeast, near the Ure River in Yorkshire, but business interests had necessitated a move to the capital. He had been here only three months and found it all very exciting. He had kept the farm, he told me, hoping to use it for holidays and such.

We had walked six blocks when he stopped abruptly, looked around the shabby, ill-kept buildings, and sighed.

"I am afraid I have done it again, Miss Weston. I am lost, hopelessly. I was sure I knew the way. I was all set to impress you with this wonderful place I discovered quite by accident, but now..." He shrugged his broad shoulders and looked at me with a sheepish grin on his face. "I can find my way blindfolded around the wild North York moors, but these London streets defeat me every time. I feel a fool."

I laughed and pointed ahead.

"If we turn left at the next corner, there is a place where we can stop. Do not despair, Mr. Palmerston," I addd as we walked on, "nor give up so easily. London streets were designed to be incomprehensible. Even after three years, I still get confused. Ah, here we are."

We had come to O'Leary's Bake Shop. Matthew Palmerston stared in patent disbelief.

"I do not credit my eyes. This is the very place to which I was taking you."

"Nor do I believe it!" I exclaimed. "It was to this very place I was heading when I so rudely bumped into you."

Laughing over the vagaries of fate, the convoluted twists that kept life interesting—I not knowing just how much human interference had been involved in this particular twist—we entered the shop and passed a most pleasant afternoon in each other's company. The next day, a messenger brought me flowers, and the following Wednesday, Matthew Palmerston again escorted me to tea.

For three wonderful months Matthew courted me, quickly becoming a permanent part of my small, loving family. He charmed Uncle Jacob utterly, his love of antiquities evinced in the reverent way he touched Uncle's most treasured volumes. They played chess for hours, pursuing each other relentlessly around the board, and argued philosophy with such relish that I once accused Matthew of using his interest in me as an excuse to see Uncle Jacob. He merely laughed, hugged me close, and bought me a ribbon for my hair.

He charmed Mollie, too, who at first approached him with suspicion, remembering the hurt dealt me by Andrew's behavior. That Matthew could not tell the tale of his crossing the street without becoming confused, endeared him to Mollie, and the fact that he was so very solicitous of me, thinking first of my welfare above all else, cemented her approval. Only Eamon's glowering face marred the warmth of those wonderful summer days, a chill I chose to ignore.

Slowly we grew closer, and even more slowly I let Matthew into my heart. I told him first about Andrew, for the wonderful Mr. Sykes was on everyone's lips, his stories seen everywhere one looked, and it was a natural topic of conversation. He listened without saying a word as I detailed the events of the last year and the months before it, to the fateful party in Lord Creswell's elegant mansion. It was the first I'd spoken of those events since Uncle Jacob had admitted to knowing of them. Tears misted my eyes when I repeated Andrew's hurting words, the vile accusation Lady Creswell had made that Andrew said he believed. There was no need to tell Matthew any of this, nor any of what I eventually did, but if there was to be more than friendship between us, then I wanted no secrets in the shadows. Little did I know how those secrets would be used against me.

When I finished speaking, he laid his hand atop mine. The warmth and strength radiating from his fingers gave me the courage to look up at him.

"He couldn't have truly loved you, Marina," he said, his voice low and soft. "If he had, he would have known how false it was, what that woman said. He would have known."

That night, Matthew kissed me for the first time.

He knew almost everything about me by the time he asked me to marry him. Everything except the true nature of my 'education' at Father's hands, and the means of his death. It was late in August, and Matthew's birthday. I had given him a work by Francis Bacon, *The Advancement of Learning*, an old volume from Uncle Jacob's private shelves that had cost me almost a month's salary. I had inscribed it and he laughed when he read it, declaring that my wisdom put all other writings to shame.

Matthew, I wrote. *Life is more than words, and answers are not found in books. Explore the pathways and enjoy the adventure, but remember: the truth lies within your own heart. Marina. 29 August, 1869.*

Uncle Jacob gave him a briar pipe, carved with his initials, and a pouch of tobacco to use with it. Then he excused himself and shuffled out into the shop, saying he had to check the ledgers, which he never looked at anymore. I shook my head at Matthew, a questioning smile on my lips. He smiled back at me and took my hands in his.

"I will confess, Marina. I asked Jacob to leave us alone for a few minutes. You see, I have decided to give myself a birthday present tonight. A wife."

"Matthew!"

"Will you marry me, Marina? You know how much I love you. You've become a part of me now. When I look into the future, all I can see is us. I cannot even imagine my life without you in it."

I looked away, wanting desperately to say yes. But my mind would not work; my body felt numb. I couldn't make my lips form the words that were in my heart.

"It is not the debt that makes you hesitate, is it, Marina?" he asked. "We will pay it off, my love, a little at a time, together. My business is more than prosperous enough, it will cause no hardship. I will not accept that as a reason for refusal, Marina. There will

A MATTER OF IDENTITY

be no stubborn pride, not between us."

Still I could not speak. He pulled me into his arms and pressed my head on his shoulder. The hand gently stroking my hair released the painful tears so long pent up inside me.

"You do love me, Marina, I know you do. What is it, then? Do you not *want* to marry me?"

"Oh, Matthew, yes. I want nothing more than to be your wife. But you may not want me, not when you know everything."

"I already know enough, my sweet love," he said, but I shook my head and sat up.

"You don't know everything, Matthew. Not everything."

And so I told him, told him just what Father had educated me for, in detail, how very little a lady I truly was. I told him, too, of Father's instability, the mental unbalance that had led to great debt, suicide, and the possibility that I, too, could grow unstable, unbalanced, as the years passed. As I spoke he listened, he frowned, his stare searched my face. Then he kissed me and repeated his proposal. He did not believe mental illness could be passed on, and he thought my 'education' boded well for our marriage.

"I don't want a lady, Marina," he said. "I want a wife. I want you."

Two weeks later we were married, in a small chapel on London's south side where the rector, an old friend of Matthew's father, agreed to waive the reading of the banns and unite us without delay. My joy knew

183

no bounds as I stood with Matthew before the altar. Uncle Jacob, Mollie and Eamon, and two friends of Matthew's, George and Amelia Percy, sat behind us and shared the happiest day of my life. We celebrated together with a dinner in a private room at the hotel Matthew was still staying at because, he said, the house which he had purchased was not yet suitable for human habitation. The food was delicious and abundant, the wine flowed steadily, and even Eamon left his glowering face outside on the steps.

Eventually, we found ourselves alone. I felt shy, despite Father's teachings, standing there before Matthew in the darkened hotel bedroom. He reached out and drew me to him. Gently, softly, he kissed my lips, my cheeks, my neck, until I stood trembling and gasping in his embrace. His eyes locked on mine, speaking his love into the velvet silence. With tender slow movements he slid the clothes from my body until I stood before him fully exposed in the silver moonlight cascading through the window. He held my arms and looked at me for a long time, his gaze devouring me, then he smiled and shed his own clothing while breathlessly I watched him emerge from the folds and drapes of fabric.

"Oh, Matthew," I whispered.

Again he pulled me into his arms, his skin sliding sensually across mine. I swayed against him, barely able to stand. He scooped me up into his arms, laid me on the bed and folded his long limbs down over me. And I discovered that what had seemed so ugly and hateful in Father's words, and in the pictures he had shown me, led to true ecstasy when tempered with love. I learned the full meaning of pleasure that night in Matthew's arms, when our hearts and our souls joined as one, as did our bodies. The past fell away in the beauty of our love, and in the shattering, glorious climax I found healing and peace. It lasted for three wonderful, ecstatic, incredible days, until the morning I woke to find Matthew gone.

Chapter Fifteen

I felt no alarm at first. I merely assumed that he was in his room, which communicated with mine through a small dressing room. He kept his possessions there, and wrote letters concerning his business at the desk below the window, but he did not stay there. Such was our closeness, our joy in each other, that we could not bear to be apart any longer than necessary. We slept each night wrapped in each other's arms, lying in the center of the luxurious canopied bed in my room, a room which even after three days I could not believe. It was over-large and elegantly appointed, with rich green velvet draperies and bed hangings, soft carpeting underfoot, comfortable chairs and even a small settee before the wide oak mantle. A fire, an unheard-of luxury for me in any room I had ever occupied until I moved above the bookshop, burned cheerfully in the grate at all hours, chasing away autumn's damp chill. I would sit snug and warm near the fire, reading, while Matthew concluded the odds and ends of the day's business in the other room.

And so I was not alarmed when I woke alone in the great bed. I stretched lazily, reaching out to the pillow where his head had so recently lain, and smiled, picturing his gleaming brown hair against the white linen, the way the lamplight caught the green specks in his eyes and made them glitter. Oh, how I loved him.

My body still tingled from his passionate caresses. I rose and pulled my dressing gown tight about me, for the day had dawned gray and rainy, the room chilly despite the fire on the hearth. I paused only long enough to brush my hair, disheveled from the night's activities, smiling dreamily at my reflection as my hand rose and fell, coaxing the thick, wavy locks into an ebony curtain down my back. Then I turned and walked through the dressing room to where Matthew waited.

"You are up early this morning, my love," I said. But my words stopped abruptly when my eyes beheld the vacant room. Matthew was not there, not in the chair behind the desk where he usually sat, nor in the narrow bed he had not yet used, nor in the armchair perched before the cold, empty grate. Frowning in confusion, I turned in a circle, searching every corner with care, my voice a hesitant, frightened whisper in the silence.

"Matthew?"

Emptiness screamed back at me. There was no sign of my husband. His silver hair brushes were gone from the bureau. The pipe with his initials was no longer on the table by the fireplace, the book I had given him missing from beside the bed. His elegant leather writing portfolio, spread careless on the desk just yesterday, had vanished. No dressing gown lay on the bed, no clothing hung within the wardrobe. It was as if Matthew Palmerston had ceased to exist.

"Matthew!"

I rushed from the room, my heart beating in fear, my head whirling in confusion. I stood, eyes wide with disbelief, staring at the great bed where only hours ago we had lain together. What had happened? Where had Matthew gone?

I do not know how long I stood there, staring in shock at the empty bed, fighting great waves of panic that almost drowned me. I remained completely unaware of my surroundings for long, endless minutes, oblivious to the fire crackling on the hearth, the rain drizzling outside my window, the muted sounds of the waking city. At long last the emotion ebbed, releasing me from the spell. I heard again the sounds of carriages and street hawkers, the hiss of the flames and the drip of water outside the window. I stared at that window, forcing myself not to think until I felt calm, then turned to the fire where we should even now be sitting down to breakfast. It was then that I saw the letter.

It lay on the small table between the armchairs, propped against the crystal wine carafe we had emptied last evening. Gleaming softly in the dim, watery light, it seemed to glow with a life of its own.

My name, flowing in Matthew's elegant hand, danced upon the pristine surface. Slowly, I moved closer and reached out hesitant fingers. A shudder rippled through me when I touched it, as if somehow I knew this was the beginning, that the evil had finally begun. Sinking into the chair closest to the fire for warmth, I turned the letter over and broke the seal.

The first thing I saw was the crest at the top of the page. I studied it, frowning; why would Matthew have crested stationery? Did not only the gentry, the titled nobility, use such devices? Matthew was not of that class. He was a sheep farmer from the north with interests in woolen mills, part of the rising middle class that earned increasing amounts of money but had neither title nor crest to their name. I looked again around the room, searching in vain for some sign of enlightenment, then sighed. He had borrowed the paper, I concluded, perhaps from a business acquaintance. That explanation did not satisfy, but it was all I could think of. Uneasy, I bent once more over the missive in my hand.

My darling wife, he'd written. *I have been called away home on urgent business. You were sleeping so peacefully, so beautiful there amidst the sheets and comforters, that I had not the heart to awaken you. I have instructed Giles to have the carriage ready for you by ten o'clock, and bring you swiftly here to me, at Stoneleigh. Until I hold you again in my arms, every second shall seem an hour, each minute a week, each day a month. Do not delay, my love. And do not worry. I shall explain everything when you arrive. Until then, my only love, I remain your Mathew, Lord Palmerston.*

Lord Palmerston.

I stared at the words, unable to comprehend them. What did he mean, *Lord* Palmerston? It made no sense. My eyes shifted to the crest at the top of the page, and my heart stood still. This was not borrowed paper, it was his own, emblazoned with the Palmerston crest. Lord Palmerston. *Sir Matthew?*

A knock sounded at the door and I looked up, pulled back from far away.

"Yes," I called. Suddenly, I couldn't seem to breathe.

But when the door opened it was only the maid who entered, bearing a tray with tea and toasted bread. I blinked in relief and drew in a breath; I do not know what I had expected, but that soft knock had set my heart pounding.

"Good morning, m'lady, 'tis me, Nell," the young girl said, for she was not more than sixteen. She set the tray on the table and smiled at me. Frowning, still lost in confusion, I did not answer her. I merely looked again at the letter in my lap, at the bewildering signature. Lord Palmerston... Sir Matthew...

"I shall come back in a short while, my lady, to help you pack," Nell said, pouring tea into an exquisite china cup. "Lord Palmerston asked me to assist you, since you've not your own maid with you this time. Lord Palmerston left instructions for you to leave at ten, so I mustn't delay if I'm to have you ready on time." She paused, looking at me; I did not know what to say. "M'lady? Is that all right? Shall I come back when you have finished eating?"

"Oh. Yes. Yes, come back," I said, my voice vague, my mind reeling, unable to cope with these bewildering events.

Nell curtsied and left. I sat on unmoving, the tea and toast cooling beside me. I had forgotten their existence. That was were Nell found me, half an hour later when she returned, still sitting before the fire with the letter in my lap, a faraway look on my face, I am sure, and my breakfast untouched. Without her help, I never would have been ready when the carriage arrived. How often now I wish I had not left at all.

Her cheerful nature and practical ways pulled me from my fog of confusion, and I decided in the end to do as Matthew had suggested and not worry about these strange happenings. He had, after all, promised to explain it to me upon my arrival at the farm in Yorkshire, and I was sure there would be good reason for his not telling me who he was. My heart lightened then, for I had not been abandoned again as I had feared, had not been left alone without explanation. These past three days had been so glorious that I had begun to believe, when I found all trace of Matthew gone, that I had merely been dreaming, that it had not been real, not any of it; not Matthew, nor the marriage, nor the wondrous nights in his arms. In my relief, I pushed aside my doubts and questions and plunged into the chore of packing my things.

There was not, in truth, very much to pack, for I had left behind half my summer gowns. I had brought the plain green wool dress that had caused Lady Creswell such distress, but I had discarded the gray foulard, for each time I saw it I was reminded of Lord D'arcy's hard fingers tearing at me, and the painful end which that event had precipitated in the park with Andrew. Indeed, I never wore gray any more at all, despite the popularity of the color, not in any shade or fabric. I knew it would be long years before my aversion to it would fade.

The two weeks before the wedding had been full to overflowing, crammed with fittings, for Matthew had insisted on buying me two new dresses to supplement my meager wardrobe. He chose a green satin for one, the skirt of which was over-draped with green silk gathered into a high knot in the back, falling to trail along the ground as I walked. It was the very latest in fashion. The bodice was low cut and square, with frilly delicate lace hiding that part of my bosom only he should see. The same lace edged the long, narrow sleeves, flaring out at the wrists to frame my hands in dainty filigree. It was a beautiful dress and I loved it, but I found the boned petticoats and the bustle that supported the back knot cumbersome and restrictive of movement. I had grown used to the freedom of my less elaborate work dresses.

The second gown Matthew chose was in my favorite shade of soft blue, and in a style similar to what Lady Creswell had once worn to the shop. The cashmere skirts were fuller, and the petticoats wider, than any I had hitherto owned. Ruffles and ribbons rimmed the dark blue underskirt hem, and the pale blue polonaise overdress scalloped gracefully in the front, pulled up by lacy bows and ribbons of dark blue and rose. The sleeves, slit to the elbow and inset with lace, were trimmed with satin ribbon, as was the deep, lace-draped v-neckline. Lace also trimmed the shoulders. I felt elegant in that dress, a true lady, and could not wait for the weather to cool sufficiently to wear it. Now, as I folded it carefully and laid it in my trunk with the rest of my clothes, which I had enhanced by the re-application of the lace and ribbons I'd earlier removed, I thought of Matthew's letter and the startling revelation it held. I knew I would be glad of these two new gowns, for surely nothing else I brought with me suited my new station in life. Was I truly Lady Marina Palmerston? I simply could not believe it.

For this day's journey I donned a chintz traveling dress in shades of brown, somewhat out of fashion with the wide pagoda sleeves I favored, a high buttoned neckline and an abbreviated train. That I wore it with only petticoats and not the hoop it had been designed for actually helped, as hoops were quickly giving way to the bustle. But for three years now I had been shamefully out of style and it didn't worry me, though Nell's eyes looked askance at the costume such a grand lady chose to wear. She helped me with my hair though it was not necessary, draping it away from my face into a snood in back and topping it with the small plumed hat on which I had spent half a month's salary. I watched her work, my gaze locked on my image in the mirror, thinking how strange it would seem to have someone else do what I was more than capable of handling on my own. But that was part of being a grand lady, having a maid to dress and undress one.

When I was ready at last, I sent her down with the trunk and sat at the writing desk in my room, pen and paper before me on the leather inlaid surface. I wished there was time to see Uncle Jacob before I left, for a letter seemed so impersonal after all he had done for me. But the hands on the mantle clock had already passed the time Matthew had requested I leave, and though I knew another half hour would not really make any difference, such was my state of identity with him I could not bear to willingly go against his wishes.

He had become my sun and my moon, my reason for being, and even more. He defined my existence, and completed me. I had submerged myself so totally in him almost from the first moment I saw him, that I no longer perceived myself as having any reality outside him. What he was, then so was I. And so blind was my love I did not see what I gave up, how easily and unknowingly I became the non-existent slave Father had trained me to be. Because it did not hurt as I expected it would, I did not see it happen nor the harm it caused from the very beginning. Almost instantly, it erased the Marina I had striven so hard to create, as easily as unwanted chalk marks wiped from a slate. And when I desperately needed her to ensure my survival, I found that she—that I—had almost ceased to exist. I was my Father's daughter.

'Dearest Uncle,' I wrote, after puzzling no little time over what to say, 'Matthew has been called away to Yorkshire. I am leaving in a few minutes to join him, for how long I do not know. So much as happened in such a short time; I cannot tell you yet, for I do not truly understand it all myself! Matthew has promised to explain when next I see him. I will write again when I arrive in Yorkshire, and tell you what he says. If I still do not understand, perhaps you can unravel it for me. Be happy for me—I have never felt such joy before, though it pains me to leave you behind. Give my love to Mollie and Eamon. I shall miss them, too, until we return. You can reach me at the house called Stoneleigh, in North York. As ever, Just Marina.'

I sealed the letter and wrote Uncle Jacob's name on it, and his address. Then I rose and looked one last time about the room where I had known such pleasure. I felt reluctant to leave, finding it difficult to believe that some of the happiness would not remain behind, leaving me the poorer. Checking to ensure I had Matthew's letter safe within my reticule, I closed the door on this most wonderful part of my life and went down to the coach Matthew had ordered.

Before I left the hotel, I gave the letter for Uncle Jacob to a young runner to deliver, along with a shilling for his trouble. From the way his eyes lit up with delight, and the way he bowed excitedly as I moved on to the door, I was sure Uncle Jacob would received it without delay. In this I was right, but I was not to know for some time to come that it was the last letter he would receive from me, though I wrote as often as I could. Nor did I ever hear from him. I came to believe that he had forgotten me.

The shining black carriage was elegant and roomy, the interior lined in soft dark velvet, seats thickly padded and comfortable. The Palmerston crest adorned the doors. The driver, Giles, an old man whose hard, craggy face and lean body spoke of years spent out-of-doors, looked grand in smart green and black livery. He held the door open for me, a scowl on his face, but the hand he offered was deferential when I took it to climb inside. My felt my eyes widen as I scanned what would be my rolling home for the duration of the long journey. There were fringed shades on the windows to pull against the glare of the sun, warm soft rugs to deflect the chill autumn air, a basket packed with sumptuous foods and wine, and even a spray of flowers in a crystal vase attached to the front wall of the coach. I wondered at the magnificence of the conveyance, in light of what Matthew's letter had revealed. What other surprises lay in store for me at the country farm called Stoneleigh? With a sharp jerk, the carriage rolled forward through the streets of London, carrying me to a destiny I had not dreamed could ever happen.

It was a long and arduous journey, despite the

comfort of the carriage. They were the seven longest days I could ever remember spending. At first I found it interesting to watch the rich and varied countryside pass by the coach windows, but by the end of the second day, with London almost sixty miles behind us, the novelty began to pall as we passed endless farms bordered by tall hedges and stone fences. They all seemed by then to look alike, and one can be amused by green and gold patchwork for only so long.

Though the road continued smooth for over half of the trip, the rise and fall of the carriage over the picturesque rolling hills set my stomach on edge, making it difficult for me to eat when we stopped for meals. Giles drove swiftly and stopped very seldom, and only for inadequate lengths of time. He seemed to be adhering to an internal timetable of his own, one that allowed for no dalliance or pause along the way. As for me, since we had a lifetime together ahead of us, I would have gratefully traded a few days of Matthew's company for a slower pace.

We stopped outside Dunstable the first night, at a small wooden inn which I found quaint and quite enjoyable. Exhausted from hours of rocking in the carriage, I slept well and woke refreshed with the dawn, ready to face another day's journey. Within half an hour, inadequately breakfasted, we were on the road.

The second night found us in Wellingborough, in a stone inn not quite as clean or comfortable as that in Dunstable. We pushed on to Wigston next day after again rising at dawn, and I felt tears begin to well at the thought of the miles still ahead. Not knowing of England's extensive rail system, expanding every year, it did not occur to me to ask why we did not journey at least part-way by that much faster, and more convenient, mode of transport. Only the thought that Matthew had passed this way himself but recently kept my resolve strong when I arose the fourth day to a cold, drizzling rain.

Giles had hoped to make Hucknall by dark, but the rain worsened as we clattered past Loughborough, slowing us so that we were forced to stop the night in Nottingham, after crossing the river Trent. But I did not care. The inn was warm and dry, and did not move incessantly as did the carriage. I wished to remain there forever. Indeed, I requested the next morning at sunrise that we stay a day or two to rest, but Giles would not hear of it. "Master said no delay," he told me, and off we went. I reread Matthew's letter over and over during those long, lonely days, drawing comfort from the warmth of his words and solace from the sight of his hand upon the paper. I vowed never to leave Stoneleigh once I arrived. Uncle Jacob, Mollie and Eamon would simply have to come to me.

For the next two days I entertained my mind with thoughts of Stoneleigh, growing closer now with each passing mile. Giles said little whenever I asked, repeating only, "ye'll see fer yerself," though I had little opportunity to ask him anyway, as he stopped but rarely on our wild rush across the English countryside.

But Matthew had told me of the farm in loving detail, and I felt I already knew it.

Nestled in emerald depths between tall, sun-drenched hills, it sprawled for hundreds of acres, supporting a large sheep herd and extensive barley and wheat fields. The farmhouse was of pale stone, half-timbered in the quaint English style, and built halfway up one of the hills, overlooking a large natural lake on which Matthew said he often fished. Though not large, the warm stone house sprawled, echoing the shape of the farm and giving the impression of graceful spaciousness. His family, he'd said, had lived there for generations. As we bumped past Wakefield, the road deteriorating as we progressed north, I enumerated to myself the rooms Matthew had so vividly described.

There was a parlor, whose walls were lined with pale pink satin—his great-grandmother's folly, the family called it—filled with oaken furniture whose embroidered covers had been wrought by his grandmother. The dining room was square, paneled in oak with family portraits hung upon the walls. The breakfast room windows overlooked the lake; it was the sunniest room in the house. Books collected for over a century filled the oak library shelves floor-to-ceiling. With dark blue velvet draperies, a Persian carpet on the inlaid floor, a tooled-leather-topped mahogany desk and jade chess set waiting on a table near the hearth, it was Matthew's favorite room. I was sure it would be mine, also.

Upstairs, Matthew's room was done in green, the

largest on the floor. It had been his parents' until they had died ten years earlier, within a few months of each other. There were three other bedrooms, all smaller and each with its own color scheme. The servants' rooms nestled beneath the attic eaves; there were a cook, a maid, a butler (who with the gardener slept in the loft above the carriages), and a housekeeper. It sounded warm and homey. I was sure I would love it as much as Matthew did. I couldn't wait to see it.

The last day of the journey seemed endless. We left Leeds, the terrain growing ever wilder, and crossed the Ure River just after two in the afternoon. I shivered in the cold wind sweeping across the bleak, barren country, my mind in turmoil. Where were the green hills of which Matthew had spoken, the prosperous farms and quaint villages that ringed his property? I rapped on the roof of the carriage and Giles stopped to poke an impatient face in the window.

"Are we lost? Where are we?" I asked, the barren landscape sending chills of foreboding into my heart.

"Yorkshire moors." Never full of words, he had grown more taciturn the closer we had come to Stoneleigh. "Be there soon, m'lady."

He stomped off, not waiting for a reply, and we moved on, the road now so rough and rutted I had to hold on lest I be thrown from my seat. Hours passed and still we rolled further onto the eerie, deserted moors. Nothing moved beyond the carriage windows. There was no sign of life of any kind, save dark birds circling ominously overhead. We could have been the only two people on the face of the earth. I was on the point of demanding that we turn back to a town before the encroaching darkness imprisoned us in this place, when the carriage slowed and turned into a narrow, well-kept avenue lined by tall hedges which blocked my view of what lay beyond them. When finally we broke out into the open again, I gasped at what loomed before me. Giles stopped, climbed down, and opened the door to hand me out from the carriage before I realized I had even moved.

"Where have you brought me?" I asked. "What place is this?"

"Stoneleigh, m'lady. As m'lord ordered."

The old man gave me a mocking grin, retrieved my reticule, burnoose and gloves from inside the carriage, handed them to me, then stomped off to the horses, leaving me staring in shock at the hulking structure crouched twenty feet away.

The massive rectangle of rough-hewn black rock had been carved into the semblance of a castle. Tall towers rose at either end, thin unlit window slits showing as darker slashes in the ebony stone. Crenellated battlements stretched between them, capping three stories of dark rock facade broken by narrow, glittering multi-paned windows that caught the westering sun and threw it back like cats' eyes. Not a light showed from anywhere within the dark stone depths. A gigantic carved entry door stood barring access atop a wide flight of steep stone steps. The great house sat in the center of the desolate moor like a spider waiting to ensnare its prey. Black clouds boiled overhead, driven streaming by a wild wind that howled mournfully, warning of doom and damnation both within and without. Had I not been rooted to the spot by terror, I would have turned and fled afoot across the shadowed moor.

While I stood motionless with shock, the door opened and an elderly woman in black dress and cap paced down the steps. She was thin and gray-haired, her bony body possessing the look of whipcord strength. Her face was long and narrow, her dark eyes hidden beneath a jutting brow, thin lips overshadowed by a painfully hooked nose. She stalked toward me, her face flooded with animosity. Involuntarily, I took a step back. She stopped five feet from me and dropped her glare the length of my body before she spoke.

"Welcome, m'lady, to Stoneleigh." Her voice was cold, harsh, and quite unwelcoming. "I am Mrs. Peele, the housekeeper. Lord Palmerston is anxiously 'waitin' you in the lib'ry."

Behind me, the carriage lurched off into the deepening gloom, and I spun, gasping.

"Where is he going?" I cried.

"The stables, m'lady." Mrs. Peele's voice held an odd, questioning note; I turned back to find her watching me, her hawk-like face frowning and wary. "Please. Come inside, m'lady. The night air can be dangerous on the moors."

I followed her hesitantly up the stairs and through the massive, iron-bound door into a huge, echoing entry hall. It looked like a Medieval fortress, with floors and walls of dark stone and huge solid beams overhead. A hearth large enough to walk into three abreast occupied a back corner, though the fire that blazed therein did little to overcome the chill of the dark rock. Medieval weaponry hung high on the walls, and suits of armor stood sentinel on either side of the doorways visible in the murk.

"This is Stoneleigh?" The tremble in my voice reflected my confusion. Where was the warm farmhouse Matthew grew up in, the green valley and cool lake?

"Of course 'tis, m'lady. Come. Lord Palmerston is waiting."

She led me through a doorway on the left and into a bewildering maze of dark, interconnecting corridors. At last she gestured to a lighted room through whose half-open door wafted the comforting sounds of quiet conversation in the cold stone darkness. I heard someone speak, the voice deep and rich.

"I do not know what to expect. That is why I wanted you both here."

The sound echoed oddly in the stone hall. Matthew? I could not quite tell.

"Oh, come now. Surely you exaggerate," someone answered.

"We'll only end up in the way, Matthew, you know that," a third voice objected.

My heart leapt. He'd said Matthew. Soon all

would be explained. I smiled at Mrs. Peele, barely able to see her sour, disapproving face in the dark corridor.

"Thank you, Mrs. Peele, for guiding me here. I did not expect a house quite so large. I am afraid it will take me a while to become accustomed to its twistings and turnings."

"Ye'll learn," came the clipped, terse reply. Her basilisk eyes stared at me. "I wouldn' keep him waitin' 'f I were you. He knows you arrived."

I blinked, startled at her rudeness.

"Yes, of course. I'll go right in to him."

She stood a moment watching me walk toward that lighted room, then turned and melted quickly into the darkness in her black dress and cap. When I looked back, I could not tell if she stood still in the corridor or not. The voices continued as I moved to the door.

"Remember, watch carefully, Boulton. I am depending on you. And you, also, Roger."

"Of course, Matthew, though I am sure your fears are groundless. Many women suffer a sort of mild shock upon marriage, but with time and gentle handling—"

The voice broke off when I pushed the door wide and stepped into the stone-floored room. It looked nothing like the warm, cozy library Matthew had described. Here, all was cold stone and dark mahogany, the carpet underfoot a plain deep red, as were the damask drapes masking the narrow windows. Only the wall behind the desk was lined with books. No chess set stood before the hearth. Two men were seated in burgundy leather armchairs on either side of the mantle, and they rose politely when I entered, brandy glasses still in hand. The one on my right was perhaps fifty or so, and short, his figure portly from years of good food and wine. His plain round face, lighting with pleasure as he looked at me, seemed open and comfortable. A half-bald pate gleamed in the candlelight. Laugh lines radiated out from twinkling hazel eyes.

The man on my left was taller, though not as tall as Matthew. He was also closer in age to Matthew, who was thirty-five; I estimated this man to be just over thirty. His sandy-brown hair had been meticulously combed, and he wore the very latest in fashion, his brown coat cut sharply away to reveal a red brocade waistcoat, his gray trousers pencil-slim and perfectly tailored. He wore a shirt sporting the latest turned-down collar and a red, blue and yellow ascot folded soft beneath his bearded chin. Cold brown eyes, holding curiosity but no warmth, stared at me from out of an oval face. His nose was the only truly noteworthy feature due to its extreme width.

But I did not pay more than passing attention to them, a quick, curious glance, for my eyes were drawn irresistibly to the third man in the room, whose back was to the door as he bent over the hearth poking at the fire. He wore the selfsame suit he'd had on the first day he'd come into the shop, his broad shoulders still straining at the dark gray cutaway as through seeking their freedom. The same gray-blue and charcoal striped trousers covered his long slim legs, and I wondered if he had remembered and dressed this way just for me. I could feel the joy shining on my face, my emotion standing clear in my eyes for the other men to see, and a shiver of love lifted my shoulders as I broke into a smile.

"Matthew!" I exclaimed.

He straightened, turned.

"Marina, my love. At last you are here. I have waited what seems an eternity."

He moved to me and clasped my hands in his, his smile full of love and devotion. I stared at him, my own smile frozen on my face, unable to look away, nor even think or breathe. He was tall, like Matthew, his body as firmly muscled and strong, his shoulders as broad and his hips as narrow. His clean-shaven jaw was square, like Matthew's, his nose proudly arched, his sensual lips half-hidden by a mustache. Sharp cheekbones angled up above smooth, hollow cheeks, and his brow was clear and wide, as was Matthew's. But this man's hair was dark, as black as my own, and lay thick upon his head without a wave or curl. And the eyes that stared at me below the straight black brows were an icy, arrogant dark blue.

He was not the man I'd married. He was not Matthew Palmerston.

Chapter Sixteen

"You're not Matthew!" I felt my eyes gape wide in shock. I could manage only a whisper. "Who are you? Where is Matthew?"

I twisted in his suddenly tight grasp, trying to free my hands, and cast a pleading look for help at the men to either side. But they stood with quiet, speculative eyes narrowed at me, making no move to come to my assistance.

"Marina, what are you saying?" the blue-eyed man holding me asked. "Of course I'm Matthew. Who else would I be?"

"No! Matthew, *my* Matthew, has brown hair and brown eyes. Please, let me go. What is happening here? Where is my husband?"

In desperation I wrenched my hands from his and spun to the door, only to find it closed and the younger of the two onlookers now leaning casually against it, blocking my way. I backed away toward the huge mahogany desk, scarcely able to breathe past the panic assailing me.

"It seems the journey has proved more difficult than you imagined, Matthew," the bearded man said, his voice toneless. "Your wife is quite overwrought."

"Wife!" I cried. "I am not his wife!"

"Of course you are, Marina," the man they called Matthew snapped, clearly wrestling with impatience. "Don't be ridiculous."

The portly man laid a warning hand on his arm, and the black-haired man drew in his breath, visibly pulling himself back into control.

"I am not your wife," I said again. "I have never seen you before. Who *are* you?"

"I am your husband, Matthew Palmerston," he answered calmly, quietly, as though to a child. "We were married by Rector Boyles," he added as I shook my head again in denial, "at St. Clement's Chapel in London. The ceremony was witnessed by your Uncle Jacob, and by Mollie and Eamon O'Leary. My friend, Sir George Percy, and his wife, Amelia, also attended. How can you have forgotten? It was only last June, Marina! A mere three months ago."

Three *months*? Was he crazy?

"That's not true. Matthew and I married just ten days ago, on September the tenth."

But how, then, does he know who married us, and where, and who was there with us? I hunched my shoulders and backed away from the disturbing thought, moaning in terror. Darkness gathered, lurking just outside my vision, waiting to pounce, the darkness that had threatened once before when Father was still alive. The blue-eyed man stepped closer, and I cowered against the desk.

"Marina, please, listen to me," he begged. "You have been very ill, and you are still confused about some things. I think Roger is right, the journey here was too much for you, too soon. I should not have insisted you come. Perhaps after a night's rest..."

He reached out for me but I twisted away, pressing against the wall beside the fireplace. He exchanged a solemn look with the portly man, who nodded and moved to the chair in which he'd been sitting. The man with the black hair again turned to me.

"Please, let me go," I begged, tears now falling down my face. "What do you want from me? I haven't been ill and I didn't marry you. I married *Matthew*. Why are you doing this to me?"

The man who called himself Matthew closed his blue eyes, shook his head, and sighed. He reached onto the desk and opened an ornate wooden box. He withdrew a folded paper which he held out to me. I slid away along the wall to my right, hands covering my mouth to hold back the terrified screams pushing from within. My head whirled. My mind filled with panic. I was trapped in this room with these men. What did they want with me?

"Take it, Marina. Our marriage certificate. Look at it," the Matthew-man demanded.

I looked at the older man, who still stood next to

the chair, an open bag on the seat beside him. He held a small dark bottle in his hand. The bearded man had moved away from the door and stood now behind my tormentor. I moved further to my right. Perhaps I could run around behind the desk and open the door before they could stop me. The Matthew-man stepped closer and shook the paper.

"Take it, Marina. Read it."

I snatched it quickly, lest he grab me again, and opened it without looking away from him.

"We were married in June, Marina, and went to France for our honeymoon. You fell ill there, and the doctors would not let you travel when I was called back to Stoneleigh. There is the proof, in your hand. Look at it. Look at the signatures, Marina."

His voice was soft, persuasive, compelling.

I looked down and blinked my eyes clear, then stared disbelieving at the paper from St. Clement's Chapel, declaring our marriage official and binding. There was Reverend Boyles' name, and ours, and our signatures, mine and Matthew's, unmistakable at the bottom. And below them, Jacob Chadwicke and Mollie O'Leary as witnesses. The darkness moved nearer, closed tighter around me, filled the edges of my mind. The cold fingers of madness touched my soul, and I gasped.

"Where did you get this?" I managed to whisper.

"Look at the top, Marina. Look at the date."

I looked. *12 June, 1869.*

"No. No, it's not possible. It can't be!" I cried. I

threw the paper from me to the floor, screaming, and curled my arms over my head. As I did so, the reticule hanging from my wrist bumped my face and I gasped. Matthew's letter! The one he'd written to me the day he left. It was there in my bag, proof that I was right, that this man was lying. Frantic, fighting the creeping darkness and panic that smothered me and kept me from breathing, I pulled the bag from my wrist and tore it open.

"Here, I have proof. I have his letter, he left it for me, the *real* Matthew, just seven days ago. You can't do this to me, you're not Matthew. Here it is, see, his letter. Look at it."

I held it out and saw an address written on the front where only my name had been before: *Lady Marina Palmerston, Rue la Mer, Chartres, France.* And stamps from the passage across the Channel, stark on the expensive white vellum.

"No!" Screaming, I tore it open. There was Matthew's handwriting, his crest at the top, his signature at the bottom. But the date! *2 August, 1869.* And the words! *My darling Marina, I pray this finds you well at last and able to travel, for we have been apart too long —*

And the darkness clamped down. Panic submerged me in an ocean of despair. I whirled and raced for the door, screaming for Matthew, pleading for his help. The dark-haired man caught me, striving hard to hold my struggling body. I struck out blindly. My nails raked down his face and he staggered back, losing his grip. I lunged again for the door, grasping the knob just as the bearded man's iron-hard arms wound around me from behind. I screamed and kicked and felt my shoe crack against a shin. He cried out in pain. I twisted free as his arms loosened, only to have the Matthew-man grab me again and pull me to the floor.

"Roger! Her arms and legs!" he shouted.

My wrists were caught in vise-like fingers, pulled down to my waist and clamped to the floor just as a heavy weight settled on my legs. I lay half on the carpet, half in the dark-haired man's strong arms.

"Hurry, Boulton! Get as much into her as you can!"

Powerful fingers grasped my face, tipped my head up. They pressed on my jaw, pinching my cheeks until with a despairing moan I gave way and my mouth gaped open. The portly man poured a bitter liquid down my throat, choking me, as I struggled desperately against the hard hands holding me. Over and over he forced my mouth open and poured the bitter fluid into me while I fought on, choking and sobbing, pleading to be let go, crying for Matthew, *my* Matthew. Finally, whatever he had given me began to take hold. I lost control of my muscles and grew lighter and lighter until I started to float away, leaving my body far behind. I heard their voices as through a long, echoing tunnel.

"I daren't give her any more, Matthew," the man called Boulton said. "I can't tell how much she's actually swallowed, but it should be enough."

"Will she be all right, do you think, Boulton?" the Matthew-man asked, his voice cracking.

"It's hard to say. We'll keep her sedated until she's calm, then let her rest. Only time will tell."

"Thank God you two were here. I don't know what I would have done if I'd been alone with her. She's so much more violent than she was before..."

I forced my eyes open. The man with the beard sat astride my legs, holding my arms motionless. The portly man set a dark bottle into a bag on the floor beside him. He bent over me, each movement seeming to me painstakingly slow, and examined my eyes. Then he laid a gentle hand on my cheek.

"You can release your hold now, Roger. The fight is gone. Keep her warm and comfortable, Matthew, and get that dress off her. I'll come by early in the morning to check on her, though I doubt she'll wake before noon."

The bearded man stood up and moved away. I watched him for hundreds of years. The Matthew-man gathered me into his arms and rose. I looked up into his cold blue eyes and shook my head.

"You're... not... Matthew," I whispered, my words sluggish, my tongue thick and uncooperative. Darkness rushed upon me, trying to pull me away from the strong arms holding me suspended in time and space.

"Not... Matthew," I again forced out, then my head fell onto his shoulder and I knew no more.

I fought. For long, endless days, through limitless tunnels of darkness, pursued relentlessly by the winds of madness, I fought his hands, his face, his voice, the Matthew who was not Matthew. I would wake slowly, rising from the misty depths of unreality in which he'd imprisoned me, to find him by my side, holding my hands, stroking my face, calling my name. I would stare at him, his face wavering in the dreamy, vaporous sea upon which I floated, and hear his words echo around me, speaking of the things Matthew and I had done, things only my husband would know. And yet, he was not my husband, for all he resembled him. Whatever he said, however he knew it, his hair remained as black as coal, his eyes a dark, icy blue. He was not my Matthew.

I would twist away, my movements feeling agonizingly slow, and cry for Matthew, plead for mercy, beat at the man who bent over me and poured more of the bitter liquid down my throat, until the room, the bed and the impostor floated away and I ceased to exist once more. When again I would return to the dark and shadowed room, the nightmare would begin anew.

Twice the portly man sat beside me when I woke. The second time, I floated down out of a spinning kaleidoscope of soft, warm colors. I did not want to leave its gentleness, and tears filled my eyes when I opened them onto the hated room where the Matthew-man dwelt. I gazed curiously at the odd, shimmering figure bending over me, realizing with slow wonderment that he was the other one, the physician called Boulton. I watched his undulating movements as he examined me, fighting desperately to break free of the imprisoning lethargy that left me immobile. At last, he sat back and smiled at me.

"How do you feel, Marina?" he asked, his voice echoing in my ears. I rolled my head on the pillow, seeking escape.

"Help me," I pleaded in an uneven whisper. "He is... poisoning me. I cannot... move... the room... wavers... the walls..."

He laid a gentle hand on my brow and smiled.

"No one is poisoning you, Marina. It is the medicine, the laudanum, that makes you feel this way. We have had to give you heavy doses to keep you quiet, so you will not hurt yourself. If you will stop fighting us, I will reduce the dosage. Will you do that?"

I wanted to agree. The words had almost left my lips when the fearful dark head appeared over the doctor's shoulder. The Matthew-man smiled at me and removed the pipe from his mouth, a briar carved with Matthew's initials—the pipe Uncle Jacob had given Matthew, my brown-haired Matthew, on his birthday.

"Good morning, my love," he said, and bent to kiss me.

"No!"

Terror pounded strength into me and I overcame the soporific effect of the medicine. My hands lifted, struck out at him. The pipe flew from his hand and clattered onto the floor. My fist hit his cheek. He stumbled back and, still screaming, I twisted away from the doctor's grasping hands. It took both of them to hold me down and pour more of the hated laudanum down my throat. I lay sobbing in the Matthew-man's arms, fighting futilely as the drug pulled me away again to a world where sanity did not exist. Dimly I heard the Matthew-man's anguished voice.

"Will this never end, Boulton? Have I lost her forever? I want her back. Oh, dear Lord, I want Marina back."

The nightmare stretched on, infinity elongating until time collapsed. It folded back upon itself, bearing me relentlessly along into hidden creases filled with emptiness, a great echoing abyss. Inside it, what had been was replicated endlessly, until life became a barren void in which reality ceased to exist and the vacuum became a wall through which I could not penetrate. Over and over the pattern repeated, until sense dwindled, extinguished like flames beneath cold water, and I vanished into a dark void that defined my non-being: A drop of darkness merging into ebony black shadows. I have no memory of anything other than the suffocating darkness; ghostly meaningless chimeras of inexistence; and undulating visions of strong, slender fingers, straight black hair, and frigid blue eyes that sought to destroy me.

Until the morning I—whoever I was, whoever I had become in that nightmare delusion—woke to a room empty of anyone but myself. I lay for what seemed hours, my restless gaze searching a room both familiar and unknown. Echoes of Matthew, of brown hair and lies and deception, whispered softly in the gloomy depths. Where was I? What was happening to me? Where did reality lie? In the wisps memory that fled whenever I tried to touch them, or in the depths of dark blue eyes and midnight-black hair?

Shaking uncontrollably, I pushed the luxurious covers away and stumbled to my feet. A pale blue silk nightdress, trimmed with lace and ribbons, clung to my body. I did not remember ever seeing it before. I groped my way around the beautiful room on legs almost too weak to hold me, wrestling with the bewildering revelations I discovered. Silver hairbrushes engraved with my own initials lay on the dressing table, hairbrushes I knew I did not own. Or did I? Elegant clothing hung in the wardrobe, gowns I had never before seen; at least, I did not think I had. I stared at them, tears filling my eyes. I could no longer be sure, could trust neither my own perceptions nor the hazy memories shimmering half-hidden in my mind. My head reeling, I staggered to the door and wrenched at the knob. It was locked, as was the door connecting to the adjoining room. I was a prisoner here, amidst luxury I could not trust was real.

Nightmares lurked at the edges of my vision and my heart thudded as I turned again to the bed. My body hurt, tiny pinpricks of pain that skittered up my arms and legs, across my breasts and belly. Shadows flitted past the corners of my eyes, but there was nothing there when I spun to look. Halfway to the bed I fell and my body exploded with agony. I sobbed, clawing at the rising pain beating from within, begging for mercy. The torment only worsened. As it did, the demons waiting in the shadows converged and plunged my mind into a chasm of horror, leaving me writhing on the floor.

For two days I fought the demons that devoured my body with pain and my mind with nightmares. I screamed for clemency, for forgiveness, for death— even for the black-haired Matthew—as the pain twisted and gouged into my soul and wrung every last drop of hope from my heart. I was aware of little save wrenching agony that ebbed and flowed but never ceased, noting with passing unconcern the progress of the sun across the floor where I suffered. When the light dimmed into darkness, the terrors engulfing me intensified. I shuddered and retched and screamed until I had no voice left to plead for surcease, but still the torment continued, through another endless day and dark, limitless night. Sweat poured from my body; bile spewed from my mouth, driven upward by the unrelenting torture. Tears streamed from my eyes until no drop of moisture remained within me. At long last, as dawn gradually lightened the sky on the third day, the demons retreated from my mind and my body, leaving a broken, almost-empty shell behind.

Not for years did I truly understand what had happened, what had been done to me. For more than three months I had lain heavily drugged on massive doses of laudanum, a highly addictive opiate. When suddenly the doses stopped, both my body and my mind rebelled. They had become enslaved to the pleasure induced by the drug, the escape from reality both physical and mental that had been my daily sustenance for long, endless weeks. The opium had assimilated me, had meshed inextricably with my being, and existence apart from it was no longer possible. Then it had been taken away and my very essence was wrenched apart, my body and mind shredded in the desolation of that inestimable loss. The desperate, deadly struggle that ensued as the opium tried to take me with it into permanent oblivion broke what little will I had left. I lay on the cold, hard floor, my body still shuddering and retching from the power of the drug, and no longer knew who, or what, I was. I could very easily have died from the enforced separation. How many times since then I've wished I had.

Slowly, as the day strengthened outside the narrow, locked windows, I became aware again of the room around me; the chill, stone, carpet-covered floor on which I lay; the body that occupied space in a reality now foreign to me. I became aware that I shivered with cold. Goose flesh raised up all over my body. My eyes blinked open and I saw before me the canopied bed in which I'd lain insensate. Warm covers trailed down onto the rough carpeting. Desperate for warmth, I forced myself to move, forced boneless limbs to drag my torso close, closer, until at last I grasped the comforter and blankets and pulled them down to cover me.

I lay cradled in growing warmth and fighting the sleep that tugged my lids down, for I feared that if I let go I would drift forever in a nebulous dark void. It was an instinctive fear, born from long weeks in the opiate stupor. I knew, without knowing how, that without something to hold onto I would vanish completely. How long I lay forcing myself to remain awake I do not know, but at long last I became aware of a small brown object that lay nearby on the floor. I reached out and picked it up, turning it over and over in my hands: a briar pipe, polished to a rich gloss, entwined initials standing proud upon the bowl: MP

It had meaning, I knew, though I had no memory of what that meaning was. The lingering smell of tobacco evoked misty images of joy and contentment, a feeling of rightness and peace. There was love here in this piece of smooth wood, but not until the sun crept close and touched it, loosing glints of gold from the rich brown depths, did I remember: Brown hair and brown eyes, glints of gold and specks of green.

"Matthew!" I whispered. Tears filled my eyes.

The door opened. I lay in the tumble of blankets, cradling the pipe in my hands, tears streaming down my face, while he stood staring at me in silence for long minutes. Unaware of his reality, I did not lift my face. Finally he knelt beside me and took the pipe from my hands with gentle fingers. I looked up into deep blue eyes.

"Matthew?" I asked.

His features wavered. I saw black-brown hair, gleaming gold where the sun's rays caressed it. I saw green flecks in the blue-brown eyes. He smiled at me and the image hardened, the brown and green fading back into the misty shadows.

"Yes, my love. It is me. Matthew," he said. He looked up at the short, stout man with him, and gave a sigh that spoke of relief.

He folded away the comforter and blankets and gathered me into his arms with tender hands, kissing my brow, my cheek, before laying me on the bed. He tucked the covers snug around me and stroked my hair away from my face. I carried his gentle smile and the feel of his hands with me into the healing caress of sleep. And the sound of his voice.

"What do you think, Boulton, is it over? When I received the letter from Alcott in America, I truly despaired. Can she have inherited the madness? Will I have to shut her away, the way Weston did her mother?"

"Only time will tell, Matthew," answered the soft, rumbling voice. "She seems to be mending now. With love and gentle care, she should recover. Though for how long…"

The voices faded away. What did they mean? I wondered. Madness… my mother… But sleep was too near for me to hold the thought, and it dissolved before I grasped the meaning. And again I slept.

Chapter Seventeen

It was a slow recovery. I was very weak, completely drained in body, mind and spirit. Matthew of the black hair and blue eyes hovered anxiously, looking, I know, for signs of the madness to show itself again, reluctant to leave me alone lest he return to find me screaming once more. But I had no will left to fight him, and in the beginning what little memory of happier times remained slowly dissipated into shadowy mists. I could distinguish neither form nor meaning in the vaporous darkness and soon no longer tried, content to drift through the empty days like a ghost myself, waiting for my strength to return.

For two weeks I lay abed, sleeping most of the time, letting odd, disparate thoughts drift through my mind when awake. I neither pushed them away nor examined them closely. I merely let them touch me with whispering fingers and then watched them dissolve back into the forbidden netherworld from whence they came. The emptiness within filled me so completely that I found room for nothing else, not even my own self. No one resided within the shell of my body.

The Matthew-man—I still thought of him thus, insensible to the deeply buried, covert denial implicit in the image—came and sat with me for an hour each morning and evening, reading aloud from books whose words made no sense to me. But the sound of his deep voice was not unpleasant to my ears. He read well, with great feeling and varied inflection, and I often fell asleep to his mellifluous tones. I said little to him, watching, from the silent vacuity which I had become, the lazy, careless gestures with which he lit his pipe, crossed his legs, turned the pages, sipped his whiskey, prepared to retire. There was nothing in these gestures that stirred the mists of memory within me, not one faint sign of familiarity. He was Matthew, my husband, and I knew him not.

The physician came, too, Sir Robert Boulton, often in those two weeks, and at first I held myself very still, my eyes on his face, fearing he would again send me to the place of nightmare. But he smiled with happiness that seemed genuine, declaring himself pleased with my slow progress and continuing docility, and the dark bottle stayed within the depths of his black leather bag. Soon I even began to look forward to his visits, for his face appeared friendly, his manner benevolent and sympathetic. I longed to speak to him, to pour out the lingering fears and doubts I dared not admit even to myself. But I remembered his hands, steel-hard and uncompromising as they forced the laudanum down my throat, and my lips remained sealed, my questions spoken only into the dark nights of silence when I lay awake and tried to sort through the conflicting realities that called to me. There was no one here I could trust, least of all myself.

It was Sir Robert who, after two weeks, insisted I be allowed to leave my bed to sit before the fire for a few hours each day, and it was that which pushed the expanding emptiness aside, creating open places to which the mists of memory could cling. Thus the past began to re-emerge in my mind. Like light through a prism, my life shimmered into ethereal colors, faint hues caressing me with warmth in the chill isolation of that cold stone room. The past, bearing vaporous nuances of the soul I had given to my brown-haired Matthew and the spirit I had lost to drug-induced madness, teased me with meanings I could not decipher. I puzzled long over each piece that was offered, turning it carefully in my fingers, inspecting every corner, every bend and fold, fitting with delicate precision each into the others until at last, after a long, mist-enshrouded week, I discovered Marina.

For three more days I sat watching visions of Marina, wondering at her, my metaphoric eyes drinking in the assuredness with which she seemed to pass each day. From a far distance I watched as her life unfolded a moment at a time, her joys and sorrows barely touching me where I reclined, stretched upon a brocaded chaise, silken throws about me to keep me warm. I wondered who she was, and why she had come to me. Each night I fell asleep with my questions unanswered. But they did not long remain so.

It was cold and barren, that huge dark house, and almost devoid of life. Giles, the carriage driver, who I learned was Mrs. Peele's husband, never set foot within the black stone walls, lurking out-of-doors or in the stables and grinning in the windows at me. Inside the house there was Mrs. Peele, who moved like an icy silent wraith through the darkness, appearing unexpectedly to stare at me with bitter, hate-filled eyes. Her feet made no sound on the echoing stone floors, and she seemed to be everywhere at once. Nothing ever happened that she did not know about. She abhorred everything and everyone but Matthew, me most of all.

The only other servant was Mary, their thirteen-year-old granddaughter, a dirty, misshapen lump of a girl, a drooling half-wit who obeyed unspoken commands mindlessly, cowering in mortal terror from both her grandparents and Matthew. But Mary never came to the upper levels of the house, and I did not learn of her existence until I began to leave my second-floor room. In the vacuum within the stone walls, the silence broken only by the mournful wind outside the windows, or Matthew's and Sir Robert's shortening visits, I found ample time in which to watch, to memorize, Marina.

Matthew found me sitting, shivering, on the edge of the bed the fourth morning after I had discovered the Marina memories, and with quick steps he crossed to me from the door that connected his room to mine.

"Darling, are you all right? Why are you sitting there like that? You should have called me."

He picked up my dressing gown and slid it up my arms onto my shoulders.

"I'm fine, Matthew. I woke early, that's all."

"How cold you are! Lie back again, Marina, before you take a chill."

He put his hands on my shoulders and pressed, but I shook my head, my fingers curling about his forearms.

"No, Matthew, please. I want to get up now. I am tired of lying around doing nothing. I want to brush my hair, please, Matthew."

He cupped my cheeks with gentle hands, searching my face intently. A slow, joyful smile grew on his lips, but oddly did not touch his dark, icy blue eyes. I wanted to smile back, I knew it would please him, but somehow I could not force my lips to lift. After a long moment, he dropped his hands to my arms.

"Come, let me help you, darling," he said, lifting me to my feet and winding a strong arm about my waist.

Leaning on Matthew, I inched across the deep red carpeting, past windows masked with heavy red velvet curtains, to the dressing table in the corner. He lowered me onto the embroidered bench and kissed my forehead.

"I will go inform Mrs. Peele we are ready for

breakfast. When I return, I'll help you to the fire. You'll be all right?"

He smiled at me and I nodded slowly, solemnly.

"Thank you, Matthew," I whispered.

I stared at the silver hairbrushes for a moment after he shut the door. They were quite elaborate, chased silver with my initials entwined in the center in elaborate Medieval script. Like the black-haired Matthew, they evoked not one shred of misty memory. Picking one up, I nestled it in my hand with a shiver as the cold of the metal radiated into my palm. Not even its touch seemed familiar.

I raised my arms, pushing my hair up away from my face and pressed the bristles against my scalp as I pulled the brush through my long-neglected locks. My head lifted and my eyes met those in the mirror; huge, sad and gray in a pale, oval face, lips still rosy despite the long illness, black hair tumbling about thin shoulders covered now with dark green satin. A beloved voice, so very long silent, whispered on the rising wind outside the windows.

… the exquisite Diedre…

Marina!" I exclaimed.

The brush dropped from my hand and marred the edge of the dressing table before it bounced down onto the carpet. I stared, shocked, at my image in the mirror, reaching out to touch my cheek, then hers, watching our hands meet on the chill surface of the glass. I gasped. *I* was Marina! *I* was the memories, the joys, the sorrows I'd watched drift gently before my eyes these last few days. It was I who had walked the London streets, I who had kept the neat, orderly ledger books, I who repulsed the unwanted attentions of a cruel blond nobleman. It was I who had been self-assured, competent and free. Before I married. Before the Matthew-man got his hands on me.

I knew, then, with blinding certainty, that he truly was not my Matthew, for in all those memories through which I had sorted there had been not one with black hair and blue eyes. That he was a nobleman I would have to accept; everyone here called him Lord Palmerston. And that he was called Matthew I would also have to accept, for that was the name Sir Robert had used, as had the bearded man who had also been in the library that first night, the one called Roger. But he was not, could never be, *my* Matthew.

Whatever it was he wanted of me, I would have to be very careful and play along, until somehow I could contrive to escape from this desolate, isolated place. I would have to pretend that I believed him, that I truly thought him my husband, and thus allay his suspicions and loosen his guard. Whatever the truth behind what was happening, I now had brown hair and brown eyes to hold onto, to keep me sane. Little did I know how close to impossible that would prove to be.

I retrieved the hairbrush and worked methodically at the tangles, finishing just as the Matthew-man returned. He stood behind me with his hands on my shoulders, our eyes locked in the mirror.

My heart beat fearfully. Could he see the knowledge in my face, did he know that I understood again who I was and who he was not? Finally, he smiled and kissed the top of my head. We breakfasted together and he did not seem to notice my uneasy silences, for they had become my way since the illness. I breathed a sigh of relief when at last he left to ride the moors as he did every day, leaving me alone in the chill, oppressive stillness of the house.

I progressed quickly then, for I had a reason now to recover. Within a week I was able to leave my room, though both Matthew and Dr. Boulton restricted me to the south wing, where our bedrooms lay above the library, a dark gloomy drawing room, and the huge echoing dining room. I did not argue, for my strength failed if I walked too far and my nerves jumped at each noise I heard in the vast stone rooms. Sir Robert also prescribed a glass of sherry at bedtime each night to calm my nerves and help me sleep, and though I hated its too-sweet cloying taste and it did not keep the night demons at bay, I drank whatever the Matthew-man gave me. I did not want to risk making myself ill again. I did not yet understand that the illness was drug-induced, and that hands other than mine controlled its onset.

Eerie shadows remained as the days progressed, despite my new-found strength. They drifted nebulously just beyond the range of my vision, eroding the certainty I had discovered in my mirror. The winds outside the house wailed in mournful lamentation, and

I began to hear voices moaning beneath the weird unremitting gusts. Despite the sherry, I would wake in the night with the darkness vacuum-still around me, and hear the wind calling my name, enticing me, luring me from my bed to the window beyond which a pale, ghostly demon waited to ensnare me. In the evenings, I sat staring at the window, hearing insistent disembodied voices call my name while Matthew read to me or we dined together. Though the voices were clear to me, it seemed he heard nothing at all. He would study my trembling body, my sweating brow and my nervous starts with frowning dark blue eyes, growing ever quieter and more watchful. Sir Robert came by a little more often. Terrified, I tried to ignore the desolate sounds, though I could not resist the pull to the windows. I spent long hours staring out at the bleak and barren landscape, my soul feeling lost, abandoned and hopeless. Every day eroded a little more of the woman I'd thought I'd found.

Chapter Eighteen

Two long, wind-haunted weeks passed before I suddenly remembered I had neither written to, nor heard from, Uncle Jacob. *How long has it been?* I wondered. I had no idea how much time had passed since I had arrived at Stoneleigh; I had not had interest enough to ask. How worried he must be! I searched my room in a panic, startling at the odd, wailing sound of the wind on the moor and the rattling of the windows in the casements, but the desk in the corner was empty, holding neither pen, paper, inkwell nor blotter. I had just decided to go down to the library to ask Matthew for what I needed when the door opened and he strode in, resplendent in gray riding breeches and coat.

"What a day for the moors, Marina!" he exclaimed, crossing to his room, throwing off his coat as he moved. "It is as wild as a nightmare out there. I was hard put to control my stallion. You would not think a little wind could frighten such a fierce animal, would you?"

I shivered, glancing at the windows. Dark clouds boiled across a leaden sky. The wind poked prying fingers into every crevice and crack.

"I can understand his fears, Matthew. It sounds as though the demons of hell are abroad, seeking souls to capture and take away." I wrapped my arms around my body. "Sometimes, when I sit here alone in this room with the stone and the silence, I hear the wind calling to me, as though it were alive. I hate it!"

"You are just not used to it, my darling, that is all," he soothed, moving to me and enfolding me in a warm embrace. "I am sure you will learn to love it, as I do. In a few weeks, spring will mellow the sound and it will be angels, not demons, abroad on the barren hills."

"Spring?" My heart skipped a beat. "In a few weeks? Matthew, what day is this? How long have I been ill?"

"It is the end of January, Marina. The twenty-seventh."

"No." I moaned, shaking my head. Matthew tightened his clasp, smoothed my hair away from my face with tender hands. "So long? So many months? I do not believe it."

"You have been very, very ill, my love. For a long time you did not even know me. There were many times when I despaired of your recovery."

"Matthew, I must write to Uncle Jacob. He will be frantic with worry. I had thought that only a few weeks had passed since I left London, but four months?

Matthew, he must have written to me in all this time. Has nothing come?"

"No, darling, there has been nothing. But that is not so surprising, is it, since Uncle Jacob believes you still in France?"

I shook my head, pushing away from him and pacing to the window. I could feel panic rise again in my breast. I began to shake and my eyes blurred.

"No, Matthew. I wrote him from London just before I came here. I told him he could reach me at Stoneleigh. He knows where I am. I gave the boy a whole shilling to deliver the letter. Why has he not written to me?"

Matthew stood very still, his body tense and wary as he watched me gasp for air. The room swam about my head; I could feel my grasp on reality begin to fade, the pain of Uncle Jacob's silence enfolding me like a smothering blanket. Slowly, cautiously, Matthew stepped closer. He did not touch me, but his intense gaze never left my face.

"Marina, darling, you cannot have written him from London. You weren't there, you were in France. You came directly here from the boat, you did not stop in London. Uncle Jacob does not know you are here."

"But he does! I wrote to him, I remember doing it. I remember what I said, the words I wrote, that you would explain—"

I broke off, aware of his eyes staring, assessing, calculating. I turned away and buried my face in the velvet drapes, my heart hammering in fear. Matthew laid his hands on my shoulders, and I prayed he did not feel me flinch.

"Marina, it never happened," he insisted, his voice calm, compelling. It was hard to know what to believe when he spoke like this. "It is the illness, it has made you imagine many things that aren't true, that didn't happen. They feel real, those dreams, I know. Very real." He turned me around and held me close, my head resting on his chest. His hand stroked my hair. "I understand how frightened you are, but you cannot let it upset you like this, Marina. Your nerves are very delicate, they cannot take any more strain. You don't want to collapse again, do you?"

I shook my head, terror closing my throat tight. I knew what he would do if I continued to seem upset. He would call Sir Robert and they would dose me with laudanum again. I couldn't let that happen. I clung tight to Matthew and willed my trembling to stop, my pounding heart to slow.

"That's right, my darling, calm yourself. It is only a lapse in memory, that is all. You *are* getting better, Marina, a little every day. Soon, you will feel strong again, and know which is real and which the dream."

"You're right, Matthew," I agreed, straightening up and pushing away from him. "It is silly to let myself get so upset. I am so grateful you understand how difficult it is, how real the dreams seem. I cannot always tell the difference."

He smiled and ran his fingers through my hair. "I can tell, Marina. And I will help you to see it, too. Are you all right now?"

"Yes, Matthew. But I should write to Uncle Jacob and tell him where I am, that I am safe with you. Even if he still thinks me in France, he will worry when he has no word from me." I looked at the nearby desk. "But I have no paper, Matthew, nor a pen. Could you not find them for me?"

"Of course, Marina, of course." Matthew smiled and moved away toward his room. "I have just what you need in my desk. I'll bring it to you. And Marina," he added, pausing in the doorway, "do not be overlong about the letter. Our guests will arrive soon for dinner. I am sure you will find them a pleasant diversion from the wind. Come down to the library when you are ready."

Guests for dinner? I stood in the center of the room, my heart pounding, my head whirling in confusion. What guests? Why had he not told me? Or perhaps he had. I cast my mind back, searching the days, turning over our conversations, but could find no trace of the words, of Matthew's voice telling me of guests, of a festive dinner party. But neither had I found memory of the hairbrushes on the dressing table, the jewels in the ornate wooden box on the desk, or of most of the clothing in the wardrobe. Yet they were real, as was the date at the top of the marriage certificate which Matthew had given me to keep on the table beside my bed. Though I remembered so clearly a September wedding in the chapel, the truth lay elsewhere, on a paper signed three months earlier. The dark illness that sought to devour me lurked ominously close to the edges of my mind, wispy shadows winding down into the core of my being, propelled by the howling, satanic moorland winds. The substance of sanity, the rock to which I clung, slowly crumbled with each passing hour.

Matthew returned, tall and handsome in deep gray and green, and set paper, pen and inkwell on my desk. I stood watching in silence, my gaze caught by the sight of the Palmerston crest at the top of the white pages. I began to tremble once more as I pictured Matthew's letter, *my* Matthew's letter, the one I had found in a London hotel room, not in France. I had held it, read it, memorized the words on the long journey to Stoneleigh. It had been in my bag, I *knew* it had been. But it hadn't been, had it, for it didn't exist. It had been another letter, from another Matthew, not from *my* Matthew.

Behind me the wind rose, a mournful, eerie wail in the darkening afternoon.

Marina...Mariinaaa...come to me....come....

I spun to the window, gasping, as my name echoed faintly across the moor. Matthew strode across the room and yanked the heavy red draperies shut, then gathered me into his arms.

"It is only the wind, Marina, there is nothing to be afraid of. You are trembling so! Come, sit down."

He led me to the chair before the desk and sat me down, caressing my face with a gentle hand, a sad, tender smile on his lips. His eyes, however, remained distant, cold and calculating. After a moment, he disappeared into his room, returning quickly with a small glass, filled with a shimmering amber colored liquid, which he put into my shaking hands.

"Drink this, it will stop your trembling," he said.

"What is it?"

"Your sherry, darling, the one Sir Robert left for you at bedtime. He told me to give you a little whenever I feel you need it. It will steady you, Marina," he insisted when I shook my head; how I hated its sickly sweetness. "You know it will. You cannot write to Uncle Jacob if you are trembling like that. He would never be able to read it."

That, at least, made sense. I looked up at Matthew and sighed, nodding agreement. If I put pen to paper now, the words would surely look written by an old, old woman, indeed. Raising the glass with care so as not to spill any, I sipped at the sugary, potent wine, feeling it spread a warming glow throughout my body. Matthew leaned against the wall, watching as my trembling faded. After a few minutes, I set the half-empty glass on the desk and gave him a hesitant smile.

"Thank you, Matthew. I feel much better now. I know it is just the wind, and yet still it frightens me. Please be patient with me a little longer. I am sure I will grow used to it, in time."

"Of course you will, Marina. Now finish the sherry and your letter, and forget the wind for tonight. My friends are anxious to meet my beautiful bride, and I know you will find the company and conversation more enjoyable than that racket outside." He bent and kissed my cheek, then strode to the doorway. In the hall he turned. "Wear the silky gray dress, Marina, the one you wore for the portrait. I love what it does for your eyes."

He disappeared, leaving me staring into the dark, empty corridor. The silky gray dress? What gray dress? What portrait? I turned my head and looked at the closed wardrobe. I had not inspected its contents closely, for each morning Matthew would select a dress for me and lay it on the chaise. I knew from what I wore each day that most of the contents were unfamiliar, but I had not yet had the courage to open those doors myself. The wardrobe held only mystery and confusion, and I could not face any more of that. It seemed that now, however, I had no choice.

I turned back to the desk and sipped more of the sherry before I bent to my letter. I kept it short, merely telling Uncle Jacob that I had fallen ill from the long, damp journey to Stoneleigh. I apologized for the lingering weakness that had kept me from writing until now, and assured him that I was almost fully recovered. 'It is cold here,' I wrote, 'and dark most days. The sun rarely shines. I miss the gold that glints from Matthew's brown hair when the sun caresses it. Do you remember how his hair would shine, and how the green specks in his golden-brown eyes would glitter? Matthew says the spring will bring the sun with it. I do hope it will, for it is hard to remain cheerful in the face of such gloomy skies.'

I stared at the words I had written, knowing they held either my salvation or my doom. Would Uncle Jacob agree with me about Matthew, or would he ask what I meant by brown hair and green-flecked eyes, tell me that Matthew had, indeed, black hair and blue eyes? I hesitated long before I sealed the letter, for I truly feared the answer. Despite my resolve the day I rediscovered myself, I had come to mistrust my own perceptions. I may have continued to hold onto the memory of the other Matthew, *my* Matthew, but I was no longer sure he was the real one, the one I had actually married. I did not know if I was ready for the truth.

At length I sighed and sealed the letter. Ready or no, I would soon find out. Laying it aside, I rose and with reluctant steps approached the wardrobe, knowing that even if it were the only gown within it, I could not wear the gray dress as Matthew had requested. I saw it, a lovely pearl gray in shimmering moiré, the moment I opened the doors. I also saw Lord D'arcy's face. I ignored the gray dress and reached instead for the green silk and satin gown Matthew himself had chosen.

But which Matthew? I wondered as I clasped petticoats and bustle about my waist and pulled the luxurious fabric over my head. It was a bit large, I found, once I had done up the buttons, for I had lost weight during my long illness, and I was glad of the deep lace ruffle around the neckline that minimized the gaping of the fabric over my breasts. I pulled my hair back and fastened it high on my head with a glittering clip from the jewelry box, letting it fall into long curls down my neck, and clasped a strand of pearls about my throat. My hands were steady when I lit a candle and picked up the letter, leaving the cold stone room, heavy red drapes, and rattling wind-haunted windows behind. With careful steps I made my way along the dark corridors and down steep stone stairs to the library below, where Matthew and our guests waited.

The library was dim and deserted when I entered, a banked fire glowing in the grate and only one lamp lighted on the desk. I laid the letter on the blotter for Matthew to post and stared around, frowning. My hands began to shake. Where was he, and the guests of whom he had spoken? They should have arrived by now, I had taken long in writing the letter, and in dressing. I stood irresolute, at length braving the silent dark hallway, my candle flame flickering in mysterious drafts, to look into the deserted, echoing drawing and dining rooms, before returning to the library.

I stood in the center of the room, listening to the wind poke at the windows, unable to move, to think, to even breathe. Where were they? Why was I alone? Suddenly, it hit me—the stables. Matthew must have taken our guests to the stables for some reason, to show them something. A new horse, perhaps. They were probably even now on their way back here, to the library. I sighed with relief, set the candle beside me on the table and sat before the hearth to wait, wondering why Mrs. Peele had not stirred up the fire to warm the room. At length I stood and poked at the half-burnt logs, bringing the fire back to a semblance of life, and sat again to wait. The candle burnt lower and the silence deepened. Eventually, even the wind outside fell silent. I fretted over what to do: remain where Matthew had told me to be, or leave and search again for him and perhaps rouse his anger. What was happening? Why had he not returned with the guests? Surely they could not still be in the stables, the dinner hour was long past by now. Then the door opened wide and Matthew stood in the opening in his dressing gown, staring at me.

"Marina, what are you doing in here? I've been looking all over for you. Why are you dressed like that?"

"You told me to come here, Matthew, when I was ready. You said the library, that the guests would be waiting, but no one was here. I've been waiting for such a long time."

"Guests? What guests? What are you talking about?"

"Our dinner guests, Matthew. You told me they were coming, that they were anxious to meet me. You said to come to the library when I finished my letter to Uncle Jacob, but no one was here. I thought that maybe you took them to the stables, but it's been such a long time. Where is everyone, Matthew?"

He crossed the room to where I sat and knelt before me. Clasping my hands in his, he looked up into my eyes. The faint light from the glowing embers in the grate and the guttering candle nearby emphasized the sharp, square planes of his face. His eyes, intense and sad, seemed as dark as his hair. He spoke softly, as though to a child.

"Marina, there are no guests. No one could come out on a night like this. We rarely entertain on the moor in winter. There will be no dinner parties until spring arrives. No one is coming for dinner, and I did not tell you to come to the library. You imagined it."

He pulled me to my feet and led me out of the library and up to my room with strong arms around my waist and shoulders. He would not listen to my protests and ignored my tears, merely stating calmly over and over that I had imagined the whole conversation, that I was overwrought and needed to rest. He pulled the gown and petticoats from my body, slid a silky nightdress over my head, and wiped away my tears while he fed me two glasses of sherry. My eyelids were drooping by the time he'd finished. Matthew tucked me in bed with a chaste kiss on my cheek, and sat beside me holding my hand until I fell asleep, whirled away by the sickly-sweet drink. He kept me in bed, and fed me Dr. Boulton's mind-numbing 'tonic,' which I had come to despise, until I stopped arguing and protesting and lay still again beneath his hands.

And thus was the pattern set. For two months I spent my days wandering aimlessly around my room, haunted by the stone, my nerves fraying to shreds as the wind called to me and shadows danced shimmering at the corners of my eyes. Things would disappear—a brooch, my hairbrush, the book I was reading—and I would search in vain, crying to Matthew for help, only to discover the object where I had left it originally, in a place barren of its presence a few hours before. I stared for hours at the portrait on the wall in Matthew's room, a portrait I did not remember sitting for, a painting of me in an alluring gray gown, glittering gems in my glossy hair, a quaint French avenue visible beyond the open window behind me.

Twice Dr. Boulton came for dinner and I was not ready, for I did not know he was coming. Matthew had not told me though he swore he had. And three times I sat waiting for the doctor because I thought Matthew had told me of a visit Sir Robert did not make. Slowly, like sand through a fine sieve, my sanity filtered away, grain by tiny grain. I no longer knew what was real and what a part of my fevered imagination. The brown hair and brown eyes were very, very far away, and very hard to touch.

Late each night I would see through my window a waiting shadow on the dark moor, when the moaning cry of the wind calling my name would wake me to roiling ebony clouds and arrows of cold silver moonlight. Misty and vaporous, the pale shade beckoned to me as though luring me out to my doom. Matthew, who somehow always knew when I had left my bed and would rise himself to lead me back to its warmth and safety, saw no sign of the evil phantom that, even as he stood looking out my window, still beckoned to me. Not wanting any more of the sherry, I did not tell Matthew of the ghost, but I could tell from the look in his eyes that he knew something was wrong.

And then one day the phantom came into the house.

Chapter Nineteen

I waited anxiously for word from Uncle Jacob, a reply to my letter, but though the days passed, one after the other, the silence remained unbroken by an answer. Finally, I could stand it no more.

"Why does he not write to me, Matthew?" I asked one night when we sat together in the library. Unnerved by the sound of my name wailing on the wind, I twisted my hands around each other. "I don't understand why I have not heard from him. Do you think he's angry with me?"

"My darling, you must have patience." Matthew took my hands in his to stop my wringing them. "It has only been two weeks since you wrote. That is not enough time for your letter to reach London and Uncle Jacob's reply to find its way back here, to Stoneleigh."

"Two weeks? Matthew, it has been *five* weeks. I wrote to Uncle Jacob five weeks ago," I insisted as he shook his head. "I *know* it has been five weeks, I have counted the days very carefully."

"Marina," he caressed my face with his strong, warm hands, "you are confused. It has only been two weeks since you wrote the letter."

"No. No, Matthew. I am not confused, it has been *five* weeks. It *has*!"

"Hush, darling, hush. You're confused. It's so easy to lose track of time here on the moor, every day seems so much like the last," Matthew said, but I slapped his hands aside and spun away to the window.

"Stop talking to me as though I were a child," I yelled. "I know how much time has passed, I'm not an idiot."

"No one said you were, Marina." Matthew's voice rang quiet and cold. "You're just confused."

"I am not confused. I'm not," I said, but the wind at my back and the beckoning phantom beyond the window distracted me, drained the conviction in my voice.

"Yes, you are."

"No. I'm not, I can't be. I counted."

He moved to the desk and poured sherry into a glass. The library door opened. Mrs. Peele stood in the opening, arms folded, malevolent eyes pinned on me, a smug little smile lifting her thin, bloodless lips. Wide-eyed, I looked from her to Matthew, to the still, watchful expression on his face, the glass of sherry in his hand.

"You're lying to me!" I exclaimed, backing away into the window embrasure. "You're trying to hurt me!"

"Marina, stop." Matthew handed the glass of sherry to Mrs. Peele and slowly came toward me, hands patting the air. "You're getting yourself upset over nothing. Calm down."

"No." The wind rose to a howl, screaming my name. I clapped my hands over my ears to shut it out. "No, get away from me. Leave me alone!"

Matthew grabbed me and wrestled me over to his chair. He sat and pulled me down on his lap, pinning my arms to my sides. Mrs. Peele handed him the sherry.

"No, Matthew, I don't want it!" I screamed, twisting in his hard embrace. "Please, Matthew, stop."

Matthew shoved the glass between my lips and sloshed the sherry down my throat until I gagged, forcing me to swallow the sweet liquor. Though almost half spilled down my dress, I could feel the warmth of what I'd ingested spread through my body, robbing me of strength and the will to fight. Mrs. Peele refilled the glass and Matthew relentlessly fed it to me. By the time I finished the second glass, I could barely hold my head steady. Mrs. Peele placed a bony knuckle under my chin and tilted my head up. The pleasure in her eyes startled me, as did the undercurrent of enjoyment in her voice.

"She's getting worse, isn't she, sir?"

"It appears so, Mrs. Peele. It appears so."

I heard it in Matthew's voice, too, that frightening undercurrent of pleasure. Fighting the soporific effect of the sherry, I turned my head and looked at him.

"Why?" I whispered.

Matthew smiled and kissed me, and I knew no more until I woke the next morning in my own luxurious bed.

I spent the morning wrapped in a fog, knowing something had happened the day before, something I needed to remember, but unable to discover what it might be. Matthew sat at the desk in his room, working on the business of the estate. In mid-afternoon, bored with silence and inactivity, wishing to fill my head with anything other than the elusive echoes with which I'd spent the morning, I rose, took a candle and wended my slow, benumbed way down to the library for a book. The demonic wind kept my footsteps company. Twice I almost dropped the candle, startled by the sound of my name wailing in the drafty corners of the hallways.

I gained the library, but once inside, distracted by the rolling mists outside, I forgot what I had come for. I stood for long minutes at the window, watching storm clouds battle each other, catching glimpses of the phantom's trailing vapors at the corners of my eyes. Finally I heard Matthew calling for me. I left the window, took up the now-guttering candle, and walked into the shadow-laden hallway.

It came at me out of the darkness. Grotesque, twisted, trailing pale, diaphanous drapes over the cold, black stone, the ghostly phantom wavered in the fitful candlelight, looming over me, hands clawed as though to choke the life from me. I screamed and dropped the candle as I backed into the wall. The hall plunged into almost-total darkness. I felt its hands rake across my robe, the fingers snagging on the delicate fabric, pulling it half-open. Terrified, I sank to the floor and wrapped my arms around my head, screaming for help, for Matthew. The demon screamed back, the echoes of our voices booming in the confined space, deafening me as I waited for it to take possession of me.

When at last it grabbed my arms, in blind terror I struck out, beating at it with all my strength. It roared on at me, words I could not understand as I struggled for my very life.

"Stop, Marina! Stop!"

It caught my fists, held them tight. I could not get free. Sobbing, screaming, I fought on, twisting away from the strong hands holding me prisoner, the hard, warm body that threatened to overwhelm me.

"Marina. That's enough. Stop!"

The words, the tone, began at last to penetrate my fog of terror. I opened my eyes. Matthew knelt over me. My hands were trapped in his. Lamplight shed a warm glow over his dark hair, sparked in his blue eyes, glinted from a thin streak of blood trickling down his cheek.

"Matthew?" I whispered, barely able to form the words. "Matthew. Help me."

"Marina. Marina, what is it?" He let go of my hands and gathered me into his arms. "What's happened to frighten you so?"

"Don't let it get me, please, Matthew. It wants to kill me. Please, Matthew, help me."

"Darling, there's nothing here," Matthew said, stroking my hair and looking around the darkened hallway. Mrs. Peele held a lamp at shoulder height. It showed the hallway stretching deserted in both directions.

"Yes, there is, Matthew, it came from the moor, it came for me!"

"What, darling, what came for you?"

"The ghost, Matthew! The demon!" I was shaking so hard, I could scarcely form the words. "It's been waiting for me, watching me through the windows."

"Ghost? Demon? What are you talking about, Marina? There are no ghosts or demons."

"Yes, there are, Matthew." I clutched his coat tight. "It came for me, came after me as soon as I left the library."

Matthew frowned and looked up at his housekeeper.

"Mrs. Peele?"

"There was no one else here, my lord." An indefinable hint of satisfaction under rode her flat, emotionless tone. "I was just coming to call you for dinner when I saw her step into the hallway. She started screaming and fell to the ground. She didn't seem to hear me when I tried to help her, so I went to fetch you."

"Thank you, Mrs. Peele," Matthew said, and

turned hard eyes back to me.

"No, Matthew, it was here," I pleaded, stroking his face. My fingers came away bloody. "You must believe me, it was here. It tried to take me, but I fought with it."

"That was me you were fighting, Marina."

"You? No, Matthew," I said, my voice quavering with doubt as I stared at the blood on my hand, the seeping scratches on Matthew's face. He laid a finger on my lips and clasped me close.

"Hush, my love. Be still. It's over now, it's over."

"No," I moaned, "it'll never be over. Never."

He gathered me into his arms and carried me up to my room. It took three glasses of the sherry before I calmed enough to sleep.

A few days later the sherry came out once more when Matthew asked if I had a reply to Uncle Jacob's letter ready to post. I grew hysterical, for I had no memory of receiving any letter, no memory of the words he had written. Matthew could not help me, for he said I had not let him read the letter, and I could find no trace of it on my desk or anywhere in my room. With feverish haste I penned another letter to him, the words reflecting my crazed state of mind. I felt my hold on reality slip further and further away, and passed my days in a fog that allowed no awareness of when one ended and the next began. The shadows danced very close around me, indeed, during that time.

At last, when the weather had warmed and the wind gentled by day, though by night it still howled as fiercely malevolent as ever, Matthew came to my room as darkness was falling. He stood staring at me where I reclined on the chaise, reading, then sighed and took the book from my hands.

"Marina, darling, you must dress. Have you forgotten? Our dinner guests are already waiting below, and they are quite anxious to meet you."

"Guests, Matthew?" My heart pounded. "Oh, yes... I must have... lost track of time."

I tried not to let him see my fear. For four days, now, I had seen no shadows, lost no objects, confused no dates or times. The sherry had stayed in the bottle. I had begun to hope that perhaps, as had the winter, the sickness was ending. I sat staring at Matthew, trying to smile while I controlled the tears welling in my eyes. I had forgotten again. It was not over, the confusion, the terror, the fear. What was happening to me?

Matthew helped me dress, for my trembling hands could not negotiate buttons and clasps, nor even brush my hair into a semblance of order. He chose the emerald silk and satin, bringing a hesitant smile to my lips as he reminisced about the day he had ordered it, the look of awe on my face as the seamstress draped lengths of the exquisite fabric around my body. When at last I was ready, having sipped a small glass of sherry to calm my nerves, Matthew kissed me tenderly and led me down to the drawing room, a vast gloomy chamber done in deep green and gray.

Nary a picture or tapestry hung on the black stone walls to soften their stark, cold impact. A fire crackled in the huge fireplace, shedding little light or warmth into the huge, square room. Mrs. Peele had placed candles and lamps on all the tables, but they did little to dispel the pockets of translucent shadows that swirled at the edges of my vision. I hated this room. It was cold, damp, impersonal, and felt sinister in atmosphere. The line of uncurtained floor-to-ceiling French doors in the back wall terrified me—by day because they exposed a vast expanse of the surrounding desolate moor to view, and by night because shifting ebony opacity hid eerie chimeras that lurked beyond the glass. The presence, now, of two elegantly gowned ladies and finely dressed gentlemen, conversing in gay tones and sipping sherry and whiskey before the fire, did nothing to lighten the oppressive air or push back the waiting darkness. A fifth man stood in the far corner of the room, half hidden in misty shadow, staring out the French doors, his back turned to the laughing company. Matthew led me up to the fire as the guests rose.

"Here she is, my beautiful American wife, Marina," he said, his arm draped about my shoulders. "Darling, this is Lady Caroline Fairfax and her husband, Sir Miles. And here is Lady Leona Francis and her brother, Sir Roger."

The Fairfaxes were an older couple in their mid-forties, he softening to flab and half bald, a bushy, grizzled beard hiding most of his face. Bright dark eyes inspected me with close interest as he bowed over my hand in greeting. Lady Caroline, resplendent in purple satin, had a long, narrow face of the type homely in youth but that grew to handsomeness with age, soft pale skin, a large well-rounded body, and a high breathless voice.

The Francises were the opposite, she looking younger than Matthew, each thin and dynamic seeming, each dressed in brown and beige, though Lady Leona's moiré shimmered in the firelight and its high-fashion exposed her pale shoulders to both the night air and the men's eyes. Her blue eyes showed a watchful attitude and held little welcoming warmth, though her words, in a tone of black velvet, were gracious enough. Her blond hair glittered with jewels, and her gaze rarely left Matthew. Sir Roger, the bearded man who had been in the library with Matthew and Sir Robert the night I arrived, was handsome in an ordinary way. His fingers held mine a little too warmly, and lingered a little too long.

"We have all been friends for many years, Marina," Matthew said, handing me a glass of sherry, "and it is a good thing, too, for we are all there is out here. There are no other big houses within a day's ride. It would certainly be tiresome to be stuck with disagreeable neighbors."

"Now, Matthew," Lady Caroline laughed, simpering at my husband, "it would be hard to imagine anyone finding you disagreeable. He has had all the unattached ladies of the entire district after him for years, and quite a few of the married ones as well," she said to me, her tone confidential and her dark eyes sparkling with malicious amusement. "You will have to tell us how you caught him, Marina, my dear, and how you intend to keep him. The moor may look deserted and desolate, but you'd be amazed at how much competition there is out here."

"As you can see," Lady Leona said, smiling with barely disguised animosity, "we are quite outspoken here in the north. You will have to get used to that, Marina. We rarely mince words."

I looked from one to the other of the women, acutely aware of the undercurrents swirling beneath their words. I felt dizzy, disoriented. The ladies seemed to waver in the flickering light, and their words confused me. I smiled my nerves at them, remained silent and sipped at the too-sweet sherry I held. The wind moaned at the windows, a forsaken howl of woeful despair that struck shivers into my soul. My hands began to tremble.

"Ah, there you are. Come meet my sweet wife," I heard Matthew say from somewhere behind me, then he touched my shoulder with warm, caressing fingers. "Darling, I want you to meet our last guest. You will see a lot of him, for he has agreed to stop a few weeks with us."

I turned around and froze in shock, my eyes on the tall, lean figure before me. Echoing from a far distance I heard Matthew's voice continue the introduction.

"Marina, this is my very dear friend, Lord Henry D'arcy.

Chapter Twenty

"Matthew, she is exquisite. I congratulate you heartily, and you are right. No words could ever do her justice."

D'arcy reached out for my hand. I jerked back with a gasp, my heart thudding. The glass of sherry slipped from my numb fingers and shattered on the stone floor.

"No," I cried, backing away. "Don't touch me."

"Marina." Matthew said, stepping toward me, but I backed further away, shuddering in anger.

"No. How could you bring him here, Matthew, after what he did? How could you?"

"What are you talking about, Marina?"

"You *know* what I'm talking about. I won't have him here. I won't!"

"Perhaps I had better leave," D'arcy said, but Matthew silenced him with a gesture.

"Stay where you are, D'arcy. Marina is just confused, that's all."

"Confused? *Confused?*" I shouted. "I am *not* confused. Do you think I could *ever* forget his face, or his name? Get him out of here."

"Marina, please, you're causing a scene," Matthew said, stepping closer to me.

"A scene? You want a scene, Matthew? I'll give you one." I darted behind a table and swept it clear with my arms. One of the books hit Matthew in the thigh. The candle bounced across the carpet. Miles Fairfax stamped it out before it could start a fire.

"That is enough, Marina," Matthew growled. "You're being childish. D'arcy is my guest and you will be civil to him."

"Never! I will not stay in the same *room* with him!"

Matthew reached out and grabbed my wrist. "Calm yourself, Marina, please," he said, adding in a low, cold voice that only I could hear, "or I will do it for you."

He pulled me closer to him and his hand tightened until tears of pain stood in my eyes.

"Matthew, stop, you're hurting me." I twisted in his grasp to no avail.

Matthew looked over his shoulder at his astonished guests. I saw Henry D'arcy watching with a detached, speculative look on his face. The others huddled near a settee, their wide eyes taking in every moment of the scandal.

"I don't know what's got into her," he said, all the while tightening his fingers until I feared my wrist bones would crack.

"Let go of me, Matthew. That hurts. Let go!" I screamed. My free hand reached out, snatched up a paperweight from another table.

"Palmerston!" D'arcy shouted. "Look out!"

Matthew turned and threw up his free arm, deflecting the heavy glass globe I swung. It glanced off his cheekbone and he grunted in pain, then caught my free hand and squeezed until I screamed and dropped the paperweight.

"Francis," he shouted, "go for Sir Robert, quickly. D'arcy, there's a dark brown bottle on the desk in my room. Bring it. Hurry!"

"No, Matthew!" I screamed, wrenching one hand from his and beating at him. "No, don't! Let me go!"

D'arcy and Sir Roger ran from the room, and I knew that in a matter of minutes I would be drugged senseless on laudanum again, and at the mercy of both Matthew and Lord D'arcy this time. Terror lent me strength. I twisted my arm and raked my nails down Matthew's face. He cried out and stumbled, his fingers loosening as he fell to one knee. I tore myself free and spun around, only to find the way to the door blocked by Miles Fairfax.

"Don't let him do this to me," I pleaded, barely able to speak through my terror. "Please, help me."

Fairfax merely stood silent, wary and watchful. He had, I could see, been forewarned of me by Matthew. In desperation I ran to the fireplace and snatched up a poker just as Matthew regained his feet.

He began walking slowly toward me.

"Don't come near me, Matthew. Don't. I won't let you give me that stuff, not anymore. Get away from me."

"Matthew," Caroline Fairfax said, her tone one of fear mixed with concern, but Matthew held up a hand, silencing her.

"Put the poker down, Marina, before you hurt someone," he said, edging closer. "Please, darling. I only want you to calm down. If you calm down, I won't give you the medicine, I promise. I just want you to be calm. Please, Marina. Put the poker down now. You can trust me, darling."

I almost believed it. His soft, persuasive voice caressed my ears. He said what I wanted to hear, and the panic began to fade. I lowered the poker.

Matthew lunged for me. I screamed, twisting away from his grasping hands and swung the poker. It shattered a lamp, spraying burning oil over a couch and the carpet. Flames shot into the air. Caroline and Leona screamed, backing away as a nearby chair caught fire. The flames quickly ate across the carpet, trapping the women on the far end of the room. Leona's dress began to burn. Miles Fairfax gave a strangled cry and ran past me to help his hysterical sister. Matthew, who had stumbled to his knees, surged to his feet and raced to their aid with nary a glance at me. The way now clear, I threw down the poker and ran from the room.

In the hall I paused, wondering what to do, where

to go. I could not go left, past the dining room and library to the stairs to my room, for Henry D'arcy was there, somewhere. I turned right and ran down the dark hall, seeking the front door and freedom. But the dark, twisting corridors defeated me. I had not come this way since the night I had followed Mrs. Peele into Stoneleigh and within minutes I was completely lost.

Surrounded by cold stone walls and almost-absolute darkness that penetrated into my very soul, I stumbled and fell more than once, tearing my beautiful gown to shreds. I ran headlong into the rough stone walls, bruising my body. There was no light save a fitful moon half-glimpsed through narrow, slit-like windows, and no sound other than my own sobbing and the wind beyond the walls.

On and on I ran, blinded by tears and fear and pursued by the wind, until at last I found myself creeping down a long, narrow upper gallery. Tall windows lined one long wall, looking down two stories to the desolate moor. On the other wall hung mist-enshrouded portraits, eerie disembodied faces that glimmered momentarily in the hazy moonlight filtering through dirty panes of glass. I reached a dead-end. The door at the far end of the gallery was locked tight. I would have to go back and try another way.

I turned, leaned on the locked door and stared down the endless length of that room. In the flickering moonlight the portraits seemed to move, to come alive, to beckon to me, veiled in shadows as alive as the wind moaning outside the windows. I forced myself to move, sobbing with fright, my hands pressed hard to my mouth to stop my wailing screams. I was halfway down the gallery when it happened. One of the painted images took form and materialized out of the cold stone wall, a ghostly mirage of transparent pale vapors that floated toward me, arms reaching to take possession. The wind rose outside, bearing with it my name echoing from fleshless lips.

Marina... Marinaaaa... come to me... to me... to me...

The walls rose and folded down around me. Shrieking, I turned and fled to the locked door and beat on it.

"Help me! Matthew, help me! Matthew!"

Only the wind heard me.

The phantom stalked closer. I sank to my knees and huddled against the door. The wind called my name and the ghostly presence drew nearer and nearer. Curling my arms over my head, I felt the first cold touch of the ungodly mists. I looked up and saw the demon's head grinning at me. I shrieked until I had no voice left as the phantom slowly enveloped me, pressing closer, smothering my mind in horror. I twisted deeper and deeper into the darkness, seeking escape, pushing my mind into tiny cracks where the wraith could not possibly pursue. When at last it lifted from my body, it took with it what little awareness I had left.

Matthew and Sir Robert Boulton found me the next afternoon, curled on the floor, pressed tight against the locked door in the portrait gallery. I learned later that together they had searched the house since dawn, Matthew cold and stoic, Sir Robert growing more concerned as the hours passed and they discovered no sign of me. At long last they entered the deserted gallery in the closed north wing and found me crumpled at its end.

I heard their footsteps echo closer but I could not move, caught still in the paralysis of horror that had kept me immobile since I'd awakened just after dawn. Matthew knelt and touched my shoulder. I cried out and cowered away, looking up in fear through the tumbled tangle of my hair.

"Matthew?" I whispered. My abused throat burned unbearably. "Help me."

"Oh, Marina," he said, his voice choked, and gathered me into his arms.

I sobbed while he held me tight, rocking me on the cold stone floor. Finally, he kissed my wet face and stood up, holding me easily in his strong embrace. I was asleep by the time he laid me on my bed. When I woke late the next morning, I was alone with the cold dark stone and the eerie wailing winds. A tray sat on the bedside table, tea lukewarm in the pot. I lay trembling, my gaze searching the murky corners, trying to sort through what had happened to me.

He had brought that man, Henry D'arcy, to the house, and tried to make me believe he was not the one who had attacked me. But he was. No matter how confused I became, or how ill, I would never forget those searing blue eyes, the cruel sneering lips, the slim strong fingers that had torn at me. Why had Matthew done that? Was he trying to drive me crazy?

I sat up with a gasp, my heart pounding. That was it, it had to be. It explained so much: my not remembering things Matthew said had happened; the memories of things Matthew claimed never had happened; the possessions I had never seen before; objects that disappeared only to mysteriously reappear; the visions of phantom figures beckoning in the darkness; eerie voices calling to me on the wind. I thought of the terror in the portrait gallery, walls that seemed to waver and bend over me, and tasted again the sickly-sweet sherry Matthew had given me as I was dressing, the second glass I'd had in the drawing room.

And I knew.

The wine had been drugged, it must have been. When rational I knew very well that there were no voices in the wind. Portraits do not move, nor descend from walls and stalk terrified victims. But it had seemed so real, there in the shadowy darkness. I had not been able to tell the difference, for the drug-laced sherry in my blood had kept misty shadows clinging too close for rational thought to emerge. I cast my mind back over the six long, endless months I had been here, and realized I must have been drugged almost the entire time. No wonder I had lost touch with reality, save for fleeting moments when the drug had worn off. I had been kept too far away from reality to even remember its existence.

Why? Why was he doing this to me? With sudden clarity I saw Matthew, *my* Matthew, standing before me, brown hair gleaming gold in the sunlight streaming through the hotel room window. I felt again his kisses, his hands on my body, his rich deep voice in my ear—*I love you so, Marina, my soul. Do not ever forget that*—and tears fell down my cheeks. He *was* real. It *had* happened. Pain twisted in my heart as I realized that he, too, must be part of the plot, but I pushed the knowledge away. If I admitted his culpability I would have nothing left to hold onto, to strengthen me until this was over, until I escaped. Without the memory of his love, I could very well end as the black-haired Matthew wished me, mad in truth.

I scrambled from the bed and raced for the door, determined to leave the house at once. But it was locked tight, as was the connecting door to Matthew's room. I was a prisoner here. Even the narrow windows would not open; I discovered later they had been nailed shut from the outside. Frantic, I paced the room, fighting despair, until I began to shiver with cold. At last I returned to the bed where I sat huddled against the ornately-carved headboard, a silken comforter wrapped about my shoulders.

I sat unmoving when Mrs. Peele opened the door, bringing the evening tray. She stared at me with wary eyes, studying my straggling hair, my crouched position on the bed, the look of fearful suspicion I knew I could not keep from my face. Carefully, she set the tray down and picked up the other, shaking her head at its untouched state.

"Y'ought to eat," she said, her voice cracking like a whip. "Y'don't, he'll force it into ye. Don't think ye'd like that!"

Her lips lifted in a faint sneer, and her cold, dark glare dropped down my body. Then she spun and left, before I could move. I sat staring at the tray and listened to the key turn in the lock. Dusk closed down outside and lengthened the shadows in my cold room. It was almost completely dark before I realized why it was so cold. There was no fire in the grate, nor did any lamps or candles remain in the room. Panicked, I raced for the door, pounding on it with my fists and crying, screaming, for Matthew. I could not bear the thought of being locked for endless hours in smothering darkness, with only the wind for company. I received no answer to my pleadings, not one sound in the corridor without, nor from Matthew's room beyond the connecting door. Terrified, I backed into the corner and slid down the stone wall, hands pressed tight to my ears to block the sound of my name vibrating on the rattling wind. After a time, I slept.

Chapter Twenty-one

When I woke, faint silver light ghosted through the half-open drapes. It was past midnight and the moon had already risen. Shaking with cold, I stood and stumbled to the bed. The tray still sat on the table, the tea icy, the cold shepherd's pie swimming in globs of fat. I drew my dressing gown on, trying to ignore the lure of the wind, and drank half a cup of the cold, unsweetened tea. Slowly, I drifted to the window and stared out at the bleak, moon-bleached moor, watching the familiar wispy phantom beckon to me, listening to its call: *Come, Marina... come... follow me... come... come...*

Who are you? I wondered as clouds streamed forth and covered the moon, plunging the moor, and my room, into darkness again. Ghosts and spirits did not exist, I knew that, except in fanciful imaginations. Now that the drug no longer clouded my mind, I fully understood that a human agency lay behind this eerie manifestation, though I had no idea how they had contrived it. Nor why. What had Matthew to gain by my insanity? I wondered, groping my way back to bed. Well, he wouldn't get it, I decided, sliding beneath the thick covers. I knew what he was up to now, and I would no longer allow his tricks to affect me. I would simply out-wait him, and remain calm and rational in the face of his machinations.

It was my hunger that defeated me. I woke the next morning to find Mrs. Peele shutting the door behind her. She had left fresh, hot food and my stomach twisted at the enticing aroma. Trembling, I poured steaming tea into the cup and sipped cautiously. There was nothing in it, no hint of the bitterness of laudanum covered by an overabundance of sugar or honey. Sighing with relief, I assuaged my raging thirst and hunger, not once considering that the dangerous medicine could be hidden in the food.

For three more days I remained locked in that dark, frigid stone room, while slowly the opiate eroded my senses. I began to shake and sweat. Shadows again flitted at the corners of my eyes. Eerie voices floated through the darkness, assailing me relentlessly as I cried and pleaded for surcease. When Mrs. Peele came, she would force me to stand against the wall while she changed the trays, threatening to beat me senseless if I moved.

"I ain't like his lordship," she growled that first evening, when she entered to find me close to the door, hoping to dart out past her. She grabbed my arms in iron-strong fingers and backed me up across the room, bending and twisting my wrists until tears streamed down my face and I cried out from the pain. She slammed me up against the stone wall.

"I don't got to be gentle with the likes of ye. I ain't yer kin, like he is. Ye stay right 'ere, against the wall, where I can watch ye good. Ye take one step toward me 'n I'll beat ye 'til ye can't stand up. Y'unerstand?"

I nodded, terrified. She let go of me and turned to her work. I felt her watching me the whole while, and when she had set the morning tray in the hall she returned and stalked slowly over to where I stood trembling against the stone. I cringed in fear as she came closer, sliding down the wall until I huddled on the floor, my arms curled protectively around my head. She merely stared down at me, then snorted in derision and left me alone with my fear and the cold and the voices.

From that time on, she would open the door and stand in the doorway until I pressed myself against the far wall, where I would stay until the key once more turned in the lock. She never again looked directly at me or spoke to me, but I knew she noted every tremble of my body and I dared not move. I saw no one else in all that time save the eerie, beckoning phantom outside the locked window.

The moon shone fitful on the fifth night after Matthew had found me in the gallery. It chased in and out behind dark clouds, casting onto the moor sinuous shadows that danced with a life of their own. I stood at the window, my heart thudding, waiting for the phantom to appear, the phantom I could not quite convince myself was not real. The memory of the clarity with which I had awoken almost a week ago, the understanding of the human plot in which I was both main participant and victim, had slowly submerged until now I caught only mere glimpses of it. Impelled by the drug coursing through my body, the landscape beyond the cold, clear panes of glass undulated in slow ripples that made my head swim. But though the wind howled mournful dirges around the house, there was no sign of the pale, misty spirit that held my destiny in its hands.

And then I heard it. My name. It echoed close, a faint ululating call echoing from the stone walls looming around me. I heard a noise behind me and spun to find the door gaping wide. I stared a moment in shock, expecting I know not what to appear and devour me, but all was still and silent. Then again, very faint, the voice echoed: *Come, Marina…come…come with me…*

Scarcely able to breathe, I moved to the open door until I stood staring out at the ebony velvet filling the corridor. My hands lifted, stroked down the satin smooth wood of the doorposts. It was real. The door was truly open. I was free. I stepped out into the dark hall and hesitated, for in my drug-confused state I could not remember which way to go. Far to my right a pale figure wavered, beckoned. Again the voice echoed faintly in my ears: *Come…hurry…Marina…*

My heart froze. My mind emptied of all emotion.

I was not free. It had come for me at last, the demon shade, come to take me away into madness. And like a sacrifice cast into a deep spell, I turned and followed the ghostly chimera through the dark and twisting corridors of stone.

I followed it for what seemed hours, hemmed in by ink-dark rock and crushing silence. My slipper-shod feet made no sound on the hard floors. At last I found myself at the top of a wide staircase that curved along the wall and descended into the huge main entry hall of Stoneleigh. The phantom paused in the open front portal and beckoned again, then disappeared into the night. I blinked at a suit of armor standing against the wall and remembered my frightening arrival in this black house of evil. Reality again rose up, breaking through my dazed confusion. Freedom lay beyond that open door, if I could escape the phantom figure that I was sure lay in wait for me beyond it. My hands gripped the cold railing as I turned my head, searching the cavernous space for I knew not what. I saw, hanging high on the wall adjacent to the stairway, the display of ancient weapons. If I could reach one from the stairs…

I leaned over the railing and stretched up as far as I could. My groping fingers touched a hilt, closed around icy metal. I lifted down a heavy, two-edged sword. Feeling courage and hope return with the weight of the weapon in my hand, I carefully descended the rest of the way down to the hall.

By the time my feet touched the floor and I

moved toward the open portal, the mists had once more submerged reality and I forgot why I was walking abroad in the night, forgot even the sword clutched tight in my hand. It was only the momentum of the movement down the stairs that propelled me across the hall, that and the lure of the moonlight outside, and my name ghosting on the wind. Wrapped again in nightmare, I stepped out into the wind-driven darkness.

Marina...Mariinaaa...

The demon vapor awaited me, calling, beckoning, and again I followed as in a trance, along the outside of the house, the cold wind pulling at my hair, whipping my dressing gown about my legs. There was no light anywhere save in the sky, a teasing glimpse of a silver moon-ship riding an ocean of boiling clouds. The misty figure wavered in and out of view, luring me on with merciless insistence. Caught in its spell, a sacrifice to doom, I could do naught but follow. Then abruptly it disappeared, leaving me alone in the dark.

Voices penetrated the mists in my mind. Not eerie, disembodied whispers but deep, solid male voices. I turned my head and saw light. It gleamed out through a long, narrow window open to the cool air. Frowning, I moved closer and peered in. It was the library. Five men sat within, clustered around a roaring fire, brandy and whiskey glasses in hand. Matthew and Dr. Bolton sat with their backs to me, Roger Francis in profile to my left. Miles Fairfax faced the window, Henry D'arcy beside him. I listened as they talked on, and gradually realized it was me of whom they spoke.

"I had no idea it was so serious, Palmerston..." Roger Francis paused to take a sip of his whiskey, "...even given what I had seen when she first arrived. The look on her face before I left the drawing room chilled my blood. Thank the good Lord no one was hurt."

"I would never have invited any of you had I realized how dangerous she has become." Matthew shook his head. "She seemed so much better those last few days before the dinner, and I had hoped a pleasant evening, meeting new friends, would be of further help."

"What I don't understand is why she turned on me." D'arcy, too, sipped his drink, his face bleak though his eyes held a curious spark of satisfaction. "I've never seen anything like it. What did she think I had done, Matthew?"

"She thought that you had once attacked her."

"What?" D'arcy's face mirrored shock and disbelief; his eyes retained their glow of satiety. The other men moved restlessly and echoed D'arcy's incredulous words. "By all that's holy, why?"

"She had been attacked once, D'arcy, she told me all about it. By a kinsman of yours, actually, though she wouldn't know that. Your cousin Jane's brother, Malcolm Wellington. She fought him off and saved her virtue, but I gather in the process he beat her quite badly. She was ill for a long time after the incident."

"But I don't look anything like Malcolm. He's

short and stout, and his hair is dark. How could she possibly think I was him?"

"I don't think she was at all rational, D'arcy," Fairfax said. "You weren't there when she started the fire. You should have seen her face—she wanted to kill us all. It was quite terrifying. Like a wild animal, she was. I don't think my sister will ever fully recover from the shock. It was truly a miracle we did not burn to death."

Dr. Bolton sighed and turned to Matthew. His thoughtful frown stood clear in my view, even though I could only see his profile.

"You said she had been attacked, Matthew?" Bolton laid a hand on Matthew's arm, and Matthew nodded. "How long ago did it happen?"

"Just over two years, now, I believe. Yes, she said it happened in mid January, in sixty-eight, at a literary gathering in Lord Creswell's house. She had gone with a writer friend. Malcolm trapped her in the library and tried to seduce her."

"That's it, then." Dr. Bolton nodded. "I've been worrying at it, searching for the trigger, trying to figure what brought on the illness. There didn't seem to be anything at all, though I've never heard of a case that wasn't set off by a nasty shock of some kind."

"You're sure, then? It's not something else? She really is going insane?" Matthew's voice seemed to hold inestimable anguish. The other men looked down, all but Henry D'Arcy. They appeared embarrassed by Matthew's private emotion, and thus they did not see the gleam of satisfaction in D'Arcy's face that I saw.

"I'm afraid so, Matthew." I could hear the compassion in the doctor's voice, and wondered why he gave it to Matthew, when I was the one so in need of it. "It seems unlikely it could be anything else, given her history. It is following a classic pattern, periods of increasingly violent hallucinations alternating with normal, rational behavior. As the years progress, lucid times grow fewer and shorter in length, until they cease completely and the patient retreats into a fantasy world of her own creation. Women, alas, are particularly susceptible to this malady. It often takes many years for full insanity to develop, but in Marina's case the progress appears unusually rapid."

"Is there no way to stop it?" Matthew bowed his head and covered his face with his hands. D'arcy's lips twitched as though he fought a smile.

"I'm sorry, there is nothing. The most you can do, Matthew, is slow the onset, if possible. She must rest, and eat well. That is essential. Do not allow her to make any decisions, or burden her with any sort of work. I've seen as little as a mistake in needlework set off an irrational episode. Keep her calm and quiet and do not let her roam free. Above all, avoid stressful situations, such as changes within the house and staff, or meeting new people. Anything of that sort may upset her unduly, which will bring on the fits that in her case only speed the deterioration—as you have already discovered. I truly am sorry, Matthew. I wish I could hold out some hope, but given what you have uncovered about her mother, there is little doubt in my mind about the diagnosis."

I gasped softly. My mother? She died when I was only five. What could she possibly have to do with this? In my puzzlement I missed what Miles Fairfax said. Dr Bolton turned to him and nodded.

"Yes, she suffered from the same affliction. Matthew received an answer to his query but a fortnight ago. It appears Marina's father—who, by the way, took his own life—was forced to put the mother into an asylum years ago. She is still there, quite mad. It is unfortunate that she passed the disease on to her daughter, but that is quite common with this type of illness."

"Is that what you think I should do, too?" Matthew's pained voice rang in the night. "Put my wife into an asylum? My beloved Marina?"

Stunned, I lifted my hands, raising the sword I had forgotten I held. My mother had been insane? She hadn't died? Father had shut her away from those who loved her, who could help her and care for her? And now Matthew would do that to me? Why?

"Oh," I keened, my voice an anguished echo in the dark night. "Oh, Mama, no."

Matthew turned to the window. His eyes locked on mine and as I backed away I could see the pleasure he derived from this game of his, even as his face registered well-feigned shock at the sight of me, my hair and nightclothes streaming in the fierce wind. The moon broke free of the concealing clouds and glinted on the sharp two-edged blade I held.

"Dear God in Heaven, she's got a weapon!" D'arcy exclaimed, setting his hand over his heart. Dr. Bolton reached out and clamped his fingers on Matthew's arm as Matthew started to rise.

"No!" I screamed into the wind, then turned and ran in terror away from the house, out onto the dark moor.

Chapter Twenty-two

I ran for what seemed forever, desperately seeking a hidden shelter on the flat, barren moor. Shadows danced around me, pushing at me, blocking my way, pressing against me with almost physical force, products of the drugged delirium that held me in its thrall. The misty white phantom darted at me from out of nowhere, trailing insane laughter, its diaphanous tendrils wrapping about my face until I screamed in horror. I whirled away from its teasing, reaching arms, falling over and over, tearing and soiling my silk and satin nightclothes, unaware that I fled at its discretion, in the direction it wanted me to go.

I lost my slippers as I ran, my feet bloodying on coarse dried grass and sharp rocks I never felt. I ran still clutching the heavy sword, even though it slowed me down and overbalanced me. I clung to it not as a weapon, but as a symbol of reality, a connection to a life that had substance and sanity. And then suddenly, out of the darkness, Matthew appeared before me.

I swerved to the left, hoping to race around him, only to find Miles Fairfax guarding the way, wary and alert, watching the sword in my hand. I skidded to a stop, backed away, and spun around again, putting Fairfax behind me and Matthew on my left. Roger Francis waited ten feet away, his face determined though his eyes looked almost as terrified as I felt. Off to my right I caught a glimpse of movement and, raising the sword, I revolved that way to find Henry D'arcy and Dr. Bolton slowly converging upon me, tightening the circle that trapped me.

"Stay away!" I screamed, whirling in a circle and brandishing the sword. The men stopped moving, exchanged a look, then again pressed inward, first one, then another, while I sobbed and spun, swinging blindly with the deadly blade, searching for a way out. I turned to face Dr. Bolton and D'arcy darted forward to grab my left arm. I screamed and slashed at him with the sword, catching his right arm and shoulder. Bright blood spurted from the deep wound, glistening black in the eerie moonlight. With a strangled cry, he fell onto the moor.

"Marina, stop!" Matthew roared. "Francis, get back!"

From beside the fallen D'arcy, Roger Francis ran at me. I jerked around. The sword followed my movement and caught him in the left thigh. He screamed and stumbled to his knees. Black blood squirted through his fingers. The doctor went to his friends' aid and I raced out of the circle through the place Robert Bolton had vacated.

"Grab her, Fairfax!" Matthew shouted, but the older man's hands missed their mark.

I went no more than ten steps when again the demon shade flew at me from the darkness, wraith-like arms reaching out for me. I struck out with the sword, hoping to part its misty shadows and clear an escape path, and felt it hit very solid flesh, indeed. The shock stopped me in my tracks, for I'd had no idea there was a living person behind the apparition. The phantom wavered, stumbling off into the darkness, trailing ruby-red blood onto the stony ground. Hard arms closed around me from behind, pinning my arms to my sides. I writhed, shrieking and terrified, trying to break free.

"It's over, Marina," Matthew growled in my ear as he wrenched the sword from my hand and spun it away into the darkness. He turned me around, clamping hurting fingers on my arm, and lifted his hand. It cracked against my face, three hard, forceful blows that buckled my knees and made my ears ring. Robert Bolton caught his wrist as his hand rose yet again.

"Matthew, stop! That's enough. Remember, she is ill."

"What else do you suggest I do, doctor? She has almost killed two of my closest friends. D'arcy may yet die. Her illness is no excuse. None. I will not treat her tenderly and bow over her hand as though she is a lady—she has forfeited that right. What I do with her now is no concern of yours. You see to your patients, and leave the handling of my wife to me."

One of the injured men moaned. The sound stopped Sir Robert's protest. He turned away into the night, and Matthew seized my wrists in his strong hands. I cried out at the pain of his grip and looked up at him from where I knelt in the coarse grass. Matthew turned his head and spoke to Miles Fairfax, who stood nearby, watching.

"Go help the doctor, Fairfax. I can handle her from here."

Sir Miles stared down at me, his eyes narrowed chips of ice. After a moment, he turned on his heel to join Sir Robert, who bent over the wounded men. Matthew brought his hands together and grabbed both of my wrists in one large hand, his fingers iron bands I had not the strength to break. My face still burned from his blows. Tears streamed from my eyes, half-blinding me.

"Matthew," I said, but he shook his head.

"You brought this on yourself, Marina. You've left me no choice. No choice at all."

Though his voice was full of anger and sorrow, his eyes declared his pleasure in what he was about to do. He turned and strode across the moor toward the distant manor, towing me along after him. I stumbled and fell, but Matthew did not stop. He dragged me over the rough ground, shredding my clothing, ignoring my cries of pain and pleas for mercy. When we reached the manor, he hauled me through a dark, gaping side door, down endless stone corridors, and up a steep winding staircase until at last he threw me to the ground near a thick, iron-bound oak door. I scrabbled to my knees, seeking escape, but Matthew pushed me flat and planted a heavy foot upon my arm, pinning me in place. My sobs echoed from the walls as he took a large iron key from his pocket and fitted it into a well-oiled lock.

"Matthew, please, don't hurt me," I begged, terrified of what he would do to me in that room. "I'm sorry, Matthew. Please, don't do this."

He ignored me and threw open the door. The resounding crash reverberated in the air, and I pressed a hand to my ear. Matthew reached down, grabbed me by my hair and hauled me into the room. A dim lantern beside the door revealed it to be quite small, and round. He threw me against the curved wall opposite the door. I hit it with stunning force and lay still, the breath knocked from my body. Matthew knelt and grasped my right hand. A chain rattled, a cold, hard band closed around my wrist, a lock clicked sharp in the darkness. He grabbed my left hand.

"No! No, Matthew, don't!" I screamed, twisting and flailing my arms, hitting and kicking at him. My blows landed, for I heard him grunt and catch his breath, and his fingers jerked on my flesh. But his grip did not loosen as again a chain rattled and an iron band closed tight on my left wrist. Without a word, Matthew rose, took up the lantern and left the room. He slammed the solid oak door behind him and turned the key in the lock, imprisoning me in dead silence broken only by the rattle of chains, my sobbing pleas, and absolute darkness no eye could penetrate.

I grew truly mad then, fighting the chains on my wrists and the smothering darkness, entombed with only unbearable terror for company. For how long I was mad I am still not sure, but long weeks passed before I became aware of conscious thought. My memories of those weeks are fragmented, filled with horror and pain, numbing cold and raw despair. I remember the chains and the feel of the iron biting into me. Marks still linger on my wrists where skin and flesh were rubbed almost to the bone.

I remember being consumed by devouring horror and cowering like an animal in filthy straw, pulling it over my shuddering body as shelter from the piercing cold. I remember unremitting darkness, blackness that closed around me like a demonic entity, darkness barely relieved at day by what little light trickled down through two tiny air slits high near the top of the twenty-foot-tall walls.

I clawed at the stone that imprisoned me and screamed for hours on end, long wailing howls of wretchedness that rose to the slits and dissipated, unheard, on the fitful winds. And I attacked anyone who entered through the iron-banded door, shrieking incoherent curses, scratching and tearing with nails honed razor-sharp against the rock. I had no awareness of who entered. They were merely the enemy, my tormentors, jailers who hit me and hurt me in ways I shudder now to think of. I remember crouching near the wall whenever I would hear the key turn in the lock, glaring through the tangle of my hair, half naked, and springing out at whomever walked through the ominous gape of the open door. Like the wild animal I was treated as, I snarled and slavered and clawed in rage and fury and fear, wanting only to kill those who kept me imprisoned and tortured me so.

Yet the injuries I inflicted were minor, for my captors had freedom of movement and strength of body. And light to see by, lantern flames that blinded my light-starved eyes. The beatings I sustained on an almost daily basis left me bleeding senseless on the cold stone floor, my body so abused and pain filled that, had it not been for the numbing cold, I would have been unable to move at all. At long last I broke. My tormented spirit could take no more. I lay after the last fierce beating, my body throbbing, my cheek split open, unmoving for days, unaware of anything around me, not even myself. Where I went during that time I do not know, but there was no pain, no fear, no torment in that place. When at last I returned to the place of my imprisonment, I wept with despair and prayed to die.

When next the jail door swung open, I recognized the man standing there, lantern in hand, though I did not know who he was, he who had locked me in this chamber of agony. As he stepped slowly toward me, I scrabbled away on all fours, cowering against the curving wall, until the chains on my wrists caught me short and I could go no further. Terrified of another beating, I dug into the rancid straw, trying to cover myself from his sight. He stood staring down at me for a long time, his expression curious, lips pursed, while I mewled at his feet like an idiot, trying to hide myself behind the rat's nest of my hair. Then he turned on his heel and left, not having spoken a word.

And so the days inched onward, early summer turning to autumn as I cringed from the very jailers I had fought before. Mute and terrified, I crouched in mindless misery, gnawing at the gristly bones and scraps of fat they threw onto the disgusting straw once a day, dwelling in fear and despair, filled with disconsolate grief, not knowing who I was, not even sure if I was dead or alive. The memories are longer in the telling than in the recalling.

I do not know what would have become of me were it not for the bird, a tiny sparrow-like creature with bright eyes and quick movements. I woke one morning to find it sitting in the straw near my head. I lay curled like a baby, my body aching from the constant damp chill of the stone. I could barely see through the snarls of hair that covered my face. I do not know how long I lay staring at the bird, unmindful of its presence, but suddenly it moved, made a quick sideways jerk with its tail. My eyes blinked and focused. For the first time since the iron bands had closed upon my wrists, I became aware of something outside myself and the nightmare in which I lived.

While I lay motionless, watching, the bird ducked

its head and grasped a piece of straw in its beak. Its bright eyes seemed to fasten on mine as I stared, then it spread its wings and was gone. Unable to move—and having no earthly reason to do so—I lay still for a long time, my mind blank and unfeeling. Then once more I caught a flash of movement. The bird had returned. Again it grabbed a piece of straw and left. By the third time it returned, I had scraped the hair from my eyes and turned onto my back, so I could watch it disappear through one of the narrow slits near the high ceiling.

Freedom, I thought, as the bird rested in the narrow slit before flying out into the sky. It looked down at me from its high perch. *If only I could fly, too.* I thought of the blue sky and realized that it still existed beyond my dark confinement, sky I could no longer see, and knew it unlikely I ever would again. Or feel the sun on my face, or the wind in my hair.

"Stay a while," I whispered to the tiny creature so high above, my voice barely audible. "Don't leave me."

It might have stayed. But I lifted my hand, the chain clanked loud in the stone-hushed silence, and the bird swiftly vanished. I did not see it again. It is possible it may have returned while I slept, or at night when I could not see it come. I do not know. But I thought my heart would break when it took fright and flew away from me, abandoning me to the empty darkness.

Still, it left behind awareness of life. Awareness of self. After an endless, immobile silence, I turned my gaze to the chains on my wrists, touching the heavy links with wondering fingers, tracing them to thick rings set solid in the wall. For the first time I became fully aware of the chamber that was now my home—the darkness, the cold, the silence. A small chamber, no more than twelve feet in diameter, its circular wall was broken only by the massive iron-bound door, the iron rings near where I lay, and the two narrow slits high above me. Filthy, rancid straw covered the hard floor, the remains of yesterday's scraps scattered about a wooden bowl set in the center of the room.

A tower, I thought. He must have dragged me to the top of one of the towers, its room prepared months earlier for the endgame, a game that from the start I'd had no hope of winning. Looking down I touched the ragged, shredding fabric that covered a body grown emaciated from starvation, and remembered the night I'd been drugged, lured out onto the moor and steered to an open window, sword in hand—though I doubt that Matthew had anticipated my having a weapon.

I wept then for what I had done, the injuries I had caused, and for what had been done to me since. How long ago? Six months? A year? I had no way to know, and no expectation they would enlighten me. Hopelessness filled me, for I knew there was no way out. Matthew had what, for some arcane reason, he'd wanted all along: a wife homicidally insane who must be kept locked in a tower. That I wasn't insane mattered not at all. I doubted Matthew would ever let anyone near enough to me to discover the madness was a sham. I sighed and let my mind go blank again, the better to survive the deprivation I must now endure.

When the door at last swung open, the faint light from above had already begun to fade. I sat shivering against the wall, knees drawn up, arms wrapped around my body in a fruitless attempt to find warmth. She stood looking at me for long minutes before she sidled into the chamber, picked up yesterday's food bowl, set today's down. She pushed it closer to me with her foot, all without taking her eyes off me. I grimaced in disgust when I looked at what she had brought: two well-carved bones, bearing little other than fat and gristle, trimming scraps such as one would give a dog, and moldy bread. Without a word, she set a small water jug beside the bowl. There was no glass to drink from, no utensils of any kind. I looked up at her, but what protest had been in my mind vanished when I beheld the acid look on her face. Then she backed up into the doorway and turned to leave, and I had to speak.

"Mrs. Peele." I kept my voice soft, though it rasped a bit from disuse. She paused at the sound and looked over her shoulder at me. "I am so cold. Could I not have a blanket with which to cover myself? Please."

She merely stared at me, then slammed the door and plunged me into my familiar darkness, for the fading day had merged into full night while she was there. I wept again, curled down onto the straw, for I knew she would not return until the next night, and bring no blanket when she did. Would she bother to tell Matthew that my senses had returned? There was no way to tell. Nor any way to know how long she would wait to inform him, should she chose to do so. Given what she brought me to gnaw and suck on, and the increasing cold as the year waned, I could very well be dead long before Matthew knew of my simple request. At length I sat up and groped for the bowl of scraps. I gnawed on the nasty bones, unable to bring myself to eat much of the fat trimmings now that I was aware of what they were. Despite my aching hunger, I could not bring myself so much as touch the green bread. I tried to fill my stomach with the stale-tasting water, then lay down again on the reeking straw, shivering.

Matthew did come but I know not how long I waited. When immured in everlasting sameness, one has no way to judge the passage of time. I counted four times that the faint light above me waxed and waned, but I slept much of the time, and sat blank and unfeeling when I did wake, and so could easily have missed how often the day came and fled. It had nothing to do with me, and so it was difficult to take note of it.

He stood in the doorway, lantern in hand, watching as I blinked at the dim light that pierced my eyes like brilliant sunshine. His face was closed, hard and angry, but his eyes held deep satisfaction to see me in such straits. We stared at each other until finally I looked away, tears welling in my eyes. He was enjoying the charade. There would be no mercy from him.

"She said you seemed better." His quiet voice sounded over-loud in the deep silence. "I could not believe it. Are you rational again? For how long, this time?"

"You would know that better than I, for it is you who dictates the bouts of madness," I replied. Matthew pursed his lips, fighting the smile that threatened to break free. I sighed. "I am sorry for what happened to your friends, Matthew. I was not, as well you know, fully aware of what I was doing, or even that I held a sword. I did not want to hurt anyone, truly. I only wanted to be let go." I paused and looked at him. He was no longer smiling. "Did they recover?"

Matthew's lip lifted in a sneer. "After a fashion. Francis' leg has healed, he has merely a nasty scar to show for your night's work. But D'arcy." I looked into his dark, glittering eyes and cringed. "He has lost the use of his arm, Marina. He almost died before Bolton and I finally stopped the bleeding and he lay abed for weeks before finding strength enough to stand again. You have made him a cripple, Marina. A broken man."

I could not suppress the quick flush of satisfaction that flooded into me. Matthew growled and took a step closer to me, his fist raised.

"Do not ask for release, Marina. You will not get it, not from me. Not ever."

"I did not think so." I looked down at the chains on my wrists, the rotting straw on the hard floor, and back into Matthew's eyes. "But is this what I truly deserve for my part in events that were shaped by others, events beyond my control? Should I not at least have edible food, and decent clothing with which to cover myself? Will you really keep me chained like an animal in filthy, vermin-ridden straw for all my life?"

"Do you expect more, my love?"

"I shall die of the cold, Matthew, if I have no blanket," I looked away, unable to bear the amused expression on his face, "or of starvation without proper food. And I do not think you want that. Had you wanted me dead, I would be. You know where the truth of this lies, and it is not in madness although it almost was." I looked at him again and could not keep the pleading from my tone. "Have I not been punished enough for something I had no hand in?"

"No hand in?" He gave a cynical laugh. "Don't be absurd, Marina. It was most certainly your hand that nearly ended my friends' lives. What you suffer now is no more than what every murdering madwoman deserves."

"But I am not insane, Matthew, and you know it. I was for a while, I will admit, after you chained me in this dark hole. You had that much success, at least. But it didn't last, Matthew, it couldn't, because it was not real underneath. I am not insane and you cannot make me insane, though you can make me believe I am for a time. And make others believe it, also." I shook my head and held out my hands. Tears fell from my eyes as I stared at the chains. "This is no longer necessary,

Matthew. You have broken me. I'll not fight you anymore. You have won. My fate is in your hands, and I will bow to your will. Surely a locked door in a windowless prison is enough to serve your purpose, whatever it is." I looked up into his smiling face. "What more can the rest of this torture gain you?"

Matthew smiled. "Satisfaction."

I gasped as the cruelty behind the smile, the word, slammed into me. Again I shook my head. The chains clanked as I raised my hands to cover my face.

"No more, Matthew," I sobbed. "Please, no more."

Matthew watched me a moment longer, then stepped forward, knelt by my side in the filthy straw and drew me against him. When at last the despair lifted and my tears ceased, he wiped my face with his handkerchief and smiled at me with tenderness in his eyes.

"I will think on it, Marina. After all, this room will be here waiting for you if you do not cooperate fully, will it not?"

He rose and left without a backward glance. That night Mrs. Peele threw a coarse but warm blanket at me when she entered the cell. There was more meat on the scraps filling the bowl and no mold on the rock-hard bread. Still it was a long time before Matthew reappeared at my prison door, two or three weeks at least that to me felt like months. He motioned for me to rise and I struggled to obey, clinging to the wall for support for my weakness was extreme. Then he pulled a key from his pocket and released the chains from my wrists, binding my hands together with a length of coarse rope he'd brought with him. Without a word, he turned and dragged me, tripping and stumbling on unsteady legs, down the spiral stairs to a room on the ground floor of the tower.

It was almost identical to my prison at the top, except for the lower ceiling. The two slits here, at the top of the twelve-foot-high walls, were almost wide enough to be called windows, perhaps a foot across. Glass panes denied entry to the elements. The brightness that the slits let in, dim though it was, blinded my light-starved eyes, and I could barely see for blinking, though I glimpsed a minuscule patch of sky through one of them. A small wardrobe stood to the right of the door, a narrow bed opposite it. A wooden armchair sat to the right of the bed.

Matthew shoved me into the center of the room, where a hip bath stood waiting, steam rising from the hot water. I stared in disbelief while he untied my hands and yanked the sordid rags from my body, grimacing when he beheld the ridges in my breastbone, the ribs marching down my sides in bony arcs. His grabbed my face and turned it to him, his fingers digging into my cheeks hard enough to raise bruises.

"Clean yourself, Marina. You're a disgrace. Then dress yourself if you remember how. I will allow you to remain in this room as long as you cause no trouble and do exactly as you are told. Keep in mind that it is a very short walk up those stairs. And if I have to put you up there again, I will never let you out. Remember that."

He let me go with a small shove, and I collapsed onto the stone floor. Mrs. Peele appeared, her mouth stretched in a nasty grin as she beheld my naked, begrimed, emaciated body. Matthew gestured at the disgusting rags he'd peeled off me.

"Burn those. And bring her something to eat in one hour. Feed her twice a day from now on, and not inedible scraps. Something...adequate. After all, Mrs. Peele, she is my wife, and despite her unstable mental condition and her murderous rages, I am obligated to take care of her. Am I not?"

They smiled at each other. The housekeeper gathered the torn, dirty remnants of my once-elegant silk and satin nightclothes, and left. Chuckling, Matthew followed her, locking me into my new, more luxurious prison.

Chapter Twenty-three

Time again inched past my prison windows in an endless round of monotony. Boredom settled over my being like a pall, for there was nothing to do save pace the cold stone floor or sit in the hard chair and stare at black rock walls, or squint through the one window slit that afforded the merest glimpse of sky on the few days the sun appeared from behind the clouds. Even had Matthew allowed me books to read—he had laughed with great amusement when I asked, and left without a word—there was not enough light to read by even on the most cloudless days, when for a few short hours the sun stood highest in the heavens. As summer ended and autumn drew her chill skirts around the moor, sunny days grew very few, indeed. I was allowed no lamps or candles with which to keep the darkness at bay, and there was neither hearth nor fire to keep me warm.

The wardrobe held but four dresses, all of which hung on my skeletal frame. Two were coarse servant's costumes in gray and brown, rough and scratchy on my tender skin. The two others had arrived with me from London; the green wool I'd worn so much that fateful winter when Lady Cresswell had visited our shop, and the dark blue, long sleeved dimity, minus the pretty trims I'd had applied before my marriage. It seemed I was not to be allowed even the solace of feminine daintiness. They provided no underthings save one thin camisole and a plain, narrow petticoat, and no shoes, though I did discover a pair of flimsy slippers in the wardrobe. Grateful as I was for them, they offered little protection against the cold radiating from the damp floor, and my legs acquired a bone-deep ache that never fully abated even when I lay beneath the covers at night.

I had no nightclothes. As the nights grew increasingly cold, I slept fully clothed. Though my dresses ended wrinkled and unsightly, at least I was warm. My disheveled state greatly amused Mrs. Peele.

The hot water and soap that had greeted my arrival in this room did not reappear. Once a week I would splash my body with cold water, kneeling on the floor over a shallow basin. I knew that soon I would begin to feel as dirty as I had in the room above. But at least I maintained a modicum of cleanliness, and had warmer clothing than shredding rags, and a bed whose thin lumpy mattress was still softer than foul straw. And things no longer crawled in my hair. I was sure that when it became necessary, Matthew would provide enough hot water and soap to keep the vermin at bay.

Food arrived twice a day as Matthew had ordered, meager meals that, though overdone and cold, held more appeal than gristly bones, gelatinous fat and moldy bread. Though just this side of edible, I was grateful for them, for I knew how bony my body was, how close to starvation I had been. I ate as much as I could, picking at the food throughout the long, lonely hours, yet at first I could not finish even half of each meal. My body simply could not hold what was brought to me. Mrs. Peele took sadistic pleasure in beating me for wasting food, and threatened to reduce my rations to inedible scraps. My greatest fear was that she would tell Matthew I was not cooperating and he would again chain me to the wall at the top of the tower. It is only in looking back that I can see how Mrs. Peele orchestrated the opportunities to beat and terrify me. She never reduced my portions to what I could actually consume. No matter how much I forced into my shrunken stomach, there was always more than I could eat on the next meal tray.

How many weeks of her cruelty I endured before she tired of the game and informed Matthew of the "trouble" I was causing I do not know, but one season had blended into the next before he opened the chamber door and stood staring at me where I lay on the bed, nursing the painful cuts and bruises the latest beating had bequeathed. I looked at him, my heart sinking, knowing what his presence signified, though I didn't even have strength enough to cry.

Shaking his head, Matthew crossed the room and sat beside me on the bed. His surprisingly gentle hand smoothed back my hair as his cold, calculating eyes inspected the damage done to my face and shoulders. Finally, he sighed.

"Did I not advise you to cooperate, Marina? One would think you were born to make trouble. What have you done now to deserve this?"

"I cannot finish my food," I whispered. "I try, Matthew, I do try, but I had nothing but scraps for so long that my stomach cannot hold all she brings. I do not mean to be troublesome. I eat as much as I can, Matthew, until my stomach hurts, but I just cannot eat it all. Maybe if she brought just a little less…"

My voice trailed off as Matthew frowned and turned his head away from me. I wanted to beg, to plead not to be dragged back up those stairs, but I could not find the breath or will to form the words, for I knew they would do no good. Matthew would do what he would do, no matter what I said or how I pleaded. It was his game, and he set the rules.

He looked back at me, picked up my hand, examined the ring of raw, scabbed flesh around my wrist. I could not breathe.

"Whatever happens, my dear, it is your own fault. I did warn you to be obedient." He rose. I looked up to see a sarcastic smile on his lips. His eyes were so cold and impersonal. "I will discuss it with Mrs. Peele, and then decide."

I did not watch him leave. Despair held me in

thrall until the slam of the door broke through and released my pent up terror. It was hopeless. If Matthew were to judge by Mrs. Peele's biased words, I would end in chains by nightfall. I cried a long time, hugging the thin pillow to my face to muffle the sound, until at length I fell asleep. It was almost full dark when the sound of the key in the lock jerked me awake.

Matthew had returned. I would be dragged up the stairs and entombed in that vile room forever. I couldn't bear the thought. My heart hammering, I scrambled up and cowered against the headboard, wishing I could disappear into the wood. If he took me up there, if he again closed the chains on my wrists, I knew I would not survive. I could barely hold on here, in this semi-civilized isolation. If that little were taken from me, if I was once again chained to the wall with only straw for my bed and unremitting darkness for a companion, my mind would truly desert me. I pressed my hands to my lips to keep from screaming as the door swung open.

It was not Matthew who stood there, backlit by the dim lantern in the corridor. Nor was it Mrs. Peele. It hesitated a moment, this stooped figure, then it sidled with shuffling steps into my prison chamber.

"Who is it?" I asked, my voice trembling with fear. The figure froze. The head turned toward me. I caught sight of a humped back, huge terrified eyes, unkempt stringy hair. I gasped. "Mary? Is it you?"

The sound of my voice saying her name caused her to jibber with fear. Her shaking hands almost dropped the tray she held. The sight of the half-wit cripple astounded me. I had seen no one but Mrs. Peele and Matthew for long months, and expected to see no one but them for the rest of my life. Indeed, I had forgotten the existence of this poor child who also suffered beneath Matthew's roof.

Mary set the dinner tray on the floor far from where I crouched on the bed, snatched up the morning tray then lurched through the door, dragging her club foot and whimpering like a baby. The door slammed shut and the lock turned before I could recover my senses.

My heart ached as I stared at the door, for I realized the poor child was terrified of me, the crazy woman in the tower. I could well imagine what she had been told, and what she might even have seen that night on the moor and heard in the tower since then. For a moment I wondered that they would send her to this duty, young and frightened as she was. Then I remembered how Mary was treated in this house—like a valueless slave, beaten and abused at every turn— and had my answer.

Sighing, I slid from the bed and groped my way to where she had left the tray. I carried it over to the hard chair, my steps cautious in the darkness, where I sat and held it on my lap. I could not see what the plates held, but that was of no consequence. I was now well used to not being able to see, having spent so much time shut in inky darkness, and it did not disturb me to explore with my hands. The plate on the tray held less than half of what Mrs. Peele had piled upon my previous plates. I knew I would have no trouble finishing what had again become, if not truly meager, then just barely enough to curb my hunger. I had, of course, to eat with my fingers, for utensils were still forbidden me. Indeed, I never expected to hold a fork or spoon in my hands again. Whatever the reason for the game, Matthew was playing for keeps.

While I ate I thought about Mary, the Peeles' young granddaughter, who I estimated to be about twelve or thirteen years of age. No one had told me of her existence. I had thought Mrs. Peele and Giles the only servants attending to the huge manor house. The first time I'd seen her was in the corridor outside the library. I had been seeking Matthew, my drugged state making me half-crazed, when I came upon her as she exited the room. The heavy bucket of ash she carried bowed and twisted her body into a grotesque shape magnified by the drug and my guttering candle. The dragging clubfoot in its coarse cloth wrapping made a slushing sound that echoed from the surrounding stone. Fitful candlelight glistened on the saliva drooling down her chin when she lifted her head and looked at me and I had panicked, screaming and cowering against the dark wall as the horrifying apparition had loomed closer, shrieking itself as though it would devour me, when all Mary sought, in her own shock and fear, was escape. Matthew and Mrs. Peele had come running, Matthew to carry me to my bed and feed me more laudanum-laced sherry, Mrs.

Peele to drive off the unfortunate child with her fists and haranguing words.

I saw her only a few times after that, for she was not allowed above stairs and I rarely left my room. When I did see her I had hoped to speak with her, to apologize for my screaming fit, but each time she saw me she had run away and hid. I was glad she did, for my courage failed me when again I beheld her obscene form. I had not until today seen her without the opiate coursing in my blood. She did not now appear as hideous as she had then.

I wondered if she would come again, or if her terror of me would overcome her need to escape Mrs. Peele's beatings. I wanted to see her in what passed for morning light oozing through the window slits, for the brief shadowy glimpse I'd just had led me to believe she was not at all the monster I had thought her to be. And I wanted to tell her I was sorry for the way I had caused her to be treated. No one, no matter what they had done or how they had been born, deserved the treatment either of us received in this hellhole.

Mary did come again, twice every day, for Mrs. Peele no longer brought my food. I saw the housekeeper only when she came to change the bedding, or brought the washbasin, her canny eyes like ice, daring me to be stupid. I stayed as far away from her fists as I could.

I was still abed when Mary returned the next morning, for the ache in my body and my fear of the room above had kept me awake most of the night. I watched in silence as the girl, brown hair dangling in filthy strings around her face, a shapeless dress of coarse brown wool hanging sack-like from her hump-twisted shoulders, set the breakfast tray on the floor and picked up the dinner tray which I had placed near the doorway the night before. She kept darting quick, fearful glances at me, poised ready for flight should I so much as move my head. Not until she had almost disappeared through the door did I speak.

"Thank you, Mary."

She froze at the sound of my soft voice, her shoulders hunching as though I had hit her. Then she scurried out and slammed the door. Sighing, I rose as the key turned in the lock. I lifted the tray, sat in the hard chair and ate slowly while my gaze traced over and over the dark planes of the stone.

The day dragged on, towing me with it, the leaden sky outside the window slits hoarding what little light there was. I passed the long hours of shadowy limbo in the chair, sitting motionless, trying to keep my mind blank. Somehow it seemed easier if I did not think. There was no sound all day save my own breathing, until Mary unlocked the massive oak door as the day was fading.

Day after day I watched her bring my trays, saying only, "Thank you," each time she left the bleak chamber. She showed no sign that her fear had eased. She was not, as I had thought, grotesque at all, though her body twisted due to the lump on her back and the club foot, and she drooled down her chin. Her eyes, though, were bright and alert beneath the dirty tangle of her hair, and I suspected that, cleaned up, with her hair washed and decent clothing on her body, she would be presentable at least.

Sometimes she would stand a moment looking at me as I sat in the chair or on the bed, and I wondered what she was thinking. Matthew had said she was dumb, and an idiot. She had never spoken, and could neither read nor write, not that anyone in that household had ever attempted to teach her, I was sure. I realized she was as much a prisoner in her feeble-minded body as was I in this thick-walled room.

One morning a few weeks after she had begun to bring my trays, I noticed the way her stare lingered on the cinnamon bun that sat on the tray she carried. I knew it would be stale and cold, and I felt little inclination to eat it, unusual a treat though it was, but from the intense longing I saw on Mary's face I wondered for the first time what she was given to eat, if she had ever before tasted even a stale sweetened bun. I smiled at her from the chair where I sat—if I were not there or in the bed when she arrived, she would not enter the room—and spoke very gently, very softly.

"Would you like to share my cinnamon roll, Mary? It's all right, I only want a small taste of it. I'd like you to have the rest, so it will not go to waste. Please."

She stood motionless, her gaze darting from me to the open doorway to the sweetened bun and back to me. Whimpering, her hands shaking, she all but dropped the tray on the floor before snatching up the empty tray and lurching through the door. Another endless day dragged on as I sat drowning in silent emptiness, but when Mary returned at dusk the icing on the bun I'd left for her glimmered in the light spilling in from the lantern she'd left in the hall.

She stood still, staring at the tray, her head bent.

"I saved it for you, Mary. Just for you. I hope you like it," I whispered from beneath the bedcovers.

I smiled at her but she did not look up. Finally, she stooped, picked up the tray and left. She neither touched the bun nor looked at me. I cried myself to sleep that night.

More time passed. I lost track, for each day and night seemed eternal in their sameness, and my ability to tell them apart failed as another autumn progressed and the skies grew constantly leaden, covered with clouds almost as dark as the stone surrounding me. I dwelled in never-changing twilight, not able to see across the room through the gathered shadows. The oppressive silence vanished, the dark now populated with the rising, fitful winter moorland wind. Not even my thick prison walls could keep it out.

I continued to talk to Mary though I had no hope of response from the mute girl. She provided a diversion, something besides darkness and stone. I also feared that the elongating isolation, and the silence now spiked with the moaning wind, was eroding my soul. As each day passed the ones before with uniform sameness, I began to feel pieces of myself slipping away. My world had shrunk to the size of this room. Nothing existed save silence and shadow and wind. The periodic invasion of Mary and Mrs. Peele left less and less impact, for neither spoke to me, nor even looked at me. I felt completely invisible in their presence, as though I no longer existed in corporeal form. Once they left I even found myself doubting their existence.

Black-haired Matthew retreated deep into the shadowy recesses of memories I rarely accessed, for he no longer came at all. As time went on and the stone walls began to feel familiar, almost safe, in their isolating coldness, I feared that soon my true jailer would become not the iron lock on the door nor the Matthew-man outside it, but my own mind. Would I someday find my small world so comforting in its stone embrace that I would refuse to leave it even were the door left open wide?

It was perhaps two months or so after I had first offered Mary the bun that she arrived to find me pacing the floor in nervous agitation. She stood in the doorway, her brown eyes solemn on my restless movements, but, stirred by the rising wind, I could not settle. Finally, knowing she would not enter until I did, I walked over and stood behind the chair, clutching the high, carved back.

"Please do not be frightened of me, Mary. I'll not harm you. I am just restless today, that is all. The wind scares me when it howls like this. It almost seems alive." I laughed, walked around the chair, and sat down and gripped its arms. "But it is not, is it? That is just my silly imagination. So, what have you brought me, tonight? Something special?"

Slowly, Mary crossed the room and laid the tray, which held nothing but plain, common fare, on my lap. I sat frozen, afraid even to breathe, and kept my gaze on the plates.

"Oh, yes. This looks good. I shall enjoy this very much. Thank you, Mary, you are very good to me."

I looked up then and gave her a hesitant smile, but her expression of trepidation did not alter. She backed away, picked up the morning's tray and moved to the door, where she paused and looked back at me. I could not help myself; tears filled my eyes and traced down my cheeks.

"I am not crazy, Mary," I half whispered. "Truly I am not. I know how it seems, what he wants everyone to believe, but my being locked away like this does not make me crazy, any more than your twisted back and lame foot makes you an idiot. We neither of us belong here, Mary. Neither of us."

Without so much as a blink of her eyes, Mary turned and shut me into my bleak life once again.

The next morning, however, Mary accepted my offer of a slice of raisin bread, standing near the bed while she ate and I talked to her of whatever came into my mind. As the days passed I told her about Uncle Jacob and the bookshop, and about Mollie and Eamon's tea shop and the wonderful treasures to be found within it.

She always stood and she never spoke, though she listened with wide eyes, and stayed only long enough to finish whatever food I shared with her. Then she scurried quickly out the door as though frightened to be away from her other duties for too long. They were wonderful days, for the look of awed wonder on her face and the shy, hesitant smile on her lips bolstered my flagging courage and gave me something to look forward to, silent and abbreviated as her visits were. Until the day Mrs. Peele discovered us and put an end to the only little happiness and hope I had.

"Here, Mary, try the scone," I said, handing her the hard round cake—hard, because I was never given anything that was not either stale or old or overcooked. I sat on the bed and she stood near its foot, nodding her delight at the slightly sweet taste of the raisin-laden dough. Suddenly, Mrs. Peele swooped into the room and grabbed Mary by her hair, spinning her around and cuffing her ears with an iron-hard hand. She threw her toward the door. Mary staggered and fell, skidding on the hard floor, skinning her hands and arms. She lay in the doorway curled on her side, sobbing.

"Get out'f here, you little rat!" Mrs. Peele shouted. "An' 'f I catch you stealing food again, or talkin' to this crazy woman, I'll beat ye until ye can't move! Go on, get out!"

I rose, indignation flashing in my eyes. Mary scrambled to her feet and loped from the room, still sobbing. I spoke without thinking, anger ringing in my voice.

"That was uncalled for, Mrs. Peele. Mary stole nothing, I gave her the scone. And she has never said one word to me. It was I who spoke to her."

The housekeeper turned and laid the back of her hand across my face. I dropped down on the bed and she hit me again, three times, then caught my wrists in her hard hands and pinned them to the mattress on either side of my head. She leaned over me and growled, her face inches from mine.

"Don' use that tone with me, missy! Don't ye even speak to me! Are ye forgettin' who ye are, where ye are? An' what I can do to ye?" She let go of one wrist and closed her clawed hand on my face, digging her nails into my cheeks. I gasped in pain that clouded my eyes with dark sparks. "If y'ever speak to my granddaughter, or even look at her, do anythin' to corrupt her with yer insanity, I'll tell his lordship 'ow much trouble ye've been causin', how much I've overlooked! Ye know what he'll do to ye then, don' ye? Where ye'll end up?" She took her hands away, then hit me again, rocking my head to the side. "Don' ye push me, missy! And don' make the mistake of thinkin' I won' do it. It'll be the last mistake y'ever make!"

She whirled and left the room, leaving me half-conscious on the bed, my breakfast spilled onto the blankets around me. There was no food brought for three days.

I did not speak to Mary again after that. We barely looked at each other, fearing that Mrs. Peele lurked in the hallway, and would beat us again for that much contact—or go to Matthew. Mary's face turned purple from the punishment her grandmother had meted out that night, and I knew my own face bore both discolorations and cuts from her vicious hands.

For long, silent weeks I paced, pursued by the strengthening wind, feeling the empty darkness chip away relentlessly at my soul. I would find myself pressed against the stone wall with no memory of how long I had been standing there, and spent endless hours in the hard, uncomfortable chair staring at the dark clouds streaming past the window slits high above, looking desperately for a patch of blue sky to give me hope. It never came.

At last I could stand no more. I broke, my heart shedding tears of blood for every drop of water that fell from my eyes. Curling down onto the cold damp floor, bundled in the blanket I'd wrapped around myself in a vain attempt to keep the chill away, I sobbed, desolate, abandoned, all hope gone. I wanted to die. I begged to die. Why had Matthew not simply killed me out there on the moor? It would have been the kinder thing to do. I was, I estimated, only twenty-five or -six years old and could see nothing ahead but thirty or more years of continuing torture, long bleak years of barren isolation and silent, cold stone walls.

My will failed. I would not survive the coming winter, I knew that, not with my spirit intact. Already huge pieces had crumbled away. Soon there would be only a shell left, a shell called Marina, a shell that held no identity, no humanity, a shell that no one loved and no one wanted. Walled up for a lifetime. Anguished misery consumed me and I sobbed on as the dismal light faded. It grew midnight-dark earlier with each passing day.

I did not hear the key turn in the lock, nor the hinges squeak when the door pushed open. Nor did I see the light shed by a lantern that entered the cell with whoever carried it. A soft touch on my shoulder made me gasp. I froze and held my breath.

"You… hurt?"

The words were hesitant, barely audible, the voice deep and scratchy. I turned my head and peered through my tangled hair, blinking my swollen, throbbing eyes to clear them, and gasped again. Mary! Had I truly heard her speak?

"What?" I whispered.

"You... hurt?"

I *had* heard her speak, her voice rusty with disuse. She was not dumb, as everyone thought, and far from an idiot. Indeed, she was bright enough to hoard a secret from those who enslaved her, and thereby snatch a tiny piece of autonomy from their cruel hands. I sat up, scraping my hair from my wet face, wiping my tears with my hands. I looked at the doorway. Mary rose, picked up the lantern and went to the door to look up and down the hallway. She closed the door and returned again to crouch at my side.

"Not there. You hurt?"

"No. No, Mary, I'm just sad. I do not want to be

here, in this room, but they will never let me go. They've even taken you away from me. I'll never have anything more than these walls, and loneliness. No one to talk to me but the wind."

Tears began again as I spoke. There was no way to stop them.

"Do you see up there, Mary, those two tiny windows? That is all they have left me of the world out there, and now even the blue sky is gone, covered by dark clouds all day. I've not one tiny thing to hold onto anymore. I will never stand beneath the sky again, or feel the wind in my hair or the sun on my face. Matthew will keep me in here forever, in the cold and the dark, until I cease to exist. They all believe him, that I am crazy, that I deserve to be locked away like this. I want to be free, I want to live, but there's no one to help me. No one will ever help me."

Sobbing, I curled back onto the floor, muffling my cries with the blanket. I felt again madness lurking close, and it was so tempting to simply go into the oblivion within its empty reaches, to extinguish my soul, surrender my spirit to the ebony darkness of non-being. Mary's warm hand on my shoulder pulled me back from the brink.

"I help."

Shocked, I sat up.

"Mary, no. You can't help me. They will hurt you if you try."

She shook her head.

"I help."

"Mary, please, don't do anything. There is no need. It is only a fit of sadness brought on by the winter wind," I lied. "It will pass. In a little while I'll be all right."

"No. I help."

"Oh, please, Mary, I don't want you to." I grasped her hands but she pulled them back. "You know how cruel they are, they'd not hesitate to kill you. How could I stand it if you were hurt because of me? There is nothing you can do to help, anyway. They're too strong, you can't fight them, no one can. But I thank you for wanting to. It helps knowing that at least one person cares about me. It takes the sadness away. It truly does." I reached out and embraced her, pressed my lips to her cheek. "Go, now, before you are missed and Mrs. Peele comes looking for you."

She climbed to her feet, grabbed the morning tray and lantern and left, locking me again into the absolute blackness. After a while I pulled the dinner tray close and began to nibble on the barely tepid food. As I ate I thought about what had just happened, the miracle of Mary speaking to me, and I prayed she would not do anything foolish because of my self-pitying tears.

She did nothing foolish, but she did help. Two days later I found a small stone on the morning tray, a stone that glittered with mica flecks even in the faint, overcast light. A tiny sprig of heather lay beneath a bowl the next day, and a short brown and white feather the next. Day by day I found new things: a three-inch-long stick with a pretty pattern in its bark; another stone whose beauty was released when submerged in water; a small unhatched egg from a bird's abandoned nest. I smiled with gratitude at that sweet, wonderful child for, since I could not go out to it, she was bringing the world in to me. Fluffy down from a chick in the barnyard joined the growing collection in the bottom of the wardrobe, and a lock of coarse hair from a horse's mane. Then came a butterfly, a tiny flower, a stalk from the basil that grew in the kitchen garden, and a leaf from the tall hedges lining the drive.

The gifts were always on the morning trays, for Mary knew the darkness in my cell was so absolute at night, I would not have been able to enjoy what she'd brought for long hours should they come at supper time. She even thought of that.

Each object brought me endless hours of enjoyment as I pictured the plant, animal or garden from which it came, stroking my fingers on the varied surfaces, feasting my eyes on the diverse colors, breathing in the aroma of freedom and life. She also made sure each item was small enough to hide easily within my hand should Mrs. Peele unexpectedly throw open the door. For the first time since I awoke to find my Matthew gone, I felt a flicker of joy and hope.

The weather continued to worsen. The cold intensified. I sat wrapped in my blanket most of the time, shivering, dreading the dead of winter. I feared I would not survive with only the one blanket, and so found the courage to ask Mrs. Peele for a second. She worked on, stripping the bed as though I had not spoken. No second blanket made its appearance in my icy chamber. I wondered how long I had been imprisoned, how many months. Or years. I had no way of knowing, and dared not ask Mrs. Peele. Had Matthew come, I would have asked him, but he had been absent in my life since he had come that one time about the food. I had to be satisfied with wondering.

The winds grew in strength, keened mournfully around the tower, and not even Mary's gifts could insulate me fully from the disquieting sound. I paced more, my nerves jumping, and slept poorly at night, restless, my dreams haunted by the unceasing wails vibrating in the stone, the memories of the wispy phantom who had called my name and beckoned me onto the moor. I was tormented by the insidious cold, my body now so chilled I could no longer escape even in the depths of the bed. And yet, somehow, I did not hear the key turn in the lock late that night, nor the faint squeal of the hinges as the door slowly swung open. Neither did the dim light from a shielded lantern penetrate through my closed eyelids. I knew nothing but restless dreams until a hard hand clamped over my mouth, jerking me roughly from sleep.

Chapter Twenty-four

"Lie still. Don't make a sound."

A man's harsh whisper. I grabbed at the hand over my mouth, trying to push away the strong, unyielding fingers. His other arm pressed on my body, keeping me pinned to the bed. I could feel his breath, hot on my face.

"Do you understand? Don't scream. I'll take my hand away if you promise to be quiet."

My heart thumped, one tremendous, painful jerk. That voice! My eyes widened, probed the shadows cast by the faint lantern light, but could not penetrate the thick shadows that obscured his face.

"Do you promise?"

I could barely hear the almost-soundless voice. I nodded and he lifted his hand.

"Matthew," I whispered. I could scarcely credit it. Matthew, *my* Matthew, come at last to me in my dreams, a dream so real it took my breath away. "Matthew?"

"Yes, my love, it is me."

He gathered me into his arms, so strong, so reassuring. I raised my hands to his face and gasped. A soft, bushy beard covered his features. Long hair fell to mask his face. This was not Matthew, not *my* Matthew. It was not a dream, it was a nightmare. I stiffened in panic and he clamped his mouth on mine to stifle my scream. I fought his embrace, but the strong arms pressed me tight to his chest until suddenly the feel of his lips penetrated the fog of fear enveloping me.

This *was* my Matthew. I could never mistake his lips, the sweetness of kisses that sent shivers of ecstasy into me, the feel of his caressing hands, the beat of his heart. Why he came to me in this guise I did not know, but I did not care. It was enough that he was here. I stopped struggling. My arms came up and wound around his neck and I kissed him back, tears seeping from beneath my closed lids.

"Oh, Matthew," I sighed when at last he broke the kiss, "I have waited so long for you. Don't ever leave me again. I shall die if you do, die in this room of dark madness without your arms to hold me."

I buried my face in his chest, unable to speak further, my heart breaking. I knew this beautiful dream was but an illusion, a cruel delusion that I feared would crush me when it vanished with the morning light.

I had clung to the vague, misty memories of my Matthew since that first might in the library, but he had never seemed so real before. To feel again his arms around me, his lips on mine, only to lose them in the light of day, would surely push me into the madness that lurked awaiting me in the ghostly wind. Knowing the time was short, that dawn would soon lighten the sky and end the dream, I tightened my arms around his neck, desperately trying to keep him from vanishing by the strength of my hold. He rocked me, stroking my hair, whispering soothing words of comfort quietly into the darkness. At length he loosened my arms and held me away from him.

"Hush, my love, be still now. We must hurry if we are to be far away before dawn."

"Away, Matthew? What do you mean? I cannot leave this room, not ever."

"Yes, you can, my darling. And Palmerston will never touch you, never hurt you again, I promise. Hurry now, Marina. Dress quickly and be very quiet. I have a carriage waiting."

"A carriage?"

I was completely bewildered. I had expected him to kiss me and then disappear back into the mists of memory, not speak of leaving my prison and waiting carriages. Mystified, I turned my head and saw the shielded lantern that stood on the floor nearby, the door that gaped open, the gleam of the stone that lined the corridor beyond—a deep ebony slash of freedom slicing through the cold thick walls of my prison cell.

"Darling, please, we must hurry," Matthew urged again, stroking my cheek with tender fingers. I turned wondering eyes back to him.

"You're really here? You are not simply an illusion, a dream? You are real?"

"Yes, my love, I am real." He laughed softly, pushing my hair away from my wet face. "I have come to rescue you, Marina, and it will be much easier now than in a few hours when the house is once more astir. Please, you must get dressed."

I was still not quite convinced this was not a dream, but even if it was, I was willing to follow it— follow Matthew—wherever it led.

"There is no need, Matthew. It is so cold at night with no fire that I sleep with all my clothes on, even my slippers. I am ready now."

I threw off the covers and slid from the bed into Matthew's arms. He held me close for a moment, then took my hand and led me toward the open doorway. Halfway there he stopped to pick up the lantern, and I slipped my hand from his.

"Wait, Matthew. I must get something."

"Hurry, my love."

I crossed swiftly to the wardrobe and took out the blue dimity dress, tore away a sleeve and knotted one end. Then I dropped into the makeshift sack the wonderful gifts Mary had so lovingly given me. Whether I was venturing into full madness or into freedom, I needed to have them, have Mary's love, with me. A moment later, dress replaced and wardrobe doors closed, I returned to where Matthew waited, lantern in hand, his gaze searching the darkness of the stone corridor beyond the room.

"We will have to move carefully, for I dare not let out any more light," he said as he cradled my hand in his.

"That matters not, Matthew, for I have not had much more light than this by day, and none at all at night for long, long months. It is quite bright enough for me."

He looked at me, frowning questions on his face, anger in his eyes. His body stiffened. But he did not ask. Instead, with a sharp inhale of breath he turned and led me down the dark corridors, through the deserted kitchen and out a side door into the kitchen garden. Extinguishing the lantern, he pulled me close against the thick, dark wall of the house.

"We cannot risk any light out here, it would show for miles even dim as it is," he explained. "Just pray the moon does not come out from behind the clouds and flood the moor. There will be no concealment for us if it does, and anyone astir in the house will see us."

I nodded, shivering, wishing I had a warm shawl to add to the thin wool of my dress. Matthew saw, removed his coat and buttoned it about me, smiling at the sight of me in the huge garment. But it was thick, and warmed from his body heat, and I was grateful for it. We set off hand-in-hand, circling around the sprawling stables and outbuildings, then striking at an oblique angle across the flat moor to where Matthew said he had left his horse in a shallow gully. The carriage, he said, waited on the road a mile further on.

"Matthew," I asked as the house grew smaller

behind us and my courage increased, "how did you know I was in the tower? And how could you open the lock?"

"You can thank your little crippled friend for that, Marina." He grasped my arm and helped me over a small outcrop of rock. I could feel my slippers shredding beneath my feet. It was that more than anything that convinced me of the reality of my Matthew's presence and our flight from the Matthew-man. "I've been out here hiding on the moor for more than a week, watching the house, hoping for a glimpse of you, for a way to get you away from him. I had no idea he'd locked you away so soon; it is less than two years since I left you. I stumbled upon her behind the barns. She had stepped on a briar and was sitting on the ground, crying. I pulled the thorn from her foot, praying she would not then scramble up and run to her master to tell about me. But she just sat there, staring at me, then she said, 'You *my* Matthew? I help.' It was she who told me where you were being kept, and she who gave me the key."

"*Mary* gave you the key? Oh, Matthew, you don't know what risk she took. She—ow!"

A sharp stone cut into my foot, for the fabric of the slippers had worn completely through. They hung now in tatters about my ankles. Matthew swung me up into his arms and I sighed, grateful for the strong arms that held me, the warmth of his body close to mine. He kissed my cheek and I wrapped my arms around his neck.

"We must take Mary with us, Matthew. They will kill her if they discover she has helped me to escape. I would rather return to that room than leave her in such danger. You must go back and get her."

"There is no need." Matthew grunted softly as he carried me down into a small, rocky depression. "She's with the horse, waiting for us."

A moment later he set me down beside a huge, dark gelding. Mary rose, her humped figure a fearful sight in the clinging shadows, for the sack-like garment she wore billowed in the sharp wind.

"Oh, Mary!" I fell to my knees and embraced her shivering body. Tears fell down my face. "Thank you, Mary. Thank you." I rose and wiped the tears from my cheeks. "You are coming with us, Mary. I'll not leave you behind. You are free, too, Mary."

Her head lifted, a wondrous smile growing on her face. She nodded and turned to Matthew, her hand extended.

"Key. I return key so they not chase soon. Back quick."

"No, Matthew, don't let her. She'll be caught."

"But she's right, Marina. If she re-locks the tower door and replaces the key, they will not know anything is amiss until midmorning. Mary told me your tray is not sent until all the morning chores are finished. It is worth a half-hour delay if it gains us a few more hours."

"Then go with her, Matthew. Take care of her. I could not bear it if she was hurt."

"All right, my love," he agreed, smiling at me. He held me close for a moment, then reached into a pocket and withdrew his watch. "Take this. If we are not back in half an hour, get on the horse and ride straight that way." He pointed east. "When you reach the road, turn left. The carriage is about a half mile further on. There is money hidden beneath the seat. When the road forks, take the coast road, the left fork, and wait at the White Gull Inn. If we are not there by tomorrow morning, keep going, Marina. All the way to London. Promise me."

I nodded, knowing I would go nowhere without him or Mary. He kissed me, a quick, rough, passionate kiss that left Mary giggling behind her hand.

"Don't wander around, you'll cut your feet to ribbons." He caressed my face. "We'll purchase shoes in the first town we come to."

And they were gone, swallowed quickly by the dark night. I stood still, straining to hear the sound of their footsteps, but the moaning wind drowned all sign of their passage beneath its mournful wail. I stood beside the gelding, shivering, leaning my head against his warm neck, praying for their safe return. Time crawled by—ten minutes, fifteen, twenty, twenty-five—minutes filled with keening wind and fitful moonlight that gleamed from behind racing clouds. Thirty minutes, thirty-five. I looked up, searching for stars. Had Matthew and Mary failed to return the key in secret? Had they been caught? If I ended in the Matthew-man's clutches again, chained at the top of the tower, I wanted one last glimpse of heaven's lanterns to keep the memory of hope alive. But the shrouded skies gave me no sign of stars. The fitful moon again fled behind the thickening cloud cover, leaving me in darkness with only shredding nerves and the wind.

Forty minutes. The moon again danced out from behind the clouds. Which Matthew would emerge from the darkness, which would hold my life in his hands? Forty-five, fifty, fifty-three minutes. A twig snapped, a stone rattled down the slope into the gully. Gasping, I whirled and pressed against the horse. The moon slid behind the clouds and blackness again clamped down. The wind fell. Eerie silence enshrouded the moor. A boot scraped over stone, echoing in the stillness. A huge shadow, monstrous, misshapen, detached itself from the surrounding darkness, stalked slowly closer. I shook my head, fearing the nightmare phantom had again come for me. And then it spoke, its voice a harsh, angry growl.

"Marina!"

I could not speak. Matthew? It must be. But which one?

"Why are you still here? I told you not to wait."

I cried out in relief. It was Matthew, *my* Matthew. He swung Mary down from his arms and clasped me close, his strong embrace helping to still my trembling.

"I could not leave you behind, neither of you," I said, blinking into his beloved face. Then I looked at Mary. "Is she hurt? Why were you carrying her? And what took you so long? I was so afraid you would not return, that I'd never see you again."

"Hush, my love, everything is all right. Mary is fine, it was simply faster to carry her, that is all. Here." He beckoned Mary closer. "She brought you these."

The moon again flooded the night with its brightness. Mary handed me a pair of walking boots. They were my own boots, kept in the wardrobe in my old room, the room beside that in which the black-haired Matthew slept. I stared at her, stunned at the risk she had taken, until Matthew pushed me down onto a rock and dusted off my feet.

"That's what took so long," he said as he laced the boots tight. "Mary detoured upstairs to find you shoes to wear. By the time I got her out of there, the damned moon kept coming out and we had to lie on the ground until it was dark and we could move in safety again. I thought for sure we'd either be seen, or dawn would break before we could make it back here. Come on." He pulled me to my feet. "It's very late. We have to hurry."

Mary sat on the horse and I walked with Matthew until my feeble strength failed and he set me behind her. Less than twenty minutes later we struck the road, turned left, and in another ten minutes came upon the waiting carriage. Matthew tucked Mary and me snug beneath a thick wool rug and hitched the horse beside its patient companion. I was almost asleep when he climbed onto the driver's bench in front of us and smiled back at me. Mary's head lay on my shoulder.

"I love you, Marina," Matthew declared softly. He turned back to the horses and snapped the reins. The carriage gave a sharp jolt and rolled quickly down the rutted road. My lids continued to droop despite the rough ride, and in minutes I was fast asleep.

I woke to the sunrise, memory flooding back as I blinked against the strengthening light. The morning dawned more quickly than my light-starved eyes could adjust to, and I sat with lids closed for long minutes until I felt able to open them without pain or tears. Mary's head lay in my lap and I tucked the thick blanket tighter around her for her dress, coarse though it was, gave even less protection against the cold than did mine. Idly I stroked back her snarled, dirty hair and looked up to study the broad back in front of me, the shoulders straining at the coat I'd given back to him when we had reached the carriage.

Who are you? I wondered, remembering the joy of his strong arms, the sweetness of his lips, the gentleness of his hands on my body. I had given him my love, surrendered my soul into his care, trusted him with my life, and yet I did not know him at all. He had betrayed me, delivered me into an endless nightmare. He was not the Matthew I had loved, but a stranger who had walked away as though I meant nothing, as though my heart, my mind, my being had no value. Now he had returned, to end the nightmare. 'I love you, Marina,' he had said. But if he truly did, would I be here now?

We pushed on through the day, not stopping at

the White Gull he had earlier mentioned, for he wanted as much distance as possible between us and Stoneleigh before we rested. He had brought food, cold meats, bread, cheese and wine, and we ate while the carriage still rolled on the moor above the wild channel coastline far below. I watched the bleak, barren winter landscape speed past the carriage on the right, and studied the way the dense fog obscured the water to our left, and refused to meet his eyes when he looked back at me. My need to hold onto the image of 'my Matthew' slowly eroded away beneath the open skies. The cold breeze and cloud-shrouded light scoured the fantasy from the painful reality that lay below it. As dusk again descended on the eerie, wild moor, I realized that he could never be 'my Matthew' again. The myth had remained behind within those thick stone walls, with the dark and the cold and the chains. I had no room left now in my life for illusion, not even the illusion of love.

Three hours later, near nightfall, we stopped at the Red Dory Inn and Matthew procured rooms for us. When Mary and I woke the next morning, I ordered a bath and scrubbed clean her pitiful body and ragged hair. She was not, as I had once thought, a big girl. That was an illusion created by the ugly sack dresses she wore, for the body beneath was rail-thin and covered with scars from years of abuse, the bones narrow and delicate-looking. Her face, beneath the dirt and free now of the mortal fear in which she'd spent her life, was almost pretty, with pale skin soft and flawless on gently rounded cheeks and chin, a small straight nose and large dark brown eyes under gracefully arching brows. Her lips were uneven, the lower one over-full and inclined to droop open, but she no longer drooled as she had in that house. An ugly scar, left by a vicious beating in the past, no doubt, marred the soft roundness of her jaw. A fainter one traced across her brow above her right eye.

But her hair was lovely, fine, straight and silky, a medium brown that glistened red in the fitful sun poking through the window. It had been hacked off carelessly just below her shoulders, more a man's than a woman's length, but with time and proper care it could well be her loveliest feature, along with her wide brown eyes. I smiled at her, combing the shining, still-damp locks with my fingers, for our rescuer—I no longer wanted to think of him as Matthew—had not thought to bring such things as combs or brushes. And I, of course, had had none in my stone prison to bring with me.

"It is nice to see there really was someone under all that dirt," I said to Mary, stroking her hair back from her face. "You've a pretty face, Mary. Nice eyes and lovely hair. You must stand straighter now and keep your head up, so that everyone can enjoy them."

She put her arms around me and hugged me tight. "I love you, Marina," she whispered.

I left her wrapped in a blanket by the fire before which her coarse wool dress hung drying, for I had washed it, too. It had been so filthy I could not have borne putting it back on her, and it was so old and ragged, I considered myself lucky that it had not shredded in the wash water. I decided that the first order of business when we reached London was to find Mary at least one decent dress, though how I would accomplish this I had no idea, for we had nothing to our names save the clothing we wore. But it would do no good to fret about it now. There would be plenty of time to worry once we drew closer to London. Perhaps our rescuer would be kind enough to advance me the price of a dress for Mary.

I took a deep breath and turned my reluctant steps toward the private dayroom where the man I had thought was Matthew waited for me. It was time for answers, answers I was not really sure I wanted to have. Still, I needed them all the same.

He rose when I entered—he was that much a gentleman at least—and my heart lurched. Even bearded he was my Matthew, his brown hair glinting gold in firelight that sparked on the green flecks in his golden-brown eyes. Tears filled mine and for strength I leaned against the door a moment before I walked over to stare out the window.

Twenty yards away the cliffs plunged down fifty feet to the coast below, where merciless waves, whipped by the whistling wind, pounded the huge rocks that lined the foot of the escarpment. The clouds, which earlier had been fluffy and white and showed teasing glimpses of luscious blue sky, now massed solid and dark across the arching vault of the heavens, churning with wind-induced fury. I shivered in the chill draft blowing in around the window frame.

"I hate the wind," I said, my voice low and bitter, "and the moor. I pray I never see or hear either again." I swung around, trembling, and faced him, my beloved betrayer, tears shimmering on my lashes. "Why? Why did you do this to me—whoever you are?"

He winced at the biting words, the hurting tone I'd not tried to veil, and rubbed his face with his hands. Then he turned to the small table and dropped into a chair, nodding. He sat leaning forward, elbows on knees, his head bowed as he stared at his clasped hands.

"Who am I? Yes, that is the best place to begin. It is time I admitted it, especially to myself. I am a coward, my love." He looked up at me with a small, self-mocking smile. "A craven, no-good coward. And my name is certainly not Matthew Palmerston."

His eyes filled with pain as he turned to stare into the fire. I remained at the window, the cold moor at my back and his chilling words before me.

"My name is Daniel, Marina. Daniel Farley. I am an actor, and a damned good one."

"I know."

I was unable to keep the bitterness from my voice. Matthew—Daniel—grimaced and bowed his head. After a moment, he again looked into the fire.

"I am not the best of people, Marina. I have been known to gamble more than a bit, and have always been ready for high adventure with the type of nobility who enjoy slumming on occasion. And I have a temper, quite a hot one. It has gotten me into trouble all my life." He laughed, a sound full of irony. "But nothing like this last trouble, my love. You see, I killed a man, Marina. I got into an argument with a Viscount's son— over a woman, a pretty little tart who cared not a whit for either of us—and though he threw the first punch, it was my hand that knocked him flying into the marble fireplace. It split his head wide open. He was dead before he hit the floor. And so was I, for although three of my companions had stood watching, two of his had, also. They had what we hadn't; money, position, a title. Who would believe us over them? We were only actors, and everyone knows actors are all thieves and liars. And I had killed the man, though it had been an accident and he had begun the fight. At the very least I'd spend half my life in prison. I knew it more likely I'd hang."

He rose, walked to the fireplace and leaned his forearms on the mantle, his back to me.

"So there I was, at the mercy of two very un-noble noblemen. It took them all of a minute to seize advantage of the situation. One, obviously, was Matthew Palmerston. And the other," he turned his head and looked at me, "was Henry D'arcy."

It had not taken them long, Daniel said, to decide how best to use the power they now had over the handsome young actor. Matthew Palmerston needed rescue from his father's restrictive dictates. The elder Lord Palmerston had died only a week before, leaving a will stating Matthew must marry within a year to inherit the sizable fortune the old man had left. But that Matthew was not willing to do, for respectability and settling down did not rate high on his list of desirable assets.

It was Daniel's uncanny resemblance to Palmerston that sparked the idea; in body and facial structure they appeared to be brothers. Within a half hour Palmerston and D'arcy had the basic plan sketched out, their friend's body looted and dumped into an unsavory alley with a bloody brick lying nearby, and Daniel ensnared, forced to carry out their orders in exchange for their silence, passage to South America, and money for a new beginning there. Two days later, they met with a solicitor who had a reputation of being helpful to those of the aristocracy in need of somewhat shady legal assistance, a man named Alfred Marlowe. When he learned that they sought a well-born young woman who could disappear without a fuss being raised by relatives, Marlowe immediately thought of me, gloating over the revenge for which he'd been hungering. Henry D'arcy masterminded the details of the plot, and Daniel said his eyes had glowed as he planned the systematic destruction of the only woman who had ever refused him.

They thought of everything, planned for every contingency. Two marriage certificates with different dates were prepared and signed by Palmerston ahead of time. With the September one lying atop the June one, covering the date, Uncle Jacob, Mollie and I had signed the fake one without knowing it, thinking we merely signed two copies of the same document. The letters, also, had been prepared ahead, each written by Palmerston—one for Daniel to leave for me, and one for Giles to switch when we drew close to Stoneleigh. Daniel had written nothing at the desk in the hotel room. Every paper I saw in his portfolio had been written by Matthew Palmerston.

Palmerston and D'arcy had prepared the tower for me, too. The chains, the straw, the austere lower room, it all had been waiting for months, as had the gauze shrouds the Peeles would wear to frighten me. Elegant clothes were made to fill the wardrobe, cut from a pattern bought from the seamstress who had sewn the green wool dress I'd had made. Hairbrushes were engraved with my initials, jewels placed in an ornate box, even a portrait had been painted by an artist who visited the shop a few times to observe me. When at last they were ready, they sent Daniel Farley to bring me to them.

And he had. That I instantly fell in love with him made it all so easy. My own insecurity played right into their hands. I gave so much of myself to 'my Matthew' that when he disappeared I was left completely adrift. It took very little to break me down. What they had estimated might take two or three years to accomplish had been over in a mere six months, though Henry D'arcy paid an unexpectedly high price for his participation. Daniel said he had turned recluse now, a lonely, crippled and bitter man who never left his estate.

"I still don't understand," I said when Daniel finished his tale. "If Matthew did not want to marry at all, why then have you marry me in his name? He may have the fortune he wants, but he also has a wife he does not."

"Yes," Daniel agreed, "one who is thought insane, who must be kept locked in a stone tower lest she again attack others with a sword, perhaps killing someone this time. People are still talking about it, Marina. I have been here less than three weeks, and at least twenty people have told me about you. Everyone knows of Palmerston's 'great tragedy.' He has his father's money and the sympathy of every woman he meets. He can take what he wants in the grand name of consolation and never have to be forced into marrying any of them, whatever happens. For he already has a wife. In the tower."

"And you knew? From the beginning you knew the plan, what they would do to me once you left?" Though I tried to remain calm, I could not stop the anger that welled up from deep inside me. It shook my voice with a force that left me gasping.

"Not all the details," Daniel shook his head, "but I'm not stupid, Marina. I had a damned good idea what would happen. But I couldn't let it influence me. It was just another role to play, that was all, a part in an ongoing play where the payment was not just money, but my life." He looked at me and shrugged. "I didn't see it as real, Marina, not at first. It was even fun for a while, playing the well-to-do gentleman, writing my own script. Even you weren't real to me. You were just another character in the play."

"You were real to me!" I cried, choking on the raging anger. My hands clenched into fists. I wanted to hit him, to hurt him as he'd hurt me. "I loved you more than life itself. I gave you my heart, my *life*, and you were just acting, just playing a *role*?"

"Only at first, Marina. I really did fall in love with you by the end, you were so wonderful. I never expected that to happen and I didn't know what to do about it. I couldn't stop, or they'd have sent me to the hangman. So I just pretended that Palmerston and D'arcy didn't exist. I made myself believe I really was who I said I was, that we would live happily together once we were married." Tears welled in his golden brown eyes, tracked slowly down into his beard. His voice dropped to a mere whisper. "I didn't want to leave you, Marina, you must believe that. They forced me. I was supposed to leave the day of the ceremony, but I couldn't. I wanted you so much, and then I found such happiness in your arms I just couldn't make it end. I lay awake for three nights, Marina, watching you sleep beside me, and I just couldn't leave."

"But you did leave!" I shouted, raising my fists as though to strike him. "You didn't love me enough to stay, to save me from them. You left me."

"I had to, Marina. You don't understand. D'arcy came in that last night, at midnight, right into the room with us. He stood for a long time and watched you sleep, then he handed me a copy of a letter he'd written to the police. He threatened to send it if I didn't do what they wanted, if I didn't leave, right then, that minute. I had to go, I didn't have any choice."

"If you had truly loved me, you never would have left. You knew what would happen to me. How can you possibly say you love me, when you let it happen?"

"I do love you, Marina, you must believe me. But I'm weak. I was scared. I didn't want to hang, so I traded my life for yours."

He held out his hands in supplication. Tears streamed down his cheeks. Anguish darkened his eyes. He stood open and vulnerable before me, but I felt not one spark of sympathy for him. My rage was too all-consuming. I merely shook my head and glared at him. He dropped his hands and sighed.

"I want you to know that it wasn't worth it, Marina, what I did. I kept seeing your face, your shining eyes. They followed me, Marina, everywhere I went, even into the Brazilian jungle. I tried, but I couldn't get far enough away. No matter where I went, or how much I drank to forget, you were always there. That's why I came back. Because I love you. I had to help you."

He moved toward me, reaching out to embrace me, but I twisted away, hitting at him with my hands.

"No! Don't touch me. Don't."

He backed away, his face wretched, watching as

my rage turned to tears and I sobbed out the pain, the agony, until at last the tears dwindled, leaving me drained and empty-feeling inside. I wiped my face with my hands and looked at him, my beloved, beloved betrayer.

"I knew what was happening, after a while," I said, my voice as bleak as my heart. "Even through the fear and the confusion, I knew that he was trying to drive me insane, but he kept me drugged and I couldn't fight him. I knew you had to have been a part of it, a big part. But I couldn't admit it, not while I was locked in that tower with nothing but silence and empty darkness. I needed to believe you were real, that what we'd had, our love, had meaning and an existence outside the horror I lived in. It was all that kept me alive. And sane." I took a deep breath and shook my head. "But it didn't have any meaning, did it? It was all lies, playacting. It was never real."

Matthew—Daniel—wiped his face with his hands. "You're wrong, Marina. It was real. It might have started as sham, it might have been Palmerston's hand on the marriage certificate, but when we stood before the altar it was real. I was the one who took the vows. I pledged you *my* love forever. *Mine*. Daniel's. That was real. I know you must hate me for what I've done, and I don't expect you to feel anything else. But please, please believe me, Marina. I do love you. Until the day I die I shall love only you."

I nodded, grateful through my heartbreak that there was this, at least, however little it meant. Then I uttered a pained little laugh.

"I wonder, given the circumstances, just which one of you I am married to."

"Neither of us, that is the great irony," Daniel said. "There never was any marriage, not officially. That was Marlowe's idea, the solicitor. He found it vastly amusing, said it was the least of what you deserved, to have all vestiges of respectability torn away from you. Boyleston was no rector, he was merely a down-on-his-luck actor in need of a few pence for whiskey. It was all a complete sham. You never were legally married, Marina. Not to him, and not to me." He glanced out the window then turned and strode to the door, once again the strong, competent rescuer. "I'll get the carriage ready. We should leave soon, we've been here too long as it is."

I stood a moment after he left, trembling with emotion, stunned at what he had told me. Not married? Not ever married? This whole thing grew more absurd with each passing hour. In a fog of confusion, I checked on Mary, whose clothes were now dry. I left her dressing and walked out to the cliff edge, hoping the whipping wind and cold salt air would clear my mind and blow away the pain. Matthew's—I could not seem to think of Daniel as anything other than Matthew—his words chased round and round in my head, and I knew not how many years it would take before they would settle painlessly into the fabric of my memory, before I understood what they meant in the context of my life. I didn't know if ever I would love again, if I could ever trust anyone with even a tiny part of myself, but one thing I did know. I did not hate Daniel Farley. Though what we had now was gone forever and could never be recalled, he was still my Matthew. He would always be my Matthew. I loved him, and would until the day I died. He deserved to know that.

"Marina!"

I heard the call lifted on the wind and sighed. It was time to press on, to put more distance between us and Matthew Palmerston. And that tower prison. I would survive this too, somehow, and find a new life in the old, back in London. Perhaps Uncle Jacob would take me in again, although I did not think so. He had not answered any of my letters. It seemed he had quite forgotten me, and rather quickly, too. *Well,* I thought, turning away from the sea, giving one last look at the birds who soared high above me in careless freedom, *there must be another Uncle Jacob somewhere in that huge city. Perhaps Mollie and Eamon will help me look, as they had once before.*

"Marina!"

The call was closer, more demanding, frighteningly familiar in its strident arrogance. My heart began to thud and I looked up to see the black-haired Matthew, Lord Palmerston, striding across the coarse winter grass toward me. His eyes glinted fury, his face a mask of mingled hatred and enjoyment.

"Marina!" he shouted again. "I've come to take you home!"

Chapter Twenty-five

I backed away as he stalked toward me, my stare locked on his cold, infuriated face.

"Leave me alone, Matthew," I shouted back. "You have no hold on me any longer. Daniel Farley told me everything. I know we're not married. You cannot force me to go with you."

"And who will believe that, my dear?" Matthew stopped within arm's reach of me and sneered. "The rantings of a crazy woman? You are mad, indeed, if you think anyone will believe a murderess over me."

I froze, shocked. I could barely find breath to speak.

"Murderess? What are you saying?"

"You killed Giles that night, my dear, with your trusty little sword. Why do you think Mrs. Peele hates you so?" He grabbed my wrist in a crushing grasp and I screamed. "And you have stolen away her precious grandchild. I'll not be able to stay her hand this time, Marina. Not that I really want to. I only need you alive,

Marina. As long as she does not kill you, it matters not what condition she leaves you in."

"No, Matthew. It's not true, he isn't dead, you're lying. Let go of me, you can't take me back." I twisted in his grasp, but could not loosen his hold.

"I can and I will, *wife*! You are my property. I can do what I want with you, and no one will dare interfere. You're going back to the chains at the top of the tower, where you belong. And this time you'll never get out of those chains, Marina. Not ever."

I fought him as he yanked me across the open ground. But I was helpless in his hard hands, powerless against his strength, and we drew ever nearer to where his huge black stallion stood waiting.

In the next moment he stepped into a shallow depression and lost his footing. He jerked sideways, arms flailing. His fingers loosened on my wrist as he fought to keep his balance. I wrenched my arm free and shoved him with all my strength. He stumbled back and fell hard on the rock-strewn soil where he lay stunned, his breath knocked from his lungs. I whirled and ran over the open ground, the inn on my left, the cliff edge on my right, heading for the out buildings behind the inn, hoping to find a hiding place somewhere within them. As I passed the side porch of the inn someone grabbed me and I screamed again, struggling in the tight grasp.

"Marina, stop, it's me, Daniel. It's Daniel."

"Daniel, help me." I clung to his shoulders. "Don't let him take me back. He'll put me in the tower, he'll chain me again. I'll die, I know I will."

"Farley? Farley!" The malicious shout thundered in the air. "You're a dead man, Farley!"

I looked over my shoulder. Palmerston was back on his feet, racing toward us and closing fast. Attracted by all the noise, guests began emerging from the inn to watch the confrontation.

"He won't take you back, Marina," Daniel said. "Not while I'm alive to stop him. He won't hurt you again, I promise. Never again. Come on."

He turned and, with my hand in his, towed me behind him as fast as he could, angling away from the inn and any possible interference from the growing crowd of spectators.

"Let go of my wife, Farley!" Matthew roared. "Stop him, he's got my wife!"

Someone might have obeyed him, but before anyone could move my foot twisted on the uneven ground and I fell, cutting my hands on the stony earth. Daniel hauled me up, but pain stabbed from my injured ankle and I sank to the ground again. Bending, he wrapped an arm around my waist and lifted me up, swinging me around beside him. Before Daniel could take another step Matthew grabbed my arm. With a rough jerk he yanked me away from Daniel, and I screamed, fear and pain both battering at me.

"You've had it, Farley. First murder, now kidnapping—you'll hang for sure!" Matthew yelled.

"Don't count on it, Palmerston." Daniel reached for me and pulled me away from Matthew. Pain shot up my arm into my shoulder. "We've a story of our own to tell. Leave her be, or I'll kill you."

"She's my property, Farley. And an escaped lunatic. She'll get exactly what she deserves."

Matthew hit me, a backhand blow that stunned my senses. My knees buckled and I fell from Daniel's arms onto the hard ground. Ignoring me under their feet, the two men attacked each other, fists pounding like sledge hammers, opening cuts on cheeks, brows and lips.

"Hold her!" Matthew grunted between blows. "Don't let her get away."

As the fight carried the men across the ground, someone ran to my side and grabbed my arms, holding me in place. I struggled, screaming, trying to crawl after the combatants, to stop the fight. Then somehow Mary was kneeling at my side, clutching me, sobbing. We clung to each other, surrounded by self-appointed guards, as on and on Matthew and Daniel fought in the howling wind. As the light faded from the sky they drew closer to the cliff until they teetered at the very edge.

The wind fell silent. The last rays of the setting sun broke through the dark clouds to glint on the blade of an upraised knife. I could not see who held it. I stared, frozen, as it descended in a glittering arc. Mathew and Daniel stood motionless in the silent light, clasped tight in each other's arms. Then they staggered, swayed, and plunged down off the cliff, still locked in their deadly embrace.

"Matthew!" I screamed, and knew no more.

For five days I lay in the inn, barely aware of my surroundings, my sprained ankle bandaged to reduce the swelling, the side of my face turning purple. Bruises dotted my arms where Matthew's and Daniel's strong fingers had yanked and pulled at me. The innkeeper had sent one of his servants and Mary to Stoneleigh with news of Lord Palmerston's death, and Mary had brought back clothing from the room next to Matthew's, a pretty blue wool gown that dipped and swirled into alluring folds. But I refused to remove the green prison dress, now torn and soiled from the desperate struggle on the cliff. I lay unmoving, staring into the distance, stroking my fingers endlessly over the rough fabric, caught in a pit of despair. Mary asked the innkeeper to send for Dr. Boulton. When he arrived he gave me a sedative that made me sleep, but it did not help. The pit was too deep for mere rest to pull me out. Once she returned, Mary did not leave my side.

I spoke not one word, for I was completely empty inside. Over and over I heard Matthew's words—*my* Matthew, Daniel—and saw his anguished face: *I know you must hate me, but I love you. I'll love you until the day I die.* He had died not knowing he was wrong, that I, too, loved him, and always would. Now, he would never know.

I heard, also, his words to the black-haired Matthew: *Leave her be or I'll kill you.* And I saw the knife, glittering in the dying sun, rising and falling endlessly, over and over, wherever I turned my eyes.

Oh, Matthew, my Matthew, I cried in the dark depths of the nights, *you should have taken me with you, too. You should not have left me behind again.*

They brought the bodies from the sea late on the fifth day, brought them to the ice house behind the inn where Dr. Boulton examined them, the bodies of who they all thought were my husband and my kidnapper. I heard the commotion outside my windows and I knew what it meant, but it took me an hour to gather the strength to stand. With Mary helping me, I hobbled out to where a crowd clustered around the ice house door, muttering and murmuring to each other. They fell silent as I approached, parting in solemn deference to let me through. Dr. Boulton emerged just as I reached the door.

"Marina, what are you doing?" His voice was soft, but the hands he laid on my shoulders were firm and determined. "Go back to your bed, please."

"I must see them," I replied, my voice wooden, my eyes on the ground. "Let me pass."

"No, Marina, you don't want to see him. The rocks were not kind to him, nor the sea. It can do no good, and it will not bring him back. You will only upset yourself, needlessly."

"I have to see him." I raised my eyes and looked into the doctor's face. "I have to. Please."

He studied my face carefully. I do not know what he saw in my eyes, but it was that and not my pleading words that convinced him. He nodded reluctant agreement, opened the door and followed Mary and me into the dim, cold interior.

He was right, the rocks and the sea had not been kind. Matthew Palmerston and Daniel Farley lay stretched side-by-side on makeshift tables, bruised, battered, bones broken, clothing shredded. Matthew's face was ugly, purple and bloated, one side of his head caved in, but other than a nasty scrape down one cheek and a cut on his forehead, Daniel's face was unmarred. The icy salt water had washed away the blood and minimized the damage done by the savage fight. But for the dead gray color of his skin, Daniel could well have been sleeping. I stared at the Matthew-man for a long time, at the cruel lips that had kissed me with feigned tenderness, the hands that had fed me drug-laced sherry, and I felt nothing, as though I were made of the stone that he had surrounded me with for so long. But I knew this numbness would not last forever, and when feeling did return, it would be agonizing.

At last I turned away to the other Matthew, *my* Matthew, and felt my heart lurch. Though Daniel's face had escaped almost unscathed, the rocks had taken their toll on the rest of his body. It was difficult to see anything human beneath the deformities. There was no numbness for me here. I took a deep breath and bowed my head, closing my eyes against the pain that began to twist inside me as I beheld his grotesquely distorted limbs.

"Do you know his name, Marina?" Sir Robert asked in a low, quiet voice.

"Farley." It was all I could do to whisper. "Daniel

Farley."

"Why did he take you from Stoneleigh? What did he want?"

"He didn't take me, I went with him. Willingly."

"Willingly? Did you know him, then?"

"No." I shook my head and opened my eyes, looking again, for the last time, on my beloved betrayer's face. "I thought I did once, long ago, but I was wrong. I didn't know him at all." I raised my eyes to the doctor's puzzled face and spoke before he could pose another question. "Which one of them has the stab wound?"

Sir Robert blinked, surprised at the question. "This one, Farley. Matthew died in the water, he drowned before the rocks battered his skull in. This one was dead before he hit the water. Stabbed through the heart."

I nodded and turned away, limping slowly to the door where I paused and looked back, my body trembling. Daniel had kept his promise, that Matthew would not take me back or hurt me again as long as Daniel lived, for he had taken Matthew into death with him. I felt a soft touch on my cheek, the tender caress of breath hot on my face, and knew that he was there, my Matthew, saying farewell. I spoke softly to the gentle spirit that once had been all of life to me.

"Good-bye, Matthew, my love. I do love you. Until the day I die I shall love you."

Trembling so violently I could barely stand, I stepped out into the cold sunshine. I did not see the gathered crowd or hear their curious murmurs. I saw only Daniel's dead face and heard the sound of the sea on the rocks. I did not see Mary step to my side, or feel her slip her hand into mine. Neither did I feel the hands that caught me when I swayed and collapsed in a deep faint.

Chapter Twenty-six

Six weeks later I sat in the drawing room of Stoneleigh, Mary by my side, facing three solicitors from Matthew Palmerston's estate. The land was entailed, and since Matthew had died without issue it would pass to the next in line of inheritance, and the title with it. As would the money he had used me to acquire, for he had also died without making a will. I, merely his wife—as they thought—was not eligible to inherit a penny aside from the dower provisions arranged for in the entailment.

I had feared to face Mrs. Peele when we returned to Stoneleigh two days after Matthew and Daniel were found, but the house proved to be empty when we arrived in the company of Sir Robert. The housekeeper's possessions were gone from her room as well as a horse and small carriage from the barn. Sir Robert offered to find a new housekeeper for me, and three days later Mrs. Eliza Greaves, a middle-aged widow, took possession, bringing warmth, laughter and unflagging optimism into the cold stone manor.

Stoneleigh's dark macabre atmosphere did not long stand against her jolly practicality and glowing high spirits. Soon the stone seemed a little less black, the air somewhat less chill. I asked her to open the north wing and prepare rooms for Mary and me, for I could not bear the memories attached to the south wing, memories of pain, fear and madness. I had not slept much since I had returned to the dark, evil house.

Three weeks after Mrs. Greaves' arrival, Sir Robert, who had been concerned about my mental stability—indeed, despite the winter weather he had made the long journey to Stoneleigh at least three times each week to check on me—entered the house to find me not in the drawing room as usual. After a long search with Mary as guide, he finally located me at the top of the south tower, in the room to which I had so nearly been returned.

I had known it would be painful to ascend those stairs, yet I had felt compelled to do so, to confront the memories head-on and defeat them, for they were coming close to destroying me. I had been alone in the dark room for close to three hours when Mary led Sir Robert up the stairs, the light from the lantern she held picking out in sharp relief the rough stone walls, the filthy malodorous straw, the chains hanging from thick iron rings, gaping open, ready still for my wrists. An icy winter wind blew in through the narrow openings high above.

I lay curled on the floor a few feet to the side of

the door, so deep in tormented memories that I did not hear them enter. Sir Robert looked down at me, his own mind, I'm sure, holding memories of that wild night on the moor more than a year and a half ago, a night of terror, blood and a swinging blade.

"Oh, dear Lord," he murmured, holding out a hand to stop Mary where she was. "Be very careful, child, she may turn violent again. I was afraid this might happen."

"She not crazy," Mary said, shaking her head. "She just sad."

She slipped by his restraining hand, set the lantern on the floor and moved to my side. Gently, she touched my shoulder. I looked up through my tears, pushing myself to sit upright once more. Mary knelt before me.

"Don't be sad. I help," she whispered.

"Oh, Mary," I moaned, gathering her close to me and rocking her in my arms while I waited for the tears to end. When they did, I kissed the top of her head and smiled into her anxious brown eyes. "Yes, Mary, you do help. My sweet Mary."

I looked up at Dr. Boulton, who stood staring with great distaste around the vile chamber, then wiped my face. I rose, straightened my dress, and greeted him quietly.

"Welcome, Sir Robert. I am sorry I was not downstairs when you arrived. The ascent to this room can be dangerous. Mary should have come and brought me down to you."

"She wanted to. It was I who insisted on coming up here myself." He looked around again and frowned. "This is where he kept you? I don't understand, Marina. Matthew assured me that you were well taken care of, that he had everything under control after that awful night."

"And as you can see, he did. Quite under control. And perhaps this is what I deserved, for I was mad then, for that little time after he closed the chains on my wrists and left me in the dark with only straw for a bed. As near as I can figure with Mary's help, for time passes differently in dark isolation than it does in normal life, I was chained to that wall for more than six months, beaten constantly and thrown rancid scraps once a day."

"I didn't know, Marina. I swear I didn't. My God, if I had seen—"

"You'd have stopped him instantly had you seen it. I know that, Sir Robert. And so did Matthew. And if you had seen me below, in what I call the prison room, a room not much better than this, you'd have known I was not at all mad. And so he told you what you needed to hear, to keep you far away from me. He would never have let you see me, not ever again. With your medical knowledge, you posed too great a risk to his plan."

"His plan?"

I did not answer, merely led him down the narrow winding staircase with its uneven steps to the austere prison chamber three floors below. He stared, shocked to the core, at the bare lifeless room in which I had passed more than a year. When we returned to the small south wing drawing room that Mrs. Greaves had opened up, an almost cheerful room done in rose, gray and white, with pretty tapestries to soften the walls, I explained everything in detail, just as Daniel had. I had discovered a locked room on the other side of Matthew's bedchamber, and when I had opened the door I found the pale, gauze shrouds Giles and Mrs. Peele had worn in their masquerades as malevolent spirits, one stained with blood; the letter Daniel had left for me in the London hotel room, and the one Giles had placed inside my reticule; the marriage certificates with the June and September dates; the volume by Francis Bacon inscribed in my own hand that Matthew had to hide because of the telltale August date; and my unposted letters to Uncle Jacob, and his to me, nine letters lying still unopened, seals unbroken, words crying out for liberation, yellowing in the isolation of the small dark room.

I also discovered a letter to Matthew from the Boston lawyer, Mr. Alcott, about my mother. Matthew had lied about her. She was not mad, and she had not been put into an asylum. She had died when I was barely five, when the carriage in which she was fleeing from Father's cruelty had overturned, killing both her and her lover. Mr. Alcott had also enclosed a receipt, showing that Matthew's payment had fully discharged the debt Father had left. It was the only kind thing Matthew had ever done for me.

I showed Sir Robert all these things and watched his face change from suspicion to wariness, to stunned disbelief, cautious acceptance, and finally quiet conviction. He had corrected me only once. I had not killed Giles on the moor that night, as Matthew had claimed, though I had wounded him gravely. He had recovered only to be kicked in the head by Matthew's huge stallion in early July. He had died a few days before Matthew had moved me down to the lower prison chamber. To the very end, Matthew had not ceased trying to crush me.

Now, all these weeks later, I smiled sadly at Mary as the solicitor droned on, which one I was not even sure, for all three looked alike to me; round and somber, with bald heads, a pince nez on each beakish nose, thick lips pushing in and out, and dark suits on short bodies. As there was no dower house on the estate, I was entitled to a suite of rooms in the main residence, said rooms to be determined by the new Lord Palmerston, and an allowance of one hundred pounds per annum. Or one hundred fifty pounds should I choose to reside elsewhere, or Lord Palmerston deem it best. They had just today located the heir, a distant cousin in Sydney, Australia, who had never been to England. Word of the inheritance and title would be on its way down under in the morning post.

I looked up when he stopped speaking, and sighed.

"I am grateful for your kindness in explaining my

position to me. It is very tempting to simply remain silent and accept the dower payment as Matthew Palmerston's widow. It is, after all, the very least of what he owes me, morally if not legally. But I do not wish to remain silent, nor live under false pretenses. I have done enough of that from when I first met Sir Matthew. I cannot accept the dower, gentlemen, for I am not his widow. We were not married."

Their mouths dropped open in shock, one after the other, then they turned to each other, abuzz with consternation.

"Please, do not distress yourselves. I will explain what that means, hopefully to your satisfaction." I poured more tea and handed the cups around, my hands steady and my heart light. Whatever hardships this decision might incur, I knew it was the right one. And as I spoke on, detailing in brief Matthew's plan to defraud the estate, a great burden lifted from me. I was truly free at last.

"I can only conclude that by arranging a contrived marriage, Matthew left himself open for declaring it false if in the future he should ever desire to marry legitimately, no doubt naming himself the innocent dupe, and me, his insane wife, the arranger of the deception. And who would question his word, or listen to protests from a mad woman locked in a tower?"

The three men stared at me, aghast, varying degrees of disbelief on their faces. I knew it would do no good to argue or protest—I was, after all, speaking of a peer of the realm—and so I merely nodded my acceptance of their skepticism.

"I do not expect you to believe only my word on this. I have proof of what I say, of the outrage that was committed, the pain and terror that I have endured at Matthew Palmerston's hands. Sir Robert Boulton, who was an observer of some of the events in question, has inspected the proof very thoroughly, and is firmly convinced of the truth I speak. He has even located the actor who played the role of the rector. So you see, I cannot in good conscience accept that to which I am not entitled. I will abide by whatever decision you make, and leave Stoneleigh whenever you say I must. I do not expect anything, but I do beg you to bear in mind that I am completely destitute. Were I to leave today, I would have nowhere to go, and no means of getting there save walking across the frigid winter moor."

I could feel tears begin to rise, and I swallowed hard to prevent them from spilling over. My distress echoed in the shaking of my voice. I squeezed Mary's hand for comfort.

"I do feel the very least I am owed is to be returned safely to London, from where I was taken. The proofs of which I spoke are there, gentlemen." I gestured to a nearby table on which I had earlier placed the items from the locked room, and rose. The solicitors scrambled hastily to their feet. "I shall leave you to inspect them at your leisure, and decide the truth of the matter for yourselves. I will await your

SUSAN TUTTLE

decision as to my future in my room."

With Mary's hand in mind, I walked to the door on trembling legs. Tears beaded on my lashes. On the threshold I paused and turned back to the men.

"The very worst of this, to my mind, is that it was a solicitor who conceived and actively executed the plan to defraud the estate, as well as participating in the destruction of the life and sanity of an innocent woman. Alfred Marlowe should be made to pay somehow for his actions, though I know there is little I can do about it. I am, after all, only the victim of his twisted hatred, and my personal pain and tragedy are of little consequence to the world. I do, however, find it inconceivable that a man of such temperament be allowed to represent the laws and justice of this country. It does not say much for your brand of law or justice, does it?"

I paced my room, waiting for the summons back to the drawing room, worrying about what would happen to Mary and me should we be put out immediately, with no money or transport provided. That she would go with me I had already decided. I could not risk leaving her here, for if her grandmother returned for her, Mary's life would once again descend into hell. She was slowly blossoming under the loving, gentle care she now received from both Mrs. Greaves and myself. Her eyes had ceased shifting in fear whenever anyone came close, and even had a sparkle in them. She stood straighter, the twist in her back seeming less pronounced. She no longer drooled at all, her speech grew clearer every day, and a smile often lit her face when we sat together working on her reading and writing, though I had yet to hear her laugh. And though she was not over-bright, neither was she the half-wit she had been treated as in the past. In these last six weeks she had learned to read the alphabet and some simple words, and was able to write not only her name, but mine as well. In my heart she had become my sister, and I would never give her up.

The solicitors agreed that I should remain at Stoneleigh until the new Lord Palmerston had been heard from, but required that all household expenses be cleared through their offices. I was given no spending money. My story, and Mary's, would be included in the letter to Sir Toby, and it would be up to someone who had never met me to decide my fate. It would be months before Sir Toby's wishes would reach us. This solution contented me, for I was too drained emotionally to be able to decide what to wear from day to day, much less what to do with my life, or Mary's.

The winter months rolled on, full of sadness and warmth, laughter and tears, memories, dreams, black stone and the wind. Always the wind, moaning pitifully through the long cold days and nights. I occupied my time teaching Mary, and used my needle to alter a few of my simpler dresses for her, for in the locked room where Matthew had stored the evidence of his cruelty, I had discovered the clothing I had brought from London, the things I had worn in Uncle Jacob's shop. And I found I was right. With proper clothing on her twisted body, Mary looked quite presentable, indeed. It seemed she stood even straighter with soft wool and challis covering her thin limbs than she had when only coarse cloth scraped across her delicate skin.

The new Lord Palmerston's letter arrived in late March. One of the solicitors, Edwin Athering, brought word to me without delay. Sir Toby declared himself appalled at his kinsman's treatment of me, and offered to allow me to stay at Stoneleigh until his arrival in late June. Should I desire to leave sooner, the solicitors were instructed to hand me two hundred fifty pounds as payment for my time as mistress of the great house and compensation for the abuse I'd suffered, and to arrange pre-paid passage for me to wherever I wished to go. I was also allowed to take with me whatever clothing and personal mementos I desired, though all jewelry and valuables would, of course, remain behind. All things considered, I found it a generous gesture. I thanked Mr. Athering for his courteous assistance and assured him I would, indeed, leave within one week's time. I had no desire to remain any longer than necessary in that house. It was only lack of means that had kept me there this long.

"I will go to London, Mr. Athering, for I have friends there who I am sure will assist me."

I might have sounded confident to the solicitor but I truly was not, for I had had no contact with anyone other than Matthew and Mrs. Peele since my so-called marriage. It was entirely possible I would find no welcome at all in London. But where else could I go?

"And I will need transport for two. Mary Peele will be accompanying me. You may take the charge for her expenses from the money Lord Palmerston has paid to me."

"I am sure there is no need to do so, given the circumstances," Mr. Athering said, rising. He knew how abused Mary, too, had been at Matthew's hands. "I doubt Lord Palmerston would deny the child that much. Indeed, I believe she is owed a few years' back wages. I will see that it is paid before you depart."

He bent over my hand, leaving me blinking in stunned disbelief at his words. If only I had gone to such a man as this when Father died, how different my life would have been. Mr. Athering kissed my hand and looked again at my face as his fingers closed gently around the scars on my wrist.

"I shall order a carriage for Thursday week, if that is satisfactory, Miss Weston, and arrange for the delivery of letters of credit for both you and Miss Peel, drawn on a London bank. It would be unwise to travel carrying such a large sum. I wish you a safe journey, Miss Weston, and in future the happiness you deserve."

I nodded, blinking, unable to speak past the lump in my throat. Mr. Athering strode to the door, turning back to me before he opened it.

"By the way, Miss Weston, I thought you would like to know that we agreed with your sentiments concerning Alfred Marlowe. We had enquiries made, and found him to be exactly as you described. The case was taken before a review board. We received word of the decision only a few days ago. Mr. Marlowe is no longer allowed to represent the laws and justice of this country. He has been disbarred."

Chapter Twenty-seven

It was mid April, the day before my twenty-seventh birthday. I stared at my pale complexion in the mirror as I brushed my hair back from my face with trembling hands and decided I looked as terrified as I felt. We had been in London a full week, but I had not yet gone to see Uncle Jacob. My courage had failed me each time I had attempted it. But I would put it off no longer. Today I would not turn back.

I had written to him in January, after I had found the courage to read the letters Matthew had kept hidden from me. Tears had coursed down my cheeks as the tone changed from one of warmth to concern, disappointment and then anger that I did not care enough to write back. The early letters had been filled with the latest news: Uncle Jacob had acquired a new assistant, David Phibbs, who also was enraptured with the new stories being printed. Mollie and Eamon were well, and anxiously awaiting word from me. Andrew's popularity seemed to be waning, and not as much made its way into print as in the early days. Eamon had burned his arm badly on the ovens, but it appeared to be healing well. Gradually, the news dwindled and the letters grew shorter as my silence continued, each asking why. Was I too grand for my old friends, now that I had money and position in the upper middle class?

The last letter, sent five months after I had left London, seared my heart, for Uncle Jacob's tone was cold, angry and dismissive. He told me in clear, harsh words of the hurt I had caused him and the O'Learys, and said he would write no more if he received no reply to this missive. *'I would not have expected such heartlessness and cruelty from you, Marina,'* he wrote. *'We truly love you. It shames me that you do not love us in return.'*

I had written to him, then, almost two years too late, though it took me three weeks to find the courage to put pen to paper. *'I have just read your letters, Uncle, and my heart is broken. There is little I can say in a letter to explain my silence. I was prevented from writing, though I do not expect you will believe that. I will be returning to London, though I do not yet know exactly when. It may not be until Spring or Summer; the decision is not yet mine to make. When I arrive, may I come to see you, to explain to you what has happened since last we saw each other? I feel I owe you that much, at least.'*

Given the anger in his last letters, I did not expect a reply, and when it came I opened it with hopeful, trembling hands. But it was terse and cold. I might have been an unwelcome stranger who cannot be avoided for all the warmth of his words.

'By all means come, Mrs. Palmerston. I will listen to what you have to say. You are right. You do owe me that much, at the very least.'

It was signed, 'Jacob Chadwicke'.

Now, I set my hat upon my head and smoothed my dress, a pale orchid silk with a high bustle and sleeves that ended in a flare of lace at the elbows. Deep purple ribbons threaded the square neckline and trimmed the fall in back. It had come from the wardrobe at Stoneleigh, for though I had not at first wanted to take any of the dresses Matthew Palmerston had provided, I realized it would be foolish to leave them behind. Like the wood and blankets from Lady Creswell, these were the very least of what was owed to me.

As with all my clothes, this gown was too big now, but I had not the skill to properly alter such elaborate creations as these. My collarbones jutted out quite noticeably, framed by the square neckline, and my skin still dipped between the bones of my bare forearms. But at least the ripples in my breastbone no longer showed, nor did my ribs. I was slowly regaining the lost weight, though it would take more than a few months to repair the damage caused by Matthew's cruel abuse. I would, indeed, much rather have worn one of the summer gowns I had brought with me when I had 'married,' but as they were simple patterns I had altered all of them—there were only six—to fit Mary.

Money for clothing, at least, was not something we should have to spend for a while. Not until winter came again would Mary need warm things.

I sighed and picked up a small package that contained Matthew's two letters, the marriage certificates, a gauze shroud, my unmailed letters to Uncle Jacob and his unanswered letters to me. I did not know if I would show any of these things to him, but the feel of them in my hands gave me the courage to leave the small room in the boarding house where Mary and I were staying. I had not left it at all in the week we had been there. I walked over to where Mary sat studying her lessons—she was making remarkable progress and was already halfway through the second primer—and I bent to kiss her shining red-brown hair.

"Keep working, Mary. I will not be long."

She turned and looked up at me with solemn, dark brown eyes.

"Do not go, Marina. It will make you sad again."

"Perhaps," I replied, smiling. "But it is something I must do, Mary. We cannot always avoid sadness. Sometimes, we have to face it and learn from it."

I kissed her again and left quickly, walking more than twelve blocks to Chadwicke's Books. It was a lovely Spring day, the sun warm and the air clear and clean, and I did not wish to waste money on a cab. Though my account of two hundred fifty pounds seemed more than adequate, I knew from personal experience how quickly it could disappear in a city like London. We had to pay for everything: food, clothing, a room; fuel when winter came again. I would have to find work soon, for I would not touch the one hundred sixty pounds the new Lord Palmerston had paid to Mary for seven years' wages, a generous amount by any standard, as she was merely a child though she had labored like an adult.

I walked along filled with cautious optimism. Surely a city the size of London must house others like Jacob Chadwicke, willing to employ a competent, able person even if she was a woman. With two hundred fifty pounds in the bank, a cheap room and a frugal purse, I had time enough to search. I strode on with my head high and my heart hopeful, looking about me with great interest as slowly the buildings grew more and more familiar.

There was the seamstress who had made my two winter dresses, and the small grocer where I had shopped for food. I passed the draper and milliner, the woodworking shop, and the wine merchant where Andrew had bought the wine we had shared beside the Thames. It was all here, just as before, as though I had never left. Nothing had changed. I detoured three blocks, my heart pounding with excitement, to pass by the bakery-teashop I loved so dearly.

It was gone.

I stopped, staring in shock at the window in which I had so often sat looking out at the busy London street. It was filled now with bric-a-brac: pottery bowls and pitchers; a spinning wheel; candlesticks and a ship's brass lantern. I tilted my head up and gazed at the sign. 'A. Lederer, Dealer in Antiquities.' I blinked and moved on toward Chadwicke's Books, the day no longer as warm or bright, my heart no longer filled with happiness. What had happened? Where were Mollie and Eamon? There had been no mention of this in Uncle Jacob's letters, but his news had ended the February after I'd left London, more than two years ago now. A lot can happen in two years, as well I knew. Too much.

My optimism had drained away by the time I approached the bookshop, my steps slowing the closer I came. Finally, I stood on the sidewalk clutching my package tight, nerving myself to open the door and step inside. My heart pounded and my head grew light. I couldn't do it. I could not face the hostility and rejection that was bound to follow my entry into that shop. I turned to flee and encountered a vivid image of my Matthew—Daniel—as he had stood before me on the day I had bumped into him, his hair shining gold in the brilliant sunshine, green specks dancing in his sparkling golden-brown eyes. Pain stabbed into me, stole my breath, and I turned and retreated into the shop to escape the aching memory.

The dimness blinded me momentarily, and I stood just inside the door blinking focus into my eyes, much as Daniel had the first day I had ever seen him. But the memory did not have time to surface completely, for within seconds a short, thin, fair-haired young man hurried forward from behind the desk where once I had worked. He looked knowledgeable and energetic, a comfortable sort of person, with wire-rimmed spectacles perched on his thin nose, a round face covered by a soft, blond beard, and green eyes bright and alert behind the shining lenses. He donned his coat as he moved toward me, over shirtsleeves rolled halfway to his elbows. His fingers were stained with ink. He bowed gracefully, if somewhat stiffly, giving the impression he had practiced the movement before a mirror, and greeted me in a high, nasal voice which was not altogether unpleasant to the ear.

"Good afternoon, Madam. Welcome to Chadwicke's Books. What may I show you, today?"

"You must be David Phibbs," I said, forcing a smile. I only half succeeded. "Mr. Chadwicke wrote to me about you. Do you like it here, in the shop?"

"He wrote you? You know Mr. Chadwicke?" The young man's voice held a wary, suspicious tone and I realized he loved that wonderful old man just as I did, and felt protective of him. I nodded in answer, smiling more successfully this time, though I knew my eyes remained sad. I had no hope of a smile reaching my eyes again, not for long years, if at all.

"Yes, I did once, long ago." I moved to the shelves and scanned the titles. "I see you have kept the same order. I used to work here, you know."

"Oh." His voice had gone flat, hostile. "So that's who you are. The too-grand Mrs. Palmerston. What do you want here?"

I kept my face turned from him, my gaze on the ornate leather spines. Despite my best efforts, my voice trembled.

"I wrote and asked Mr. Chadwicke if I might stop by when I arrived in London. He agreed to see me. Is he here?"

"He's not seeing anyone, he's been ill. I won't have him upset, not by the likes of you."

David Phibb's cold voice slashed at me, but I barely noticed it through the alarm that surged in me. I whirled to face the antagonistic young man, my heart pounding.

"Ill? How ill? Have you called a doctor? A good one?"

"That is no concern of yours, Mrs. Palmerston." He pronounced my name with extreme distaste. "He is mending slowly, though more slowly than need be if the truth were known. It seems someone has destroyed a good part of his enjoyment of life—and his trust in people."

He glared at me, then turned on his heel and stalked away. I bent my head, fighting tears, biting my lips to keep from crying out.

"He sees only special customers, now," David Phibbs told me from where he stood beside the desk where the account ledgers lay. "Those he can still trust, who he feels are worthy of his time. I doubt you fall anywhere near that category, Mrs. Palmerston."

I raised my head and looked at him, holding myself very still lest I break in half.

"Please, will you not at least ask him if he will see me? I doubt I can find the courage to come again."

Phibbs stared at me a moment, then turned and disappeared behind the curtain. Long minutes passed. My fear rose and began to overwhelm me. I knew I could not do this, could not face Jacob Chadwicke. Mary was right, it would only make me sad, break my not-quite-healed heart once again. I should not have come. I was not ready to experience that level of pain yet again. Perhaps I never would be.

I turned toward the door, but before I could take a step David Phibbs emerged from the back sitting room and spoke, his voice like ice.

"He will give you ten minutes, Mrs. Palmerston, that is all. I will keep a close eye on the clock."

I almost refused, almost ran out despite Uncle Jacob's agreement to see me. But I forced myself to into calmness, swallowed back my tears, and turned to follow the assistant's stiff back into the so-familiar sitting room. *You must see it through, Marina*, I told myself, *for it is your own fault*. Though I knew that was not true. It was Matthew's fault, and Mr. Marlowe's, and Lord D'arcy's. And Daniel's. Not mine.

Nothing had changed. The sitting room looked just as it had always looked, cluttered and worn and comfortable. Each corner was crowded with wonderful memories: to my left, the parlor set where we shared tea; beyond it, the door to my upper room, now closed; in the back left corner, the table where we ate together, laughing and talking; and in the right back corner the reading nook still piled with books. Nothing had changed.

Then I turned my head to the right and saw Uncle Jacob, sitting where once in my great illness I had sat, in the rocker before the fire, a thick blanket over his knees. He looked so much older, so thin and delicate, his skin stretched like parchment over his aged, brittle bones. Much of the roundness I remembered had vanished, eaten away by the severe sickness. My heart sank so at the sight of him, wan and drained in the chair, that I quite forgot myself.

"Uncle Jacob!" I cried and took a step toward him, but his searing look froze me in place again.

"Ah, Mrs. Palmerston. How good of you to condescend to visit my humble abode. That is a lovely gown. Quite a step up from the simple things you were forced to wear before, isn't it?"

"It was not my choice, believe me," I said, looking down at the intricate folds of luxurious silk. "I much prefer what I had before, when I was here."

"Indeed? But then I should have guessed by your *silence* how *important* all this is to you. Should I not have?"

I looked at him, a protest on my lips, my eyes swimming with tears, but he spoke on, gesturing at the package I held, animosity further hardening his face.

"If you think to soften me with gifts, Marina Palmerston, you have wasted Matthew's money. I want nothing from you but an explanation, and then your permanent withdrawal from my life."

I gasped at his words, the scorn beneath his tone. I shook my head and backed up. Tears spilled down my face to darken the bodice of my gown.

"I should not have come here," I choked. "It was a mistake. I cannot bear to have you look at me like that. I'm sorry." I turned away.

"Marina! Sit down!" he barked. "You will explain to me, and I will endeavor not to look at you. It should not be difficult, as I have little desire to see your face, anyway. Sit down!" he snapped again as still I hesitated, remained turned toward the curtain. Instinctively, I obeyed, groping for a chair, sobbing uncontrollably. He waited with patient indifference until at long last I brought myself under control, wiped my eyes, and sat back with a desolate sigh.

"It is so hard. I do not know where to begin."

"Try starting with this." Uncle Jacob handed me the letter I had written to him in the hotel room.

"Yes," I agreed, "it is a good place to start, though it really began a long time before this was written. But I did not know it then, and so I will tell it to you as it happened to me."

And I did, sparing no detail, no matter how small, reliving as I spoke the horrors I wished only to forget. I showed Uncle Jacob the letter Daniel had left for me, and the one I'd found in my reticule upon my arrival at Stoneleigh. The marriage certificates with the June and September dates. The gauze shroud that, in the ebony shadows, had so terrified me in my drugged state. The still unopened letters I had written to him that had never been sent. The letters from him I had not been given, and that I had only recently read. The scars around my wrists left by the rough iron bands.

I also had a letter from Sir Robert Boulton, attesting to the accuracy of my story. I gave that to Uncle Jacob, too, though he laid it aside, unread. At last I ended, my story done, all feeling drained from inside me. I knew I would not again repeat these words, not for long, long years, if ever. The past was done. Now it was time to move on.

"And it was Marlowe who did this?" Uncle Jacob asked after a brief silence, his voice quiet and thoughtful.

"Yes." I looked over at the settee where the solicitor had once sat. "Because I had compromised his honor. And Lord D'arcy, because I had refused his lust. And Matthew Palmerston, from greed and Daniel Marley from fear." I looked back at Uncle Jacob, and gave him a wistful smile. "And me. I understand now that I had my own part in this, because I loved too much. I lost sight of who I was. I gave away too much of myself to Daniel and had nothing left to fight with, nothing of myself to hold onto. All I had was an illusion, and illusions disappear when you try to pin them down."

I rose and tied up my pitiful package, leaving out the few unopened letters I had written to Uncle Jacob. I draped my shawl over my shoulders and smiled at that dear, wonderful old man I knew I would never see again.

"I will leave these letters for you, along with Sir Robert's. Perhaps one day you will want to read them.

Mine are probably quite incoherent, for I was heavily drugged when I wrote them, but there may be something in them that is worthwhile. I don't know, for I do not remember. Thank you for listening to me. I wish," I lifted my shoulders in a rueful gesture, "that it was a more believable tale, but when the truth is all one has, then it has to do, however strange it seems. I'll not bother you again. Good-bye."

Uncle Jacob, I added silently, turning away. He waited until had I reached the curtain before he spoke.

"Marina." I turned and looked back at him. "That boy out there." He waved dismissively toward the shop where, I was sure, just beyond the curtain David Phibbs stood guard over my meeting with Uncle Jacob, listening to my every word. I wondered how believable my tale had been to him. "He does not live here, you know. He has a place of his own, somewhere. Independent, that's what these youngsters are. Your room is empty up there, even the clothes you left behind hang still in the wardrobe. It is a big room, if you remember; big enough for two. Of course, you will need another bed, but that is your problem."

He stopped and we stared at each other. I could hardly breathe, could not believe what I had heard. I shook my head in confusion. What *was* he saying?

"It is lonely here at night without you, Marina. Come live here, you and the girl. Please. Come home and be my Just Marina again."

I ran to him and buried my head against his chest.

Chapter Twenty-eight

It was the most wonderful birthday I had ever had, for the next day I came home; home to my wonderful room above the bookshop, home to the myriad books waiting like old friends to greet me, home most of all to Uncle Jacob, to his arms and to his heart. He even employed me in the shop, working on the ledgers, for he declared David Phibbs, who was marvelous with customers and ingenious as a salesman, a total incompetent with figures. He was right. It took me more than two months to straighten out the muddle the accounts were in.

Uncle Jacob was merely civil to Mary at first, being somewhat uncomfortable with her deformities. But as time passed he grew used to her shuffling gait and twisted back, recognized her sweet nature, and eventually came to love her as did I. After a year, when she had progressed sufficiently in her studies, he employed her as an assistant to David, who was kind and gentle with her, and as protective as a big brother.

She shelved stock and located books, lettered signs and designed window displays, and never once lost her awe of the printed word. And I never lost my amazement at Uncle Jacob abdicating responsibility for lunch to Mary. It was a mark of true affection and respect that he allowed her to touch his stove. It was a wise decision; our meals were markedly improved.

David Phibbs and I learned to coexist within the shop, but though I tried my best to win him over, he remained cool and somewhat suspicious of me until the day we parted company. At odd times I would feel his eyes upon me, or catch a speculative expression on his face when he thought I wasn't looking. I knew, from a few things he let slip over the years, that he had in fact eavesdropped on my confession to Uncle Jacob, and I wondered if he perhaps blamed me for not reacting differently to what Matthew Palmerston had done to me.

Not that anything I could have done would have changed what had happened, for Matthew had determined my fate long before he sent Daniel to me. From the moment my hand was upon the marriage certificate, I was doomed to walk the path he had so carefully prepared.

But perhaps that was not it at all. Perhaps David blamed me for coming into Uncle Jacob's life in the first place. Perhaps he simply blamed me for being me. I wish he could have found, if not liking, then at least forgiveness in his heart, for though we worked hard at being cordial for Uncle Jacob's sake, his attitude made those years in the shop a little less happy for me than they could have been.

David's friendship was not the only loss I suffered during those years of peace and quiet joy. I cried bitter tears when Uncle Jacob told me of Eamon O'Leary's death. He had collapsed one afternoon the August before I returned to London, while I languished in my stone prison. He had been taking a batch of sweet cinnamon buns from the oven. He died three days later without regaining consciousness. I remembered how he had instantly disliked Daniel Marley, who we all thought was the wonderful Matthew Palmerston, and my heart ached that I had not listened to him, that he had died without knowing he was right, and with my silence heavy on his heart.

Their son had inherited the shop, for Mollie, who had shared Eamon's life and labored by his side for more than thirty years to build their business, could inherit neither money nor property because she was a woman, and his wife. Sean had sold the shop and taken his mother back to Ireland to live with his family, an arrangement that suited Mollie very well, as she now had time to spare for the four grandchildren she had seen only twice before. Sean kept what he considered her money apart from his, for he had no patience with ridiculous laws that left women bereft and helpless after working all their lives. He was, truly, an enlightened man.

It took me three weeks to gather the courage to write to Mollie, explaining in brief what had befallen me after my marriage, and expressing my grief and pain at Eamon's loss. Uncle Jacob told me she had been quite angered by my silence, for Eamon, who had taken me into his very cautious, shielded heart, had grown more and more short-tempered and bitter when it became obvious they would have no word from me. The hasty line penned to them in the one brief letter to Uncle Jacob before I left London, passed by Eamon almost unnoticed. And though Uncle Jacob did not say so, I felt sure Mollie must blame me in part for Eamon's death. I know I did; I had, in a very real way, unknowingly broken his heart.

I hoped only that she would understand, and perhaps soften her harsh feelings toward me. I had no expectation she would write back. I did not know, however, that Uncle Jacob had also written to her two weeks before I did, describing to her in great detail, just as I had to him, the terrors I had undergone. She said nothing of this in her letter—I did not discover what he had done for more than five years—but her unconditional forgiveness, her motherly warmth, and her great empathy with my pain despite her own personal grief, unleashed tears that fell daily for almost a week. A protective emptiness had filled me since that day on the cliff when Daniel had died, an emptiness that held in check the anger and self-pity that threatened to overwhelm and destroy me. In returning to the tower room I had faced the anger and defeated it. In facing Uncle Jacob I had erased the self-pity. And so the tears Mollie's letter brought were of healing, tears of love and peace and acceptance. They washed away most of the fear that remained, and eroded a bit of the distrust with which I now faced life, for her words were of hope, of the growth to be found in pain, and of building on the sorrows of the past to create a future filled with confidence and joy.

'We are never alone, Marina,' she wrote, 'not if we can still love. There is always something true, something beautiful and real, even in the greatest illusion. What this man Daniel did to you was despicable, base and cruel beyond belief. But if you search your heart, you will find the truth. He may have been weak, but that does not make his love for you any the less. Remember, he did come back. He did save you. Take the beauty, Marina, and let it heal you. Forget the rest; it is not worth remembrance.'

She was right. I followed her advice, difficult though it was, letting the tears heal my heart and wash clean the love buried so long beneath the pain and anger. In the end I discovered it had not been all illusion. The love we had shared, my Matthew and I, stood separate, deep and pure, apart from the pain and confusion and betrayal. The joy we had known could not be fabricated. It alone was real, solid and permanent in a world filled with loss. It alone would last forever, though my Mathew—Daniel—was gone and I, too, would fade away in time. That love had made everything else endurable, and worthwhile.

They were five wonderful years, those last years with Uncle Jacob. Our business thrived, David Phibbs married a lovely girl named Nancy and had a son whom they called Jacob, and Mary grew into an attractive young woman despite her handicaps. Her desire for knowledge was insatiable, and it was hard to get her nose out of the books she constantly devoured. She developed an affinity for philosophy, and though she still read slowly she understood even the deepest writings and often amazed Uncle Jacob and me with her insights. She had come a long, long way from the cowering, shambling, drooling half-wit who had haunted the stone corridors of Stoneleigh.

Uncle Jacob's life was as full and happy as ours, and although he never did regain his full strength after his illness, his health continued unimpaired. He died quietly on a warm early June afternoon in 1876, while he sat reading Plato and smoking his pipe. It was David's half-day off, and Mary and I were tending the shop. When we closed at seven-thirty and went into the sitting room, we thought at first he had fallen asleep, he looked so contented and peaceful. And though my grief was deep and everlasting, it was also as gentle as his passing had been, for I knew his love would live on and color every day of my life.

It was then, in the long letter of condolence that Mollie sent, that I learned of what Uncle Jacob had written her five years before. I thought again of the gray hair ribbon he had recovered from Lord Creswell's mansion, and realized he had been a man of uncommon depth and courage. His passing left a very large, empty space within me, adding to those left by Daniel and Eamon, and by Andrew's untimely death almost four years earlier.

But I still had Mary, and half the bookshop, for Uncle Jacob had left it to both David and me equally, along with the money he had saved over the years, quite a sizable sum. I found it ironic that it was due to Mr. Marlowe's deviousness in ensuring I had never married that left me single and free to inherit. However, David Phibbs found it neither amusing nor comfortable to be in partnership with me. The suspicion and distrust which Uncle Jacob's presence had held at bay slowly grew into barely disguised animosity, and the tension between us rose daily. It did not surprise me then that, feeling alone and friendless once again, I began to long for Boston. Without Uncle Jacob, without Eamon and Mollie, London no longer seemed like home to me.

In late July, much to my relief, David agreed that he would buy me out, and with the profit I realized I purchased books with which to stock the bookstore I hoped to open in Boston. In late September I booked passage for Mary and me and the many boxes that contained our dreams for the future. It was a pleasant voyage, the seas calm despite the lateness of the year. Mary and I passed the long, lazy days making plans amidst laughter and hope. Three weeks later, one late afternoon, I stood at the rail watching the Boston skyline slowly emerge from the mists, my mind filled with memories of Father, my heart hammering from fear.

What was I doing, a woman alone, responsible for

a handicapped English girl, thinking I could carve a life for myself in the fabric of a society that did not allow for such things? What I wanted was simple, but impossible. A small house, large enough for Mary and me and the one or two others like her I hoped to find, rescue and love, unfortunate, rejected children whose only sin had been to be born different. A shop with shelves stocked with books both new and old, to give pleasure and enlightenment to others. A sign, 'M. Weston, Bookseller,' proclaiming to the world that I existed, that I was real, that I had value despite the fact that I was a woman.

It was not truly that much to ask of life, a place to stand independent and on my own, but suddenly I felt myself panic. My heart quailed. I could not do this, not me. I simply couldn't. I was incompetent. I would fail, I knew I would.

Then I felt Mary's hand slip over mine on the rail. I looked at her and smiled. Her touch had silenced the doubts, destroyed the echoes of Father's voice. I thought of the colorful pebble I carried in my bag, one of the gifts she had given me in that cold stone room, a symbol of hope, a pledge of love and life in the dark emptiness of despair, and I knew. I *could* do this, I could build a life for myself. I would have to, for no one else could do it for me, or it would not be my life. And if the venture failed, there would be other options, new opportunities to be had.

Failure would not make me less, for I am not the things I have, nor even the things I do. I am the hopes and dreams, the thoughts and emotions, the joys and sorrows that lie within me. I am the help and pleasure I give to others through whatever I say and do. I am uniquely me, and my value is as inestimable as anyone else's.

I turned my gaze back to the enlarging buildings. The fresh sea breeze caressed my face. I had been away for ten years. I had left in excitement and confusion, unsure of who I was and fearful of a future I felt I had no control over. Now I returned confident and hopeful, calm and independent, secure in myself and in charge of my life. I would find the house I needed, and I would open my shop. I would take in what children I could, and with Mary's help mend their lives. And if love found me I would not turn away, for I was ready at long last to love again. I was still somewhat young, just turned thirty-one years old. I wanted to feel a man's arms around me once more, his body close to mine. Despite what Daniel had done to me, I was no longer afraid of love.

Life without love is not life; it is merely existence. It is love—not just for a mate, but also for a child, a friend, or a parent—that makes all living worthwhile. I had finally come to understand that what I had done with Daniel, plunging all of myself completely into him, was not the best kind of love, for it was filled with fear, with abdication of self, and a turning away from the responsibility to take care of that self. To truly love, one must have a piece of being from which to love, an inviolate core that stands secure and independent, that gives to and gains from but does not join with any other. When next I loved, it would be with a love worth having, for the matter of my identity had now been resolved. It was owned and defined by me, and I would never again give it completely away.

I turned my hand beneath Mary's and twined my fingers into hers.

"We have finally arrived, Mary," I said. I could feel my eyes shining. "This is America. Boston. Isn't it wonderful? Your new home, Mary. We have come home."

BOOKS BY SUSAN TUTTLE

All of Susan's books can be ordered through any bookstore, as well as ordered through Amazon.com.

FICTION BOOKS

Tangled Webs: Teenage Lia Willett, daughter of a serial killer, left town under a cloud of suspicion and animosity, leaving behind a dead classmate and unanswered questions. Seventeen years later, bizarre circumstances bring her back to Mercerville, where the hatred directed toward her in the past slowly escalates into ever-more-lethal vandalism and threats. Wanting only to live a quiet life, Lia finds herself stalked and menaced by the town and plagued by nightmares of a frightening past she only half remembers. As events spiral out of control, to save both her sanity and her life Lia must unearth the terrifying, long-buried memories of what happened before she left Mercerville. And in the process answer the most important question of all: Is Lia Willett, like her father, a murderer?

Available in both print and Kindle format from Amazon.com

Proof of Identity: an indieB.R.A.G. Medallion Honoree. Danae Holloway is arrested for the stabbing murder of a man she's neither heard of nor met. But the police have eyewitnesses who saw her leave the scene, and her fingerprints are on the murder weapon.

Legal Aid attorney, Collin Montgomery, gets her released on bail and another murder occurs. Again her fingerprints are found at the scene and she has no alibi. Collin, believing Danae innocent, desperately searches for answers to exonerate her. But will the truth he uncovers only cement her guilt? Is the court-appointed psychiatrist working to help Danae, or does he have his own agenda? Most importantly, what happens when the facts and the truth don't agree? Just what constitutes proof of identity in a digital age?

Available in print and Kindle format from Amazon.com

Sins of the Past: Sabrina Compton's sheltered life is shattered when her beloved husband is brutally slaughtered. And though their home has been ransacked, nothing appears to be missing. Unable to face the memories the house holds, Sabrina flees to her great-grandmother's cottage on Gaffe Island, off the coast of South Carolina. But the peace she tries to recover there is crushed by the revelations of an intrusive FBI agent, and her life is forever altered by the weight of her husband's devastating betrayal. As a hurricane bears down on Gaffe Island, she discovers her husband's killer is now after her. Will Sabrina survive both the storm and the killer's rage? Will the presence of the F.B.I. agent be enough to protect her? Or are the sins of the past destined to destroy her, too?

Available in both print and Kindle format from Amazon.com

Piece By Piece: When high school teacher Ken Reed meets a woman a woman suffering from total amnesia, who is terrified of getting help, he feels compelled to bring her into his home. He names her Julie and wants nothing more than to keep her protected and safe. But soon her troubling past begins to return in disjointed flashes of horrific memories. And people around Julie start to die. Is Julie simply the victim of a tragic accident, or did she have a hand in the terrifying events her memories uncover? Who wants Julie dead? Why is she so afraid of the police? Most importantly, what is left for Julie and Ken to hold onto when the past intrudes on the present, piece by terrifying piece?

Available in both print and Kindle format from Amazon.com.

It Takes Class: (coming late Winter, 2015) An anthology of short pieces written during timed (15 to 20 minutes each) exercises in the writing classes I teach. These pieces run the gamut from character sketches, to intriguing scenes, to mini-stories. Realistic, romantic, mysterious, dark, arcane or fantastic, there's a genre here for everyone, especially those who like their fiction in short bursts. This volume is a fascinating look into a "slightly twisted" writer's subconscious mind at work.

Available soon in both print and Kindle format from Amazon.com.

Death in the Valley: (coming June, 2015) A collection of three award-winning short suspense stories that take place in the San Joaquin Valley, California. In "The Telltale Death," a ringing antique phone spells disaster. In "Beef Killington," a gourmet tri-tip contest offers a bored housewife a way out. In "Hydro-synth," the discovery of mummified bodies in the desert launches an investigation into horror.

Available soon in both print and Kindle format from Amazon.com

NONFICTION BOOKS
These books are available from Amazon.com in print format.

Write It Right Workbook #1: Character, Setting Story offers 26 lessons and exercises in the first 3 of the 12 skills needed to craft compelling fiction and creative nonfiction. ***Unit 1: Character*** contains 9 lessons and timed exercises that help you create characters who are fascinating, flawed and filled with vision and desire, characters that readers will want to know about. ***Unit 2: Setting*** presents 7 lessons and exercises that show you how to design vibrant settings and landscapes that will capture and enthrall readers, settings that are fascinating and evocative. ***Unit 3: Story*** offers 10 lessons and exercises designed to help you discover stories that will grip readers and not let them go, stories that will live on in the minds of readers.

Write It Right Workbook #2: Point of View (POV) presents **15 lessons** to help you navigate the murky waters of ***Unit #4: Point of View.*** You'll learn the difference between straight, emotional omniscient and classic omniscient POV, and understand the strengths and drawbacks of each one. You'll gain experience in first, second and third person POVs, and work through the differences in shifting, close and alternating POVs. You will learn how to identify which character can best tell your story, and how to remain in that character's viewpoint consistently.

Write It Right Workbook #3: Plot, Dialogue contains Unit #5 and Unit #6. ***Unit #5: Plot*** contains 8 exercises on crafting flawless, intricate plots that sizzle off the page. Discover what constitutes a viable plot, and how to spot an idea that doesn't have enough depth before you start to write. Learn the importance of a through line, how to analyze ideas for viable plots, and where and how to find plots in the world around you. In ***Unit #6: Dialogue*** you'll find 8 lessons/ exercises that show you how to write sparkling dialogue that sounds perfectly natural while still addressing the six necessary ingredients that make dialogue an integral part of the story. Learn how to write for your audience, make your characters' voices unique, use idioms to infuse verisimilitude, tag properly and incorporate subtext into what your characters say as you write realistic dialogue that serves the purpose of your story and leaves readers amazed.

Write It Right Workbook #4: Scenes, Voice/ Style offers 20 lessons and exercises. ***Unit #7: Scenes*** presents 11 lessons/exercises that take you through the 9 different scene structures and into the scene question and transitions between scenes so that your stories truly live in the hearts and minds of hour readers. *Unit 8: Style/Voice* presents 9 strategies to help you develop your own unique writing style, a clear, consistent voice that will stand out among all the others and be readily recognizable as yours alone. Unlock the essence of voice and style that lies deep within you, innate natural storytelling qualities that, once realized, will enable you to tell a story as only you can tell it. A voice that is uniquely yours.

Write It Right Workbook #5: Conflict/ Tension, Subplot presents Units #9 and 10 in a series of 17 lessons and exercises. All stories, not just mystery and suspense, need tension to sustain reader interest. *Unit #9: Conflict/Tension* explains in 9 tension-filled exercises the necessity of tension and conflict in stories and explores how to inject the proper amount of tension into any situation to keep readers reading. The 8 strategies contained in the *Unit 10, Subplot*, will show you how to derive organic subplots from situations, characters and the main plot, how to use subplots to reflect, refine and deepen the major themes of the main plot and how to create an effective and compelling series that satisfies readers as it pulls them through one volume to the next.

Write It Right Workbook #6: Brilliant Beginnings/Extraordinary Endings offers 8 lessons/ exercises in each of the last two units of the program. In *Unit 11: Brilliant Beginnings* you will learn the 8 different strategies for crafting a dynamite opening line that will hook readers immediately, methods for

SUSAN TUTTLE

completing a compelling first paragraph, and techniques to craft an entirely gripping first page and chapter. These techniques will capture readers and make them continue turning pages. *Unit 12: Extraordinary Endings,* takes you through 8 lessons/ exercises on the second most important part of your story: the ending. Learn the secrets to choosing the proper ending for whatever story you write, 8 types of endings that will so satisfy your readers that they will eagerly pick up your next story.

ABOUT THE AUTHOR

Susan Tuttle, an award-winning writer, is a freelance editor, writing teacher and the slightly twisted author of suspense and paranormal suspense novels (listed in the Books section). Short pieces also appear in the anthologies *The Best of SLO NightWriters* from San Luis Obispo's premier writing group, and *Somewhere in Crime* from the Central Coast Chapter of Sisters in Crime (SinC).

Her critically acclaimed, 6-volume *Write It Right: Exercises to Unlock the Writer in Everyone* workbook series for fiction and creative nonfiction is based on her weekly writing classes. Each workbook contains lessons and exercises for writers of all levels, in fiction and creative nonfiction.

Susan is past president of SLO NightWriters and the Central Coast Chapter of Sisters in Crime, and is presently the newsletter editor for both organizations. In her fiction life, she is working on two YA fantasy series, and a mystery series featuring her psychic detective, Skylark, who will debut in the short story "Murder Under the Oaks" in the upcoming new SinC anthology, *Deadlines: Murder and Mayhem on the California Coast*. That volume should be out in June of 2016. Then look for two Skylark novellas to follow in late Summer or early Fall: *The Somewhen Murder* and *Dead Ringer*.

Susan is active in her church, where she is the head of the music ministry and works as the church's office manager. She also writes spiritual songs and is working on two spiritual meditation *Lord, Let Me Walk* series: *A Journey With Jesus Through the Parables*, and *A Journey With Jesus Through Lent*.

A Buffalo, New York transplant, Susan lives on the Central Coast of California with her imaginary cat in a house filled with her (mostly unfinished) handmade quilts and (mostly finished) knitted scarves. Find her on LinkedIn, Facebook (susanwriter), Twitter (stuttlewriter), and follow her writing blog with its weekly writing prompts (Write Over the Hump) at www.SusanTuttleWrites.com.